A SPELL FOR THE REVOLUTION

TRAITOR TO THE CROWN

D0831416

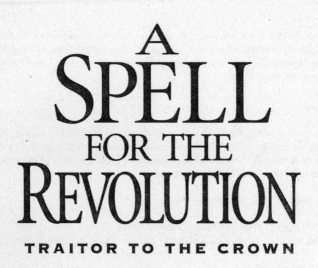

A SPELL FOR THE REVOLUTION

TRAITOR TO THE CROWN

C. C. FINLAY

BALLANTINE BOOKS • NEW YORK

A Spell for the Revolution is a work of fiction. Names, characters, places, and incidents are the products of the author's imagination or are used fictitiously. Any resemblance to actual events, locales, or persons, living or dead, is entirely coincidental.

A Del Rey Mass Market Original

Copyright © 2009 by Charles Coleman Finlay
Excerpt from *The Demon Redcoat* © 2009 by Charles Coleman Finlay

Published in the United States by Del Rey, an imprint of The Random House Publishing Group, a division of Random House, Inc., New York.

DEL REY is a registered trademark and the DEL REY colophon is a trademark of Random House, Inc.

This book contains an excerpt from the forthcoming book *The Demon Redcoat* by Charles Coleman Finlay. This excerpt has been set for this edition only and may not reflect the final content of the forthcoming edition.

ISBN 978-0-345-50391-6

Cover design by Jae Song. Inset illustration by Craig Howell.

Printed in the United States of America

www.delreybooks.com

OPM 9 8 7 6 5 4 3 2 1

for Jacob and Hannah
go make history

Chapter 1

August 1776

Proctor Brown urged his horse into the shallows, fording the Potomac River an hour before sunset. Water splashed up and soaked his shoes; after ten days in the saddle, with his stockings almost as stiff as his legs, he hardly noticed wet shoes. If he found the Walker farm tonight, he'd have a chance to dry off and clean up. Assuming he was welcome.

The jarring lunge up the far bank reminded him that he was more accustomed to being behind a horse, hitched to a cart or plow, than on top of one. He grunted, shifting weight from his sorest parts to those parts almost as sore. A day of rest could be a good thing. It might take that long to convince Alexandra Walker to return with him to The Farm outside Salem, Massachusetts. It depended on how vividly she remembered the assassins sent to kill them during her last visit.

Proctor wanted her help, in case the killers came again. It took a witch to defeat witchcraft, and Alexandra was stronger and more experienced than any of the other witches he'd been able to find this past year.

When they reached the road, Proctor's sturdy little bay mare turned toward the smoke and rooftops a mile away. "No, Singer, the other way," he said.

With a weary toss of her head, Singer circled onto the cart road that led south into the Shenandoah Valley. Even this late in the day, the August air lay on them like a damp wool blanket, one that had been warmed by a fire and filled with biting insects. Land stretched out around them, lush and green, all the way to the mountains.

So this was Virginia, the home of General Washington and half the leaders of the Revolution. Last night about this time, Proctor had arrived in McAllister's Town, Pennsylvania, where the innkeeper at The Sign of the Horse bragged about Thomas Jefferson's visit the previous April. Jefferson had praised the inn's sausages, which were made by the innkeeper's cousin. The sausages were good, but Proctor doubted that he'd slept in the very same room as Jefferson, no matter what the innkeeper claimed. Still, it had been worth the extra half a shilling to get that close to the author of the Declaration of Independence.

Proctor pushed back his hat and wiped the sweat from his forehead as he scanned the landscape. He was a bit twitchy, wary even. This was the farthest he had ever been from home. The crickets chuckled at him from the safety of the tall grass that lined the trail.

Something rustled through that grass, startling him from his thoughts. Proctor reached for his musket, but by the time he sighted down the barrel, whatever had been there was gone.

He tried to convince himself that it was only a stray dog, or maybe a pig loose from some nearby farm. He knew that he'd been jumpy ever since the battles with the Covenant last year. Being this far from home only made him jumpier.

Not that he needed more reasons to be jumpy. As a young man in Massachusetts, he'd been forced to conceal his talent for magic lest his neighbors turn on him. But ever since the battle at Lexington, he'd needed that magic to spoil the plots of the Covenant, a mysterious group of European witches who wanted to crush the American rebellion. The Covenant's ultimate purpose remained hidden, but the stakes were so high that they'd murdered other American witches and had tried several times to kill Proctor. Not just kill him, but turn the magic in his blood into a curse against American soldiers.

He rolled down his sleeves to cover the pink scars on his forearms, a memento from that particular encounter. Thanks to Deborah, he'd survived and they'd reversed the Covenant's spell before the battle at Bunker Hill.

Deborah Walcott. Prior to the war, Proctor had been engaged to Emily Rucke, the beautiful daughter of a West Indies merchant, the kind of young woman everyone noticed. These days only Deborah filled his thoughts, though she kept herself plain as a Quaker and tried, like every witch he knew, to go unobserved.

What Deborah couldn't hide was the spark inside her. When the Congress signed the Declaration of Independence, she perceived the new danger.

"The Covenant will strike back hard," she told Proctor. "Only a third of Americans support the rebellion. If the Covenant can make a mockery of independence and break our will to fight, people will go running back to Mother England like chastened children."

Which was why they needed every witch who could detect or break a spell, including Alexandra Walker—who, when they'd seen her last, wanted nothing to do with magic ever again.

One of the farms ahead, rooftops silhouetted against the sky, must be hers. The sudden return of his thoughts to the present caused him to tense. Something was wrong.

The crickets had fallen silent.

A figure loomed suddenly beside the road, and Proctor raised his musket. Then he realized it was only a scarecrow, made real by the twilight.

As he relaxed, a small flash of light revealed the creature's distorted face, with intense, malevolent eyes and a sneering mouth.

Proctor started in the saddle, jerking on the bridle, and Singer flared her nostrils and came to a stop. The figure that he'd taken for a scarecrow emerged from the shadows as a man, his face lit red by the hot coal of his pipe.

"Good day," the stranger said, lifting his pipe stem. He wore a pair of calfskin gloves, even in this miserable heat.

"Good night is more like it," Proctor said. It was no wonder he had mistaken the man for a scarecrow. The stranger's jacket was of foreign cut, plum-colored with relics of silver embroidery on the cuffs and pocket-flaps. A golden velvet waistcoat was mismatched to a red silk scarf tied about his throat. His tattered wig was topped by a ragged bicorn hat sporting a cock's feather. The feather was surely the freshest piece of the motley ensemble.

"It's good to see a young man heading away from the war, instead of rushing off to join the rebels," the stranger said. His voice was hollow, his accent as odd as his clothes.

Proctor bristled. He'd risked his life in the war, and he had been cut off by his mother for using magic to fight it. He believed it was the right thing for the country and was glad the Declaration of Independence had been issued, even if it meant renewed fighting.

"I've served as a minuteman and would rather be thought a patriot than a rebel," Proctor said. "Do you have something against independence?"

"No, just against—" He puffed out a cloud of tobacco smoke, pausing as he searched for the right word. "—*pointless* bloodshed. No offense intended, young man."

"None taken," Proctor said, though the *young man* irritated. Singer stamped her hooves aggressively, the way she did when strange dogs came too close. It would be best to move on. "I'm looking for the Walker farm. You wouldn't happen to know where it is?"

"The Walker farm?" A smile spread slowly across the stranger's face. "That's a coincidence. I've just come from the Walker farm. Follow the trail up to the big oak with the blaze on it. Then turn to the left and climb over the hill. That's where you'll find it."

"Is it far?" Proctor asked. He wondered how the stranger knew the Walkers. The way Alexandra talked, her parents and brothers were all ardent patriots.

"It's a mile, maybe a bit more," the stranger said. "Be careful or you'll miss it in the dark."

"May I have your name?" Proctor asked. "So that I may remember your kindness to me to the Walkers."

The stranger puffed on his pipe again and blew out another small cloud of smoke. "Bootzamon," he said finally. He chuckled, as if at some private joke. "Folks around here call me Bootzamon."

"Thank you, Mister Bootzamon," Proctor said. With a tip of his hat, and more than a bit of relief, he kicked Singer's sides and headed up the trail.

A hundred feet on, he stole a glance over his shoulder. For a second Bootzamon once again appeared to be a scarecrow standing at the edge of the road. Then the coal flared in his pipe, destroying the fancy, and Proctor turned away from the strange man.

He followed the ruts of the road to the blazed oak standing on the little knoll just where Bootzamon said it would be. Proctor tried to stand in the saddle to look through the trees for some sign of a house, but soreness constrained him to craning his neck. The wind shifted and brought to his nose the scent of cheap tobacco. It smelled like Bootzamon's pipe; the stranger had probably refilled his tobacco pouch at the Walkers.

He rode down the trail until the dark shape of a primitive house emerged from the trees. Rough-hewn logs, chinked with mud and stones, supported a roof with a single chimney. The plank door stood wide open, but no light shone within.

The hairs tingled on the back of Proctor's neck. He reached into his pocket for a handful of salt, in case he needed to cast a quick protective spell.

"Hello," Proctor shouted. "Alexandra. Mister Walker,

Missus Walker." His voice carried past the house, bringing back no reply but the chirping of the crickets.

Nothing appeared wrong. The garden looked well tended, as much as he could see of it in the twilight beyond the split-rail fence. So did the field of corn just past the house.

He dismounted slowly, grunting as he hit the ground. After tying Singer to a narrow stump that seemed meant for that purpose—it was next to a trough made from a dugout log—he limped over to the house.

"Hello," he cried again, leaning into the open door.

Something smelled wrong, sharp and metallic, but the smoke-stench from the hearth overwhelmed it. It was too dark to see anything without a light. He suddenly wished that he'd done a scrying before continuing his journey today, but he hadn't seen a need and he hated to risk doing magic where he might be caught.

He stepped cautiously inside.

"Hello! Is anyone home?"

Nothing.

His nose wrinkled again at the smell. The shadows within marked out two rooms. He stepped into the one on his left and slipped in something on the floor. His shoulder banged the wall, but he caught himself before falling.

He rubbed his sore shoulder. A few coals glowed red in the hearth, enough to start a fire for some light. He still had that wary itch at the back of his neck, but he dismissed it. That odd Bootzamon fellow had just been here, and he'd mentioned nothing wrong.

Proctor shuffled forward, moving his feet carefully to keep from slipping again or tripping over some stray piece of furniture. When he reached the hearth, he groped in the dark until he found the iron poker. He repeated the effort until he located the basket of tinder and wood. Using the poker to stir the coals, he blew on them and fed them dried twigs and branches until they leapt into flames.

Outside, Singer whinnied. Proctor knew he needed to go out and remove the mare's saddle and rub her down. Or maybe it was the Walkers returning.

"Hello, in here!" Proctor called. He added wood to the fire and prodded the coals until the room glowed orange and red.

Singer whinnied again. Proctor turned his head toward the door, conscious that the crickets had fallen silent.

His gaze shifted from the door to the room.

Not all the red was cast by fire.

He jumped back. The iron clattered off the stone hearth as he dropped it. Blood was smeared everywhere. He checked the bottom of his shoe—he'd slipped in a pool of wet blood on his way in. It was fresh. A woman's body lay under the table. The top of her head was missing. A man's broken body, cut to bloody ribbons, was folded against the wall.

"Jesus," Proctor whispered.

"Funny, that's who they called on too," said a voice that made Proctor jump again.

Bootzamon stood framed in the doorway. For just a second he looked like a scarecrow. Then his pipe flared, and he blew out a stream of smoke.

"Mister Bootzamon," Proctor said, trying hard to keep his voice steady. "What happened here?"

Bootzamon shook his head sadly. "It appears to be an Indian attack. Exactly how old are you, young man?"

"Turned twenty-two this past month," Proctor answered in reflex. He looked for a way past Bootzamon, remembering that the Covenant's assassins had come to The Farm dressed as Indians last year. "What makes you say it's Indians?"

"See, that's too bad," Bootzamon said. "My master wants young witches only. 'Catch the young ones, kill the old.' I couldn't find the Walker girl, but I got to thinking you might be young enough to take her place."

His cockfeather brushed the lintel as he stepped through the door. One arm hung at his side, the gloved hand casually dangling a bloody tomahawk.

Proctor saw the weapon, but he felt *magic* tickle the back of his neck. Worse than murder had been done here already. He reached into his pocket for his bag of salt while his thoughts raced for the right protective spell. Keeping his eye on Bootzamon, he sprinkled salt in a quick circle around himself. "The Lord is my rock and my fortress, my deliverer. Deliver me from my strong enemy—"

"Bosh," Bootzamon said around the pipe stem in his lips. He removed the pipe and blew smoke toward Proctor. A wind slammed through the house, banging open the window shutters and scattering Proctor's circle of salt.

The wind died, and Bootzamon stood there, tapping the tomahawk against his palm.

"You're a witch," Proctor whispered, and then felt foolish for saying it. His own use of magic was too slow, too useless for this kind of fight. He bent down quickly and snatched up the iron.

"Not precisely a witch," Bootzamon said. "But I may be a ghost—boo!"

Proctor twitched.

Bootzamon chuckled and danced closer to Proctor. "Or I may be an Indian." The last word came out with a sneer as he swung the tomahawk at Proctor's head.

Proctor banged the tomahawk aside with the iron, then reversed his swing and slammed the metal bar into his attacker. It was like hitting a bag of sticks and straw. The tomahawk flew one way and Bootzamon the other. He hit the far wall, crumpled to the floor, and then popped up again, pipe in mouth. He reached up and recocked his hat, then licked his gloved finger and ran it along the edge of the feather.

"What are you?" Proctor asked.

"What are *you*?" Bootzamon retorted. "I'll tell you what

you are—you're nothing but a miserable bag of snot and bones, piss and *Scheiße*. And, sadly, too old to be of use to me."

Bootzamon stretched his hand toward the tomahawk. The weapon slid toward him across the floor, the blade scratching a line through the blood, and flew up into his hand. The flickering light from the fire cast a sinister glare over his features, distending and exaggerating them.

He blocked the only path to the door.

Fear shot through Proctor like fire through dry grass. He turned and leapt headfirst through the open window. He slammed into the ground, and the air crashed out of him, but somehow he held on to the poker.

Singer snorted.

Bootzamon flew through the window and landed nimbly on his feet next to Proctor.

Proctor rolled away, rising, swinging the poker as he stumbled upright. Bootzamon was either a witch, doing magic, or he was a creature made from magic, like the animated corpses that had attacked Proctor and Deborah on The Farm that dark night the year before. Either way, the magic had a focus. Break the focus, break the spell.

He retreated around the corner of the house, watching Bootzamon follow him with an almost casual step. The coal from the pipe cast a thread of light along the cockfeather in his hat. Roosters were the focus of all sorts of black magic. The cockfeather must be the focus—it made perfect sense.

"I smell you," Bootzamon said. "Even a corncob nose can smell the stink of sweat and hunger, fear and death on you." He pulled the pipe from his mouth and held it down at his side. "I smell you—"

Proctor lunged and knocked the hat off Bootzamon's head, dodging the tomahawk as it swung at him. Holding the iron bar in front of him like a shield, Proctor snatched up the hat and yanked out the feather, crushing it in his fist.

Bootzamon stood there, unfazed.

"If you think my hat looks better than your own, you're welcome to it," he said, jamming the pipe in his mouth. "It can cover your naked skull once I peel off your scalp."

"The feather's not the focus?" Proctor said, stunned. But then what was—?

Bootzamon laughed. He made a quick lunge toward Proctor. It would have been deadly but the creature froze mid-step. The dark light in his eyes began to fade, and his body suddenly grew more lumpy and shapeless. He pulled out the pipe and saw that it was extinguished.

"Dickon!" Bootzamon cried.

A horned, man-shaped shadow the size of a cat swirled up out of the earth. Its left fist was closed around a burning coal that illuminated a webwork of veins in the back of its hand. With a screech of anguish, it smashed the coal into the pipe. Then it disappeared in an upward spiral of smoke, leaving behind the stink of saltpeter and brimstone. Proctor suppressed a shudder of revulsion—it was one thing to believe in imps and demons, but another thing entirely to see one summoned by name.

Bootzamon drew deep on the relit pipe and puffed out another noxious cloud of cheap tobacco.

The pipe. Of course. Proctor should have guessed that first. He could try to smash it, but he didn't think he'd get a second chance to hit Bootzamon in the head. He backed away, slowly, measuring his step, making sure of his footing. If he went around just one more corner, he could make a dash for Singer.

Bootzamon chuckled at him, then coiled and made a leap that carried him over Proctor's head. Proctor ducked, swinging the iron wildly. When Bootzamon landed, Proctor charged him.

The creature leapt back again, another fifteen feet, and held out his arm, the tomahawk hanging limp in his hand.

"What are you going to do?" Bootzamon taunted. "If

you break me, my master can put me back together. If you destroy my limbs, I can find replacements." The tomahawk snapped upright in his fist. "You, on the other hand, are neither so durable nor so easily repaired."

His arm snapped back, and he threw the tomahawk at Proctor, who twisted aside, dodging it easily. Now was his chance—he charged at Bootzamon.

Something in the glitter of the dark eyes warned him.

He ducked as the tomahawk returned, passing through the space his head had just occupied, landing with a soft *thwack* in Bootzamon's fist.

"Ah, that worked on the woman," Bootzamon said, sounding either pleased or disappointed.

Proctor circled to the right.

"You wouldn't know where I could find the girl, would you?" Bootzamon said, dancing jauntily from side to side, holding the tomahawk ready to strike. "I could promise to make it quicker for you if you tell me—"

Proctor attacked in the middle of Bootzamon's sentence, and the creature reacted by leaping backward again.

"It's not polite to interrupt—" Bootzamon said as he landed next to Singer.

He was interrupted by the mare, who lashed out with her rear hooves the instant he landed. The blow sent Bootzamon flying off in several directions—an arm one way, body another, pipe a third.

Proctor dropped the poker and dived for the pipe.

Bootzamon popped up to his feet and swung an empty shoulder socket toward his life spark. His other hand still clutched the tomahawk. "Give that back to me," he growled.

"You didn't say please," Proctor said. He snapped the pipe in half.

"You stinking peasant farmer—"

The words died on the creature's lips. His head shrank to a dried gourd with a corncob nose, his remaining arm flopped loose like a broken flail, and his legs turned stiff, not bending at the knees. He ran straight-legged for Proctor, raising the tomahawk above his head in a wordless scream.

Proctor plunged his hand into the trough. Steam boiled up around his fist as the pipe was extinguished, and Proctor jerked his hand out with a yelp.

Gourd, scarf, clothes, and straw fell in a jumble at Proctor's feet. The tomahawk slid across the ground to the edge of his bloody-soled shoe.

In the grasses nearby, a cricket ventured a chirp.

Proctor shook his hand. His knuckles hurt, as if he'd punched someone in the jaw. After retrieving the fire iron, he poked carefully through the pieces—a broomstick, an old thresher's flail, and pieces of chair legs knotted together formed Bootzamon's scarecrow bones. Only when Proctor had knocked them apart did he dare breathe easily.

The sound of the crickets rose in grateful chorus.

He went over to Singer. She had froth around her mouth, but her eyes were calm again. Proctor stroked her neck and fetched a handful of oats from his saddlebag. As she nibbled from his palm, Proctor said, "Thanks."

Singer rubbed her head against Proctor's shoulder and pulled at her tether. He gave her another handful of oats.

Unfortunately, he wasn't done here just yet. He took a long look at the pieces of the scarecrow scattered on the ground. It was so dark now, he wasn't sure he could see them all. Wasn't sure they hadn't moved or collected themselves.

The fire in the cabin had faded, leaving no more than a dim glow through the open door. Taking the gourd and broomstick first—the skull and backbone—Proctor carried the pieces inside and shoved them one by one into the flames until the creature was completely destroyed. If he concentrated on the work and watched where he put his feet, he didn't have to look too closely at the dead bodies.

Still, by the time he fed the last bits of straw into the fire, he had seen enough. The woman had auburn hair, the same color as Alexandra's; the man was lean and broad-shouldered, just the way she'd described her father. Though he turned out Bootzamon's pockets before burning the clothes, he had not discovered the missing scalps and could not give the bodies the final dignity of being complete. With the stink of burned wool and silk strong in his nose, he searched the second room and the sleeping loft, but he found no sign of Alexandra or her several brothers.

He stood in the doorway and leaned his head against the jamb, breathing fresh air and staring out into the night. Poor Alexandra—she was going to be devastated, just as Deborah had been when the Covenant killed her parents.

Deborah! What was the phrase that Bootzamon had used? *Catch the young witches and kill the old.* The Covenant knew the location of The Farm. If Bootzamon had been sent after Alexandra, then The Farm wasn't safe. He had to get back home *now*.

He retrieved a purse full of salt from one of his saddle-bags, brought with him to create a protective circle around him as he slept. He used nearly all he had left around the perimeter of the small house, saying, "Let there be no remembrance of former things, neither let there be any remembrance of things that are to come with those who shall come after."

The words trickled out of his mouth like the salt from his fist, starting over again each time he dipped his hand in for more. Anyone who came here now would turn away, forgetting why they came. The house would be all but invisible to them, for at least a time.

When he finished, he stood at the door and whispered a silent prayer to God, begging His forgiveness and asking Him to consecrate the bodies inside in place of a proper burial. All his aches and soreness, forgotten during the fight with Bootzamon, came rushing back, amplified by his new bruises. Night was no time to travel, but he couldn't stay here.

He walked toward Singer and found her at the end of her tether, well away from the trough.

A red light glowed in the bottom of the water. The pipe.

Proctor plunged his hand into the water, still teakettle-warm. He fished out the broken bowl-end of the pipe and took it to the splitting stump. Using the heaviest piece of firewood he could find, he smashed the pipe into pieces. Then he took the butt-end of the log and ground even the pieces into dust until there was no flame left.

"Good night, Mister Bootzamon," he said.

He turned toward the house one last time—and didn't see it. He knew better, but it was still unsettling. Deborah had done a good job teaching him after all.

Proctor walked over to Singer and climbed back into the saddle. She seemed as eager to leave the farm as he was. They had to push through the thick, oppressive air and the dark to find the cart road and turn north again. About an hour later, they came to the ford on the Potomac.

"Didn't think we'd be back again so soon," Proctor said.

Singer plunged down the bank and splashed into the water. Proctor rubbed his eyes to stay awake as they crossed. Five hundred miles away, Deborah and the other witches were in danger already. And they didn't know what was coming.

Chapter 2

The afternoon sun warmed everything, even the dust that rose from the narrow road as it wound between familiar stone walls. Proctor smelled like a man who'd been in the saddle for the better part of a month. Two days' stubble roughened his face. He was sore in places he didn't even know he had. But as he rode Singer to the crest of the hill, there was a smile on his face.

He had never been so glad *not* to see a place.

Below him, a great oak tree leaned over the road. Knolls crowded together behind it, with a bog on one side and forest on the other. Uncultivated land. Nothing more.

The spells that Deborah used to conceal The Farm and protect it from strangers were still intact. She and the others were probably safe.

"We're almost home, girl," he told Singer, reaching down to pat her neck. Her head hung low, and she didn't respond to his touch. She was nearly spent, and he felt that he owed her one more healing spell to restore her strength. He knew to keep that strength for himself—just in case.

He checked his musket, knife, and tomahawk, which were all sparkling clean even if he wasn't. Then he tapped his shoes against Singer's side, and she started down the road toward the shade of the oak.

As soon as they came down the hill, Proctor felt a tingle pass over his body, like hundreds of tiny pinpricks. Singer nickered, her ears flicking and her skin twitching all over. Her tail whacked at invisible flies on her flanks.

That hadn't been there before. Maybe he'd been too quick to feel relief.

He dismounted beneath the oak, next to a solitary post that had no apparent purpose along this empty stretch of country road. After three weeks in the saddle, Proctor felt much shorter all of a sudden. The ground, steady as it was, seemed to rock beneath his feet.

Proctor gripped the weathered gray knob of the post. As soon as his skin connected with the wood, he heard distant chimes, almost like fairy bells. The landscape flickered as if a veil were removed from his eyes. The knolls receded from one another, growing into hills. Between them a gate appeared, set in a wall of fieldstone. Behind the wall, at the spot where the two hills joined together, rose the rooftops of a house and barn and outbuildings, surrounded by gardens and orchards and pastures. The Farm.

Already halfway from the house, walking toward him, was a welcome face.

With Singer's bridle in hand, Proctor hurried through the gate. "Deborah!"

She grabbed up her skirts and started running; he dropped Singer's reins and, forgetting all his aches and tightness, sprinted up the path toward her.

They stumbled to a stop ten feet apart from each other.

Deborah was dressed plainly, in the drab grays and duns typical of her Quaker upbringing. But her face was as bright with life as the flowers that she loved, and her nut-brown eyes had more intelligence in them than in all the schoolteachers Proctor had ever met. She smiled at him for just an instant, then reached up and straightened her plain cap, feeling with her fingers to make sure all her hair was tucked in. She glanced over her shoulder. Her half a dozen students were neatly lined up on the porch of the house.

Proctor rubbed his chin, self-conscious of the stubble and the dirt from the road. Just once, he wished Deborah would look at him with the same exuberant expression

Emily used to have when she saw him. Things had been awkward between Proctor and Deborah for a while, growing worse as more people joined them on The Farm. For months, they had both been so busy with work that they'd stopped trying to find private time together. "You've worked hard while I was gone," he said.

"Thank you, but the credit belongs to Ezra and to Magdalena." She looked past him. "You're alone."

"I couldn't find Alexandra." He'd let it go at that for now. "How did you know I was coming?"

"I added a second warning spell, farther out, along the ridge of the hill. For the past few days, someone's been poking around the borders of our spell—"

"Who? When?" Fear pushed its icy fingers into Proctor's heart as he thought of Bootzamon or another creature like him. "Have they gotten in?"

"Of course they haven't gotten in," Deborah said disdainfully, as if he were questioning her ability. She paused, peering at him more closely. "Why do you ask? Did something happen on the road?"

Singer had walked over to Proctor's side and nuzzled his hand for a treat. Proctor rested a hand on the saddle, next to his musket. He was still thinking about his answer when a voice came down from the house.

"Is everything all right?"

Squat, bandy-legged Ezra, the only other male witch at the school, stood halfway down the hill.

Proctor waved to him. "I'm home—"

"It's only Proctor," Deborah shouted. "Go back to work! We'll be up shortly." Turning back to Proctor, she said, "What happened in Virginia? You're scaring me."

"We've got reason to be scared," he said. He took a deep breath. "Alexandra was already gone—I don't know where. But an agent of the Covenant got to her house before I did." He paused, then decided to say the next part straight. "He murdered her parents."

Deborah's hand flew to her mouth. "May the Light shine on them," she whispered. "The poor girl."

Deborah's own parents had been murdered by the Covenant just a year before. The wound had not entirely healed over; it might never heal. Not that she ever let anyone see that side of her. Proctor was about to say something comforting, but the horror faded from her face and was replaced by her more usual intense thoughtfulness.

"How do you know it was the work of the Covenant?" she asked. "Are you guessing?"

"No, unfortunately, it's no guess. The murderer was still there when I arrived at their house."

Her hand darted out to touch his arm, but he was too far away, so she pulled it back. "What?"

"It was the uncanniest thing I've ever seen, a scarecrow brought to life and animated by some ghost or spirit. He said his name was Bootzamon. Magic made a man of him, at least to look at, and he had gift enough to blow away my protective spell as fast as I could sprinkle salt, and he could call things to him—"

"What kind of things?"

"The tomahawk, after I knocked it out of his hand." He might as well be honest. Deborah understood more about witchcraft than anyone else, and if they were going to stop the Covenant this time, she had to know what they were facing. But he didn't give her a chance to dwell on it now; she would do that plenty later. "And he could summon this imp or demon, a creature named Dickon, that kept his pipe lit. The pipe was the focus of the spell. When I realized that and broke the pipe, Bootzamon turned back into a scarecrow and fell apart. Then I came back here as fast as I could."

Deborah's hands were clenched in fists at her waist. The news had scared her, though she only looked angry. "Why didn't you stay and look for Alexandra? If the Covenant is moving, we need her skills with us more than before."

"I told you, she was long gone. Bootzamon tortured her parents before he killed them, and they didn't say where she was. Bootzamon said something else too: he said his master wanted him to *capture the young witches and kill the old*. I was already too old for him. I was worried about you, all of you," he added, with a gesture toward the porch, where the neat line had turned into a clump with heads bent together, talking. "That's why when you said someone was poking around the borders, I worried more."

Deborah shook her head, puzzled. "I'm not sure I understand completely. Was this Bootzamon a puppet?"

"A puppet without a puppeteer. There was no one pulling the strings, no biloquist casting his voice. He mentioned a master, so maybe he was more like a slave than a puppet."

Deborah turned her face east, squinting against the wind. "Maybe it's best if we say nothing about this to the others."

"We can't keep this from them," Proctor said, shaking his head. "We agreed on that at the very beginning, after last summer. Everyone who comes here has a right to know exactly what dangers we face."

"Just don't scare them more than necessary." Her voice was almost pleading. It was always so hard for her to ask for anything.

Singer nudged his hand again. He took her bridle and started to lead the horse toward the barn. "I guess I'll get her out of this saddle and get her rubbed down and fed."

"Proctor?"

He turned, expecting her to say thank you. Maybe expecting her to express amazement that he'd just ridden a thousand miles in twenty days, because she'd asked him to, because he was worried about her. "Yes?"

But she had that thoughtful look on her face again, as if she was trying to keep track of everything. "Ezra needs help out in the pasture, repairing the fence. The clearer our borders are, the stronger our protective spells will be."

He looked past the barn, along the line of the hill, where the rail fence had tumbled down. Proctor's back ached from the saddle, and his legs felt too stiff to walk much farther, but she was right. The Farm needed a strong border to protect them. "I'll get to it as soon as I can," he said.

"Good," she said, sounding relieved. She hurried past him, heading for the group on the porch, probably to lecture them on the evils of laziness when there was work to be done.

"Come on, girl," Proctor said, rubbing Singer's neck as they plodded toward the barn.

He should feel happy to be home. Their garden beds overflowed with carrots and cabbages, lettuces and leeks. In the orchard, branches sagged with ripening pears and apples, with the plums ready for picking. Beyond the orchard, rows of field corn stood shoulder-tall and thick with ears. Half a dozen pigs dozed contentedly in the shade of the barn, out of the hot August sun, while the oxen and sheep grazed in the lower pasture where the fence was still intact. A lot of this was his work coming to fruition. He had taken the run-down farm Deborah inherited from her parents and turned it into someplace prosperous enough to feed all of them. He knew that he should feel proud.

Instead he felt like a sand castle at the tide, about to be overwhelmed.

He paused at the barn door and looked across the yard and the well at the house. Deborah had already shooed the other witches back inside for lessons, but his attention was drawn to the rear, where a new wing rose as big as the main building. Ezra had made a lot of progress the last fortnight. He'd been a ship's carpenter most of his life and hated the farming chores, but he tackled the building projects with skill and enthusiasm.

The overwhelming tide retreated for a moment at the

prospect of a real house to sleep in again, instead of the barn. No one could say there was anything improper about him and Deborah sharing space under one roof, not when the men would have a separate door and separate rooms from the women.

A small tug at his shirt hem made him spin around. A girl of ten or eleven stood there. She was small for her age, with dark straight hair cut short like a boy's. Darker skin and almond-shaped eyes hinted at a mixed heritage.

"Hello, Proctor," she said.

A knot melted in Proctor's jaw. "Hello, Zoe."

"Watch this."

She closed her eyes and furrowed her brow, her hand held out in front of her. After a couple of seconds, a spark popped to life in her open palm.

His hands darted out and squeezed her fingers shut, extinguishing the flame. "*Never* do that near the barn."

"I'm not in the barn," she said, pointing at the door to indicate that she was a few steps outside.

"I said *near* the barn, not *in* it."

She jerked her hand away and cradled it against her chest. "You're just like my father. And yes, I'll never do it near the barn or in a house or anything like that. I just wanted to show you."

He sighed, realizing that he was reacting to his memory of the widow Nance, the Covenant agent responsible for, among other things, the scars on his arms. "I'm sorry, Zoe. That just reminded me of a very bad witch who could make fire appear that way. She used it to hurt Deborah's mother and father. I was scared for a moment, and I reacted too strongly."

"Well, that's stupid," she said. "I'm not a bad witch."

That brought a smile to his lips. "No, you're not," he said. He reached out and mussed her hair. She leaned into his hand, almost like a cat.

"Can I pet Singer?" she asked.

"Of course," he said. "How about I put you in the saddle for a minute? Then when you get down, you can help me take off her saddle and brush her."

She nodded eagerly, and he grinned. He lifted her onto the mare, who bore this further delay with a toss of her head and a nip at Proctor's hand. *Capture the young witches and kill the old ones.* He didn't know what the Covenant wanted with witches, but if Alexandra was young enough at fifteen or sixteen, then Bootzamon's master would be even more eager to have someone like Zoe. Proctor wouldn't let that happen.

"Who's giving you your lessons today?" he asked.

"Ugh. They *all* fuss over me, telling me what to do," Zoe said. She sat perfectly still, her hands braced on the pommel. "Can I ride her in the pasture?"

"Not right now. But tomorrow or the day after, I promise. None of them have children of their own, you know."

"Neither did the sailors, but they didn't fuss so much." Zoe's father was Captain Mak, a merchant engaged in the China trade; once her mother died, he had taken her aboard his ship to look after her. When Mak discovered that she had a talent like Ezra's, he entrusted her to the carpenter's care and sent her to The Farm to learn how to control her gift. Zoe shifted in her seat, leaning forward to brush Singer's mane. "Miss Walcott, she—"

"Zoe Mak."

Deborah stood at the front of the house, her hands planted firmly on her hips. Zoe slipped off the horse and dodged behind Proctor.

"Come on, I'll go with you," he said. He took Zoe's hand, and they walked over to Deborah. "She came out to see Singer," he explained. "I told her it was all right."

Zoe let go of Proctor's hand and ran around Deborah, slipping through the door without a word. Deborah stared at Proctor for a moment, then lowered her arms and sighed, following Zoe inside.

Proctor went back to the barn, walking as if he still had a horse beneath him. It would be a while before his legs straightened out again, he thought. He took off Singer's saddle and gave her a thorough rubdown, then put her in the stall. As he filled her feed bag with oats, she lifted her muzzle and slobbered on his cheek. He scratched her ears then went to store her tack.

His work was interrupted by an odd *thump*. He glanced around, taking it for one of the cats, then went back to rubbing oil into the leather.

Another *thump* was followed by the sharp knock of metal on wood. He lifted his head. "Hello? Ezra, is that you?"

He stepped away from the saddle and froze.

A sickle lay on the ground, several feet from the spot on the wall where he kept it stored. There was a line through the straw, too much like the line Bootzamon's tomahawk had drawn through the blood at the Walker house. The sharp, curved blade caught a piece of light from outside, almost seeming to wink at him.

The constant buzz of summer insects fell silent, just like the crickets in Virginia.

His hands started to sweat and shake.

Then something pushed up against his leg and he spun, tense, ready to strike. It was one of the barn cats, the rangy black one with white spots. It lifted its head and meowed at him, and all the sounds came rushing back at once: the insects buzzing outside, the bleating of sheep out in the pasture, the cries of birds in the orchard.

The encounter with Bootzamon had him spooked, constantly braced for another attack. He would be fine as soon as he realized he was safe here on The Farm. As safe as he could be anywhere. He rubbed his sweaty palms on his breeches and petted the cat's head.

"You knock that off the wall?" he asked.

He retrieved the sickle and hung it back in its place, then finished storing the tack. Then he cleaned his weapons and left them on the workbench while he walked to the well to wash up. He was drawing up a bucket of water when the warning chimes tinkled. He let go and the bucket splashed into the water below. Nothing was visible down by the gate—the same charm that disguised their location made the land beyond the boundary blurry.

The door banged open, and Deborah ran out to the porch.

"Somebody's here," he said.

"And they didn't set off my outer warning," she said. Her face looked worried.

"That's not possible, is it?"

"It shouldn't be."

The rest of the students poured onto the porch. Magdalena, the old witch from Pennsylvania, hobbled to the front, steadying herself with her cane. She came from one of the Pennsylvania Dutch religious groups who dressed so plainly they made Quakers look as sumptuous as a French royal court.

"You won't keep me in the dark this time," she said in the singsong German accent so many Americans had. *You von' keep me in der dark dis time.*

"The dark has no place here," Deborah answered. "Proctor and I were just going down to see who has come by."

"Then I am coming you with," Magdalena said, lifting her cane in a gesture of exclamation. She had been a student of Deborah's grandmother and a friend of Deborah's mother, who had helped her hide witches and move them to safety along the Quaker Highway. In her mind, she was the person best suited to run The Farm; she distrusted Deborah's youth and opposed many of the changes Deborah had made, especially the decision to recruit witches and bring them together instead of helping them escape and hide.

She was also still weak from injuries suffered during the Covenant's attack on them a year ago. Lifting her cane unsteadied her, and she began a slow but inevitable topple to one side.

Ezra, who, at sixty, was closest to Magdalena's age, hopped forward to steady her. He moved with that peculiar rolling gait that Proctor had seen on other men who'd spent most of their life at sea.

"But of course you're welcome to come," Deborah said as Ezra caught the old woman. Then she turned and left, walking away at a speed that Magdalena couldn't possibly match.

Proctor sprinted to catch up.

"So you two are still fighting?" he murmured under his breath as he reached Deborah's side.

"We are not fighting," she said firmly. "And no one is holding her here against her will. If she does not approve of the way I do things, she is welcome to leave at any time."

The view beyond their gate grew clearer as they approached. The dark, blurry shape of the oak tree resolved into sharper detail, as did the post beneath it. But the entrance in the wall was empty, as was the road beyond it. No one was there.

"This isn't right," Deborah said.

"Maybe it was a stray animal, or—"

"The spell on the post only works at the touch of human skin."

Proctor knew that, but he was disinclined to be shaken again the way he had let himself get spooked by the sickle at the barn. "So maybe a traveler came down the road, leaned on the post to rest, and was startled away by what he saw," he suggested.

"Then why didn't he trip my outer spell?"

A good question. "There's got to be an explanation."

Zoe appeared beside them. "What's that?" she asked.

"What?" they said simultaneously.

Magdalena, with Ezra at her elbow to help her, hobbled up as fast as she could move, the other students clustered behind her. "Right there, on the post," Zoe said.

Proctor had been expecting to see a person, so he had glanced past the bit of dark rag draped over the gatepost. Now that his attention had been drawn to it, he saw that a small envelope was also attached. He jumped through the gate before anyone else could react, intending to grab both items for inspection. His hand was stretched out to take them when the breeze ruffled the fine auburn threads attached to the rags, and he recognized them for what they were.

"What's the matter?" Deborah asked, stepping forward.

He flung out an arm to stop her. "Don't pass the gate. We aren't safe out here, beyond the wall."

"What? Why?"

"Get back behind the gate," he said, scanning the road, the tree line, everywhere for any sign of danger. The tone of voice made her step back at once, before she had come all the way through.

He grabbed the envelope and touched the post well clear of the other items, which he left behind as he stepped back through to the safety of their sanctuary again.

"What is it?" Deborah asked.

He lowered his voice, turning his body away from the others so they couldn't hear. "Scalps. The Walkers."

His attempt to be discreet was for naught. Zoe, hanging at his side where he didn't see her, blurted out, "It's scalps! Can I see?"

"No," Proctor said. He put a hand on her back and moved her away from the wall.

"Was it Indians?"

"No."

"Well, who was it?"

He didn't answer, because his attention was turned to their border. He castigated himself for coming to the gate without a weapon—no musket, no knife, not even a stout club.

The others were already shaken. Deborah had grown pale, lost in thought as she stared at the scalps. Magdalena stomped over to him and snatched the envelope from his hand. She tore it open, unfolded the letter, and read it. Angrily, she shook it in Proctor's face. "What is the meaning of this?"

He took the letter from her. In elegant script, the letter read:

Dear Mr. Brown,

As a token of our memorable encounter, I deliver these items, which, due to the press of time or your hasty departure, you neglected to collect on your recent trip to Virginia.

I look forward with some relish to the occasion when we meet again.

With warmest feeling,
Yr. Indian Friend

P.S. Please remember me to the dear ladies.

"So it was an Indian?" Zoe asked, reading over his shoulder. "You said it wasn't an Indian."

"No," he said, turning the letter away from her only to have Deborah snatch it from his hand.

Magdalena glared at him. "You two," she said, jabbing her cane at Proctor and Deborah, "have been keeping secrets. Why does your friend call himself an Indian? Who is he?"

"He's no friend. He said his name was Bootzamon—"

"Proctor," Deborah said warningly.

Magdalena snorted. "Bootzamon? Surely that is some kind of joke, a very bad joke."

"That's what he said men called him. Why is it a joke?"

The color drained out of Magdalena's face and she took a step backward, leaning into Ezra's arms to steady herself. "No, I can see, you are joking me not." She used her cane as a focus for her spells, and now she held it in front of her, scanning the road and the trees around them. "Back in the old country, my people had a tradition, the bootzamon. He was a, what do you call them, a scarebird—"

"Scarecrow?" suggested Zoe.

A chill ran through Proctor.

"Ya, that is it, a scarecrow. But not just a scarecrow. The spirit of a dead witch is captured in the bootzamon. Bootzamon is a man witch. A woman witch captured that way would be called the bootzafrau."

"What do they do with the captured witches?" he asked.

"The spirits are slaves to whoever captured them. In the old country, the bootzamon and bootzafrau would protect a village from evil, and then be released from this world when their duty had been done." She drew a deep breath and looked at the scalps. "But I do not think this is a protective spirit."

"No," Proctor admitted grimly. "Bootzamon killed Mister and Missus Walker, Alexandra's parents." He stole a glance at Deborah, who had crossed her arms and would not meet his eye.

"But not the girl?" Magdalena asked.

"No," Proctor said. "I could find no sign of her, but it appeared that she had been gone for some time. All her brothers too."

The old Pennsylvania Dutch woman digested this information. She watched Deborah out of the corner of her eye for a moment before she spoke. "We must have a meeting. You will tell everything that happened on your trip to Virginia."

"Yes," Proctor said. "I'll tell you all the whole story, everything that happened. But let's do it up at the house."

"Ya, that is wise," Magdalena said. Beckoning the others to follow her, she turned to go.

"I'll be along in a moment," Proctor said, and the old woman paused. "First I want to give some decent burial to the last remains of the Walkers."

She nodded agreement and continued on her way. Zoe bounced at his side. "Can I help?"

"No. Now scoot," he said, shooing her after the others. She trudged away with the hangdog look of the perpetually disappointed.

The last to go was Deborah. "I know you had to tell them," she said. "But I'm the one who has to protect them here, make them feel safe, on the same ground where my own mother and father were murdered. Just keep that in mind when you tell them the whole story up at the house."

"We don't even know what the Covenant's new plans are yet," he said.

"Is that supposed to make us less afraid, or more?"

When he didn't answer, she turned away and followed the others. He watched her back dwindle toward the house before he steeled himself to step out and collect Bootzamon's horrific trophies.

Chapter 3

Proctor buried what was left of the Walkers in a tiny hole next to Deborah's mother and father at the edge of the orchard. As he carried the shovel back to the barn, he realized he was tired of digging graves. And he didn't feel like waiting in one spot while the Covenant kept killing his friends and their families.

He went to join the others, who had crowded around the hearth in the main room of the farmhouse. Deborah handed him a serving of chicken potpie.

"Did you make this?" he asked, surprised.

"Don't worry," she told him. "The sisters cooked it."

Deborah's mastery of spells did not extend to cooking. Luckily, the others were willing to help. Proctor waved his thanks to the "sisters," two middle-aged women from western Massachusetts who were actually cousins. Sukey Ballard was a stork-faced widow, while Esther Pettingal was an old maid, pale as a cracker and shaped a bit more like a cracker barrel every day. Along with Abby, another young woman, they formed the rest of Deborah's students. He broke off a piece of the flaky crust, letting it melt on his tongue before he said his grace and sat with the others at the long table.

Magdalena interrupted his last spoonfuls of gravy. "You must tell us what happened in Virginia."

Proctor wiped his mouth and told the story again, just as he had told it to Deborah. They had questions—

Magdalena had the most—but there was little that he could add to his original version.

"Bootzamon's master, whoever he is, that's our real enemy," he said. "If this Bootzamon creature is from the old country, one of the German provinces, then maybe the master is too."

"I thought it was the British what wanted to stop the rebellion," Ezra said.

"They do," Proctor answered. "But the Covenant has different goals from the Crown. The widow Nance made it clear that they consider themselves better than the rest of humanity. She said their powers—"

"Our powers," corrected Deborah.

"She said our powers came because we are the offspring of angels and men. I don't know if that's true, but I think divine birth trumps divine right in their minds."

The group fell silent, more thoughtful than scared, he hoped. Either the meeting exhausted him, or three weeks of travel finally caught up with him, but when they were done he went out to the porch and tilted his head back. The first stars had already appeared in the sky. A yawn split his face and he lifted his hand to cover it as Deborah came out and stood beside him.

"I'll go fix the fence in the pasture," he said.

"Magdalena and I will set extra wards around the buildings tonight," she said. "It'll be enough until tomorrow."

"I'll get my musket and take first watch then."

"Ezra will take care of that. Just like standing watch on a ship, he said. Maybe you should get some sleep."

"But—"

"You'll be of more use to us tomorrow if you get some sleep tonight."

"I do feel like I could use a week's worth of sleep," he admitted. Or a week and a half. He hadn't slept well the whole journey back, startled awake by every rustle in the grass or set on edge every time he smelled pipe tobacco. So he said his good nights and retired to his room in the barn, where he fell onto the mattress still half dressed.

He jerked awake, grabbing for a weapon, just as he had every night since Virginia, but this time, at least, it was morning. By the time he had his tomahawk in hand, ready to strike, he remembered where he was. The pounding sound that he had taken for Bootzamon's fist on the door was only Ezra, hammering on the new addition to the house.

He felt more groggy than awake, more stiff and sore than when he'd lain down, so it took him a moment to pick the straw out of his hair and notice the double serving of breakfast that had been left beside his blankets. Thank you, Deborah. He spooned the boiled oats into his mouth, savoring the molasses. The coffee was cold and weak, but nothing could be done about that. They had to water it down; everything was in short supply because of the war.

He left his jacket in the barn and washed up at the well, blinking at the bright sun. Another hot day. The others bent to their own work in the gardens and around the house. Even with the Covenant leaving threats on their doorstep, they had to take care of their everyday tasks.

Proctor rolled his sleeves to his elbows and unbuttoned his collar. The best way to protect them would be to strengthen the borders. And that meant fixing the fence.

The fence rails along the steepest part of the hillside pasture lay in a tumble. Ezra could have fixed it in minutes, but the old man had spent his whole life in the small confines of ships. He'd paced out an area that encompassed the house, the barn, and the necessary, and it was hard to budge him beyond the rails of that imaginary "deck." So he'd left The Farm unprotected. Proctor shook his head and started restacking the rails.

Ezra was a bit peculiar, but to be truthful, most of their students were peculiar. Living in fear, forced to hide their special talents, warped them all in some way, the way it had warped Proctor's mother. Deborah's idea to start a school was smart. Maybe younger students, like Zoe, could grow up without fear and shame.

Assuming they had a chance to grow up.

The woods beyond the fence loomed dark and ominous. Bootzamon—or some other agent of the Covenant—could be out there right now, just waiting for a chance to get past their protections. He finished repairing the rails and stepped back to size up his work. He and Deborah could come out here later and restore the protective spell—

One of the posts started to slide. A second later, the fence toppled, and all the rails rolled down to his feet.

There was nothing sinister at work. The fence uprights rested on a flat rock that followed the slope of the hill—as soon as the weight of the rails pressed down, they slipped loose and the whole thing collapsed. He shouldn't have been so hard on Ezra. The old sailor probably fixed it two or three times, then decided to leave it for "the one what knows how to farm."

A walk along the edge of the pasture confirmed that the whole length of the slope was rocky. If he shifted the fencerow, he was likely to end up with the same problem in another place. So the rock had to go.

He used a post-end to scrape dirt away from the edges of the rock. Then he jammed the post under the rock and tried to lever it up. The rock didn't budge. He scraped deeper and tried again without results. He needed help.

Down at the house, the women headed inside for their lessons. Ezra was climbing off the roof of the new addition to go join them. Proctor shouted and waved his arms to get the old carpenter's attention. Ezra waved back to Proctor, and mimed tying a bowline. Ezra thought rope could fix anything that couldn't be hammered right, and he'd made Proctor learn how to tie a variety of sailors' knots. Having made his suggestion with the gesture, Ezra went inside.

So much for that.

Proctor skipped lessons because Deborah had already taught him the basic skills she was trying to teach the others. Today they were working on lifting—

It was hard to shake twenty years of upbringing. He was still thinking like a farmer when he needed to think like a witch. With the proper focus for a spell, he could use magic to move the rock.

And he could find a focus in the woods beyond the fence. The tall hardwoods beyond the boundary of the farm were blurry, even when he looked at them directly. But the hedge of hawthorn trees just past the fence appeared in sharp detail because they were inside the limits of Deborah's protective spell. Anyone who came through the woods, pushing through the spells of forgetfulness and the illusion that nothing was there, would set off the alarms and then run immediately into a thorny hedge too thick for anything but a rabbit to pass through.

But would those spells stop Bootzamon?

Proctor braced himself as if he expected an immediate attack, and stepped over the broken fence. He waited, tense and anxious for Bootzamon to appear, until a pair of warblers zipped past him and snapped him back to his senses.

He found a nest tucked in the crook of some branches. Though he reached in carefully, the thorns scraped his bare arms as he pulled a gray pinfeather from the nest, the smallest, lightest one he could find. Then he tore a couple of leaves off the nearest branch and shoved them in his mouth. The sharp taste as he chewed on them made him feel more alert. No witchcraft to that, just his mother's herblore.

He stepped back across the fallen fence and shoved the feather under the edge of the rock. The sharp end of the post fit in the same spot for a lever. Folding his hands around the wood, he bowed his head to say the spell. He wasn't as good as Deborah at pulling out the right Bible verse on a moment's notice, so he simply asked to do God's will and prayed for the strength of Samson. He had come to realize that the words were less important than the images in his head. He pictured what he wanted to accomplish and ran it over and over in his thoughts, like a dog wearing a path around the edge of a pen.

When he felt the power rising in him, like water bubbling up from a spring, he stood, took a deep breath, and heaved on the lever another time.

The stone rose a few inches and stuck.

"It's as light as a feather," he murmured to himself. He let the power flow through his hands and down the rail. They needed the fence repaired, needed the protection against intruders. "Light as a feather, light as a feather." He heaved again, pouring all his energy through the lever.

The rail splintered, and, at the same instant, the stone popped out of the ground, spraying dirt everywhere as it fell back down with a *thump*.

Proctor had flung his arms up instinctively to protect his face from the splinters, but his knees buckled beneath him and he fell to the ground, dizzy and nauseous. The thumping pain in his skull half blinded him, and he tingled all over with that familiar pin-cushion sensation.

But it had worked. The stone—no, the boulder—was bigger than a cider keg, and it had been planted deep. He laughed through his dizziness. He had moved it with magic. Well, magic and his own strong back. Now he could fill in the hole, brace the cross posts against the stone, split another rail, and be done with the fence.

Of course, to do that he needed his shovel and hatchet, which were down at the barn. He stood to go get them, but he had only taken one or two steps when black spots swam before his eyes. He tumbled back to his knees.

He crawled on his hands and knees halfway down the slope, then stood and staggered unsteadily to the well. Though he lifted the rock with magic, his body ached as if he had done it with bone and muscle. His arms were almost too weak to haul up the bucket. The ladle of water tasted like copper coins scraped against his teeth, and he spit it out.

They knew so little about magic. It drew on a source—Deborah, like his mother, insisted that the source was God. Unlike God, the source was not infinite, and drawing too much could leave you as defenseless as a child.

Which was why evil witches drew on the power of others. A year ago, Proctor had stood at this very well with Cecily Sumpter Pinckney, an aristocratic lady from Charleston, South Carolina. They had all thought her an ally, come to The Farm to learn how to use her gift. But she had been an agent of the Covenant, spying on potential enemies in the colonies. She drew her power from her slave, Lydia, and none of them had known it, though Lydia had tried to warn them. Their blindness to her warnings had left Deborah's mother and father dead.

Cecily was nothing compared with the widow Nance. Nance used death magic. In John Hancock's slave cabins, on the night before the battle of Bunker Hill, she had murdered a small boy, planning to draw on Deborah's power as she spilled Proctor's blood, sealing a death spell on the patriot leaders and destroying the rebellion. Just thinking about it made the scars on Proctor's arms itch.

Magic flowed both ways in a spell between two witches, like tidewater at a river's mouth. When Deborah broke the widow's spell, all the magic flowed the other direction, killing Nance. The widow was dead, but Cecily was still out there, still drawing on Lydia's power to augment her own. Ever since their encounter with the widow, Deborah had become obsessed with the drawing spells, how they worked, how they could be broken. None of them wanted to be fooled by anyone like Cecily ever again.

And now Bootzamon was out there somewhere too. His

master was out there. Proctor looked down at the gate. How many enemies did they have?

He took another sip of water. This one tasted palatable enough to swallow. He still felt weak, but not as dizzy as he had a few moments before. In fact, he thought he ought to go brag to Deborah about moving that boulder.

He walked carefully over to the house, like a drunk trying to keep his balance. His head still throbbed, leaving his vision tinged with gray. The door stuck in the frame. He braced his shoulder against it and shoved—he meant to nudge it quietly so he wouldn't disturb Deborah's lesson, but it banged open and he stumbled into the house.

He looked up in time to see all seven witches sitting around the table, holding hands in a circle. Seven candles were lit—he didn't have to count them because he knew how Deborah used the flame as a focus. There'd be one for each. Inside the circle of candles, a smooth river stone, the size of a large yam, floated above the table.

Zoe squeaked at Proctor's entrance.

The stone thunked to the wood.

Deborah released the circle, practically flinging the hands away from her. "That was excellent," she said. "The best lifting you've done yet. Next, we'll try it individually."

Yes, he had advanced far beyond the other students.

"It's too hard—my head aches," Abby complained. She was the next youngest, after Zoe. "We work so hard, I feel like I'm getting weaker, not stronger."

Magdalena placed her liver-spotted hand over Abby's. "There, there," she said. "It will be all right. You are doing well. Deborah, if you must be busy, I could the lesson continue."

"This will only take a moment." Deborah rose, stomping across the floor toward Proctor. "I assume this is of life-or-death importa—oh, you're bleeding."

"No, I'm not," Proctor said, looking down at his hands.

She rushed to his side and reached up to his cheek. "Be still—"

"Ow!"

"You're such a baby," she said, softly enough that no one else could hear. She held up the bloody splinter for him to see. He'd been too numb and dizzy to notice until she pulled it out. He reached up to feel the wound. "Be *still*," she said.

She touched his cheek and it tingled a different way, like bubbles rising up in a pint of beer. The pain lessened at once. The blood turned to a scab, and the scab began to dry as if it had been there several days. But the sensation dizzied him, and he flinched away before he collapsed.

"How did you do—?"

His question was interrupted by a single bell—Deborah's outer boundary warning. Someone was approaching The Farm. Before they could react, the invisible chimes tinkled.

Someone was approaching in a hurry.

Her eyes met his. The hiding spells should also protect them, but last year Cecily had betrayed their secrets and let in assassins. Did someone know the way through again?

"I'll get my musket," he said.

Her face hardened again instantly. "I'll prepare to meet them just beyond the well. Magdalena?"

"Ya, ya, we all know what to do—now go!"

The panic in the old woman's voice chased Proctor out the door. He was not going to risk a repeat of yesterday, when he'd gone to the gate completely unprepared. But the effort of running across the yard dizzied him. He crashed against the barn door, holding on tight to keep from fainting.

Deborah walked slowly and deliberately past the well. She was tucking her hair under her gray bonnet and smoothing the front of her dress. She slipped her right hand into her front pocket, where she kept a protective charm that she had never let him see.

The barrier shimmered down at the gate, and a rider appeared on a dark horse. Proctor's vision was still blurry, and everything was gray. But he could see that the rider's jacket had a military cut with epaulets, and he was armed with guns and had his hand on the hilt of a sword. He trotted crisply straight toward Deborah.

Proctor lurched through the door and grabbed his musket from its spot at his workbench. It was a Brown Bess that had been passed down from one hand to the next since the war with the French and their Indian allies more than twenty years before—a good, reliable gun. He slung his hunting bag over his shoulder and began loading the weapon as he turned back.

He hoped, if there was an attack, it was just the one man. Unless the man on the horse was a diversion. Other assassins would come at them from behind, across the pasture with the broken fence.

That thought raced through his head as he rammed the shot down the barrel and ran outside.

In the yard just past the well, the rider loomed over Deborah. He was pulling his sword from its sheath. Deborah took a step back, glancing over at Proctor. Her hand was in her pocket, clutching her protective charm.

If he brought the rider down with one shot, he could reload while he rushed out to block the next attack from the fence. Proctor lifted the barrel, aimed, and—

The musket jerked up into the air as he squeezed the trigger, discharging harmlessly. It had been magic, an invisible hand, that ruined his aim. The horse tossed its head and took a few steps back. Raising his gun like a club, Proctor started forward.

Only to be stopped by the sight of Deborah. She stood there, with her arm outstretched, palm open. She was the one who had deflected his shot.

"Proctor," she said. "It's our friend."

At first the phrase meant nothing to him. She was a

Quaker and called everyone *friend,* even some people who weren't. Then he heard the rider speak.

"I'm glad to see you're ready to defend yourselves."

Relief flushed through Proctor, and for a moment he thought he might topple over. "Paul Revere."

Chapter 4

Before the Revolution, Paul Revere had been one of the guides on the Quaker Highway, the secret network of ministers and others across New England that helped move accused witches to places of safety. Revere belonged to the Masons, the Sons of Liberty, and served on the colonial committees for intelligence and alarms, which was how he'd come to ride a horse out to Concord the year before to warn that the Redcoats were coming. Revere knew everyone worth knowing and any news they might want to know.

He sat comfortably in the saddle, his round face tan from a summer spent out in the sun. He wore the blue jacket of a Continental army officer, something new since the last time Proctor had seen him.

The door to the house opened. Ezra stood there, shoved forward by Magdalena. The faces of the other students were pressed to the window. "Is everything all right?" Ezra asked.

"There's no alarm," Deborah answered. "This is our old friend. Give us a moment with him, please."

The corners of Revere's eyes crinkled. "So, Mr. Brown, you mistook me for a Redcoat? I should be glad your aim has worsened in the past year."

Proctor leaned on the gun to steady himself. "I didn't recognize you in your new duds."

Revere ran a quick thumb down the buff-colored trim on the lapel. "You like them?"

"Eh, they're all right," Proctor said drily.

Revere laughed and showed Proctor and Deborah the hilt of his officer's sword. "You behold the Continental army's most newly commissioned captain. Although I expect to be a colonel by Christmas."

"Congratulations," Deborah said.

"It seems like a prodigal use of your talents," Proctor added, thinking of Dr. Joseph Warren, the best physician in Massachusetts, who'd been killed right before Proctor's eyes defending the barricade at Bunker Hill. "Plenty of other fellows can stop a musket ball."

Revere dismounted with ease and tied the horse up near the trough. "I'll be working with artillery. It's a continuation of the gunpowder research I did for General Washington over the past year."

Proctor had seen General Washington once, during the siege of Boston, though he'd never met him. But Revere tossed his name off with the familiarity of a neighbor or near acquaintance.

"You didn't come all the way up from Boston just to brag about your commission," Deborah said. "You've got better audiences than us for that."

Revere held out an open hand. "I would have sent you a letter, but—"

Proctor winced, knowing what was coming next.

"Absolutely not," Deborah said. "You know what we do here. We must never write anything down, give no one any way to find us or 'prove' we're witches. That rule has preserved our lives for four-score years."

"I understand," Revere conceded. "But with the war heating up again, I may not always be able to get away."

"Then you'll have to send word by a friend of a friend, the way we have always done," Deborah said.

"You're running out of friends," Revere said. "Bowditch is dead—"

"Dead?" asked Proctor.

"Of an apoplexy," Revere said. "Happened without warning. Cartland's son took over his section of the highway, but he was killed at the battle of Trois Rivières. And Whitcomb has gone missing, didn't return from his trip to the Ohio country."

"There's always the Reverend Emerson," Deborah said.

Revere shook his head. "Emerson is going to serve as a volunteer pastor at Fort Ticonderoga. He won't be available for the duration of the campaign."

"Good news for the soldiers at Ticonderoga, but bad news for us," Proctor said. All of it was bad news for them. He hoped that it was coincidental, but what he had seen at Alexandra Walker's farm worried him. Her family had also been guides, just like Bowditch, Cartland, and Whitcomb.

"I've heard much about the witchcraft of the Indians in that part of New York," Deborah said. "Perhaps Emerson can find out something for us."

"Perhaps," Revere conceded. "But my point is, our options for communication may become very limited. The war is heating up again, what with Howe landing his troops in New York—"

"Wait a minute," Proctor said. "Howe did what?"

Revere looked at him as if he were senseless. "Have you not heard? How removed from the world are you here?"

"Like a papist monastery," Proctor said.

Revere took off his hat and wiped the sweat from his balding forehead. "Admiral Howe has landed his brother's army on Staten Island. Thirty thousand men."

"That's half again as many soldiers as Washington has in the whole army," Proctor said.

"Do the British hate us so much, that so many of them want to come here to fight us?" Deborah asked.

Revere sat on the edge of the well and splashed water on his face. "They're not all British," he said. "Many of them, maybe half, are battle-tested mercenaries from Germany. Mostly Hessians."

"But we're safe here, in Boston, and north of Boston?" Deborah asked.

"We're not safe anywhere if they overrun General Washington," Proctor said.

Revere nodded his agreement. "As soon as the weather's right, they'll attack Long Island or Manhattan. We knew the blow was coming, even before the Declaration of Independence was published. But it takes so much time to move messages, much less men, across the ocean." He paused, then looked at Proctor and Deborah. "Is there any chance we'll be able to count on your people for aid?"

"Yes, absolutely," Proctor said.

Deborah said, "No, no chance at all."

Revere sipped another ladle of water, looking over the rim of the bowl at the two of them. Finally, he lowered it and said, "Which is it?"

"One army will have to take care of the other," Deborah said. She glanced over her shoulder at the house. "We're preparing to face the Covenant, and I can tell you, we're not ready."

"None of us is ready," Revere answered. "But we all do what we can, to the best of our abilities. Do we know any more about our enemy yet?"

"We know that if the Continental army is defeated, then they've achieved their goal," Proctor said, more to answer Deborah than Revere.

Deborah slashed her hand through the air, in firm negation. "The witches we faced last year, the widow and that southern woman"—Deborah never spoke of Cecily by name—"they had incredible power. They could control what we saw, making our own eyes lie to us. They could make thousands sick with a single spell. They could animate the dead." She looked suddenly lost and fragile, and her voice dropped to a near whisper. "I don't have that kind of power yet. These others that we've gathered for training, they don't have that kind of power either."

"And let us hope they never do," Revere said. "Those are evil powers and should never be used."

"Exactly," Deborah said.

"Which is all the more reason we need your defenses," he said compellingly. "General Washington can find a way to beat the British and their mercenaries, but only if his men are well enough to fight. He can't defeat another witch's spell."

Proctor could see why some men decided it would be easier to kill all witches than sort out the good from the bad. "We're doing what we can," he said. "We've had trouble gathering even the witches we know. The Covenant is sending its agents to capture or kill all our friends and allies."

"And still you will not act?" Revere said incredulously.

"We act every day that we stay in safety here, preparing to meet those who wish us harm," Deborah snapped.

Proctor wasn't convinced they were doing the right thing. Why stay here in hiding while the Covenant hunted down their friends? Better to go out and find them, destroy them where they were.

Revere, however, decided not to argue the point further. "I'll give you my bit of news, in hopes that it will help you on several fronts, both in gathering students and finding our secret enemies. There's an orphan."

The word froze Deborah, who was an orphan now. Proctor stepped over to her side and let his arm dangle where the edge of his hand grazed hers.

"An apprentice-aged lad, about eleven or twelve," Revere said. "He's named William Reed, and strange things have been happening around him. His neighbors call him haunted, but it may be your sort of gift he has."

"Where?" Proctor asked.

"Down on the western tip of Long Island, southeast of Brooklyn, at a town called Gravesend," Revere said.

"What sort of strange things?" Deborah asked.

Revere rubbed the back of his neck. "A wagon broke and fell on his neighbor, pinning him to the road, but this boy lifted it by himself, preserving the neighbor's legs, if not his life. Sometimes lamps go out mysteriously; others flash on with no agency or explanation. Stones have been seen to float around him."

Proctor leaned on his musket for balance. If the boy was an orphan, he might have no idea what was happening to him or why. He could be terrified.

"That's hardly proof that it's his gift," Deborah said.

"No," agreed Revere. "But the parties interested in him point in that direction."

"What do you mean?" Proctor said.

"Less than a week ago, a certain Cecily Sumpter Pinckney was in New York City, asking questions about the boy and looking for someone to lead her to him."

Deborah's hand pulled away from Proctor and darted into the pocket where she kept her focus.

"So if you plan to retrieve this boy, you may want to go before General Washington's troops engage Howe's army," Revere continued. "And if she's planning some kind of witchcraft, it'd be best to take the powder from her gun before she fires."

Proctor agreed. He didn't want to see Cecily doing to anyone else what she'd done to Lydia. "Can we invite you inside?" he asked. "It's a bit early for supper, but we'll feed you well enough if you'll wait."

"Thank you, but no," Revere said. In one smooth motion, he remounted his horse. "It's a big war, and I've other folks to visit yet this evening, especially if progress here is slower than we hoped. I have to report back to Boston the morning after tomorrow."

"God speed," Deborah said.

Revere turned the horse toward the invisible gate, pausing to tug his cap back tightly on his head. "And to you, also, if you go to Long Island."

With a tap of his heels into the flanks of his horse, he headed away. He was nearly to the gate when he turned and came back.

"I almost hate to mention this," he said. "But I saw the oddest thing in the woods on my approach here. At first I thought it a scarecrow, but who puts a scarecrow under the trees, away from any crops? So I took him for a beggar."

Bootzamon. Proctor gripped his musket in both hands and felt his teeth grind together.

"You know who I'm describing?" Revere said.

"We do," Deborah replied with a forced smile. "And it's nothing for you to worry about. Thank you again for going out of your way to see us."

He tipped his hat and rode away. When he passed the gatepost, his image scattered like a reflection in a pool of water shattered by a rain of stones.

Proctor frowned and felt the scab on his cheek crack. He turned to Deborah to ask her what she thought about Bootzamon.

She stared after Revere. "Another orphan," she growled.

"So who was that?"

Proctor and Deborah spun as they heard the question. Ezra had taken a step off the porch. His voice was tense, and a large mallet dangled from his strong right hand.

"That was Paul—"

"It was a friend," Deborah interrupted. "A guide on the highway, with some bad news." Picking up the hem of her dress, she stomped toward Ezra, who took a step back, startled. She chased him up the porch and back into the house.

The door banged shut before Proctor gathered his wits enough to follow. He still felt weak, but his head had stopped hammering and his balance had returned. He climbed the steps carefully and propped his musket against the house before going inside.

"—don't just sit there all fish-mouthed," Deborah said.

She stood at the end of the table, her back to Proctor, with her fists on her hips, staring at her students. "We're not done with the lesson yet."

The other students lowered their eyes, but Magdalena glared back from the opposite end of the table. Her plain gray cap had come unpinned on one side and sat slightly askew, spilling her thin gray hair. Her hands were clenched in fists on the table in front of her.

"I think you must tell us what is the news," she said.

"I told you already that it's nothing we need to talk about this moment," Deborah said. She tapped her fingers on the table, and the candles, which had been snuffed, twitched back into flames. "Our lives could depend on these skills, now more than ever. So I want to see all of you try again. Use the flame as a focus and raise this stone."

Sukey reached out to squeeze Esther's hand, to show that they were united in whatever she was about to say. "That was Mister Paul Revere Junior, the Boston silversmith," Sukey said, lifting her long, narrow nose with an air of authority. "A fancy new coat can't hide that man's smile."

"Yes, it was Revere," Deborah admitted. "Now. If we could return to our lesson."

Seventeen-year-old Abby turned her blunt, square face to Deborah and said, "You want us to raise this stone?"

"If you please," Deborah said.

Abby snatched it up off the table and held her fist at Deborah. "Here—it's raised!"

They all froze for a moment. Little Zoe sat wide-eyed and openmouthed, her head pivoting to stare at each person in turn. The others were grim, waiting to see how Deborah reacted. Even Proctor felt a bit stunned. He had never seen them all challenge Deborah's authority at once before.

Deborah stared straight at Abby, who grimaced back for a long moment. Finally, Abby's eyes flicked to either side of the table to see what the other women were doing. Her resolve shattered, and she dropped the stone onto the table. Pallid Esther flinched at the sharp sound.

Deborah took a deep breath and lowered her voice. "The Covenant is still out there. They killed my mother and father, they killed Alexandra Walker's family, and they mean to kill us, if they can. We must develop our skills."

"See, that's just it," Sukey said. Her voice was high, and as thin as her bony arms and hands. "Esther and I have been talking, haven't we, Esther dear?"

"Yes, oh, yes, we have," Esther said, her plump cheeks quivering.

"If these people, whoever they are, are hunting for witches," Sukey said, "then wouldn't we be better off where we were, in our own communities, unnoticed, instead of someplace they've attacked before?"

"Yes, yes, exactly," Esther said, nodding her round head vigorously.

"If you're here, then you weren't exactly unnoticed in your own community," Deborah said. "Someone accused both of you, correctly, of being witches."

Esther, always eager to please, said hesitantly, "Yes, yes, they did."

She winced as Sukey gave a hard squeeze to her hand.

"If they attack me, and I need to defend myself with a rock," Abby said, "then I'll pick one up and bash their stupid heads with it. Teach us something useful."

She pushed back from the table, knocking her chair over as she stood up to leave. Deborah's back knotted up just like a cat's, and her hand shot into her pocket. The chair righted itself from the floor and shot forward, knocking Abby back into her seat and scooting her to the table. She sat there, pale and shaken.

Magdalena's chin trembled in barely suppressed fury.

Proctor understood the point Deborah intended—once you learned how to lift a rock, it was easy to move other things. But all the women in this room were proud of their independence, and with tempers strained at the moment, all Deborah had accomplished was to make them feel insignificant. And afraid. Her point was going to be lost in a flurry of argument and resentment if he didn't do something fast.

He cleared his throat.

"I'll go pack my bag while you folks sort this out," he said, waving good-bye. "I'll be back in a few days."

Everyone reacted at once.

Zoe jumped up from her seat. "I'll go with you!"

Abby slapped the rock, knocking it onto the floor, then sulked back in her chair, arms crossed.

"But, son, I was counting on your help to finish the roof," Ezra said.

"You can't leave us here alone," Sukey said, raising her fist to shake it at Proctor. Her long bony fingers were still clutched tightly around Esther's plump hand, tugging her halfway over the table.

"Must we all shout?" Esther whimpered, her eyes closed.

"Sopperlut! What is going on?"

Magdalena pounded her fist on the table just like she was using a mortar to crush her potions in a pestle. Proctor knew she was upset—she'd started using that Dutch lingo none of them understood.

"Oh, Deborah will explain it all to you," he said. "Well, I'll be going then."

He turned toward the door, dragging his feet just enough to let Deborah slam it tight with magic before he reached it. He permitted himself a small smile while no one could see him, then wiped it off his face before spinning to face her.

She stalked over to him, tilting her head back to look at him eye-to-eye. She was very angry. The little crease on her forehead was a dead giveaway. "This is no time for wild goose chases," she said.

"What do you mean?" he asked.

"I mean this is no time to run off to other states again, away from The Farm for days or weeks, looking for another witch who probably isn't even there." *Not with Bootzamon out there.* But she didn't say that.

"Not even when we know the Covenant is looking for him too?" Proctor asked.

The room fell silent for a moment while the group digested this new bit of information. Finally, Magdalena broke the silence. "Who or what this wild goose is? Tell us everything."

"Revere brought word of a young boy, an orphan, on Long Island, who may be a witch," Proctor said. "He shows the talent. His neighbors have started to fear him."

Abby was the first to speak. She came from a family of eleven, with both her parents living, and her grandparents not half a mile away; more often than not, she seemed to think that if she didn't speak first she would never get the chance. "Oh, the poor boy," she said.

"We don't need another child here," Deborah said.

Zoe thumped down in her seat so hard everyone stopped to look at her. She ducked her face behind her bangs, glowering.

"I only mean, he'll be in danger," Deborah explained quickly.

"He's already in danger," Proctor said. "The British army is on Staten Island, and battle is expected any day. And we know the Covenant wants him. Cecily Sumpter Pinckney has been seen in New York, looking for him, just a few days past."

"We could use a boy," Ezra said. "We always had boys on our ships—they're good for all kinds of work."

"Chores are nothing," Abby said, with the attitude of someone who rose before dawn every morning to do the milking. "But that boy must be so frightened. I know how I felt when my talent first started to show. I was surrounded by my family, with my mother and my aunt born with the talent, and them telling me what to expect. But this boy, I'm sure he's got nobody."

Her pride in her family showed in her voice. She was the daughter of Margaret Lamb, a friend of Deborah's mother and a witch who lived up the Hudson River in New York. They were good people, Proctor thought, even if their talent for magic didn't extend much past easing childbirth and remedying a few common ills. Abby had more talent than the rest of her family combined.

Sukey shook her head. "I have to agree with Deborah this time. If there's danger here, we have no right to bring a child into it."

"Oh, that would be so wrong," Esther squeaked.

"This Sissy person, she's the one who tried to kill you last year, right?" Abby said.

"Yes, she is," Proctor said.

"Well, then he's in danger there," Abby said, exasperated. "We have to do something."

Zoe popped out of her chair. "Yeah!"

"Don't be fools," Sukey responded. "He could already be dead. It's a wild goose chase."

"This orphan boy might not have parents," Proctor said. "But he's staying with somebody's family. I don't want anyone else to stumble into a scene like the one I found at the Walker farm in Virginia."

"And you think you're powerful enough to stop this Bootzamon creature?" Deborah asked. She glanced at the others. "If he's there with Cecily."

"I did it once," Proctor said.

But he was also thinking that he could draw Bootzamon away from The Farm. All he had to do was let the creature know where he was going, and why.

And then survive.

Chapter 5

Deborah's mouth was pursed to argue more when Magdalena, the only person who had yet to voice an opinion, interrupted.

"I think we should call a meeting. We must find the way forward until we come to a unity."

Deborah's face went still.

Meeting was a habit that Deborah's mother had borrowed from the Quakers. When the witches on The Farm needed to decide something, they prayed and discussed it together until they reached a consensus. Deborah had continued the practice, but Proctor could see it was beginning to chafe with the way she wanted to run things herself.

The others were familiar with the practice too. As soon as Magdalena suggested it, tempers began to cool down.

"That's a good idea," Proctor said.

"That's a *very* good idea," Sukey said, her long narrow hand absentmindedly patting Esther on the arm. "It'll be just like a town meeting, dear."

"I don't care for town meetings or politics," Esther said meekly, with her eyes downcast. "But I should very much like the shouting to stop."

"But what's the point? We'll all agree that we have to help him," Abby said. Zoe stood behind her, nearly obscured by the larger girl, but her face peeked over Abby's shoulder and she nodded agreement.

Deborah bristled. "We will not—"

"We will be quiet," Magdalena snapped. When Deborah

clamped her mouth shut, the old Dutch woman repeated herself, more softly. "We will begin all of us by being quiet."

Proctor pulled up a chair and squeezed in at the corner of the table between Abby and Magdalena. He held out his hands palms-up, ready to grasp his neighbors' hands for prayer. Zoe hopped back into her seat on Abby's other side.

"If we captained a ship this way, we'd never find our way out of port," Ezra grumbled. "But this is what we're fighting England for, isn't it? The right to rule ourselves. So if this is what we're doing, I'm for it." He fell into his seat, next to Esther.

The only empty chair left was Deborah's, at the end of the table opposite Magdalena.

The two women stared at each other, the old one sitting, the younger one standing. There was so much suppressed anger between them, Proctor thought the air might burst into flame. Finally, Deborah sighed and took her seat.

They had neatly divided themselves, Proctor saw. Magdalena sat at one end of the table, with Proctor, Abby, and Zoe at her right hand. Deborah sat at the other, with Ezra, Esther, and Sukey at her right.

Seven candles burned on the table, the greasy threads of smoke twisting upward into a single cord. This group was not going to find unity that easily, Proctor thought. Getting all eight of them to agree would be powerful magic indeed.

"Let us pray," Magdalena said at the exact same moment Deborah said, "We'll begin with prayer."

The two women glared at each other, and each nodded her head in deference. Then, at the same time, both held out their hands to start the prayer.

Proctor grasped the hands on either side. Magdalena's knuckles were swollen, her grip arthritic but determined. Abby took his other hand like a farm boy, ready to crush his fingers.

When the circle was completed, he felt a tingle flow from hand to hand, like water moving through a waterwheel.

"Friends," Deborah said before Magdalena could speak. "We are gathered here to seek God's will regarding the orphan boy on Long Island who may be a witch." She bowed her head. "Lord, we pray for guidance, that we may come to a clear understanding of Your purpose for us, so that we may walk in Your light and do Your will."

"Amen," Abby said.

They released hands and the tingle stopped.

The opening prayer was followed by silent prayer, so that all the members of the circle could find their inner Light, the voice of God, revealing His will. Proctor lowered his head, but he couldn't keep his eyes closed. Every time he shut them, he saw the bodies of Mr. and Mrs. Walker, scalped and bloody.

He was moved to say something about that, and why it was a reason to act, but Deborah cleared her throat.

"It's important that we be united in this," she said. "Yes, this orphan boy is in danger. But so are many others, and we can't go running off after all of them. The fact is, we're in danger. We need to study and get stronger, then we can be prepared to help others."

It was considered polite to wait after someone spoke at meeting, to give everyone time to digest one set of thoughts before hearing another.

Abby started to talk the second Deborah finished. "If we're going to help people eventually, let's start with this boy right now." She looked around the table. "When the talent first started to show for me, it came in my dreams. I would dream that I was flying and then wake up floating above my bed."

"And today she can't lift a single stone," Sukey murmured to Esther.

Abby scowled across the table. "It's not funny. I feel like

my power's been drained since I came here. It's so frustrating."

"You shouldn't worry about that," Deborah said. "It happens to everyone when they start to study and think about their talent. It's only temporary. We can talk about it another time, if you like. But right now we need to come to unity about the boy."

"But it's the boy I'm talking about," Abby said passionately. "Look how hard it is for me to take the reins of my talent, and I'm surrounded by people who understand. He has to do it alone. It's not right."

She fell silent. Proctor agreed with everything she said, but he had a more compelling reason to act: if Cecily and the Covenant wanted this boy, they shouldn't be allowed to get him. He was opening his mouth to speak when Sukey waved her hand in a circle encompassing the table.

"No offense to the younger members here," Sukey said, with a nod to Abby and Zoe, "but I think we should listen to the wisdom of the elders present. Yes, it's frightening for the boy, and yes, he's in danger, but many others are too, and we should protect ourselves here first. Esther was telling me the exact same thing. Weren't you, Esther?"

Esther sat silently until Sukey jabbed an elbow in her side. "Yes, I was," Esther said. "I'm frightening. I mean, *it's* frightening, very, but we . . . we . . . What do *you* think, Mister Dillingham?"

Ezra shifted uncomfortably at the mention of his proper name. His sunburned face wrinkled in deep thought. "I say the ship has sailed. Thems what's in port get left behind in port."

"See," Sukey said. "We are in complete agreement with one another."

"No, we're not," Zoe said. She reached across the table and punched Ezra, knocking over a candle. Esther caught the candle and set it upright as Abby dragged Zoe back into her lap.

"You can't mean that," Zoe said. "You wouldn't leave me behind, would you?"

"That's not my meaning," Ezra said.

"Don't worry, Zoe," Proctor said. "We'll never leave you behind. In port. Or . . . wherever."

"So would you leave this other boy behind, just because we don't know him?"

"No," Proctor said. "I won't."

"We haven't come to that unity yet," Deborah said, firmly.

"And we won't," Proctor said. "For eighty years, the Quaker Highway has been taking witches out of Massachusetts. For the past year, we've been trying to gather them again, but the guides are dead, and the witches are missing." He paused to gather his thoughts. "If the only talent we have is for healing, that's reason enough to gather people. There's a war on, and there's more healing needed than all of us here can do, even if that's all we did. I know because I've been there, firsthand, in the front lines, and it's bloody work."

He knew his voice was shaking, that he was upset, but he had to finish what he wanted to say.

"What the Covenant has done, that's even bloodier. We don't know what their plan is, but we know the kinds of magic they use—murdering children as part of their spells, breathing life into corpses to make killers of them, trapping the ghosts of witches inside the bodies of scarecrows. It's all death and ghosts, and every breed of evil." He pointed at the door. "The Covenant is out there right now, working on their plan. If Cecily wants this orphan, then it's for the Covenant. And if the Covenant wants him, then I say that's reason enough for us to get to him first."

"Proctor," Deborah said softly.

He knew his voice had been rising, that he sounded angry. He calmed himself. "That's all I have to say."

That was the longest speech Proctor had ever given at

one of their meetings, probably the longest speech of his life. The group sat silently for a moment.

"Well, Mister Brown is certainly very eloquent," Sukey said. "But I fear that he lets his heart's passions run away with his head. Martial ardor is not unexpected in a young man, though I hesitate to call it a virtue. But we are not the witchcraft militia, ready to muster off to battle. We are healers, no matter what Mister Brown may think. Isn't that right, Esther dear?"

"Absolutely," Esther said. "I know I'm always ready to heal."

"That's a dear woman," Sukey said, patting Esther's hand. "We didn't come here to play parlor tricks with flames and pebbles. The only proper use of our talents is to heal people, to make them well when they are ill, to ward off evil influences. I must believe that. Young Mister Brown may stay if he pleases, or go after this boy if that pleases him more. Whichever he does, I say we turn our attention to basics here and learn things that can truly help people."

"We can't let him go alone," Deborah said. "With no one to watch his back or stand guard while he sleeps." She turned to Proctor. "The Covenant will kill you the first opportunity they get."

The fearful look in their eyes said the rest: *Bootzamon is already waiting out there, just beyond our barriers.*

"Well, then," Proctor said. "I promise not to give them any opportunity."

"I'll go with you," Abby said.

Everybody at the table turned their heads to the farm girl. She had picked the river stone up off the floor and turned it over in her hands.

"To be honest, I'm no good at the lessons you're setting for us, Miss Deborah," she said, smacking the stone down on the table. "And I'm tired of being cooped up here, with no neighbors to visit, no town to go shopping in, and no meeting on Sunday mornings. If it's dangerous, it can't be any more dangerous than living out on the edge of Indian country."

Deborah shook her head firmly no. "Your mother wouldn't approve if I sent you on a journey with a young man and no chaperone. In fact, she'd have my hide."

"Oh, no, she'd understand if *you* explained it," Abby said. "She said you were the only young woman she ever met who she trusted completely around my brothers."

Proctor glanced at Deborah in time to see her blush.

"You just tell her that Proctor is like your brother," Abby said. "She'll be fine with it if you tell her that he's like a brother to all of us."

Proctor stared at his feet and felt something like a ball of ice form in his stomach. Was it true? Had he and Deborah worked so hard at staying proper around each other, they'd become like brother and sister? Maybe Deborah had even said as much to Abby.

"You're too young," Deborah said firmly. "I made a promise to your mother to keep my eye on you, and I can't do that if you're not here. Besides, it's far more dangerous than the frontier. Your mother would not approve, even if Proctor were one of your brothers."

Abby's shoulders sagged.

"Ezra will go," Zoe said. "Won't you, Ezra?"

"Aye, I will," he said. He pushed his chair back from the table. "If those are the captain's orders. What time's the tide?"

"We have no captain here," Deborah said.

"It's a foolish suggestion," Sukey said. "I will not have both men gone at once, and not just in case this Bootzamon creature returns. There is too much to be done. Furthermore, I hope you don't mean to suggest that Esther or I should undertake so arduous a journey after this elusive orphan. Esther could do it, I'm certain. She has the strength and endurance of an ox, an absolute ox. But my own delicate constitution . . ."

"I, no, I," Esther sputtered, her eyes wide with dismay.

"Of course not," Deborah said. "That's exactly the problem. Proctor can't go alone, but there is no one here whom we can spare to go with him."

Another silence followed this statement.

Magdalena, who had not spoken since the opening prayer, sighed. Everyone looked at her. She shrugged and opened her hands palms-up.

"It is exactly as Deborah my friend describes," the old woman said.

Deborah stiffened in reflex as soon as Magdalena spoke; she had an instinct to argue with everything the old woman said just to show that she was in charge.

"He cannot go by himself because it is too dangerous," Magdalena said. "But there is no one to go with him. I cannot walk at all. Zoe and Abby are too young, and Sukey and Esther, they are too old. Neither Ezra nor you, Deborah, can be spared. We cannot go one day without you. So, sadly, we must forget about this orphan boy."

"You can go without me for a day," Deborah said, even if it was mostly politeness that required her to say it.

"Of course we could," Magdalena said. "Sukey could teach your lessons for a day. She knows more about healing wounds and fevers than I do."

Deborah spoke without thinking—Proctor could see it in the way she leaned across the table. "My mother always said that no one knew more about healing wounds and fevers than you do. And she said you were the best midwife she ever knew."

Magdalena shrugged indifferently. "It is true she thought that once. She used to have me teach the new students for her. But that was a long time ago."

"Deborah could go with Proctor," Abby suggested.

"I'm not sure," Magdalena said. "They don't have a chaperone."

"They don't need one," Abby said. Looking at Deborah,

she added, "My apologies, Miss Deborah. But who is there to worry about your reputation? Neither of you has parents or family around, you don't belong to any church or meeting, you don't even have neighbors. There's nobody but us, and we know the two of you are just like brother and sister."

"I think it's a marvelous idea," Sukey said. "We could get a different perspective on the healing arts."

"I would like that a great deal," Esther agreed, completely unprompted.

Ezra looked at Zoe. "Seems like somebody should go fetch this boy. And we could use an extra hand in the rigging."

"Do you even realize we're not on a ship anymore?" Zoe asked.

"I don't want to be the only one holding back," Magdalena said. "Not when the rest of you have made your opinion clear. I can never be the teacher that Deborah is, but I will do my part to do her work while she is gone. Are we in unity?"

Sukey and Esther, Abby and Zoe and Ezra affirmed their unity at once. Seven faces turned toward Proctor. He suppressed a smile. He admired the way Magdalena had planted the field and then waited to harvest it. All she wanted was a chance to teach the students. He suspected that they would all do better with a brief change.

"I am in unity with the rest of you," Proctor said. "I believe we have to stop the Covenant's plans, whatever they are. But I'll feel better with someone to help me."

"Deborah?" Magdalena said.

She sat for a long time, trying to think of a way out. Finally, she smiled and ducked her head toward Magdalena. "I don't want to be the only one holding back. Not when the rest of you have made your opinion clear."

Magdalena nodded. To her credit, she didn't smile or

gloat. "That is what we shall do then. You will reinforce our borders before you leave."

Proctor and Deborah went outside without the others. They walked past the well and the pile of stones toward the barn. He carried his musket and looked across the horizon to the high blue skies aswim with shreds of cloud.

"Is it true?" he said. "Are we just like brother and sister now?"

The whole mound of stones rose into the air at once, from pieces the size of marbles to chunks bigger than his fist. Deborah flung her arm, and they flew at the barn like grapeshot from the barrel of a cannon. The smaller stones clattered against the clapboards like hail, and the bigger stones tore holes in the wood. The pigs squealed, disturbed from their afternoon slumbers into a brief melee in the mud as they dodged for cover.

Proctor stopped in his tracks. A bit angrily, he said, "That's a lot of extra work for me, just to fix that."

Deborah turned her head away to hide how upset she was. "She led me by the bridle, right where she wanted me to go."

"Is that so bad? She studied with your mother—"

It was the wrong thing to say. The scattered stones rose from the mud and hovered in the air.

"I'm sorry," he said softly.

The stones thudded to the ground. The big sow walked over to one and rooted through the mud, turning it over with her nose to see if it was worth eating.

"You've grown powerful this year," he said. He knew that she practiced every day, always pushing herself. But it was a different thing to see her use that power.

Her head sagged. "I'm afraid it's not enough."

"You can only do so much."

"I have to do more." Her head came up. "The widow—she cast a spell that stretched all the way around Boston, making all the militiamen ill. She was going to place a curse on an entire army. And she said that her master was more powerful than that. How do I fight that? Come on."

She led him to the cornfield, where she started pulling husks from the ears and tying them in knots.

"You don't have to fight it alone, for one thing," he said. "I'm glad you're coming with me. What are you doing?"

She held up a little doll, made from the corn leaves. "This Bootzamon creature is out there, looking for us. When you and I leave, I'm going to make him think we've all left. If he thinks The Farm is abandoned, he'll follow us."

Proctor whistled appreciatively. "That's better than what I had planned."

"What did you have planned?" she said.

"I was going to bang some pots and pans in hopes of scaring him."

Chapter 6

Before dawn the next morning, they gathered in the main room of the house. Deborah lined up the dolls she meant to use as a focus. She needed a hair from each person to complete the spell, and she yanked the hairs out by the roots to preserve their living essence.

"I'm certain that hurt unnecessarily," Sukey said, rubbing her scalp.

"Complain again and I'll take another," Deborah said as she knotted the hairs to each doll.

Few other words were exchanged. Deborah gathered up the dolls and slipped them into her dress pockets. As they stood at the door, Magdalena said, "In a week you will be back."

"That may be as fast as we can manage," Deborah said.

"It will depend on how hard this orphan boy is to find," Proctor said. "If Cecily has reached him first, we may have to locate them both and—"

"It was not a question," Magdalena said. "In a week, you will be back."

"Yes, ma'am," Proctor said.

Deborah faced the window. "It is almost dawn. Time to make a very noticeable departure."

She opened the door and stepped onto the porch. Proctor followed with their biggest pan and a large wooden spoon. He banged on it as hard as he could. The sound echoed off the hills and disappeared into the trees.

"C'mon!" he bellowed. "It's time to go! Everybody out here now!"

Deborah muttered her spell, and six other figures appeared around her. It wasn't a convincing illusion. Up close, they were a bit gauzy, and their legs did not seem to touch the ground quite right. But as she walked off past the well, they looked solid enough.

He dropped the pan and the spoon inside the door and pulled it shut behind him. The others wouldn't venture outside again until Proctor and Deborah were well on their way. He picked up a bag with some basic items for their journey, slung it over his shoulder, and ran to catch up with Deborah. He made a point to step around the apparitions that followed her.

"Do you have everything?" Deborah asked.

"Yes, enough for ten days," he said. "I'd feel better with the musket." He knew that a gun would draw too much attention on their journey, just as his tomahawk would also be hard to explain, but he carried the largest knife he owned. He walked with his hand on the hilt.

"What good would a gun do against a creature without flesh or bone? Besides, we're supposed to be traveling as Quakers."

"I know," he said. "I fixed the fence out in the pasture and set the spells there. Are you ready?"

She closed her eyes for a second and nodded.

They didn't know if Bootzamon saw and heard things as people did, or if he was sensitive to magic. The pan-banging had been in case the former was true. The latter would require a little more effort at convincing.

"You go first," Deborah said.

Proctor nodded, and then, braced for an attack, he stepped through the gate. A few birds flew from the grass to the trees in the dawn light.

Deborah followed after him, stopping long enough to place a large flat stone against the gatepost.

"Hold out your hands," she said. She stood directly across from him and showed him the gesture she meant. The apparitions flowed around them, completing the circle. It looked like Magdalena held his hand on the one side and Abby on the other, but he felt nothing.

Then the tingle flowed through him, the way it did when they were all joined in a true circle.

"Let the root of evil be sealed from this place," Deborah said, using a Bible verse from Esdras for her spell. "Let weakness and the moth be hidden from here. Let all corruption flee into hell to be forgotten. Until we return."

Proctor could feel the power bubble out from them, spreading over The Farm like a blanket covering a bed. The apparitions of the other witches began to fade, and Deborah dropped her hands. At once the images returned.

Proctor followed her gesture. He saw a bead of sweat trickle down her forehead and across her cheek. "Paradise?" he asked.

"What?" she said. She seemed dizzy, almost out of it.

He stepped over to help her, but she waved him away. "That verse. You used a protective spell that compares The Farm to paradise?"

"It is the only paradise I shall think of until we return here safely. And it was the strongest spell I could conjure to protect The Farm in our absence." She glanced at the dark shadows of the woods around them. "Come, the . . . others will be stronger if we keep them moving."

"Are you strong enough to keep moving?" he asked.

"I'll get stronger as we go," she said, setting off down the road toward Salem. The apparitions followed her like ducklings after their mother.

Proctor checked over his shoulder and scanned the woods for movement. Seeing so many people depart might draw Bootzamon, but then it might also make him wary enough to keep his distance. Proctor spied no sign of the creature, and he hurried to catch up with Deborah.

They had only been walking a short distance when Deborah said, "Stop looking over your shoulder so often."

"But I want to see him coming," Proctor said.

"So don't give him any more reason to conceal himself."

She was right—a wary Bootzamon would be invisible. Better to keep up the illusion that they were all leaving The Farm out of fear. Proctor bided his time, stealing glances back as the road turned, but there was no sign of Bootzamon until they came to the junction with the Salem Road.

As they joined the larger road, Proctor stepped to the side, pretending to make way for the women in their group. Fifty yards back, the shadow of a man wearing a large-brimmed hat stood just inside the trees.

"There's someone behind us," Proctor told Deborah.

"A farmer or a woodcutter maybe?"

Proctor glanced back just in time to see the figure leap twenty feet across the road and behind the cover of a stone wall. "No, it's most certainly—"

"Take your hand off your knife and turn back around," Deborah said. "We're trying to draw him away."

"And he'll follow us farther if he thinks we're not aware of him," Proctor said. "I know—it's just hard not to . . . after what he did in Virginia . . ."

If he felt the strain, he saw that she did too. They passed a field of wildflowers—a riot of purples and yellows and blues, with butterflies dancing from blossom to blossom. It was exactly the sort of thing that always drew Deborah's attention and often made her stop. But she kept her eyes straight ahead on the road, and her hands in the pockets where she stored the dolls. They traveled the miles in silence, both lost to their own thoughts.

He was glancing over his shoulder when she said, "This is your family's territory up ahead, isn't it?"

His head whipped around. "My parents both came from Salem Village, but I don't know which part."

"I think the Proctors—that's your mother's family?"

"Yes," he said.

"They lived farther north. This area is called Shillaber's Plains," she said, pointing to flatlands ahead as they came out of the hills. "Giles Corey, the man who was pressed to death with stones during the witch trials, lived there, near the lake."

"What about the Browns?" he asked.

"The land hereabouts is thick with Browns," she said. "Most of them descended from Goodman Brown and his wife, who lived in the village near the meetinghouse, back when it was first founded."

"Were any of them—" He paused in his question as a farmer on a wagon loaded with milk rattled by them, heading eastward toward Salem city. The farmer looked at their little group twice, then shook his head like someone waking from a dream and turned away.

"Did any of them share our talent?" Proctor asked.

"I don't know," Deborah said. "They must have. Your mother has the talent, and your father must have carried it in his blood too. But my mother never spoke of others by name, not unless I'd met them. It was part of her rule, like the injunction to never write things down. We have always been afraid that if one of us was taken, all would suffer."

If Bootzamon captured and tortured them as he had done to the Walkers, Proctor had no doubt he or Deborah would reveal their subterfuge, and then everyone still at The Farm would be in peril. The less they knew, the more danger they were in; the more they knew, the more danger they were to their allies.

The cluster of buildings and the roof of the meeting-house loomed protectively just ahead. People moved about their daily labor—hanging out laundry, picking vegetables, painting houses. Proctor felt a little safer. Bootzamon surely wouldn't try anything with so many about.

"He's come closer," Deborah said.

Proctor started to turn his head, then stopped. "What?"

"I saw him—sensed him actually, and then saw him, in the doorway of the butcher's shop. It's easier for him to blend in now that there are more people about."

She was pale from the effort of maintaining the illusion. The skin of her face was as soft and delicate as the petals of lady's slippers. "Let's get to the docks," Proctor said. "He can't fly, and I don't think he can swim. Once we're on the ocean, we'll leave him behind."

The city of Salem gleamed like polished silver and smelled like fish and seawater. Proctor and Deborah walked down Derby Street, which ran the length of the small peninsula that contained the city. The left side of the street was lined with large brick houses painted shining white. They had gable-ended roofs, topped with weather vanes and gilt-railed widow's walks. Spacious front yards overflowed with fragrant summer flowers. The right side of the road was lined with the docks that served the fishing fleets that had made Salem rich. The street was busy, and the strain of holding the illusion told on Deborah. Rather than risk a conversation or inadvertent encounter, they stepped aside for groups of young women in pink-ribboned caps, for slaves and little servant boys in rough clothes running errands, and for old men with half-empty wagons moving from dock to dock.

But the docks themselves sat empty. Small boats, none more than twenty feet in length, bobbed in the shipyard, and a few fishing boats unloaded their cargo. A fat man stood outside the customhouse at the far end of the largest pier, staring out to sea.

"We have a problem," Proctor said. "If none of those masts at the far docks is sailing south, we may have to go to Marblehead."

"We face a more significant problem," Deborah whispered, turning her body aside. She pointed discreetly.

Twenty yards ahead of them, Bootzamon leaned casually against a lamppost. In the daylight, he looked like a foreign prince, wearing an old-fashioned hat as an affectation while he puffed merrily away on his pipe.

Proctor's hands shook. He wasn't ready to fight Bootzamon again, not yet. Some wagons loaded with fresh cod rattled toward them. Proctor pulled Deborah to the side of the road.

"Quick, give me the doll for Zoe," he said.

She reached into her pocket and slipped him the knotted leaves. He leaned over in front of the little girl's image, just as if he were talking to her. "What are you doing?" she asked.

"Make sure Zoe runs away—keep her running as long as you can," he said. A wagon loaded with fish bumped by at just that point. Proctor stepped out behind it and, using his body to shield his action from Bootzamon, dropped the husk in the open back with the load.

The image of Zoe turned and skipped down the street after the wagon. The wagon picked up speed as it rounded the bend in Derby Street, and Zoe started to run after it.

"The skipping was an artful embellishment," Proctor said.

"He's supposed to bring back young ones alive, right?" she said. Her voice was strained, and her fist was in the pocket where she kept her hidden charm. "I had to be convincing."

He glanced over his shoulder. "He's gone. We'd best hurry."

They walked toward the masts at the far end of the street. Deborah dropped the dolls one by one into trash-filled water lapping the edge of the nearly empty docks. One by one, the images turned away, appearing to enter the buildings, or step down into boats, until only the two of them were left.

A small group of men dressed like militia, in their work clothes but carrying their muskets and bags, marched past

Proctor and Deborah. Proctor checked for Bootzamon and said, "Come on, there goes our passage."

Deborah fell in with him. "Why? Because those soldiers are headed to New York?"

"No, it's because if Bootzamon comes back, I want to be surrounded by men with guns." He glanced over his shoulder again. "Although the other thing had occurred to me too."

The men thumped up a plank to a hundred-foot schooner, as long and sleek as a sturgeon. Crewmen were in the rigging of both masts, making preparation to sail— an even better sign. The name painted below the dolphin figurehead proclaimed it the *Bluejack,* out of Marblehead.

Proctor and Deborah stepped up the plank. The militiamen were storing their gear aft. The rest of the crew was small—about half a dozen men who appeared to be related, with the same sun-darkened faces, square jaws, and thick mustaches, plus a similar number of black men and Indians, including one fellow who looked like he might be either.

Proctor cupped his hands to his mouth. "Can I speak to the captain?"

A man on the mainmast cried, "The captain's wanted!"

A black man on the deck leaned in the hatch and called, "Captain, someone to see you!"

A squat, weathered man climbed out of the hatch. He had a face the color and shape of the block part of a block-and-tackle. There was a gray wool fisherman's cap on his head, and salt and pepper in his mustache. "Natty Hammond," he said. "You wanted me."

Proctor tilted his head toward Deborah. "My sister and I are looking for passage to Long Island, to Gravesend if possible."

Hammond looked them over. "You're not Tories, are you? Long Island is full of Tories."

"That's why we want to go fetch our aunt from Gravesend. She sent us a letter—she's been afraid ever since Admiral Howe landed with the British army on Staten Island."

"She asked us to come bring her back," Deborah said.

Hammond's mustache twitched as he rolled this information around his mouth to see how it tasted. Finally, with a glance at Proctor, he said, "You look like you're fit enough to fight if you're such a patriot. We're taking some other fellows as replacements for Colonel Glover and the Fourteenth Continental Regiment."

This was the hardest part of the lie for Proctor. He felt like he was doing his part to help fight the war, but he couldn't explain it to other men. "We're Friends," he said.

Hammond studied them for a moment. "And your aunt lives in the Quaker town at Gravesend?"

"Yes," Proctor said, and Deborah said, "Yes, she does."

"I figured as much when I saw your dress and heard you mention the town by name. There's a good harbor there for small boats. It's where we're headed, in fact."

"Can you give us passage?" Proctor asked. "We're willing to pay."

"I can't promise a voyage back," Hammond said. "And I'd hate to leave you stranded there."

Proctor started to answer, but Deborah interrupted. "We can come back overland if we must. The important thing is to get her out of harm's way as soon as we can. May we please come aboard?"

Hammond looked at Proctor. "Can you keep your stomach down and pull on a rope?"

"Anything that you need," Proctor said.

"Then that'll cover your passage. We all help each other out during war." He waved them on board and called to one of the blacks, "Cuff, can you pull up the plank before anyone else wanders aboard? Then see what knots this fellow knows. We'll use him to haul ropes on the main deck."

Cuff accepted the orders with a nod. He had a round, intelligent face, with a knot in the side of his jaw that made it look like he was used to keeping his thoughts to himself. His big hands were scarred and callused. He bent to take up the plank, but Proctor beat him to it. When Proctor went to hand it to him, Cuff rolled his tongue in his cheek, then indicated where it should go with a tip of his head.

Proctor stored it. When he looked up again, he saw Bootzamon standing on the shore. One hand was on his hip; the other held his pipe. The wind swirled, carrying the smell of cheap tobacco across the deck.

Proctor's heart began to race, but then Cuff put him through some drills. After Proctor showed that he could tie a thumb knot, a bowline, and a figure eight, he went aft to check on Deborah. She sat watching Bootzamon, who paced back and forth on the shore.

"Has he seen us?" he whispered.

"Did anyone in Salem *not* see you running around the deck, showing off? I thought you were doing it on purpose." She checked to be sure no one on the deck stood too close, but still she lowered her voice. "I made Abby's face appear out of the hatch twice, when I thought he was watching closely."

Bootzamon stood watching the ship until they raised the sails and followed the tide out to sea. The city shrank in the distance, and the tiny figure of Bootzamon finally turned and walked away from the docks.

Proctor stood next to Cuff, in case he was needed to haul ropes. Cuff said, "So who was that fellow watching you from the docks?"

Proctor clamped his mouth shut. He couldn't lie to Cuff without losing the man's respect, but he didn't have an answer ready.

"At first I thought maybe you owed him money and were running away," Cuff said as he coiled a rope. "But the way he was dressed—nah. He couldn't loan anyone anything except an excuse. And if his cause was lawful, then why didn't he just come right up to the ship?"

"His master means us harm," Proctor admitted. "They're allied with the Loyalists."

"You've got unusual enemies for Quakers," Cuff said, storing the rope. "You might want to check on your sister. She don't look well."

Deborah leaned over the railing, watching Salem shrink behind them. Proctor leaned beside her. The wind was steady enough to kick foam off the whitecaps. "They noticed Bootzamon following us, but I don't think it makes a difference. How do you feel?"

"Better if I look at something very far away," she said. She lifted her head to the northeast and wrinkled her nose. "There's a storm growing out there."

"You've got a nose for weather?" Hammond asked, coming up suddenly to join them. Proctor tensed, expecting their talent to be discovered, but Hammond's words held no double meaning. He squinted at the sky. "Aye, there's a nor'easter brewin'. Might be trouble for them as is fishin' the banks."

"It won't make landfall," Deborah said softly. Then added, quickly, "I mean, will it?"

"No, ma'am, I don't think it will. Still, we'll sail close to shore and safe harbor, well clear of the storm." He reached up with his hand and smoothed his bushy mustache on either side of his lip. "If it gets rough, you two should head below."

"We will," Proctor assured him.

Hammond looked him in the eye. "I just spoke with Cuff. I don't appreciate any trouble brought aboard my ship, especially not when I'm doing a man a favor."

"You won't have any trouble on account of either of us," Proctor said.

"I won't ask you to swear to it, because I respect a man's

beliefs, and I know you Quakers don't hold no account with swearing," Hammond said. "But I don't hold no account with lying either."

"Neither do we," Proctor said. The little lies they had to live with each day ate away at him. "If you can drop us off in Gravesend or nearby, we'll be grateful."

Which was all truth. Hammond nodded his acceptance and went back to the quarterdeck.

"Thank you," Deborah said under her breath. "I know how hard it is for you, all the lying. You were raised in an ordinary household, as part of a community."

"It's hard for me because it's wrong," Proctor said.

"I've lived with it my whole life, since before I can remember. The need to hide who you are from people, to hide everything you're doing."

Thinking about that made him think about The Farm, and the six people left there. Would they be safe? Would Bootzamon try to follow him and Deborah south, or would he return to The Farm and try to break through the seal on its borders? They wouldn't know the answers to those questions until they returned from their journey.

"Why do you suppose they want to capture young talents?" he asked.

"They have some plan that requires great power, more than anyone wields alone," she said. "They need the power of slaves. It must be a plan of extraordinary proportions."

That was not a comforting thought. The ship rocked over another swell, and the wind came from a new direction. Deborah lifted her head and said quietly, "I don't think the storm will come this far east at all."

"How can you possibly know that?"

Deborah stared at the waves and the skies for a while before answering. "My mother had the talent to a degree." Proctor thought about the rain that had poured over her mother at her father's funeral. "But it's as though, as my talent grows, I can see the hand of God moving about the earth, arranging the bowls and spoons like a cook in a kitchen. Almost as if I can nudge them. It's . . . unsettling."

The ship plowed through a large wave, sending spray over the sides. Proctor's stomach felt unsettled too.

Chapter 7

A hand gripped Proctor's shoulder, gently shaking him awake. He lifted his head and felt the deep imprint on his cheek of the coiled rope that had served as his pillow. Out at sea, with the rocking of the boat and no way for Bootzamon to reach him, Proctor had slept well for the first time since Virginia.

Cuff knelt beside him and shook him again. "Captain Hammond, he wants to see you."

Proctor shook off the slumber and stood up. The sky above was middle-of-the-night dark, with clouds blotting out many of the stars. Another ship floated nearby, and a dinghy was tied up alongside that. The motion of the waves made it tap against the side of the hull.

Captain Hammond held a lantern, the light reflecting off several new faces. Hammond was talking in low tones to them. "This is the *Silver Molly*, out of Sag Harbor," Hammond said when Proctor arrived. Then, to the other men, "Tell him what you told me."

"Black Dick," one man started, and then looked over his shoulder as if naming the devil might make him appear, even though Black Dick was merely the name for British admiral Richard Howe. "He started landing troops on Long Island, at Gravesend, a day and a half ago."

"So we won't be able to make landing there?" Proctor asked.

Hammond shook his head. "Black Dick's got three hundred ships in these waters. He hadn't closed off the northern passage or the Narrows as of yesterday morning, but he will as soon as they're done moving troops. The *Silver Molly* is making sail for Boston, if you want to go back with her."

"No, we still have to try," Proctor said.

"There's going to be fighting. You'd best think of your sister as well."

The door to the tiny cabin creaked open, and Deborah stepped out. "His sister agrees. Our aunt is elderly, and she said she would wait for us. We have to reach her if we can. We're not part of the battle, so we should be safe."

"I wouldn't count on that overmuch, miss," Hammond said.

"How close can we get?" Proctor asked.

"I plan to sail north for the Narrows and land the men and supplies in time to help Colonel Glover. We could put you ashore near Oyster Bay. I don't think we can get you any closer than that, and I won't have the lady aboard once we pass Hell Gate. Black Dick's ships are likely to fire on us anytime from that point south."

The other sailors climbed back into their dinghy. The oars dug into the waves as they rowed back to their own ship. Proctor turned to Hammond and said, "How soon can we make it to Oyster Bay?"

Hammond shrugged. "That'll depend on the winds."

As he walked away, Deborah whispered to Proctor, "Now that I'm rested a bit, I think I smell a good wind coming."

Deborah went to the mainmast and stood with her hand against it, and her head bowed in prayer. Several of the sailors and passengers gave her curious looks. When Cuff walked by, Proctor mumbled, "She's very devout, prays every morning."

He had the feeling that the sooner they were off the ship, the happier everyone would be. The sky lightened toward dawn, turning from indigo to steel gray in the east. Sunrise brought bits of clouds torn off a great mass like sheets ripped off a clothesline. The waves rose, slapping the sides of the ship as they shoved her forward. The sails snapped and billowed, pulling the ship on.

Deborah removed her hand from the mast. She looked drained, with dark circles under her eyes as if she had not slept at all the night before. One of the mates nearby yelled out orders, and she winced instantly—Proctor knew her head must be aching to burst.

"How do you do that?" Proctor whispered to her.

"You don't want to know," she said. "You don't want to pay the price. I'll be in the cabin, asleep in the hammock."

She staggered off, barely able to keep her balance as the ship bounced over the waves. Proctor didn't know if he could pay the price or not, but he wanted to know how she did it, he was sure of that much.

The ship sailed west that whole day, entering Long Island Sound. The long, low horizon was broken by frequent bays and sandbars covered by clouds of gulls. Small ships moved back and forth like birds skimming the waves. Shouting trumpets called out the latest news.

Deborah emerged late in the day, looking pale but a little more rested. "The British still haven't commenced their attack," Proctor told her. "It takes a long time to move thirty thousand men."

"Maybe we'll have time to reach Gravesend, find . . . our aunt, and escape again before they do," she said. "I would like to be back at The Farm as soon as we can manage."

"Yes," Proctor said. "I'm worried about them too. There was a dolphin swimming along the ship a little while ago."

"Oh!" Deborah ran to the railing. He joined her, pointing to the spot where it had last appeared. When the sleek nose pushed out of the water and the dolphin started sewing its way through the waves, Deborah's face lit up like a lantern in a dark room.

Proctor found himself smiling with a glad heart for the first time in the longest time he could remember.

The wind whipped her hair out from under her cap, and he was tempted to reach up and catch it for her—he knew how she liked to have everything orderly and just so. But brothers didn't do that for sisters, and he kept his hands to himself.

It was in the hours before dawn when they set anchor in Oyster Bay like smugglers so they could go ashore.

"I'd wait until morning," Hammond said. "But we can't afford the delay."

Cuff rowed the dinghy up onto a beach strewn with shells. Proctor climbed out of the boat and helped Deborah leap from the prow to the shore without soaking the hem of her dress.

"Which way do we go?" Proctor asked.

Cuff pointed over the dunes, past a gray, weatherworn house. "Go that way until you find the road. When it curves to the west, take the footpath south toward the ridge. It's about nine miles to Jamaica Pass. From there, you'll find King's Road to Gravesend."

"Good luck," Proctor said.

"Same to you," Cuff replied. He hesitated, then leaned forward and offered Proctor his hand. "Hope you make it a ways before she stops to do her morning prayers."

Proctor smiled as he shook the other man's hand, then helped push the boat back into the waves. Deborah hiked across the wide, flat stretch of sand.

"The sooner we finish, the sooner we can go home," she said. "I don't want to leave my students in Magdalena's hands any longer than I must."

"Why do you have such a problem with Magdalena? Your mother trusted her to teach. She knows a thing or two about the talent."

"It's the wrong things. She knows protective charms to

keep your milk cow from the dropsy, or how to heal your baby from an ague, but what can she do against power wielded by the likes of that southern woman? She ran out of the house in fear the night she found that black altar. My mother died chasing after her."

Proctor understood. Deborah didn't trust Magdalena because she blamed the old Dutch woman for her mother's death. "If Magdalena hadn't woken and run outside in a panic, everyone would have died," Proctor said.

Deborah's hand knotted into a fist and slammed into her pocket. But after a moment, she said, "Maybe you're right."

"Have you given thought to how we're going to get home?" Proctor asked.

Given a practical problem, she relaxed. "The Lake family has served as guides on the highway, I know that much. I'm hoping that if we make contact with them, we can follow Friends north until we reach home." She stumbled over a rut in the road, but caught herself before she fell. "There will be a lot more walking, I expect."

"Walking's not so bad if the company's right. How many guides on the highway, do you know?"

So she told him about the Quaker Highway. She started with her earliest memories, traveling with her father as a small girl when he guided witches to new locations, because a man, a woman, and a child together were invisible, unlike a man and woman. The night raced by while they traded stories and covered the miles to Jamaica Pass. Deborah laughed several times, and Proctor found himself smiling more often.

Dawn pressed up against the windowpane of the sky, peeking over the horizon as they passed through lightly forested hills very close to the pass. Birds sang in the trees. Deborah stopped to inhale the fragrant white blossoms clustered thick on a climbing vine.

"I swear you'd stuff a mattress with those if you could,"

Proctor said with a laugh. "What flower is it, that you love it so?"

There was just enough light in the sky to see her blush. "You're mocking me," she said.

"No, really I don't know. What is it called?"

"Virgin's bower," she said.

She dropped the blossoms in her hand. When she looked up at him again, with all the wariness and worry erased from her face, his heart wanted to spill out of his chest. For the moment, he felt like they had become man and woman again instead of brother and sister. He held out his hand for her.

Her fingers were outstretched to clasp his when they heard the tramp of boots on the road. They yanked their hands back and stepped out of the way as a unit of British troops approached.

"Who goes there?" the British officer shouted at them as his men set up a barrier across the road.

"Who are you?" Deborah asked. The hard lines had returned to her face. "We're on our way home."

"Hurry on, then," he said. "You'll want to keep your heads down and stay out of the way today, miss. God save the king."

"God save us all," Deborah said, picking up her skirts and hurrying past them.

"I don't know the land hereabouts," Proctor said quietly when they had passed the soldiers. "But Redcoats, this far north, it can't be good. Do we continue to Gravesend or do we try to help Washington's army?"

Before she could answer, they heard the tramp of more feet. There was a crossroads just ahead. Files of Redcoats passed through, followed by horses pulling gun carriages. There were so many, an overwhelming number. Suddenly guns boomed in the east, startling the birds to silence.

Proctor met Deborah's gaze. "If the British win this battle," he said, "the Revolution will be dead in the cradle. The Covenant will have the victory it wants."

"We can slip behind the British," she said. "Make our way to Gravesend."

Proctor shook his head. "Why don't you go?" he said. "The roads will be safe behind the lines. Or you can wait here for me, at the tavern down the road. But I have to go see what I can do to help."

"What difference can one man make in a battle of thousands?" she said.

"I don't know," he admitted. "But I have to do something. I won't feel right if I don't. If I can't make any difference, I'll turn around and come back."

She looked angry enough to strangle him. "If you're going, I'll come too. Lead us where we need to go."

He turned west and cut through the woods along a trail that followed the line of the ridge. The trail reminded him of the race through the countryside during the battles of Lexington and Concord. The sound of guns and artillery echoed over the hills. From their vantage, Proctor and Deborah could see the British take position on the hillside. A group of Americans advanced on the road below, unaware of the danger.

The familiar cry of "Ready! Aim!" sounded from the hillside. The Americans would be cut to pieces.

Deborah stretched out her arms. At the cry of "Fire!" she flung her hands into the air as though she were tossing seed.

Fire jetted from the ends of the British guns. One American pitched backward, and another fell, spinning, but most of the lead whistled overhead, tearing up the leaves and branches. The Americans beat a quick retreat to cover, and Deborah collapsed to her knees.

Proctor's knees felt shaky at her display of power. He rushed to lift her to her feet.

"It's no use," she said. "I don't have the strength or focus to move all that lead every time they fire."

On the opposite hillside, the British fired a second volley at the retreating Americans. Despair marked Deborah's face.

"Come on," Proctor said. "We'll try to find some spot where we can make a difference."

Easier said than done. They scrambled along the top of the ridge, chasing the battle and trying to catch up with the American retreats. Eager to make a difference, Proctor pushed forward too far. As soon as he heard lead ripping through the leaves around his ears, he dragged Deborah to the ground and rolled under the edge of a log. They cowered there for what felt like an hour while shot whistled overhead and thudded into the deadwood that sheltered them. Then artillery began to fall, shaking the ground again and again. Every time the ground shook, Deborah stifled a cry and pressed herself against the flimsy shield of Proctor's body. The only sounds that broke through the thunder of the guns were the cries of the wounded on the hillside below them.

Finally, the shelling stopped. Still Proctor shielded Deborah with his own body, and they didn't move until the shelling resumed farther up the road. They stumbled to their feet, covered with leaves and twigs. Deborah had dirt smeared across her face. Proctor took hold of her arm to lead her away from the battle. She pulled away and stood transfixed. A line of abandoned dead stretched along the road away from them. At the edge of their view, a small group of Americans no bigger than ants defended a wooded knoll.

"What we just went through," she said, absently brushing twigs from her dress. "That's what they . . ."

"They can shoot back," Proctor said. "Which is more than we could do. Let's go."

"No," Deborah whispered. "I need to see this."

The Redcoats flanked the knoll and moved artillery into position. The monotony of the gun and cannon resumed, and soon dead men littered the hillside under the trees like pieces of fallen, broken fruit. Proctor could not bear to watch, and turned away.

"Was this what it was like for you?" she asked. "At Lexington, at Bunker Hill?"

Proctor remembered watching old Robert Munroe fall in the first volley on Lexington Green, and seeing his friend Amos Lathrop die at Bunker Hill. "A bit," he said. His body ached as if he'd been reaping hay all day. "But this is twentyfold, thirtyfold larger."

Deborah held her face in her hands. "No," she said.

"We can't do anything," he said. "It's too big."

"No, I do not accept this." The set of her mouth was angry, but tears ran down her cheeks. "I do not."

She pulled her cap off her head and crawled on her hands and knees, sweeping aside leaves and grasses to form a circle. Then she found a damp spot in the ground and scooped up fresh mud, which she smeared on her cheeks and face.

Proctor thought maybe she had gone mad. "Deborah?"

"You stay right here beside me, all the way through this," she said. "You promise me you'll stay right here."

"I'll stay," he said, shaken.

She knelt with her hands clasped in front of her for prayer and tilted her head to the sky. "Behold, waters rise up out of the north," she said. "And shall be an overwhelming flood, and shall overflow the land, and all therein."

A tingle shot through Proctor as he recognized the verse from Jeremiah. He looked up at the sky, expecting it to crack open at once. When he rose to walk over to her, his legs buckled and he fell into a kneeling position at her side.

She dropped her head and repeated the verse. The tears running down her cheeks made streaks through the mud.

The crack and thunder of the battle came close for a while and then moved away from them. Still they knelt there while Deborah repeated her spell. The wind changed first, from fitful to firm, growing colder as it whipped around them. The wind alone would keep the British ships from taking the Narrows and cutting off the Continental army's escape.

In time the sky grew dark as the clouds rolled overhead, blotting out the sun. If the rain came, and if it poured hard enough, it would be impossible to keep the powder dry. The roads would bog down, preventing the movement of the gun carriages. Men would stop fighting, at least for a while.

Deborah sagged forward, barely able to stay upright. "Help me," she whispered, holding out her hand.

Proctor reached out and took hold.

Something like lightning shot through him. Not affection, not the thrill he felt in her presence, not the tingle of ordinary magic. It started in the soles of his feet and vibrated through him, setting all his hair on edge and shooting out his hand. He'd felt it before.

When the widow tried to steal his life energy.

"Deborah?"

"I need you," she said in a small, raw voice.

In fear, he tried to pull his hand away, to force her to talk to him. But she gripped him too tightly.

And then he was rooted to the spot while the lightning shot through him again and again, like thunderbolts falling from the sky on the same tree. His sense of time warped, like a piece of wood in the rain, bending back on itself. He saw the clouds roll in, until the whole sky was dark. He felt the sharp cold shock of raindrops as large as shillings splash across his face. The rain sluiced down like a waterfall: one moment his shoulders were damp, the next he was soaked to the skin, as if he'd been dropped, fully dressed, in a tub of water.

He was shivering, bitter cold, more hungry than he'd ever felt before. Somehow it had gone from noon to night. The sound of artillery boomed in his ears, but maybe it was only an echo from earlier in the day or perhaps it was the sound of thunder. In time, even that faded, replaced by the steady patter of raindrops on leaves mixed with the random splashes of water spilled off the leaves and into the puddles that filled every crack in the ground.

His head was lifted in wonder, and at the same moment he felt so dizzy he thought he might tip over. He reached out to steady himself, and his hand came to rest on a wet pile of clothes. It took him a second to realize the pile of clothes was a woman.

"Deborah?" he said, trying to find her heartbeat without taking liberties. He lifted her hand to his face. It was a limp, dead weight. "Deborah!"

She didn't respond to his first gentle shake. His eyes had adjusted to the dark now, enough to see that she was curled up on her side, like a newborn baby. He shook her harder, calling her name, and she flopped over on her back. She was so cold and pale.

He tugged off his jacket, even though it was soaked, and wrapped her in it. Then he rubbed her arms and legs, trying to bring feeling back to them. He looked around, seeking shelter of some kind, a place to dry off, find food. But it was impossible to see far in the rain and darkness.

Gathering her up in his arms, he stood—and staggered sideways, almost falling. She tumbled out of his arms, sprawling across the wet ground.

Even that was not enough to bring a reaction from her. She lay there as motionless as she had been when he awoke.

Chapter 8

Proctor knelt again and lifted her carefully this time, casting her arm around his shoulders and holding tight around her small waist. He peered into the dark rain until he thought he spied the direction of the road.

"Come on, Deborah, you have to try to walk."

She didn't respond, so he set off anyway. Light as she was compared with him, he carried her only a few yards. Her feet dragged, her arm slipped off his shoulder, and she sagged out of his grip.

He caught her and lowered her gently to the ground. He looked around for landmarks, but he still felt confused, disoriented. There was a tavern a mile or more back down the road—he didn't think they could make it that far. Besides, it was probably overrun by the British and used as some kind of headquarters.

He squinted into the rain, making out the dark outline of the heights. The lingering smell of black powder was damp and stale. The earth itself smelled churned up, freshly plowed. If the battle was that way, that's where he'd find their fellow Americans.

Soaked as he was, his throat felt dry and cottony. He licked his lips, lapping up the rain that streamed down his face. After a moment, he lifted his head to the sky, squeezed his eyes shut, and opened his mouth. Fat drops rolled down his tongue, slaking his thirst.

He sighed, lowered his head, and summoned all his strength and will. Then he knelt down beside Deborah, rolled her up into a tight bundle, and held her close to his chest. Though she weighed less than he expected, he was weak and struggled to his feet. He came to a road and proceeded slowly, making sure of his footing with each step, not daring to fall or stumble.

He saw no campfires, no sign of either army. Was the battle already over? Had Deborah's storm made any difference?

Off in the trees, he thought he spied the outline of a woodcutter's shed. He left the road and headed for it. He had gone only a dozen yards when the air prickled on the back of his neck and he froze as still as a boulder.

A human figure in a broad-brimmed hat moved quickly along the road, as if he were impervious to the mud sucking at his shoes. He made no noise as he passed, and Proctor could not tell if he was British or American. Although it was August, Proctor began to shiver.

The figure disappeared around a bend and was gone.

The hair settled on Proctor's skin, and he took a deep breath that stilled his shaking. He looked down at Deborah—she still hadn't moved.

He thrust aside any thought he had of weakness or rest. The path across the hillside required all his concentration just to keep his balance.

His head was up, trying to pierce the gray shroud of the landscape to find the cottage again, when Deborah's weight shifted. For a split second he panicked as he thought they both might spill, tumbling down the slope. But she was only stirring. She took a shallow breath and burrowed her face against his chest.

Relief flooded through him—she was alive! Until that moment, he had been acting as if she were, but he had been so afraid she wasn't. A laugh of joy popped from his mouth at the same instant his feet slipped out from under him. He cradled Deborah to himself, taking the brunt of the fall on his shoulder, and losing her as he rolled down the rest of the hill, cracking his arm on a rock, clipping his head against a tree. He came to rest in a puddle at the bottom of the slope, with Deborah rolling down on top of him a second later.

"Who goes there?"

The voice that shouted the challenge was unmistakably English, and not above ten yards away.

"Proctor . . . ," Deborah whispered. He clamped his hand over her mouth and pulled her close to him.

"Show yourself, you bloody rebel, or we'll shoot!"

The voice was half the distance closer. Proctor could see the man's silhouette now, and the gleam of the bayonet at the end of his musket. Deborah was conscious enough to see it also, and she nested closer in his arms.

"They won't believe that threat," a second voice said. He walked up beside the first man, his dark overcoat open in front to reveal the white cross of the straps against his uniform. "Not if their powder's as wet as ours."

"They're bound to attack us again," the first man said. "They're trapped between here and the Narrows—they've no place else to go."

"Exactly," the second said. "That's why we'll march on them in the morning and accept their surrender. Then this bloody war will be over and we'll all go home."

"Or off to the next spot where there's fighting," the first man said. He lowered his musket and tilted his head to the sky. Proctor realized he was looking to the east for a sign of sunrise.

"There's no one out here," the second man said. "Come back to camp."

The two sentries left. Deborah reached up and peeled Proctor's fingers away from her mouth.

"Not so tight," she whispered. The whites of her eyes seemed even larger because her face was so dark and sunken around them. What had the magic done to her? "Where are we?"

"West of the British lines, I think," Proctor whispered back. "We haven't surrendered yet." By *we* he meant the American army, but he could see that Deborah understood. "What did you do?"

She pushed away from his chest, sitting upright. "I'm sorry," she said. "But I had to make a circle with you. If I stopped to explain, it would have broken my focus."

"No, I understand why you did that," he said, glimpsing over his shoulder to make sure the British sentries hadn't returned. "Though it near scared the life out of me. What did you do to call this storm?"

She shrugged, looked away over the hill. "You remember the storm forming out over the ocean? I nudged it westward."

Proctor wanted to laugh. "What, you just whistle for it like a dog and it comes?"

"This is not the time," she whispered.

The sentries stirred again, their shadows moving just past a fencerow of trees. The damp lumps of tents, their shoulders hunched against the drizzle, were visible just beyond the sentries. It was too wet to keep any fires.

Deborah was right. This wasn't the time, not when they were caught in the middle of the British lines instead of beyond them. But she would have to explain to him later how she had moved the clouds across the sky like pulling a blanket across a bed.

"Can you walk?" he whispered.

"Yes," she said. She attempted to rise to her feet, and stumbled, dizzy. "Just give me a moment."

He reached out to help her up. After a long hesitation, she accepted his hand. He flinched when she touched him, but no lightning shot through his body this time. He pulled her to her feet. Proctor bent to retrieve his coat, and then, with Deborah leaning on his arm, they climbed back up the hill. In a dense copse of trees, where Proctor had spied it once before, they found the woodcutter's small cottage.

The door had no latch. Proctor pushed it open and they went inside. There was a chair and a little bench, and an empty jug that still smelled like rum.

Deborah collapsed into the far corner. "This is as far as I can go," she said.

He set his shoulder bag on the table and brought out the food they had packed. He handed the cheese to Deborah, who broke off a piece and chewed it greedily. The bread was soaked through and fell apart in his fingers, but he still shoveled it into his mouth. His canteen was empty so he thrust the rum jug out the door where the rain was running off the roof until it was full. He took a sip, then passed it to Deborah.

She hadn't answered his question the first time, so he asked it again. "Deborah, what did you do?"

She fumbled in her pocket for her cap, and covered her head with it. Dark hair spilled out, framing her exhausted face. Then she wiped her muddy cheeks on her sleeve. "I did what I had to do," she said. "I always do what I have to do."

"Did you know this would happen to you?"

She looked away. "I knew you would be drained with me. I didn't know how badly. I knew it wouldn't be as bad as me. Does it matter?"

"It matters to me," he said. He moved the chair in front of the door and sat down on the dirt floor across from her. They divided up the rest of the food—cooked sausage, dried berries, wet crackers. "I'm frightened for you."

"I'll recover, if I have time and rest."

"Can I do a healing spell—"

"No." She laughed. "I doubt that either of us could do much of a spell at the moment. In any case, you can't heal magic with magic, not that way."

He stared at her until she shifted uncomfortably.

"Using magic is like riding a ferry," she said. "You cross

from this side of the world to the shores of spirit. Someone has to pay a toll."

"I know that," he said. "When I lifted the boulder in the field with magic, I felt exhausted, like I had lifted a heavy weight. But no one throws a rope around a cloud and drags it across the bay. How do you pay the toll for that?"

"I've paid it!" she shouted back. She stared at him until he looked out the door to make sure no one approached. "Look at me. Can't you see the price I've paid? I'm emptied, to the bottom of my bowl."

"You're lucky to be alive."

"Don't you think that's the price I paid?"

She was surprised to wake up, he realized. She was so appalled by the sheer amount of death and carnage taking place that she would have sacrificed her own life to prevent it.

He didn't know whether to slap her or kiss her hand. "Don't you ever do that again," he said.

She broke their gaze first, shifting her position to curl up on the floor. "I need some sleep."

He knew that he should stay awake to keep watch, but in a few minutes when she was as still as death, he realized he was too drained to stay awake either. He curled up opposite her, with the legs of the table between them, and fell asleep.

He awoke shivering and cold. It was day, but the clouds were thick and icy rain drizzled out of the sky, months out of season.

Deborah was curled up on the floor, but she must have been up. His jacket hung over the chair to dry, and most of the food was gone. He ate the rest, and then was too tired to stay awake. Bootzamon haunted his dreams, coming through the trees, looking for him. Proctor snapped awake in total darkness, reaching for a weapon, sweating despite the cold. The rain poured in torrents again, lashing the sides of the cabin.

"Proctor?" Deborah whispered.

"Yes," he whispered back.

"I can't get warm."

He reached out his hand and found her. Wrapped his arms around her and held her close in the dark and the driving rain. "I'm glad you didn't choose a verse about Noah for your spell," he said.

"Wait another thirty-seven days," she said. When he pulled back, she almost laughed. Instead she swallowed it and snuggled back against him. "We can't stay here."

"Because we have no heat, or because we have no food?"

"Because someone's been out in the woods, searching. I don't know if it's for us, but—"

"Why didn't you wake me?"

"Because I'm still weak, and we'll need your strength to get to the American lines."

"I wasn't sleeping that well," he admitted.

"I know. Are you all right, Proctor? Ever since you came back from Virginia—"

"I'm all right." He didn't want to talk about it any more than he had. "We can leave whenever you're ready."

She pressed up against him. "I'm not quite ready yet."

He kissed the top of her head, and she pressed back against his lips. He kissed her again and again, until she pulled away, saying, "We mustn't." But she didn't rise. They sat that way until day brightened the blackness into dismal gray. He fell asleep again with her in his arms, waking only when she finally stood. He helped her slip his jacket on again for warmth, and they stepped outside the cabin.

Somewhere nearby, drums tapped out orders. More than likely, the British camps hadn't moved since the rain started. He and Deborah set out west, avoiding barking dogs and anything that looked like a camp or a residence.

Deborah's strength began to flag. She staggered often,

leaning more and more on Proctor, until, with his arm about her waist, he practically carried her along. As they passed one small farm, a rooster crowed in the yard, his voice cracking the still shell of the morning.

The sound froze them, and in the same instant they saw two shadows leaving the farmhouse. One of them wore a broad-brimmed hat. Both of them carried the bobbing coals of lit pipes.

Deborah shuddered and pressed closer to Proctor, who shifted his body to shield her. He wanted to whisper something reassuring to her, but his tongue felt bolted to the roof of his mouth. In a moment the figures reached the road and disappeared. Proctor felt the fear flow out of him; in his arms, Deborah relaxed at the same instant.

"We have to cross this road," Proctor whispered.

"Not yet," Deborah answered. "I'm not ready yet."

While they waited in a hollow behind a fallen tree, the two figures returned. They were shadows in the twilight who could be anyone, but the man in the hat reminded Proctor of Bootzamon. The second looked like a woman.

It was a long time after they passed before Proctor felt ready to continue. They dashed from the tree, across the road, and down the other slope. Although they waited in hiding, they didn't see the strangers return.

The path west was slow and arduous, with frequent long breaks in improvised shelters during the worst of the driving rain. During the course of the day, they descended from the heights, crossed a road guarded by British sentries, and passed a range of low hills. Proctor didn't think it was more than five or six miles as the crow flew, but they went back and forth, over the most difficult terrain, just to avoid the soldiers. They were soaked and plastered with mud. Proctor's shoes squished with every step, and his toes were wet and itchy.

Deborah's strength was fading when Proctor finally spied a rise in the land ahead, a dark bump on the horizon set against the dark sky. "There it is," he told her. "That's the American line."

"How do you know?" she asked.

"Because we've gone far enough that we either run into the Continental army or we fall off the edge of the island into the bay," he said. The air smelled like mudflats, so if that wasn't the American position, falling off the island seemed like a very real possibility.

They crept forward slowly until they came to another road. Nearby, someone coughed and cursed the wet. More British sentries, to judge by the sound of his voice. Other voices joined him.

"What are we waiting for?" asked one voice. "They can surrender in the rain just as easily as when it stops."

"Maybe General Howe doesn't want to get wet when he accepts this upstart Washington's sword."

"No," said a third, gruffer voice. "This weather is perfect. We want to break their spirits before they surrender. Let 'em watch a few more of their friends die in the mud, let 'em be cold and hungry. These colonists, they've never known nothing but luxury and ease. When they see what war's really like, they'll break and that'll be an end to their rebellions."

Proctor started forward, not with any specific idea of showing them what luxury and ease had done for him, but just out of anger. Deborah gripped his arm and stopped him.

"They're right about one thing," she said.

"What's that?" he snapped.

"The plan is to break the army's spirit so there will be no more rebellion. Whatever the Covenant is planning, they'll set it into motion here."

Proctor glanced ahead through the rain again. Maybe she was right. But he couldn't imagine what the Covenant's plan might be. They'd used sickness to weaken the siege at

Boston. What could they use here that would be more powerful?

Proctor waited until the rain came down thick again, driving the sentries back under shelter. Then he wrapped one arm around Deborah's waist and dashed over the road, half carrying her with him and dropping her on the other side.

"I feel like a sack of meal," she whispered

"I'm hungry enough, I wish you were a sack of meal," he said, feeling the pangs in his stomach. A hill rose in front of them. Hastily thrown-up defenses topped the hill, similar to the fort at Bunker Hill. Hats and muskets peeked out along the barrier—it was thick with defenders. "You go first," he said.

"*What?*"

"They won't shoot a woman." As she started toward the steep embankment, he muttered, "I hope."

He followed Deborah, steadying her as she climbed the hill. At the steepest part of the slope, he pushed ahead, offering her a hand up. They were right at the top when a musket poked out over the muddy rampart. Sometimes he hoped for too much.

But the musket was followed by a hat with a drooping brim. The brim spilled water as the head beneath it leaned toward them, and the man offered them his free hand. He pulled Deborah over the rough wall first, then reached back for Proctor. Proctor rolled across the rampart and landed on his back.

The soldier clearly hadn't shaved in several days. His eyes were rimmed with red, as if it had been even longer since he'd slept, and he had an almost haunted look about him. "You folks are running the wrong direction," he said in a slight Virginian accent. "All you civilians were supposed to go over the wall the other way."

"I never was one to follow others much," Proctor said as he stood up.

"Keep your voices and your heads down," the soldier said.

Proctor dropped into a crouch and scanned the length of the wall. There was only one man every twenty or thirty feet. The rest of the "defenders" were hats on sticks and muskets propped over the barricade.

"On second thought," the soldier said. "Maybe you should just come with me." He exchanged gestures with the next man in line, indicating that he was going.

Deborah looked at Proctor questioningly, but he shook his head. As the soldier led them away from the fort and down toward the shore, Deborah leaned in close to Proctor. "There's something wrong here," she whispered.

"I know," he said. "Where are all the soldiers?"

"That's not what I mean," she said.

Now that she had mentioned it, though, he became aware of the same thing: it was a sensation he had felt on their trip through the woods—a prickling of the skin, a distant chill, a creeping sense of fear. He had thought it was just a reaction to seeing the man who reminded him of Bootzamon.

He was watching her face when he tripped over something, and their guide said, "Careful now. You don't want to look too close."

Proctor glanced down at his feet and jumped back. The thing he had tripped over was a dead man's leg.

And not just one dead man, but dozens, perhaps hundreds, lined up in a row on the hill behind the rampart. They lay face up, some with arms across their chests, others with arms at their sides, their eyes closed, their eyes open, their mouths closed, their lips parted in pain or prayer. Some had ragged holes in their chests, some their faces ruined, and some were missing limbs. None had weapons or anything to cover their heads. Proctor saw now where all the extra muskets and hats had come from.

"Deborah, don't look," he said.

She had stepped close to his side. "I've seen it already."

Their guide had gone on ahead of them. He waved them to follow. "You don't want to stay up there, miss. Come this way."

They stepped carefully around the bodies and crossed to a slight rise where they could look across the East River. The rain had thinned to a mere lace of drizzle. A mile away, across the water, the low, dark outline of New York City shouldered its way through the mist. In front of the city, the choppy water, blue-gray flecked with white, was broken by the dark shape of a dozen small boats, moving in both directions, struggling against the current to keep to a straight line.

Directly in front of Deborah and Proctor, the land sloped down sharply to the river. The shore was crowded with thousands of Continental soldiers. They were dressed in a motley of uniforms—some wearing their farm clothes, some wearing finely tailored jackets, and some wearing peacoats more suited to the sea. Many were bandaged, or leaning on crutches, and showed other signs of recent injury. All were covered in mud. The slope, from the fort all the way down to the shore, was a pig's wallow of mud. Heavy cannons mired too deep to move lay stuck in the hillside, abandoned.

Despite the rain and the mud and their wounds, the soldiers stood in orderly lines. The rear ranks faced outward, toward the fort, braced for the inevitable British attack.

The silence struck Proctor with more force than the sight of all the dead bodies. The soldiers waited without banter or protest, standing quietly in line for their turn to embark into boats as varied in origin and condition as their uniforms. When they boarded, they did so with a minimum of sound, soft steps muffled by the sound of the water. Even the boats made little noise as they came toward shore: the oarlocks were padded, and the sailors dipped and pulled the oars with such deliberate skill that even the splashes sounded ordinary.

"This is the whole of the American army?" Deborah asked Proctor in a whisper.

"Yes," he said.

"May the Light shine on us," she whispered.

Proctor couldn't imagine what the Covenant could do that would be worse than this. All the British soldiers had to do was march through the dark, come over the undefended ramparts, and pin the Americans on the beach. That would be the end of independence.

"May the Light shine," Proctor said. "But not until we've all crossed safely."

"That's not what I'm referring to," Deborah said, in a small, frightened voice.

Chapter 9

Deborah stared back, across the row of dead bodies, to the rampart beyond. Bits of mist or fog seeped over the wall.

"Don't you feel it?" she asked.

Her voice was so low he had to lean forward to hear her, and the act of falling silent, of listening to the quiet, allowed him to feel the very thing she mentioned.

Something moved in the air. It feathered across his skin, chilling him. But it moved opposite the direction of the wind coming off the water, which tugged at the coats and cloaks and banners around him.

Voices murmured in his ears. Yet the men around him were quiet, even the wounded men, not daring to cough.

"This is no natural fog," Proctor said softly.

"No, it is not," she agreed.

The fog marched over the walls, creeping at the pace of a funeral procession. It slid down the slope, over the bodies of the dead. It wrapped around Proctor, sending an unnatural shiver through his skin. He saw the same thing happen to Deborah. Then it slipped past them and flowed into the lines of the living soldiers, where it lingered.

Deborah half closed her eyes and shuddered. When she opened them again, she said, "Do you see it now?"

"The fog?"

"Close your eyes, and look with your spirit."

He closed his eyes halfway, just as she had shown him. He shivered again, but this time it was not from the cold.

The fog that advanced over the rampart was formed of ghosts, the souls of the men killed in battle. Their spirit forms were horribly wounded, disfigured by the same blows that killed their physical bodies. They crept like a mob across the battlefield, cuffing themselves to the living.

Nearby, a wounded man, his chest bandaged and his arm bound up, sat with his back against a cannon stuck in the mud. Above him on the hillside, a single ghost detached itself from the mob. It wore a hunting shirt, draped in tatters over its shattered ribs. It flowed down the hill and crawled up onto the cannon like a cat about to pounce on its prey.

"Deborah . . . ," Proctor said.

She shook her head numbly. She had no better idea of what to do than he did.

The ghost dropped off the cannon and into the body of the wounded soldier. Immediately he clutched his chest and went into convulsions. When he tried to rise, his wound burst and blood poured out through his bandages.

Deborah held her elbows tight to her sides, her hands up covering her mouth.

Proctor stepped close to block her view.

Then, as he watched, the spirit of the hunter rose from the body of the dead man. It dragged along a new ghost, one with its chest wrapped in bandages and its face contorted in pain. They hung in the air together for a moment, then flowed off in different directions toward other living men.

"What is this?" Proctor said in a quiet voice.

"It's a curse," she whispered. "This is the Covenant's plan. This is why they needed that orphan with the talent."

He glanced around, but no one else seemed to notice what they noticed. "Why are we the only ones who can see it?"

"Because it's done with magic, and we're the only ones who have the talent to see that," she said.

The ghosts continued to come over the ramparts as they

watched, hundreds, even thousands of them. Some were clearly Hessians and Redcoats. Some were women and children.

"Why are they not all soldiers?" he asked.

"The necromancer who did this uses whatever materials he has to hand, I think." She watched the ghost of a baby squirm by, squalling and miserable. "See how we're not affected. It's meant for the army. He wants to break the spirit of the army so there can never be another rebellion."

"But that wounded soldier who died—?"

"I think he was so near death already, it was easy for the ghost to drag him over to the other side."

"This is . . . it's . . ." He couldn't find the right words for something so wrong. "We have to do something."

"You can come with me," the soldier said behind them.

Proctor jumped at the voice. Spinning around, he saw the unshaven, hollow-eyed soldier who'd helped them over the rampart. He was haunted too. The ghost of a Redcoat missing its right arm at the elbow followed behind him.

"I'm sorry," Deborah said.

"I said, you can come with me," the soldier said, twitching as the ghost tried to turn his head to show him the stump. "The genr'l will see you now."

All the officers were busily engaged, keeping the men in order as they boarded the boats. One man on horseback rode up and down the muddy beach, checking on the officers.

Proctor had seen George Washington once before, from a distance, during the siege of Boston, but it didn't prepare him for the man up close. As the general approached on the sorrel horse, it took Proctor a moment to realize how big both were. Washington stood well over six feet tall, but he looked even taller in the saddle because he was so lean. The sorrel shared his proportions. He moved so easily on the horse's back, with so little obvious communication, that the two appeared to be fused together. He seemed a giant among men.

Washington took off his hat the moment he saw Deborah and ducked his head to her. He had thick brown hair, pulled back in a bow. His face was sun-darkened, more like the farmers Proctor knew than the gentlemen he'd met. His high forehead gave the impression of deep intelligence.

"My apologies for the inhospitable condition of our present habitation, ma'am," Washington said, in the same tone he might use to greet an unannounced but welcome guest to his home. His face was neatly shaven and his demeanor was perfectly calm, even relaxed, despite the weariness and tension all around him.

Washington's stillness attracted a ghost whose shattered body had been rent by musket balls and chain shot. It wore the neat uniform of a Virginia gentleman, but there was no way to tell who it may have been—the lower half of its face was gone. It climbed over the back of the horse, making the sorrel stamp its feet and try to move away. Washington stilled the animal with the slightest pressure of his knees. But it gave the ghost a chance to fasten on to Washington's shoulder.

A second ghost, built like a New York blacksmith, came along with a slave chain in his hands. He clamped one shackle around Washington's ankle and the other to the ghost already there. Then he clapped the chain to his own ankle and joined them.

The third ghost to arrive was gut-shot. Its hat and jacket reminded Proctor of the militiamen he knew from Connecticut and Massachusetts. The ghost writhed and twisted, stuffing its intestines back into the cavity of its torso, only to have his head fly back as if shot and all the organs spill out again. The blacksmith grinned as it clapped a chain around his ankle.

Washington's eyes flickered as if he felt a slight pain, but he revealed no more than that. "Is something wrong, ma'am?" he asked. "I mean, beyond the obvious circumstances. You seem dismayed."

"It's no, no problem," Deborah stammered.

"The New York ferry is presently engaged for our use, along with numerous other craft, as you may see. With your permission, I will offer you a seat—"

"General, General," another officer cried as his horse galloped in, kicking up mud with his hooves and digging in for footing while it slid to a stop. The ghost on his back was a young man who had died in fear, and it shared that fear with its new host.

Washington lifted his head, clearly unhappy to be interrupted, though it was no more than a hardening of the lines around his mouth, the disappearance of what was no more than a hint of a smile.

"General, you must embark at once," the officer insisted.

Washington put his hat back on and turned his horse toward the new officer. The stiffening of his body, the way he rested his hand on his saber—all of it made clear that one did not tell Washington what he *must* do.

But the new officer, as frightened as Washington was calm, was not to be deterred. "Sir, the rain has lifted. The British could break camp at any time."

Washington still had not spoken. When he did, it was slowly and calmly, as if there were no need at all for worry. "You keep an eye on our British friends and let me know when they start to move. I think they may be settled in for the night. Tallmadge and his men can hold them if they need to. Until then, we'll keep moving the men in the order that we've planned."

"But, *sir*. With the storm lifted, the British fleet could come up the East River at any moment. All the boats in the water will be cut off, and we'll be stranded here."

"I'll have Colonel Glover and his men keep an eye out for the British on that front."

The officer opened his mouth, thought better of what he was going to say, then closed it again. He scanned the lines of men waiting to board the boats. The lines of men, in turn, watched the exchange between Washington and his young officer intently. At that moment an empty boat returned from the New York side, driving up on the shore with a muted *thump*.

Washington sat on his horse, making no gesture to move toward the empty vessel. An instant later the next men in line began to quietly board.

The young officer overcame the fear caused by his ghost for a moment. He sat up crisply in his saddle and saluted. "Yes, sir."

Washington returned the salute. When the officer departed back to his duties, he went at a slower, more deliberate pace.

"With your permission, I will offer you a seat in my boat when I cross," Washington promised Deborah. "But there may be a wait until that happens."

"I understand," she said. "As civilians, we're not in the same danger from the British as your men."

The ghosts tugged at Washington's back, trying to divert his attention, but he was unmoved by them. "I'm glad to see that you are a woman of discernment. What's your name, young man?"

"Proctor Brown."

Recognition flashed in Washington's eyes. "Proctor Brown, of Concord, lately of Salem?"

Proctor's heart caught in his throat as if he'd been named by the minister during Sunday worship. "Yes, that's me."

"Paul Revere spoke very highly of you," Washington said. He studied Proctor closely, sizing him up. To the soldier who waited on them, he said, "Provide them every comfort we have to offer."

"Yes, sir," the soldier said.

Washington looked back at Proctor and Deborah. "And the two of you are . . ."

"Brother and sister," Deborah said quickly.

"I see," Washington said. "It is a pleasure to meet you, Mister Brown. The next time I see you, I hope it will be in the uniform of a Continental soldier."

Proctor stood at attention just as if he were at militia drill. He said, "I can't promise that. But I am willing to do my part for the patriotic cause."

"Honestly spoken," Washington said. A slight smile played at the corner of his lips. He tipped his hat to Deborah, "Ma'am."

They watched him head away toward the rear guard that protected their retreat. Proctor knew that the situation was quite grim. Still, Washington's manner was infectious—he made you want to be as calm as he was calm, as confident as he seemed to be.

"Is there anything you need?" their soldier-guide asked. He looked at Proctor differently now.

"Clean water," Proctor said. "And a bite to eat."

He knew it was a lot to ask for under these conditions, but the guide promised to see to it immediately and ran off. A short while later he returned with half a canteen of fresh water and two dry oatcakes.

"I'm sorry we can't spare more," he said. "If that covers it, then I best go back where I'm needed."

"Thank you," Deborah told him.

"Yes," Proctor said, downing a sip of water. "Thank you."

"The honor is mine," the soldier said. He saluted Proctor, and then, without waiting for a response, turned back to the ramparts. He used the butt of his musket to steady himself as he climbed the slippery hillside. The ghost riding his shoulder turned its head and watched Deborah and Proctor as he left.

"What is that about?" Deborah said.

"I'm not sure," Proctor admitted.

"Do you think Revere told him about The Farm?"

Proctor shrugged. "Maybe he just told him about what I did at Lexington and Concord, and at Bunker Hill." The truth was, he was proud of his service with the militia. He knew that what they did now was important too, maybe more important. But it galled him sometimes not to be able to serve with the other soldiers.

They went and sat against one of the abandoned cannons, tearing off pieces of the cake and chewing slowly. They passed the canteen back and forth to wash down the dry mouthfuls. If he did not exactly feel his strength returning, Proctor no longer felt so weak. Another group of boats departed, but there were thousands of soldiers still waiting their turn, including Washington and his officers and all the rear guard.

"Deborah?"

"Yes?"

Her voice was distracted. Now that they no longer had to concentrate to keep themselves going, would she collapse again? Would he? "Can we do something?"

She looked up at him, as if this was exactly the question she had feared. "I don't know what we can do."

"It has to be clear what the strategy is." He lowered his voice to a whisper. "The Covenant places this curse on the army at night. The men are filled with fear, demoralized. At daybreak, the British mean to charge over the ramparts and defeat them."

She nodded her head to the shore, where the men stood in patient, orderly lines. "They don't look filled with fear or demoralized to me."

"You know that's only temporary. They're so exhausted by the rain and the battle, they can't sink any lower. And Washington hasn't rested a moment. He's everywhere, making sure the men see him, setting an example that they want to follow. The moment he's out of their sight, the ghosts will do their work."

She looked away from him, so he stood and walked in front of her.

"You see how long those lines are, how slow they're moving. Morning will come and British ships will sail up the river, and British troops will march over those walls, and Washington and all his best men will be caught and killed. Can't we make it rain again? Bring down another storm, just long enough to cover the rest of the retreat? One or two hours is all they need."

She turned her body away from Proctor. "I've got nothing left in me."

"Tell me how to do it."

"I . . . I can't."

"Can't or won't?" He looked at the men waiting in line, the men who were fighting when he didn't. "I'll take the risk, whatever it is."

She shook her head and moved away. When he advanced again, she put up her in hands, prepared to push him away. Some of the soldiers around them were watching closely.

"What are they going to think?" she said to Proctor, indicating the soldiers. "You don't want to draw attention to us. You *don't* want to do that."

"I want to do *something*."

"Sometimes there's nothing we can do."

Proctor paced up and down the beach, the mud sucking at his feet. Boat by boat, the soldiers were slowly ferried to safety, but the night was passing rapidly and dawn would come early in the clear skies. The east was starting to brighten. Across the ramparts, from the British lines, came the distant sounds of morning drums. He went back to Deborah. "It's not enough—they're not all going to make it."

She held her hands open, helplessly. "I've tried everything I know how to try. I have nothing left inside me right now."

A low voice whistled behind them. "Hallelujah."

The speaker was instantly ordered to silence, but his sentiment was shared by others.

A mist was rising. Out on the water, over the boats, settling in around the men waiting their turn. It grew thicker as he watched, until the shore disappeared from Proctor's view.

A splash sounded as someone missed a step getting into his boat. It was followed by quieter splashes as the boat moved away from shore.

The soldier who had spoken to them before came by. "We're leaving the wall now, last troops to go," he whispered, his voice hushed even more by the fog. "It's a miracle. There wasn't enough night, but this will keep Black Dick's ships at anchor and give us a chance to get away."

Boats ran ashore unexpectedly, several of them at the same time, and voices sorted out positions and began boarding. Proctor and Deborah drifted toward them.

"This is not a natural fog," Proctor said softly. It was clammy on his skin and made his heart race.

"No, it isn't," she agreed.

"Did you do this? By accident, perhaps?"

"No," she said. "The Covenant did it."

When she said it, he saw what she meant. The rowboats full of soldiers took a cargo of ghosts with them every time they crossed. The cold from all those spectral bodies drew up fog from the water. The magic itself was drawing up the mist.

"We are saved," he whispered to Deborah. "And at the same time we are cursed."

"We can't cross," she said.

"Why? Because of the mist?"

"No, because of the curse. We have to stay, we have to find the orphan, and we have to break this curse. This is evil, Proctor. This is evil twice, because it does wrong to the souls of the dead as well as the spirits of the living."

"You're right," he said. "We'll find the orphan and break the spell."

Down on the shore, Washington climbed aboard one of the last ferries to leave Brooklyn. He beckoned Deborah to him.

"Here is the seat I promised you," he said.

"I appreciate your hospitality," Deborah said. "But my brother and I have decided to stay behind. We have a relation here. Seeing all this death, it only firms us in our conviction to remove our relative from harm. We are sorry if we troubled you tonight."

She had her arms wrapped tight around her chest. Despite wearing Proctor's jacket, she shivered so much her teeth chattered.

"Are you sure you wish to remain behind?" Washington asked.

"We are," Deborah said.

"Then keep an eye out for the British," Washington said. He regarded Proctor deliberately. "If you're the patriot I think you are, I'll expect you to find me and report after you rescue your relation."

Proctor fought the urge to snap to attention, salute, and say *yes, sir.* "I'll do what I can."

Washington gave him a nod that felt like a salute. With unhurried grace, he turned to the boat and spoke with similar deliberation to each man there. A slave in a red turban, a short dark-skinned man built like a cannonball, rode his horse toward the ferry, leading Washington's sorrel behind. He dismounted on the run, rolling into a smooth walking motion, and led both horses aboard without breaking stride.

It was an amazing feat of horsemanship, Proctor thought. Washington laughed to see it, and the slave returned his laughter with a grin.

The Massachusetts sailors pushed off from shore and began their silent journey across the river.

Deborah stepped close to Proctor, still shivering. "Let's move away from the water," she said. "It's too chilly here for an August morning."

"Where do you want to go?"

"To break this curse?" she said. "I think we start in Gravesend."

Chapter 10

Gravesend was a collection of houses on a long, low slope overlooking the ocean on the southern shore of the island. When they reached town that day, Proctor and Deborah split up to search for the orphan.

"The best thing we can do is find him within the hour and be on our way," Proctor said.

"I'll call on the Lakes," Deborah said, referring to the Quaker family that had connections with her father. "Maybe I can arrange passage home for us using the highway."

Hours later, they met again in the main street outside the church. Deborah sat by the side of the road, looking tired and worried. Proctor was worried for her. She lifted her head as he approached. "Did you have any luck?" she asked.

"Nothing," Proctor said. "Were you able to find your friends the Lakes?"

"No, they've left town because of the fighting." Her face was drawn and desperate. "There's no one here we can turn to for help."

"I'm sorry," Proctor said. He wanted to say something reassuring, but he couldn't think of anything.

She pushed herself wearily to her feet. "I did find something interesting. Walk down this street with me."

He followed her down the street to an empty lot. "What am I looking for?"

She reached up and held his head straight. Suddenly a

squat two-story house with a porch across the front and three dormor windows up above appeared in front of him. He could have sworn it wasn't there a moment before.

"That's Van Sicklyn's house," she said. "It's being used by a German lord who's here as an adviser to the Hessians." She pointed to another house across the street, a mansion with red and blue regimental colors hanging out front. "Those are the headquarters of Colonel Johann Rall, commander of the Hessian grenadiers."

"You think the German lord is our man? The source of the curse?"

"What do you think?"

He looked again and the house was gone. "Um."

"People become very vague when I ask about it—as soon as they begin to speak about the Van Sicklyns, or their house, or this German lord, they forget what they're saying."

Proctor nodded. "How did you get them to point out the house? Is there a spell that returns memory? Or—"

"I convinced an old midwife to walk down the street with me," Deborah said. "I asked her to tell me about the babies delivered in each house, and I settled on the spot that seemed invisible to her."

"Ah." Deborah was very clever. "How do we get inside to check?"

The door slammed open and a ratty-haired boy of about ten ran out. Proctor grabbed Deborah's arm and pulled her back behind a tree. This could be their orphan, but it would be a mistake to act too quickly until they knew for sure.

The boy stumbled to a stop at the edge of the yard, just like a dog on an invisible leash. His pants were too short, riding well up his shins, and his feet were bare. His shirt was too big, with the sleeves rolled up to free his hands.

The door opened a second time, and a rail-thin black woman in a simple check dress walked calmly after the boy. She stopped at his side and rested a hand on his shoulder.

"Lydia," Proctor whispered.

Deborah nodded.

Lydia had studied magic with them on The Farm. She was the slave of Cecily Sumpter Pinckney, and a source of magic for the other woman. She appeared drained, exhausted even worse than Deborah.

A small blond woman followed Lydia out the door. She wore an elaborate yellow velvet dress more suited to some governor's mansion than a farmhouse in a small town. Cecily. *That southern woman.* Someone they had trusted as a fellow witch, and a necromancer who'd tried to kill them. Her face was beautiful in its composition and terrifying in its wrath. Proctor winced as a halo of spiked fire seemed to form around her head.

He was not the only one to notice. Lydia flinched and dropped her head between her shoulders. The little boy covered his ears and screamed. Pebbles trembled on the ground near the boy's feet, then rose in the air.

Proctor braced to see them fly at Cecily.

Cecily held up her hand, delicate lace trailing from her wrist. She made a gesture with her fingers, and the pebbles fell to the ground. Then she closed her hand in a fist.

The boy fell silent instantly. He began clawing at his throat, trying to breathe. Proctor pressed through the bushes, ready to bolt forward, but Deborah pulled him back.

"Not yet," she whispered.

Cecily opened her hand and the boy gasped for air. The second he started to cry, she shut it again, cutting off his breath and his voice.

Lydia, her face a mask of sad acceptance, stroked the boy's hair while he choked and started to turn blue. She bent and whispered to him. Proctor couldn't tell what she said, but he thought she was telling him not to struggle.

"We're not ready," Deborah whispered, her eyes locked on Cecily. "I'm not ready."

Cecily opened her fist, and the boy dropped to his knees, gasping for air. Lydia knelt beside him, slipping her hands under his arms and helping him to his feet. Together they walked back toward the house, the boy hiding behind Lydia as they passed Cecily.

When they had gone inside, Cecily turned and looked up and down the road. Her gaze lingered for a moment on the spot where Proctor and Deborah were hiding. It felt like a thousand ants were crawling across Proctor's skin, and he and Deborah both ducked their heads, hoping to remain hidden. Cecily called into the house.

A soldier in a green jacket came out. A pistol was tucked in his waist along with a large fascine knife.

Proctor recognized him as well. It was the man called Jolly, who had attacked them on The Farm and then worked for the widow Nance before Deborah killed her.

Deborah's grip on Proctor's arm, which had not lessened, now bit deeper still. He took her hand in his and pulled her away, creeping along the shadow of the hedge until they could turn the corner and conceal themselves behind another farmhouse.

"Did you recognize—?" she whispered.

"Yes," he answered. "Cecily, Lydia, the orphan, Jolly—it's all our enemies and everyone we ought to rescue, all in one spot. Cecily must have replaced the widow."

Deborah shook her head. "Cecily doesn't have enough power to put that kind of curse on Washington and the whole Continental army."

Proctor opened his mouth, then snapped it shut again.

"See," Deborah said. "You know I'm right."

"You're right," he admitted. "Even drawing on Lydia's magic, and the boy's too, she didn't have that kind of power. The widow did, and you could feel it."

"Exactly," Deborah said, glancing back over her shoul-

der to see if they'd been followed. She stopped. "I'm guessing it's that German lord that people meet then get vague
about. He's the key to the curse."

"Can't we just free Lydia and the orphan? Won't that
break the curse?"

"It's a curse—he only had to draw on their power to create it. Now it has a life of its own. But unless we free them
too, our work will be wasted. Even if we break the curse,
he'll just perform the ritual and set it again."

Proctor shoved his hands in his pockets and looked
away. "What are we going to do then?"

"First we have to find this German," Deborah said. She
slumped down in the grass and buried her face in her
hands.

Proctor knelt beside her. Softly he said, "First, we have
to help you regain your strength."

Deborah looked up at him. "What?"

"It makes strategic sense," he said. "Nobody can discover anything in a small town until they have a place in it.
Our place will be servants, refugees from the war. And it'll
mean food and a place to stay."

Her shoulders lifted hopefully. "Food and a place to stay
will be good."

"If you want food, we'll have to take it out of your
wages, and it won't be cheap, not with all the British soldiers who need feeding," the farmer said.

His name was Stymiest. He had a narrow face with a
high forehead and ears that looked like they'd been
grabbed and twisted often in his childhood. He looked at
Proctor, who was standing at his doorstep with Deborah.

"And the only place I could offer you to stay is quarters
in the barn," he added.

Proctor had almost grown accustomed to barns. "That'll
do just fine," he said. "What about my sister?"

"She would have to sleep on the floor in the loft with the children," Stymiest said, scowling.

"That will be fine," Deborah said wearily.

Stymiest turned to his wife. "No," he said. "No, I just don't think we can do it. It just won't work."

"But they've agreed to *everything*," she said. Her hair and clothes were indecently unkempt, as if it was simply too much work to keep up with everything. "I need help with the children. You need help with the harvest."

"The British haven't come this far out of town yet, but they will," he said. "They're quartering troops in everyone's homes. There's no way we can provide room and board for troops, and room and board for servants too."

That was the crux of the problem. Proctor and Deborah had been turned away from every house and farm they called on because people felt the strain of quartering the British troops and their Hessian allies.

"So if we have to quarter troops, we'll release the servants," Mrs. Stymiest said reasonably.

"We'll offer no complaint if that happens," Proctor interjected. In truth, he hoped they would be gone long before then.

"No," Mr. Stymiest said firmly.

"Then you can cook your own meals and make *your* bed out in the barn," Mrs. Stymiest yelled. She stepped back inside the house and slammed the door on him.

"Darling," he yelled through the door. He tried to open it, but it was latched shut from within. "Pumpkin!"

"Don't you pumpkin me," yelled his wife.

"All right, all right," he capitulated. "We'll hire them, but only under the conditions I gave." He looked at Proctor and Deborah. "And you're dismissed the moment the British want to be quartered."

"Believe me," Proctor said. "We'll be out of here."

The door opened. Mrs. Stymiest offered her cheek for a very chaste kiss, which Mr. Stymiest provided. A little barefoot girl ran out the door and began tugging on Deborah's hem for attention.

"Let go that dress, Sissy," Mrs. Stymiest said. She took Deborah by the hand and dragged her inside, saying, "We're going to be such good friends."

The farmer looked over Proctor. "An older sister, huh?"

"What? Oh. Yes."

The farmer sighed and rubbed a hand behind his left ear. "I could tell. They always get their way. Well, best show you where you'll be staying."

The barn was in worse shape than Deborah's father's barn had been. It would have to do for the next few days.

Deborah took weeks to recover.

She fell ill the day after they arrived. Mr. Stymiest would have dismissed them both on the spot, only Proctor did enough work for two people. He had practice turning run-down farms into neat and productive properties. By the end of that first day, he had taken on enough extra chores to make himself indispensable.

Fortunately, Mrs. Stymiest took to Deborah like a child to a sick bird. She put her in a bed, made the children stay out of doors, and nursed her back to health. Proctor was allowed to see her once or twice a day.

"When will you be able to help me?" he asked whenever he saw her. Meaning help him rescue Lydia and the orphan, help him break the curse.

Every time he asked, she said, "Tomorrow."

He did what he could without her, stealing into town on Sundays and watching the house. But no one emerged again, not while he was there. And without Deborah's guidance, he was wary of breaking the barrier for a closer look. The same way he hoped that Bootzamon was wary of breaking the barrier at The Farm.

If there had been any way to send a letter to Magdalena, he would have. She and the others must have been worried sick. The only way he could think to reach them was by sending a note to Paul Revere. But the mail was entirely in the hands of the British and their Loyalist sympathizers. No letter he sent would reach Revere.

By the third week, Deborah was up and moving about again. She came and found him repairing the siding in the barn. He was so relieved to see her up and walking, he dropped the hammer and jumped off the ladder. Face-to-face, he thrust his hands in his pockets just to keep from embracing her.

"It's good to see you up," he said. "What happened?"

"I suffered a spell," she said, and shrugged as if that was all the explanation she'd offer or effort she'd expend.

It was the cost of the magic she had done to end the battle at Brooklyn. She wasn't going to talk about it, and maybe it didn't matter. Not as long as she recovered. "Are you sure you should be up already?"

"Yes," she said. "We have to break the curse."

That was so like her. She still appeared too pale and thin to him to do anything strenuous, but she was eager to get started. It was one of the things he admired about her.

"How have you been?" she asked.

"Stymiest doesn't want a servant, he wants a slave. He doesn't seek my opinion or my permission, he just uses me." He forced his fist to unclench. He didn't want to think about that now that Deborah was well. "I've not minded so much, because they've been taking care of you."

Deborah shuffled her feet uncomfortably. "I have to do something, Proctor," she said. "All the time I've been in bed, I've been thinking about . . . the unjust burden carried by our friends."

The curse. "Can you get away from the house for an hour or so?"

"Why?" Deborah asked.

"A fellow named Increase lives half a mile down the road. You have to meet him. He carries a ghost. He must have been at the battle of Brooklyn, only no one here knows. After the battle, he came home again and simply went back to work. I've talked to him in the fields. He's sick, maybe unto death."

"If we can cure him," Deborah said, "then we'll figure out a way to break the curse."

"That's what I was thinking," Proctor said. He shoved his hands deeper into his pockets. "Thank God you're all right, Deborah. I don't know what I would do if—"

She glanced back at the house as if she hadn't heard him. "Let's go now," she said. "Before they notice I'm gone."

He led her away at once. They found Increase sitting in a chair outside his own dilapidated farm. His skin was sallow and unhealthy. He blinked up at the sunlight, like a turtle on a log trying to get warm.

"Deborah, this is the fellow I was telling you about," Proctor said. "Increase, this is my sister Deborah."

Increase stirred, but only a little. His ghost was hard to see in the sun, but it had been an immense man in life, half a foot taller than Increase and five or six stone heavier. Its only wound was one small hole through his leg. The shot must have hit an artery, causing him to bleed out.

"Have you been sick?" Deborah said.

"Heartsick," Increase replied with a wan smile. "Your brother said you were a healer, but I doubt you can heal that."

Deborah had brought some fresh mint with her for a focus. "The scent will distract him," she explained to Proctor. She asked Increase to cup his hands as she poured mint into them. "Lean forward, close your eyes, and breathe in the fragrance," she said.

He did as she directed. When his eyes were closed, she poured the rest in a circle around him. She created a thick line at his back, where the ghost hung over his shoulder. Then she said to the ghost under her breath, "Devil, I cast thee out."

The ghost erupted in fury, beating its big hands as if Increase's head were a drum. Increase spilled the handful of mint and grasped his temples.

"What did you do?" he cried. "It hurts so bad, I want to die. What did you do to me?"

The ghost continued to beat on his head until Deborah retreated from him. Proctor apologized profusely, and they made their excuses to go.

"That didn't go well," he said. "Why didn't it work?"

"I think it didn't work because the ghosts aren't devils. They're just trapped souls. But I don't know what verse or spell to use to break that." She looked sick again herself, weary to the point of fainting. "I am sorry, I am so sorry."

"It's not your fault," he said. "Your intentions were good. Don't you always tell me that intentions matter?"

"They do—but he is in so much agony. His spirit is sick. Do you think all the soldiers are afflicted like this?"

"I wish I knew," he said.

"Let's stop at The Farm and get our things," Deborah said. "We'll go back into Gravesend and try to find the orphan and Lydia. I only hope that Lydia can help us."

"Is she free enough to do that now?" Proctor asked. "She wasn't last year, on The Farm."

"I don't know," Deborah admitted. A grim determination forced its way past her sickly pallor. "But I know we have to do something, and do it soon."

"That's God's truth," Proctor said. They walked along fields ready for harvest. "I wish we were back at our farm."

She looked at him oddly when he said *our farm,* and immediately he regretted it. "See what kind of food you can gather from the garden or the orchard," she said. "I'll see what I can get from the kitchen."

They split up when they returned to the farm. Deborah went into the house, while Proctor gathered their few belongings from the barn. He went out to the garden and the orchard, filling their travel bag with carrots and squash from the garden, the last few plums, and some almost ripened apples.

When he returned to the house for Deborah, he saw a one-horse shay tied up out front. He stopped on the doorstep before entering. There were voices in the parlor. One of them spoke clear English, but it was slightly accented, like a foreign spice in a familiar dish. Proctor leaned against the house, creeping closer to the window until he could make out words.

"M-m-my lord, my lady," Mrs. Stymiest stammered. "We're not prepared to receive such grace in our humble house. Let go that dress, Sissy!"

"The house would be adequate if you would but teach the children manners," said a cold, familiar voice.

That southern woman.

"We understand that you have two new servants working for you," said the slightly foreign voice. If Cecily was here, the other voice had to be the German.

"Y-y-yes, my lord."

"They are my indentured servants and have escaped my service."

"Y-y-you must be mistaken. They're Quakers, brother and sister. The young man has a Massachusetts accent—"

"I'm not mistaken."

"I knew they were trouble the moment I saw them," Mr. Stymiest said. "The worst sort of thieves and scoundrels. They lazed around, pretending to be sick. Hardly did any work at all."

"I want them returned immediately," the German said. "We are departing for Manhattan to rejoin the army, and I wish to take them with me."

"Yes, my lord," the farmer said.

"There will be a reward for any loyal subject who assists me. And consequences for anyone I find who has aided these servants in their rebellion."

Fear shot through Proctor. He had to bind this man inside so he could find Deborah and escape, but he didn't have any salt to hand. What did he have?

He ran to the feed trough and scooped handfuls of millet into a basket formed by holding up the front hem of his shirt. It had just been harvested, so that would draw extra strength into it.

He crouched, spreading a circle around the house as he went, saying an entrapment spell. He was nearly around the third corner when he heard the door open and jerked back just in time. The farmer called out their names.

The door banged shut.

"They're off hiding from work again," the farmer said. "But we'll find them."

"I-I-I still don't believe it," the wife said. "She seemed like such a sweet young woman—"

"Many things are not what they seem," the German said. "They are thieves and vandals."

And you're murderers and necromancers, thought Proctor. He crawled around the corner, sprinkling grain and focusing on his spell. He was concentrating so intently he barely heard the whispered "Psst."

He froze, glancing from side to side.

"Psst."

The sound was louder and directly above him. He looked up and saw Deborah climbing out of a second-story window. As soon as she caught his eye, she dropped. Her skirts slapped the clapboards once, and then he threw out his arms, wrapping her tight and rolling to the ground.

Cecily's voice came from inside. "What was that?"

"Is there someone upstairs?" the husband asked.

"I'm sure there isn't," his wife said. "All the children are down here. I checked when I went up there and they said it was empty."

Deborah tore herself free of Proctor's surprised grip. She snatched up the spilled grain and repaired the circle where they'd disturbed it, whispering a spell under her breath.

"Those two servants are closer than you think," the German said. "Perhaps you should take my lady with you and look again."

Proctor grabbed the rest of the grain and tossed it across the doorway to reach the circle on the other side. He thought he'd done a good job, and he nodded toward the road. But Deborah repeated his motion with more grain, lips moving to her own spell, before she took his hand. They crouched off together toward the barn.

He felt angry that she didn't trust his spell. Before he could decide whether to say anything, Cecily shouted triumphantly from the upstairs window.

"There they are."

Cecily stood there, dressed in purple silks, her hand pointing out the window Deborah had just dropped from.

The door opened and into its frame strode the German. He was a large man in every dimension. His clothes were well made, cut to his frame, but not as ostentatious as Cecily's. It was impossible to look at him for long, just as it was impossible to stare at the sun without going blind. Proctor averted his eyes and found his memory of the German fading as quickly as he looked away.

Deborah pulled at his sleeve.

The German took two long strides forward and reached the barrier of Proctor's spell. He slammed into it like a sled hitting a tree and staggered back, bowling into the farmer and his wife, who had followed him through the door.

"Hurry," Deborah whispered.

Proctor ran after her. His improvised barrier would not last long against a witch with that much power. The German stepped up to the ring of seed and, just as Bootzamon had done, summoned a wind to blow it away.

"Get down!" Deborah cried, pulling Proctor off the road into the cover of a hedge.

Wind rushed in from every direction at once, tearing birds out of the sky and branches from the trees. It thundered like an avalanche into the house, with a sound like a thousand hammers hitting a thousand planks. The German and the farmers were slammed off their feet and back through the door. The shutters fell from the house and clattered to the ground. A single child began to cry.

"What just happened?" Proctor asked.

"Later," she said. "That doesn't buy us more than an extra quarter hour."

She took off running down the road, but Proctor heard a horse whinny anxiously at the side of the road and spotted the German's shay. He ran to it, freed the reins, and climbed aboard. He steered the horse onto the road after Deborah, reaching down to pull her aboard as he caught up.

"We'll hang for thieves," she yelled, holding on to her cap. The rattle of the carriage and the pounding of the horse's hooves all but drowned out her voice.

"That may be a better fate than the one awaiting us if the German catches us first." He looked for the whip and snapped it against the horse's flank, driving them at a dangerous pace up the road. "What happened back there?"

"You almost trapped me inside the house with your spell," she accused.

"They said you weren't there."

"When I saw *that woman* coming, I cast a hiding spell and made the children forget they'd seen me. But once the German entered the house, I was afraid he would detect me."

"How? How can he do that?"

"How should I know?" She sounded frightened. "I've never encountered a talent so ablaze."

"The Light of God?" Proctor asked.

"More like the fires of hell. I added a spell to your barrier—and may I ask, why grain?"

"That's all I could find."

"You might as well tie a horse with string as hold him back with grain," she said.

"What spell did you add?"

"I remembered how that Bootzamon creature summoned wind to wreck your circle of salt," she said, looking back. The Farm was too distant to be seen now. "I suspect the creature came from this man, and I took a chance he would use the same spell. So I used the grain to make the next spell cast increase by tenfold, twentyfold, a hundredfold."

"So the grain was perfect," Proctor said smugly.

He reined the horses in abruptly, bending them around an old man with a cart. As they rattled on down the road, people came out of their houses to see them and shout at them to slow down. Proctor turned to Deborah to ask her how she'd done the spell and saw her speaking a new one under her breath. She touched the sideboard, her knee, his knee.

"There," she said. "Those who see us pass will think we are the German and Cecily."

A shiver, perhaps of revulsion, ran through Proctor's body. "I'm not sure I like to be mistaken for either one of them."

"Better that than being caught."

"True." At the back of his brain, he had a niggling worry. How had Deborah become so powerful she could improvise spells like that in the heat of the moment? He still needed practice, and it went better when he could stay calm. But she didn't seem to need any of that. "We'll be caught anyway," he said.

"What makes you think so?"

"They'll follow the carriage and find out where we've gone. We can't hide it, or our passage."

"Oh," she said.

The road was so rough that it rattled his teeth nearly out of his head. He reined in the horse and slowed to an easier pace. It wouldn't do to be too sore from riding to walk. And it wouldn't do at all if they broke a wheel or cracked an axle before they had gone very far away.

"Thank you," Deborah said, relieved at the slower, less bone-jarring pace.

"You're welcome," Proctor said. He touched the scar on his neck, thinking of the musket ball that had nearly taken his life at the battle of Lexington. "That was a bit too close."

She nodded, her face drawn. "It will get closer still before we're done."

"How's that?" he asked.

"We've found the witch who is powerful enough to put the curse on Washington and all the Continental soldiers. But we still have no idea how we can break it."

Chapter 11

The carriage rolled into the town of Jamaica. Long Island towns were less orderly than the New England villages that Proctor knew. Normally, he looked for green, meetinghouse, and taverns, in that order. But Jamaica was laid out along the length of the road like a market. The principal church in town was a stone edifice with a steeple topped by a weathercock. The building was so vain by New England standards that Proctor mistook it for a merchant's mansion.

"We need to find someone to take the carriage east for us," Proctor said. "To throw them off our trail while we double back to the west."

"We'll have to be careful," Deborah said as they rolled past a group of British soldiers. "Most of the people who remain here are probably Tories, just as in Gravesend. What are we going to tell them?"

"I've been thinking about that," he said. "We'll say that we're loaning it to a British officer in Sag Harbor, for his use here."

"There's an inn there, Howell's Inn—we'll say that's where he's staying," Deborah said.

Proctor nodded. "With luck, someone there will actually claim it."

The plan was easier to form than to put into action. The British soldiers occupied the largest houses in town and quartered their soldiers in the rest. Both they and the local residents stayed in groups while they sorted out this new arrangement. The rest of the people were much like Proctor and Deborah, strangers to the town—worn and penniless refugees from the recent battles, dust-covered merchants come seeking profit from the war, and young men trying to make up their minds which side they would volunteer for. All of them were wary.

"What about him?" Deborah asked.

She tipped her head, indicating a peddler laboring under a sack large enough to contain several changes of clothes in addition to his wares. He had dark, unruly hair and a wild, furtive cast to his face. But he observed everything, and his eyes didn't flinch from theirs when they met.

"Excuse me," Proctor said.

"Harvey Birch is the name," the peddler said, immediately swinging his sack off his shoulder and setting it down before him. "Can I interest the lady in some silk? Comes straight from China."

"No thank you, Mr. Birch," Proctor said. "We were hoping we might engage you to deliver this carriage for us. We've come as far as we mean to go, but we promised it to a British officer in Sag Harbor for his comfort. He's at Howell's Inn. You could take it there, and ease your journey along the way."

"I see," Birch said, closing his sack. "And this officer's name?"

Proctor hesitated.

"Major John Morse," Deborah said at once. "He's an old friend of my father's."

Birch studied her face, then shook his head. After glancing around to see that no one stood too near, he said, "That makes no sense."

"I beg your pardon," Proctor said.

"The regulars are moving west into Manhattan, crossing at Hell Gate. If he's moving west too, he'd want the carriage taken that way. If he's going to be stationed in Sag Harbor, he'll hardly need a carriage. It'd practically stretch from one end of the town to the other. Anywhere else he needed to go, he could sail to."

"Forgive me, sir," Proctor said. "Clearly you know more than we do about the military situation."

Birch regarded him suspiciously. "I tell you what. The British soldiers stationed here, they send messages east daily. One of them could deliver the carriage for you. Why not come with me and I'll introduce you."

Proctor hesitated again.

"Say no more," Birch said. "I know not what your game is here, but I see you are playing one. I'll not be a party to any underhanded business."

"Sir, please," Deborah asked.

"No, ma'am. Whatever you are about, it's a dangerous business in the midst of a war." He shouldered his sack. "A piece of advice for you, from a seller of wares: I suggest you line up your facts before you ply your story again."

He turned and walked away.

"Maybe he's got a point," Proctor said. "Why don't we just leave the carriage someplace in the woods?"

"It'd be cruel to the horse," Deborah replied. "And it would be found in almost no time at all. We must find someone to take it off our hands."

"I saw a stable at the other end of town. Why don't we see if we can store it there?" he said.

"That's a good thought," she said. "But we should ask if they have someone who can deliver it for us. I still think it best to take it as far from us as possible."

"Whatever we do, we must do it quickly," Proctor said. "Or the German will arrive behind us while we're still trying to decide."

Proctor turned the horse and steered the shay back to the stable. The doors were open, and he could see that most of the stalls were empty. Half a dozen boys idly kicked a football around the yard.

When they pulled up in front, the stable master rose

from his seat in the shade. He was a large-bellied man with short legs and eyes set too close together. Proctor asked him for help delivering the wagon.

"How much can you afford to pay for these services?" the stabler asked. Proctor named the price that he and Deborah agreed they could spare from their purse.

"No, sir, can't say as I can help you for those rates," the stable master said. "I might be willing to buy that team and carriage though, if the price is low enough."

"I'm afraid they're not for sale," Deborah answered. "We promised to see them delivered, as no one else was available, but I've not been feeling well and think I need to return home."

She hesitated as she spoke the phrase *not been feeling well* in a way that indicated it was some feminine problem she was too modest to explain.

"Hmph." The stabler squinted at them as if he could see through the image Deborah cast. "Why didn't you just send your own servants?"

"They've run off," Proctor interjected. "Joined the rebels."

"By God," the stabler said, glancing at the yard. "If I caught any of my boys doing that, I'd whip him to next Sunday and leave him so sore it'd take him to the Sunday after to heal up. And then I'd whip him again."

The ball rolled away from the boys and past the stabler's feet. He tried to kick it and missed. A brown-haired boy, thin as a stick, chased after the ball. The stabler kicked at him too, but missed another time. The boy picked up the ball, then paused to stare at Proctor and Deborah.

"We'll get new servants, I'm sure," Deborah said. "In the meantime, do you know anyone who can deliver the carriage for us?"

"No, I don't," the stabler said. "But I'll give you a piece of advice. Report your servants to the British officers. They're moving into Manhattan and will roll up this rebellion within a month. They won victories at Kip's Bay and Harlem Heights this past week. They'll punish all the rebels and runaways."

"You believe it will happen that fast?" Proctor said.

"Mark my word," the stabler said, swinging his hand at the boy and chasing him off. "The news I hear is that the rebels know they can't win. They're broken, all but a few men desperate to avoid justice. The rest are leaving the army as fast as they can sneak away. If you wait another week, your servants will come crawling home like dogs with their tails between their legs."

Proctor wanted to argue with the man, but he was afraid he was right. The curse was doing its work, driving the soldiers away from the American army.

"Perhaps that's what we should do," Deborah answered.

"You won't go wrong." He held up his meaty fist. "And you won't go wrong either if you show them the business end of a whip when they do come back."

"Thank you," Deborah said.

"We appreciate your help," Proctor said.

"I can tell you aren't persuaded," the stabler said. "So if you've a mind to ask someone else for advice, I say be careful who you trust."

"Why is that?"

"There's a rumor that there are rebel spies all over the island, masquerading as Quakers and such."

Proctor's throat tightened, and he felt Deborah tense up beside him. "You don't say?" she said.

"I do say. I heard it from one of Roger's Rangers. All my horses are loaned out to his men, so they can search for the spies. A spy like that might take your carriage off your hands, but he'd only deliver it to that rebel Washington. So I'd be careful who you trust."

"We appreciate the warning, sir," Deborah said. She emphasized the *sir*, knowing it marked her as a non-Quaker. To Proctor, she said, "I don't feel well. May we go?"

"Of course," he said, taking up the reins.

"There's a tavern just down the road on the left," the stabler said, "if you need a place to rest a bit."

Proctor thanked him again and then snapped the reins, sending them on their way. The stable boys had stopped their game and watched the carriage depart.

"We have to get rid of this," Proctor said. "It marks us as sure as a beacon on a hill."

"I agree," Deborah said. "If we take it north to Flushing and abandon it there, maybe they'll think we took one of the ferries across the sound to Connecticut or Massachusetts."

"That's an excellent idea," Proctor said. Relieved, he turned the horse north, onto the Flushing Road. As they bounced along, he said, "I can't keep the lies straight anymore. I keep forgetting, are we brother and sister, or some German and his lady guest?"

Deborah let his comment pass away without remark. After a moment, she said, "The German is too strong for me to face."

A bump in the road jarred Proctor. "You don't have to face him alone. We can face him together. Maybe the two of us—"

"That's what I meant. I meant, he's too strong for *us* to face. I think we have to try to break the curse from the other end."

"How do we do that?"

"The spirits of the dead aren't naturally tied to this world. They're trapped here." She put her palms together and then opened them. "If we can release the trap, they'll depart and move on, exactly as they should."

Something in her voice sounded uncertain. "It sounds like a good solution to me. What's the problem with it?"

"It means we'll have to find and treat every single soldier touched by the curse."

Proctor whistled. "That's a lot of spells."

"Yes," Deborah said. "But if it's the only way . . ."

A fellow in a brown coat stood by the side of the road. He took off his broad-brimmed hat and waved it at them. Proctor slowed down for him.

"Dost thou mind offering me a lift, friend?" the man asked.

The words were Quakerish, but the accent was pure Connecticut Yankee. The young man was about Proctor's age and height, with pale skin pinked from the sun. His hair was the color of flax and his eyes as blue as flax flowers. He had a large mole on his neck, the kind that marked a man as unlucky, likely to find a hangman's noose.

"We're happy to offer you a ride as far as Flushing," Proctor said. "Although we'd be glad to offer you private use of the carriage if you would but deliver it to a British officer out at Sag Harbor for us."

The young man straightened, like a pointer finding a covey of birds. "You work for the British?"

"We have agreed to send this carriage eastward for an officer's use," Deborah said.

"How many British troops are on the island now, dost thou think? Surely, they'll have to leave some behind to occupy it when they move east to engage General Washington's forces."

"We can't say," Proctor said.

"Can't say?" the earnest young man asked cagily. "Or won't? Come now, share. We are all friends here."

"I detect in your voice the sounds of the Society of Friends," Deborah said.

"Art thou Friends also?" the young man asked.

"Friends of Friends," Proctor said quickly, remembering the stabler's warning about spies. "What is your name?"

"Nathan Hale. I left Connecticut because of the rebels there." He held up a large lesson book, with a quill tucked in the binding. "I'm a schoolteacher looking for work."

"An honorable calling," Proctor said.

"I'm hoping to find out where the British are strongest," he said. "I think the best opportunities for teaching will be there. Thou art coming down the Jamaica Road. Canst thou tell me the disposition of the troops there?"

"I think we should be going," Deborah said, with a glance over her shoulder.

Proctor agreed. "Friend Nathan?"

"Yes?"

"Do not go farther down this road. Please turn back for your own sake."

"I am sure I don't know thy meaning," Nathan said.

"Then may we offer you a ride with us to Flushing?"

"I am sorry I troubled thee," Nathan said. "I only hoped for information, not for transportation. I am committed to visiting Jamaica today, and hope to try Huntington Bay to-morrow. If thou truly wish for someone to deliver thy carriage, however, I saw someone a few miles back who may be of service to you."

"Yes?" Proctor said.

"He was an odd character, dressed like a raggedy man and sounded a bit foreign. Said his name was Boots something."

"Bootzamon?" Proctor asked. Deborah's fist tightened on his sleeve.

"Dost thou know him?" Nathan asked.

"No," Proctor said. "No, it's a common name, that's all."

"Well, thou won't be able to miss this fellow. He's a prodigious pipe smoker. He was in a tear. If thou catchest up with him, I am sure he will be willing to help thee." He tipped his hat to Deborah, the way no Quaker would. "Now if thou will excuse me, I'd best continue on my way."

When he had gone, Deborah said, "If he's a Quaker then I'm a goose."

"I hope I am not as poor a liar as he is," Proctor said.

"Although it shames me to wish to be a better one. I would not have thought a fellow my own age would risk being taken as a spy. A man will risk being shot, but no one wants to risk being hanged."

"And yet we risk hanging every day just because of our talent," Deborah said.

"No witch has been hanged in eighty years," Proctor offered.

"Because of the work of the Quaker Highway," Deborah said. "Problems are fixed quietly before hysteria develops. Do you really think it's Bootzamon?"

"Yes," Proctor said. "We have to get rid of the carriage and head west as fast as we can."

"Hey," shouted a voice behind them. "Hey, stop right there!"

Proctor and Deborah both turned at once. Proctor reached for his knife. But it was only the brown-haired stable boy, thin as a stick.

He stopped when he got to the carriage and bent over, hands on his knees, trying to catch his breath. "I done been running after you all the way down the road, ever since the stable, and you ain't heared me or waited."

"I'm very sorry," Proctor said.

"Is there a problem?" Deborah asked.

"I thought you wanted somebody could take that carriage out to Sag Harbor," said the boy, a little angrily.

"We do—" Proctor said.

"Well, whatcha riding away from me for, then? I can take it that far for you. But you gotta pay me enough to make it worth my trouble, and to buy my meals on the way back."

Proctor hesitated. It was awkward. "If you mean to leave your master—"

"Do I look like a slave to you? No, sir. My father, he's as free as a seagull, comes and goes as he pleases, accounting to no man. Mostly goes, which is why my mother says he's a no-account. I would have said something to you there, but the stable master won't let me hang around his boys if'n he knows I'm taking work away from them now and then."

"We'll be happy to take you up on your offer," Deborah said, reaching into her purse. She counted coins into the boy's palm. "Will this be quite enough?"

"I think you ought to give me a few shillings more," the boy said.

"I'm sorry, but that's all that I have."

"Then it'll be plenty," the boy said, shoving them in his pocket.

Proctor jumped from the carriage and offered a hand to help Deborah step down after him. The boy bounded into the seat, and repeated the destination back to them several times to make sure he had it right.

"The sooner it gets there, the happier the major will be," Proctor said.

"I understand," the boy said. "I know the roads all the way out there, and can make the trip as fast as anyone." He snapped the reins. "Yah!"

The carriage bounced down the road, across the rural landscape, quickly diminishing into the distance.

"I hope we have not put the boy in any danger," Proctor said.

"We are in too much danger ourselves," Deborah replied. "Let us hope that the carriage leaves a trail that misleads Bootzamon for a day or so, while our feet carry us as far away from him as we can go."

They walked to a crossroads and turned westward. "Did you really give the boy the last of our coins?" Proctor asked.

"Yes," she said, looking stubbornly ahead.

"How could you do that?"

"I didn't bring much money because I didn't expect us to be gone this long," she said.

"We'll need something to get across the river to the city," Proctor said. He tried not to be angry, but their options were narrowing rapidly just when they needed more.

"We'll figure something out," she said. "Besides, it was all I could do for putting him in danger."

Chapter 12

It was five or six miles from the place they'd left the carriage in Flushing to the western shore of the island. Proctor felt unnaturally tired even before they started, likely a reaction to the surge of fear he'd experienced back at the farmhouse on the arrival of Cecily and the German. But Deborah was even more weary. He worried about her. It was one thing for him to travel this way, exposed to constant dangers. But he didn't think it was right to do the same thing to her. By rights, she ought to be back at her farm.

Or was it *their* farm? As he helped her along, offering her his arm, steadying her when she seemed ready to topple, he wondered if it truly was their farm. Where did things stand between them now? The lie was becoming the reality. The more they pretended to be brother and sister, the more their relationship became like that of siblings, a bond of strong affection and shared experience, but no more.

"What are you thinking about?" she asked.

"I'm sorry," Proctor said, shaken from his reveries.

"I've asked you twice what we will do once we reach the coast, but you haven't heard me. You seem so pensive."

"I was thinking about The Farm," Proctor said.

Deborah nodded her head. "It has been much on my mind as well."

"How so?"

"Thinking about my students."

"Ah," Proctor said.

"If I'd had to worry about protecting them too when we faced that woman and the German, he might have taken us all."

"I hope they're safe," Proctor said.

"Yes," Deborah agreed.

They both fell silent as soon as she said it, and they both knew they had no way of knowing. A different vision of The Farm crossed Proctor's mind, one more like Alexandra Walker's farm. The fields abandoned, the doors hanging open, bodies tossed like clumps of bloody rags into corners and under tables.

Deborah knew what he was thinking, because she reached out and squeezed his arm to reassure him. At the touch of her fingertips, he felt some of that old electric spark pass between them again. "They're safer there than they would be anywhere else," she said. "We've put every protection we know into that farm."

"But as you said yourself, is it enough? Can we really stand against the power that the Covenant possesses?" He regretted the question as soon as he asked it. While Deborah was still forming her response, he answered his own question. "Yes."

"What?" she asked.

"Yes," he said. "Yes, we can stand against that power. The colonies united can stand against the king and all his might. And our school, small as it is, can stand against the power of the Covenant. This is our home. We have courage because we stand on our own doorstep and tell the unwanted guests they cannot enter. We will never be bullied at our own hearth."

His fists were clenched by the time he finished speaking. He glanced at Deborah, almost embarrassed by his outburst, but she stared at him, suppressing a smile, her face aglow.

"I like you that way," she said.

"What way is that? Spouting off at the mouth?" he said, feeling slightly deflated. Remembering that they were in a Loyalist stronghold, he looked quickly up and down the road to make sure no other travelers were close enough to hear them.

"No, that way you have of filling up with light until it spills over, light so bright it makes me want to shield my eyes to look at you."

"Now you're mocking me," he said.

She shook her head.

"But it does make me think—maybe we've been wanting too little."

"What do you mean?"

"All we want is to prevent this Covenant from doing harm to us. We want to be safe from them. That's not enough."

Her mouth fell open. "It seems like a tall order to me right now."

"We ought to prevent them from doing harm to anyone. They come from overseas, from Europe. The widow, she was from London. Cecily's new master sounds like he's from one of the German states."

"Hesse, maybe, like the soldiers?"

"Maybe. I don't know. But the point is, whatever evil they mean to do here, they're doing over there as well. When we defeat them here—and we will defeat them—we need to take the battle to the rest of them, and not let them murder or take from people the way they've taken from us."

"How're we going to do that?"

"You've said that you want to get through the war and then turn The Farm back into a school for healing, the way your mother ran it. But that's not enough. All the years she ran it, the Covenant was out there, unchecked, using their unnatural talents to do the devil's work. I think we're called to stop them."

"Don't be too hasty," she said. "Let the Light—"

"The Light already shines in it, can't you see? Why were we introduced to the widow, and allowed to defeat her? There was providence at play, and not just luck. The same thing when I encountered Bootzamon at the Walker farm. He should have been able to kill me easily, but I turned the tables on him. And back at the Stymiests' farm—if we'd had to depend on my spell alone, we would have been captured. Was it chance that you were in the house, or that I used the grain, or was it divine will?"

Deborah walked on silently, her head lowered. At last, she said, "I will have to think on this."

"I know you long for a return to peace, to the old way that your mother and father did things—"

"I said, I will have to think on it."

That would have to do for now. He let her fall silent.

The channel that separated Long Island and Manhattan was called the Narrows. It was formed by the confluence of the Harlem River and the East River. Their currents churned around an island. British ships moved up and down the channel, into both rivers, their masts as thick as the trees of the forests.

"How are we going to cross that?" Deborah asked.

"If we were squirrels, we could cross over as easy as jumping from branch to branch," Proctor said.

She fell silent, chewing her lower lip as she stared out across the water.

"Um, you aren't planning to transform us into squirrels, are you?" he asked.

"No."

"Because I'm not always sure what you can and can't do anymore."

"I can't do that."

"Remember how the widow Nance made us think she was a panther and then a bear—"

"And a flock of crows. But all of those were just illusions."

Illusions or not, the widow Nance's transformations and escape had been Proctor's first glimpse of the real power of magic, and it had shaken him and everything he knew. Or maybe it was just his first meeting with Deborah that had shaken him.

"Too bad illusions won't get us across the channel," he said. "What were you thinking about?"

She hesitated. "How important is it for us to get across there today? At all?"

"Important," he said. "We've got the German and Cecily and Bootzamon behind us, and the curse on all those Continental soldiers ahead of us. We need to escape the one problem and fix the other."

"We have another problem," Deborah said hesitantly.

"Yes?"

"Money."

"Do we have any friends on the other side? People who might know you from the highway?"

"My mother traded letters with a Mary Murray. I don't know that she has a talent, but she was a correspondent of my mother and a friend to peace."

"Where is she?"

"Somewhere near Kip's Bay, wherever that may be."

"That's south of here, near where the Redcoats beat the Continentals. But I think the army's retreating north."

Deborah lowered her head. She looked so fragile.

"We'll figure out a way," Proctor said. "I'll find work for a few days if I must. We'll go throw ourselves on this Mary's mercy. We'll find someone else to call on." He knew someone else in Manhattan now, but he didn't want to think about calling there for mercy. Not yet. Not at all. "It'll be all right. I can find work again."

She released her breath and touched her heart. "Let us

take nothing for our journey. Neither staffs nor scrip, neither bread nor money."

Her knees wobbled as she spoke, and he reached out to catch her. A slight thrill ran through him again, the way it did whenever he touched her. It caught him off-guard, and he staggered a step before he righted her again.

"Idly quoting scripture?" Proctor said.

"It's no idle quote. I was trying to cast a spell for luck."

"Trying?" She seldom tried things she didn't succeed at.

"I'm too drained. But there," she said, straightening herself and smoothing her dress. "There, I think that will do just fine."

Seeing the strain still on her face, he said, "As long as you aren't turning us into squirrels."

"That would be lucky," she suggested in the same serious tone of voice.

Proctor laughed, then felt wrong for laughing. He glanced over his shoulder at once to make sure the German or Bootzamon hadn't stolen up on them in that instant that he let down his guard. He reached into his pocket and pulled out a large coin.

"I have a single dollar," he said. "I've been saving it for an emergency."

"Now *that* is lucky."

They found a sailor to take them across in a little sixteen-foot boat with a single sail.

It tacked and dodged the bigger ships like a dog in a herd of sheep. It bounced and skipped over the wakes, fighting the churning currents as they flowed over the mass of submerged ledges, rocks, and underwater traps.

"Why is it called Hell Gate?" Proctor asked.

"Because everyone who crosses here intends to reach the other side."

Proctor was puzzled.

"And we all know the way to hell is paved with good intentions."

The sailor was still chortling at his joke when the boat bucked again, then cracked sharply off a rock. Deborah gasped and clutched the sides of the boat. Proctor worried too. "Is there something I can do to help?"

"No," the man said. "She can take worse beatings than that. It's just a little tricky when the tides change—"

He stopped talking and pushed his shoulder into the rudder as the current tried to spin them around sideways.

"Dear God," Proctor said. "Will you please rebuke the wind and the raging of the water?"

"There you go," the man said. "You can never go wrong with a bit of prayer."

The waters went slack for a moment, as still as the surface of a lake on a windless morning. The sky and the clouds showed in the surface of the water, and beneath the surface lurked the ominous bulks of keel breakers.

The boat shot forward. When the sailor had landed them on the far shore, he turned to Proctor. "You got the ear of the Lord?"

"No more than any other man," Proctor said.

"I never saw anything like that, all the years I've been crossing the Narrows." He reached into his pocket and gave them their dollar back. "I was going to cross anyway. That's for an easy voyage."

Deborah reached out and snatched up the coin. "Thank you, friend."

They found a road and started walking across the island. "Do you think it really made a difference?" Proctor asked. "My spell on the boat? Your spell for luck? How can we tell when our spells work, and when events have happened to fall in our favor?"

"I don't know about your spell on the boat," she said. "But my spell for luck, I have every confidence that it helped us, that it will continue to help us."

* * *

"I'm so sorry I can't help you," Mary Murray said. She was a soft-spoken woman with a pretty face for her age.

They had gone to the Quaker woman's farm, hoping for help from Deborah's friends on the highway. But the farm had been ruined by battle. The crops had been torn up, trees chopped down, and wounded soldiers, British and American, still occupied her rooms. The house smelled like vinegar and cabbage.

"I don't even have food to spare," she apologized. "Right now I can barely feed the men here who are too wounded to move. You have other choices open to you. I know you understand."

"We understand," Deborah said, and pressed her hands around the other woman's hand.

"There's a tavern just down the road," Mary said. "The proprietor is a friend. If you have a coin or two, he'll feed you well and take care of you."

As they walked down the road, Proctor said, "I guess it's lucky we got that coin back after all."

"I told you so," Deborah said, but without conviction. Her spirits had been dashed by the reception at Mary Murray's house.

They found the tavern where she had said. It was a small narrow room, stinking of unwashed bodies, burned food, and bitter smoke. It was crowded with twice as many people as it could safely hold. Most were other refugees from the war. Proctor was bumped from both sides at once, by men who didn't stop to apologize. The same thing happened to Deborah. Finally, they arrived at the counter and called for the proprietor.

Deborah reached down for their single coin. She checked one pocket, then the other, then the floor.

Her eyes brimmed with tears. "My purse has been stolen."

"What can I get for you?" the proprietor yelled, leaning over the heads of other patrons.

"Some luck," yelled Proctor.

The proprietor cupped a hand to his ear. Proctor waved farewell to him. Taking Deborah by the elbow, he led her back out to the street.

"What are we going to do?" she asked.

Proctor sighed reluctantly. "I know another person we can ask for help."

Chapter 13

Tired, sore, and hungry, Proctor and Deborah trudged another eight miles down Bloomingdale Road and then the Broad Way toward the Battery at the island's southern tip.

"Who is it?" Deborah asked as they walked.

Proctor didn't want to answer. "An old friend," he said.

"A friend of your parents?" Her voice was sharp and curious.

"A friend of mine," Proctor said. "But I don't want to bring bad luck on us by talking about it. I don't even know if we can find our way there."

Finding their way to the right neighborhood proved easy enough. Loyalist refugees from all the colonies had gathered in the south and west wards of the city, packing too many people into wooden houses that already crowded the narrow streets. The towering steeple of Trinity Church was visible from miles away, but their slow approach to it only made their journey feel longer. It was after dark before they reached the neighborhood.

"How do you know the address?" Deborah asked.

Proctor knew the address because, while Paul Revere had always obeyed her instructions not to bring letters to The Farm, the Reverend Emerson, before he joined the army, was of a different mind. After the British evacuated Boston, Proctor received half a dozen letters sent by way of Emerson. All had the same return address in New York, in the neighborhood near Courtlandt's Sugar House.

"Directions were given to me," he said.

The five-story sugar house sat across the square from the church. From there he followed the directions, just as he had memorized them, through the filthy, narrow streets. People slept on front stoops, leaned out of windows in their shirtsleeves, and begged—or worse—on every other corner. Proctor and Deborah's dirty clothes matched the dirty clothes of the refugees who jostled them in the streets. The hungry rumbles of their bellies were echoed in other bellies all around them.

When they were a block away from the address, Proctor had second thoughts. He didn't want to do this in front of Deborah. "Can you stay here?" he asked.

"*What?*"

"Just wait here." He looked up. A big wooden sign hung over the street, a carving of two cocks with spurs slashing at each other. It creaked in the wind that came off the nearby harbor. "I'll meet you back at this tavern."

"Don't you know what men will take me for?"

"Please," he begged. "I'll be back as fast as I can."

When she relented, he practically ran down the street. The address was a townhome, the nicest on the block. He hammered on the door. It was answered by a servant, who closed the door on Proctor before he even had a chance to speak.

Proctor blocked it open. "Please. I'm a friend of Mister Thomas Rucke and Miss Emily, from Boston."

The servant regarded Proctor skeptically, but he turned to the house and called for her. "Miss Rucke—there's a beggar at the door who claims to know you."

Emily came to the door in a simple but elegant dress. She had changed in the past year. Her prettiness had matured into true beauty, but the lines of her eyes and mouth had lost some of their winsomeness. She looked at Proctor, puzzled.

"May I help you?" she asked.

It was clear that she didn't recognize him, even though

they'd once had an agreement to become engaged. He took off his hat and held it in his hand. "Emily, it's me—Proctor."

She startled, putting a hand on her heart.

Quickly, to put her at ease, he smiled and indicated the servant who stood behind her. "Where's Bess?"

"Father had to let her go," she said.

"You mean sell her?"

He was, he realized, as uncomfortable as she seemed to be. He knew the question, intended only to resolve his confused reaction to her statement, was the wrong thing to ask as soon as the words slipped out of his mouth. But slavery bothered him much more now than it did a year and a half ago, and he puzzled when people spoke of slaves as servants.

"Yes, he sold her," Emily said. Her hand fell back to her side, and she composed herself. "We couldn't afford to keep her anymore, not with so much trade disrupted. Did you come all this way just to be critical of something perfectly legal that my father did to help provide for me?"

"No, Emily, I'm sorry," he said, dropping his eyes. He glanced up at her again, then looked away. "I'm here in New York with a friend. Our money was stolen, there's no work to be had. The war's affected everybody—"

"If I recall correctly, Mister Brown, you played some part in starting this war," she said sharply.

More than she knew . . .

He dropped his head. "Emily, I'm sorry. We're in desperate circumstances. We need help. A few coins, something to eat . . ."

His words trailed off and he dropped his head, looking only at her feet.

She took a breath. "Permit me to be certain that I understand you correctly," she said after a moment. "We came to an understanding and started to plan our future together. Then you ignored my earnest plea for you to obey your

lawful sovereign, and helped the rebels start this war.
When my own home and security were threatened, I risked
revealing myself to the mob in order to treat your injuries
and save your life. You made no effort to express any appreciation. I forgave you all these things, and found you in
Boston to inform you that my affection remained constant.
You disappeared. Finally, I wrote you half a dozen letters,
seeking only to ascertain your health and well-being, and
to come to a peaceful resolution of the feelings we once, I
was still certain, shared—"

"Please, Emily," he interrupted softly.

"Let me finish!" she said, slamming her fist against her
hip. "That you received my letters is made evident by your
presence on this doorstep, because otherwise you would
not know where to find me. And yet the first thing you do
when you come to see me, after all this time, is beg for
money?"

Everything she said was true, although it had seemed
more complicated than that at the time. It seemed more
complicated than that now. When he spoke again, his voice
started to shake. "You deserved—you deserve—better
treatment than I've ever given you. But we have turned
everywhere, and have nowhere else to turn. My—"

He had started to repeat the lie *my sister and I,* only
Emily knew better. She peered around him to see if anyone
else was standing there.

"Good night, Mister Brown," she said.

She slammed the door on him.

He turned away, his shoulders sagging. He didn't know
where they would turn to now for food or shelter. But he
was glad Deborah had not been here to see his humiliation.
Then he glanced up and thought he saw the back of her
dress disappear down the next street.

She had followed him. He started to run after her, but
someone else stepped out of the shadows, an old woman in
rags smoking a pipe. The coal dimmed for just a second,

but in that second she looked like a sack of old clothes stuffed with straw. Then she puffed it back to life.

Just like Bootzamon.

Was there another creature like Bootzamon on the loose? She followed the same street Deborah had taken. Proctor ran after her, dodging a couple of barefoot apprentices with open sores. He rounded the corner and lost her. Then a rowdy bunch of drunken sailors moved on and he spied her again.

He stepped into a doorway and watched her small frame totter down the street. He felt the tickle of magic on the back of his neck.

The streets grew narrower, the houses more ramshackle, the smell of human habitation more intense. Raw sewage mixed in the gutters with rotted food and animal droppings, and the smell of cheap tobacco was all around. Voices came from every dwelling. Despite the late hour, children ran in and out of doors, and played games in the street. The scarecrow woman glided past them, past displaced farm wives and painted whores. Proctor edged closer to her, hiding behind a broken crate, a rain barrel, a grocer's stall.

The scarecrow woman paused in front of a tavern to puff on her pipe. The Fighting Cocks. Where he'd left Deborah standing. His heart raced in panic. Deborah was nowhere to be seen. He turned to look back the way he had come.

A tomahawk slashed at his head and he dodged it just in time. The steel slammed into the wood of the stall.

Proctor looked at the gloved hand that still held on to the handle of the tomahawk. At the other end of the arm was a scarecrow in an old farmer's jacket with a gunshot hole through the chest.

"Bootzamon."

The eyes flared fire, followed a second later by the coal in the pipe.

"Not expecting me, were you?" asked the odd, disembodied voice. The creature tugged with both hands to pull the tomahawk loose.

"I thought I killed you," Proctor said. He took a step, intending to run away, but he staggered as if all his power had been suddenly drained from him.

The tomahawk came loose.

"I was already dead," Bootzamon said. "All you did was ruin a nice suit of clothes."

Proctor groped for a weapon, closing on a dropped piece of firewood. The tomahawk slashed at him again, and he barely blocked the blow. A shock rippled from the firewood through his arm.

Bootzamon swung at him again and Proctor jumped back. Behind him, the street started to empty. Anxious faces peered from windows and doorways, but no one came to help.

The tomahawk slashed at him again, and again Proctor deflected the blow and retreated. The next swing bit into the wood and stuck. A low, rumbling laughter started somewhere in the hollow of Bootzamon's body and echoed off the narrow streets.

"You should see the fear in your face—it's marvelous," Bootzamon said, and he blew a cloud of smoke from his inhuman mouth. Then the scarecrow shrugged his invisible sinews and tore the wood from Proctor's hand.

Proctor searched around desperately for another weapon or any way to escape. He dodged behind a broken crate, shoving it at Bootzamon. The scarecrow leapt nimbly over the debris, casually pulling the firewood off the end of his tomahawk and tossing it aside. Proctor grabbed a rain barrel and tipped it over, splashing it across the scarecrow's legs.

"I don't dissolve in the rain, like some sugared candy," Bootzamon said.

With a roar of effort, Proctor picked up the nearly empty

barrel and dumped the remaining contents over the scarecrow's head.

He dodged the falling barrel, but his pipe was extinguished. The illusion of his human features disappeared.

"Dickon!" Bootzamon cried. "My pipe!"

There was a crackle of electricity, and the smell of brimstone and saltpeter. The horned and human-shaped demon, no bigger than a cat, popped out of the ground like he'd been shot out of a cannon from hell.

Proctor caught the creature by the throat as it flew into the air.

Dickon screeched like a rabbit caught in the teeth of a big dog. It thrashed and twisted, scorching Proctor's hands and slashing at him with its tail. The hot coal began to burn through Dickon's hand, and it screamed as it reached out to smash it into Bootzamon's pipe.

Proctor ran the other way, still holding tight to the imp Dickon.

"Release him," Bootzamon said, his voice rustling like straw in the wind. "Release him or your death will be longer and infinitely more painful than your life."

He raised the tomahawk to strike Proctor, but with his pipe out, the magic binding his body together had begun to fail. His straw hand, too weak to hold the hatchet, dropped it in the street.

"Dickon!" Bootzamon cried. His knees buckled and he fell in the street. "Dickon, come to me! At once!"

The imp lashed like a snake. It smashed the hot coal against the back of Proctor's hand. "Everything that can endure fire, you shall put through the fire, and it shall be clean," Proctor recited. His well of magic felt empty, but he dug down deep and pulled everything he had into the protective spell. "Everything that can endure fire, you shall put through the fire, and it shall be clean . . ."

The imp's struggles grew weaker. The coal in its hand

faded and grew cold. Bootzamon struggled once more to reach him, rippling like a sack of straw full of mice.

And then he fell still.

"Sorry, Dickon," Proctor said. But he was afraid that now he would be stuck with the imp, cursed to carry it forever.

With a piercing wail of despair, the imp smashed the coal against its own head, destroying it in a rain of ash and soot. Then Dickon turned to smoke, pouring through Proctor's fingers and sinking back into the ground.

When it was gone, Proctor stood there, panting, looking at his hand. The back of it was covered with scratches, and he had burns halfway to his elbow. But he had done it—he had beaten Bootzamon again.

"Proctor?" The voice was soft, tentative.

He spun around, clenching his fist, ready to strike.

Deborah stood there, holding so much power she shone like a lantern in a steeple top.

"Are you all right?" she said.

He released his fist and dropped his hand to his side. "I'll be fine," he said.

"I . . . I saw it attack you. I . . . I didn't know what to do," she stammered. "Was that . . . ?"

"Yes, that was Bootzamon."

"Is it dead?"

"I don't know," he said. He remembered his failure to get any aid from Emily. "Deborah, I—"

He was interrupted by another voice that said, "Deborah?"

Only the voice sounded like a curse. The scarecrow woman knelt beside Bootzamon's limp body. Her pipe was clenched firmly in her artificial mouth, and she breathed forth a stream of smoke.

"Who—?" Deborah asked.

Her words were cut short by a shrill scream of rage that seemed to come from the scarecrow and from everywhere around them at the same time. The scarecrow lurched to her feet and flung herself at Proctor and Deborah. She had fists full of straw pulled from Bootzamon's body.

"I offered you power!" the scarecrow screamed. "I offered you life! And you repaid me with this . . . this *curse!*"

The coal in her pipe flared. For a second she took on more nearly human features, like the ghost of a person behind the mask of gourd and rags and straw.

"The widow Nance," whispered Proctor.

"But—" Deborah said.

He grabbed her arm. "Run!"

The straw in her fists erupted into flames. They had taken only a few steps when the first ball of fire whizzed wildly past their heads and burst against the side of a tinder-dry house. The second fireball missed them too, splashing flames across the wood. Fingers of burning magic jumped out of the flames, skittering up the walls and across the rooftops.

"She's trying to trap us," Deborah cried.

Proctor covered her with his body and dragged them to the ground as another fireball flew over them, singeing his hair.

"Fire!" someone shouted nearby. The Fighting Cocks was already ablaze, and a second house was rapidly catching flame. Another voice screamed, "Fire!"

Proctor scooped Deborah up around the waist and looked for a clear way out of the inferno that crackled all around them. He carried Deborah into the next street, but the widow Nance pursued them.

"Run!" she screamed. "I'll burn it all down around you—I'll burn it all!"

Proctor dragged Deborah with him, dodging through the warren of alleys and streets. The widow Nance followed them like an avenging angel, snatching any material at hand and setting it ablaze as she hurled it after them.

"That way," Deborah said, pulling Proctor toward a broader street. "I think the river's that way."

Nance cast the fireballs ahead and behind and to either side, so that flames surrounded them. Panicked crowds surged past them, running the opposite way, desperate to escape their matchstick houses. Proctor held his elbow across his mouth, choking on the smoke, stumbling blindly through the stinging ash.

Deborah clutched Proctor's arm and dragged him back. "We're trapped—this is a dead end."

She was right. Rickety tenements, their rooftops already on fire, surrounded them on three sides. They turned back, but it was too late.

The widow blocked their way. She walked down the alley, cackling as she came. Her rag and straw body had caught flame at several places.

"I hope your death is as painful as mine was," she screamed. "I hope you linger for days, burned beyond healing."

Her head turned from side to side, searching for something to throw at them. Seeing nothing, she reached into her chest and pulled out a fistful of her own stuffing. She raised it above her head, speaking words of power.

Deborah fumbled through her pockets for salt, stammering a spell of protection. Proctor wrapped his body around Deborah to guard her.

The straw in Nance's fist flared bright as sunrise. In an instant, the flames ran down her arm and turned her into a torch. Her clothes whipped away in fire and ash. The charred dowel-and-spindle bones that held her together clattered to the street. Only her mad laughter, hollow and bodiless, remained, mixing in with the roar of the fire until Proctor heard nothing but the flame.

A building collapsed, sending a shower of flames and sparks across the narrow street and lighting another house on fire.

"Can you call the rain?" Proctor asked.

"Not this fast, not with this weather," Deborah said. Tears streamed from her eyes.

"Then we must save ourselves." He grabbed Deborah by the hand and skirted the burning pile of the widow's remains. The flames seemed to jump at them, but they ran by and escaped the dead-end alley.

Outside in the street, a crowd fled in one direction, carrying Proctor and Deborah along. Soon they found themselves in a street without flames, and then came to one without smoke, and then north to an open commons where men were running the other direction in an attempt to fight the fire and keep it from spreading to the rest of the city.

Proctor and Deborah stumbled free of the crowds and stood in the dark on the trampled grass. Their faces were black with soot, and they smelled of smoke.

Deborah turned back to look at the fire, clearly visible over the nearer rooftops. A thick column of black smoke roped its way into the darker heavens. Her jaw was set, and her face was grim.

"There's nothing we could have done," Proctor said.

"Did she give you the money?" Deborah asked.

Proctor hesitated for a moment. "Did who—?"

Deborah's face grew blacker, but she continued to stare at the flames.

"You mean Emily Rucke," Proctor said. He swallowed, his throat raw from the smoke. "She said no."

With her head hung despondently, Deborah turned and walked away from him.

Chapter 14

After a moment, he followed her without speaking, trailing her the way he'd trailed the scarecrow through the city streets.

The crowds were thick—refugees once turned refugees twice. Those who'd lost their homes because of the war now lost their shelter because of the fire. But wherever she went in the crowd, Proctor found her again. A chain of energy seemed to bind them, the way that lightning connected sky and earth. Whenever he lost sight of her, he would close his eyes for a moment and sense the energy, then follow her to it.

They spent the night, with other newly homeless families, in Artillery Park. The area around the park had been untouched by the flames. Neighboring families offered sheets and blankets to the refugees.

Deborah simply found a place on the grass and lay down. Proctor sat beside her, watching the crowds for enemies.

"I'm not sleeping," she said after a while.

"Neither am I," he said.

"We've got no food. We've got no way home. We've got no one to turn to."

"I'll find work," Proctor said.

"I'm sure it'll be easy to find work, what with only hundreds or thousands of men in the same spot you are, now that their homes have burned. Charity will be just as easy to come by, I'm sure."

Proctor leaned his face against his hands and rubbed his eyes. The action hurt the hand, slashed and burned by Bootzamon's imp, and it rubbed soot into his eyes and made them sting and water. Near them in the park, a mother gathered half a dozen children to her. The youngest cried inconsolably in her arms while she tried to comfort the others and make them lie down. The only thing that came to him was a Bible verse that Deborah had quoted recently.

"And he said unto them, Take nothing for your journey, neither staves, nor scrip, neither bread, neither money; neither have two coats apiece."

Deborah lay still for a moment, then she too sat up, facing the mother with the crying children. "Are you chastising me or saying a spell for luck?"

"Neither," Proctor said. "Just reminding myself that if Jesus sent out His disciples with no food, no money, and no extra clothes, and they could still fight evil and change the world, then we might do as much."

"He sent them out to heal the sick," Deborah said.

"The soldiers under that curse are sick," Proctor said.

"We have yet to heal one of them." She gestured at the mother with the children. One of her boys was throwing a tantrum and threatening to run away. "Meanwhile, we've burned people's homes and ruined their lives."

"That's not our fault."

"Isn't it?"

The mother didn't even have a dress, only her nightgown. Proctor guessed she wasn't more than a year or two older than he was. All the children were under the age of seven. The boy throwing the tantrum—the oldest—ran away. Her shoulders sagged, too weary to give chase.

Proctor cut off the boy with outspread arms.

"What's your name?" he asked, smiling.

The tears and the screaming stopped. The boy's eyes went wide and his mouth dropped open. He turned and ran back to his mother, hiding his face in the hem of her gown.

The mother scowled at Proctor in warning, then hurried her children off to another corner of the park.

Proctor stood there, deflated.

Deborah chuckled at him.

"I was only trying to help," he said.

"The people we're trying to help don't want our help."

The mother in the nightgown glanced back to make sure he wasn't following her. "Why not?" he said.

"Because they're afraid of us," Deborah said. "If you saw yourself right now, you'd be afraid too."

He looked at his hands, which looked the way his hands always did, if a little worse for wear, then over to Deborah, hoping for an explanation.

"You look as scary as that bogeyman creature you fought outside the tavern—your clothes are ragged and dirty, you haven't shaved in a couple of days, you're covered with soot and blood, and you stink of smoke and sweat."

"What's a little dirt?" Proctor said, trying to brush the soot from his sleeves and pants. He made up his mind to find a stream in the morning and clean himself up.

"It's not just the clothes," Deborah said, more softly. "Your eyes are sharp with a hint of madness, and your voice has the raw edge of anger to it when you speak."

Proctor flopped onto the ground, rolling up his hat for a pillow and stretching out with his head on it. "You'd be angry too if you were hungry, dirty, and stinky."

"Believe me," Deborah said. "I *am* hungry, dirty, and stinky."

"You're not as dirty or stinky as I am," Proctor said.

"That's true," she admitted, stretching out. "But I hold myself to higher standards than you, even under normal circumstances."

They lay there quietly while small groups of people

nearby whispered to one another, and groups farther away shouted something indistinct. Bells still rang, warning people of the fire and calling volunteers to help fight it. A heavy weight settled down on Proctor, and a chill ran through him, so much that he started, checking to see if a ghost had settled on him.

But there was nothing there except the smoke-hazy sky above. "They really are afraid of us," Proctor said.

"So much so that they killed our ancestors, murdered those with talents just like ours," Deborah replied. "They would rather die from things they cannot see than knowingly accept our help."

"Does it make you sympathize with Miss Cecily Sumpter Pinckney then, or with her German master? Do you wish you were on their side, that you had taken advantage of the widow Nance's offer to join her last year?"

"No," she said at once. She rolled over, moving away from Proctor and turning her back to him. "But maybe I wonder if it's worth it to do what we're doing. Back at The Farm, teaching women how to heal the sick, that made a difference."

He let her have the last word. Even if he had a reply, she would have said something else to get the last word anyway. Then they would have gone on all night, as they had times in the past, and he was weary now beyond hope.

Exhausted as he felt, he wasn't sure that sleep ever came. He jerked alert at every sudden noise or movement around them, and then, just when he thought he might fall asleep, it was dawn, with the birds screaming at one another from the branches, and the drum cadence of British soldiers marching on the field.

The park was not large. At the other end of it, a black boy was on a ladder, tying a noose to the largest branch of a huge tree. A mansion with a greenhouse on one side sat on a hill overlooking the open space. Carriages gathered in front of the mansion, with the bright coats and full hats of officers running in and out. A formal guard of soldiers in their red coats stood outside, but there were just as many Rangers in their green jackets milling about.

"What's going on?" asked Deborah, sitting up and looking as if she'd slept no more than Proctor had. She woke up farther away from him than when she'd fallen asleep, as if she'd tried to escape him that night.

"I think they mean to hang someone," Proctor said.

The word had spread. People packed the park around the tree, crowding up against Proctor and Deborah. The owner of the Dove Tavern set up barrels outside and sold drinks to the crowd. Unlicensed vendors offered sweet rolls and fried chicken. Proctor's stomach rumbled, and his throat ached; Deborah licked her lips, feeling the same discomfort.

"It looks like there's a stream over there," Proctor said. "Let's get something to drink at least."

The edge of the park sloped downward into a line of trees along the bank of a brook. They scooped the sharp, cold water into their mouths to slake their thirst, but it only made Proctor's belly feel more empty. He splashed water on his face, scrubbing it as best he could, and scraped off his beard with the edge of his knife. He even splashed water on his clothes, trying to clean them a bit, but it only seemed to soak the dirt into the fabric and make them uncomfortable. Deborah sat patiently until he was done.

"We should be going," she said. "We can make our way back to Salem, stopping at Quaker homes along the way and begging their charity. We should be there in a couple of weeks, and we can talk to the others and decide what to do next."

Proctor wasn't sure that was the best plan, but to be honest, he didn't have a better plan at the moment. They hadn't rescued the orphan, hadn't lifted the curse on the Continental soldiers, and hadn't stopped the Covenant; even

Bootzamon and the scarecrow widow were only temporarily stopped by the destruction of their straw bodies. The German witch who held their spirits in chattel would bring them back to life and set them after him and Deborah once again. Maybe he already had.

"Do you have a problem with my plan?" Deborah asked.

"I didn't say anything," he protested.

"It's when you don't say anything that I start to worry," she said. "I can never tell what's going on in your head when you don't say anything."

"There's nothing going on in my head," Proctor said. He bent his hat back into shape and jammed it onto his head. Without saying anything else, he started walking back through the park, circling the crowd.

Deborah came after him. They were halfway across the park when he felt her tug at his sleeve and whisper his name.

He turned, and she pointed at the gallows tree.

He glanced at it once or twice, but he had no desire to see another man hang to death. He was earnestly sick of death today. Even though he looked where she pointed, he didn't look closely enough until she spoke again.

"It's him, the man we saw on Long Island."

It was. The schoolteacher they had asked to take the carriage east for them. The poor liar. His flaxen hair gleamed like sunshine, and his skin was as pale as a ghost in the light. He stood on a box, in the shade of the tree, with the hangman's rope coiled around his neck.

A heavy British officer was reading out the charges against the man.

"Nathan Hale," the officer boomed. "You are accused of being a spy for the Continentals. You are, by your own confession, an officer in the rebel army, and were caught behind the lines of His Majesty's army dressed in civilian clothes for the purpose of spying with the intention of using such intelligence to bring them harm."

The crowd growled at this. Spying was dishonorable. An officer caught in civilian clothes could expect nothing but his execution. Men sometimes begged for a stay of execution, but Hale stood unmoved by the charge, his head held high despite the noose around his neck.

"Furthermore," the officer shouted, reading from a prepared statement, "you are accused of, last night, working with your fellow conspirators to set diverse fires throughout the refugee quarter of the city—"

The crowd roared for blood at this charge. The officer waited for this roar to subside.

"—you are accused of setting diverse fires throughout the refugee quarter of the city as part of your spying efforts, in order to destroy His Majesty's army's base of operations, and to bring suffering and hardship to your fellow countrymen who remain His Majesty's loyal subjects."

The crowd roared again, a pulse felt in the movement of a thousand fists shoved forward in anger. Deborah shrank close to Proctor and slipped her arm around his elbow.

He looked down, his eyes meeting hers. They were thinking the same thing—if this crowd thought that the two of them had caused the fire, no gallows would be needed. They would be torn apart or beaten to death.

"Do you have anything to say for yourself?" the officer shouted at Hale, and the crowd fell silent.

Hale stood calm and dignified, looking not out to the crowd but beyond it, with his head lifted as if he were addressing the heavens.

"It is the duty of every officer to obey the lawful orders of his commander in chief, even if it should bring great risk. We should all of us be prepared at all times to meet death, in whatever form it appears. As for me, I regret that I have only one life to lose in the service of my country."

That silenced the crowd. The black boy, large for his age, climbed back up the ladder and tightened the noose around Hale's neck, giving it a jerk to make sure it was snug. Then he clambered down the ladder and folded it, carrying it away.

The British officer declared the sentence against Hale. *Death.* A green-coated Ranger—another American, like Hale and Proctor—kicked the box from under Hale's feet. Hale dropped suddenly, and the rope snapped taut.

Deborah's hand closed tight on Proctor's arm.

The fall didn't kill Hale instantly. He dangled there, struggling to stay still and dignified, until reflex overcame composure. He kicked and twitched until his face grew dark, and his tongue popped out of his mouth. Finally, he hung limp, swaying back and forth.

Deborah turned her face away and buried it in Proctor's arm. The suddenly somber crowd broke apart, drifting away in clumps of twos and threes and fours. Proctor took Deborah's arm and guided her onto one of the roads out of the city.

"That could be us," she whispered.

"That is what happens to honest men with no taste for lying," Proctor said.

"That *should* be us," she snapped. "We're responsible for the fire—"

Proctor spun to face her, cutting off her sentence. "No, it should not. We did not start anything, not even to defend our own lives."

"But—"

Despair was written across her face, but he felt a surge of anger toward it, rather than compassion. "Listen to me. Yes, we could be dead. We could be dead any day. People could kill us just for being witches."

Her eyes flicked around them, looking for anyone who might overhear. But at this moment, Proctor didn't care who overheard or not. His voice grew in intensity.

"They could kill us for being spies. They could kill us just for being patriots! But there's nothing special about that, nothing different from our ordinary lives. On any ordinary day, we could fall under the wheels of a cart and be crushed, or kicked by a mule and broken, or caught in a fire and burned to death. We could catch a fever and burn to death in our heads. Every morning we wake up, any one of those is a possibility. Every day we draw a breath, that breath could be our last."

He had her full attention now. "And what's your point?"

"Life is always a fatal affliction. No one knows the hour of his going. It's not how we die that matters—because death will come, and it can come anytime, any day, in an infinity of ways. No, it's how we live that matters, and what we do with our lives."

"We are doing something with our lives already," she said.

"No, we aren't! We're running scared, without a plan, without a hope of winning. The British would rule us like tyrants, make us afraid to choose our own destiny. I'll not settle for that. Their army is huge and their navy is the largest in the world, and they may win this war, but I'll not just give it to them without a fight. And they aren't even the worst of it. This Covenant, this secret cabal of sorcerers— the widow, this German, Cecily—they think themselves the equal of God Himself. They would rule all of us, and all of Britain, and every other country in the world, making slaves of all ordinary men so that they can live like the gods they claim to be. How can I oppose British rule, and fight against that, yet not oppose the Covenant, fighting it to my final breath?"

Something in his intensity made her take a step back. He reached out and took hold of her arm.

"I would give my life to stop this German and the Covenant he represents. To keep the British alive and free, even if it means they rule over me but stay free men instead."

She jerked her arm free and whispered, strongly, "Proctor."

He followed her eyes past his shoulder and saw Emily standing there in the same dress she been wearing the night before, but with several shawls thrown hastily over her shoulders. Her face was without sleep. A small group of servants was arrayed behind her. They were hastily dressed in an odd sortment of clothes, and all had soot or ashes in their hair and on their faces. They were laden with bags and small trunks of various sorts.

Her unexpected presence startled Proctor and he tightened up, unsure what to say.

"Are you quite well, ma'am?" Emily asked Deborah.

"Yes," Deborah said, dropping her gaze. "He was just making sure I understand how strongly he feels about something."

Emily's look at Proctor was cold enough to freeze a pond. She answered Deborah's reply with a nod and took a step forward. When she held out her hand, one of the servants—very reluctantly—placed a small purse in it. She opened the purse and dipped her small hand inside. It emerged with several shillings. She took Proctor's wrist with her free hand—her touch made him jump again. The coins slammed into his palm, and she folded his fingers around them.

"W-what's this?" he stammered.

Emily let go of his hand and took a step back. "It seems petty to care about a few wins when my home and everything in it was destroyed in the fire."

Deborah covered her mouth, and then said, "Oh. Oh, I am so sorry."

"Have I had the pleasure of being introduced to you before?" Emily asked.

"Emily, this is Miss Deborah Walcott; Deborah, Miss Emily Rucke," Proctor said quickly. "The two of you did meet briefly in Boston."

"Ah," Emily said, her eyes filling with recognition.

The three of them stood in awkward silence for a moment, until one of the servants shifted the weight of his bags and cleared his throat.

Proctor jumped forward and held out the handful of coins to Emily. "Here, you've lost everything. I can't take this under these circumstances."

She kept her hands folded in front of her, and her eyes on Deborah. "No, you manifestly need it more than we do. The British officials"—she nodded at the mansion on the hill—"will help me until my father arrives to take me away. But I doubt they would do the same for you, not if you're still in a state of rebellion against them." She turned her head back to Proctor, her eyes large in her heart-shaped face. "You're not still—"

"Emily," he said softly, cutting off her question.

Her head fell. "Yes. Well, then."

"Here," he insisted, thrusting the money toward her another time.

"No," she said firmly, stepping back over to her servants. "I did not want to remember you as a beggar, desperate and in need. Now I have had the opportunity to do what I should have done when you visited last night. Chance alone did not bring me this way. God Himself meant me to find you. And perhaps you will not think so little of me now."

"I have never thought little of you," Proctor said.

"No, of course you haven't," she replied sharply, her small chin knotting. "That's why you never replied to any of my letters asking after your health, not until you needed to borrow money."

"That makes me sound so petty," Proctor said.

"The facts speak for themselves. Now, I have people to

look after and find shelter for," she said, waving her servants onward. They moved again with audible sighs of relief. "We will meet again someday, Mister Proctor Brown. I hope to find you more like the young man I thought I knew once."

"Emily," he whispered.

She had already turned away, dipping her head toward Deborah as she passed. "Miss Walcott," she said. "May fortune find you in better circumstances also, should we ever meet again."

"Thank you," Deborah said. "God be with you."

A small, sad smile crossed Emily's lips, and then without looking back she took long strides to catch up with her servants and pass them, leading them on toward the British headquarters on the hill above the gallows ground.

While Proctor stood there, dumbly watching her go, feeling numb and foolish, Deborah came over and prized the coins from his hand. She took a few strides north on the road, then turned back toward him.

"Aren't you coming along?" she asked.

"But Deborah—"

"These coins won't last us very long. We need to make the most of every day, friend Brown."

After all they had been through together, to call him *friend* like anyone else was so formal. "Friend?"

"For now," she said, then turned and kept walking. He stood watching her go until he realized she wasn't stopping, wasn't going to even look back, and then he ran to catch up. As he ran, he looked over his shoulder and saw Emily's small figure shrink in the distance while she made her way up the hill to the British.

Chapter 15

Two British pickets stopped them north of the city, as they made their way toward Washington Heights. They weren't the only refugees headed north after the fire, and most, like Deborah and Proctor, had nothing more than the clothes on their backs.

"Are you sure you want to be going?" the first soldier asked, blocking the road. They were young, skinny boys with acne still on their faces. Their weapons were propped against a fence, close to hand, but not as if they expected immediate use.

"We're sure," Deborah said. Proctor stood behind her in the road. They hadn't spoken since taking their leave of Emily miles ago.

The second soldier smiled at Deborah. "General Howe, and the royal governor, they're certain to do something to help folks if you give them a day or two to come up with a plan."

"It was a dirty trick them rebels did, burning the city that way," the first one said. "Hurt their own folk as much as they hurt us."

"Shows what kinds of scoundrels they are," the second one said.

Proctor had no desire to chat. He was sore and tired and hungry. And something worse—the encounter with Emily, the way Deborah had treated him since, it all left him feeling hollow inside and angry. He reached down inside himself, searching for the source of his magic, and into his memory for a verse that might cast a spell to help them on their way.

He felt a tickle of magic rise in his belly and start to flow rapidly through him. Turning his head to the side, he murmured, "For their ears are dull of hearing and their eyes they have closed."

Deborah and the two soldiers stared at him.

"Well, my ears ain't so dull of hearing that I couldn't hear that," the first soldier said, and they both laughed.

"Are you two related?" the second one asked.

"Brother and sister," Proctor snapped. "Our home in the city was destroyed in last night's fire. We're on our way upstate to stay with some relatives there."

The second soldier didn't hear anything after *sister*. He turned his attention back to Deborah and smiled at her with teeth that were white, if crooked. "The name's James, James Hanigan, miss, although everyone calls me Jimmy. You ought to think about sticking around—"

Without waiting for permission—or Deborah—Proctor walked around both soldiers and continued on the road north.

He was a quarter mile on before he heard Deborah's voice.

"Slow down, will you? My legs aren't as long as yours, and they're already aching."

He stopped where he was, lowering his head and rubbing his face. As soon as he saw her out of the corner of his eye, he started walking again, but at a slower pace he knew she could keep up with.

"What's wrong with you?" Deborah asked sharply.

"What isn't?" he snapped back, thinking of everything they'd gone through—the travel, the battle in Brooklyn, the German's attempt to kill them, the fight and the fire with Bootzamon and the widow Nance's scarecrow puppet. The last conversation with Emily that left him feeling so pitiful and inadequate.

Deborah let that pass. Maybe she was thinking similar thoughts. They continued walking.

"I reached for it and it wasn't there," he said, more softly, as if admitting a terrible guilt.

"What?"

"The magic. Back there, I reached for it, so we could pass those British soldiers, and it just flowed through my hands like water."

"You didn't even need to use magic. They would have let us pass regardless."

"That's not the point."

"It is the point. It's not something you need to worry about."

"What if it never comes back?"

"It'll come back. Believe me, you still have the talent within you, like water in a deep well."

"It's not just this one time. Back there with the guards, in the alley when I was fighting Bootzamon—"

"You had it back at the farm, when the German arrived."

He had, hadn't he? What had been different about that time? He wasn't sure. "That's just once. For weeks, every time I've reached for it, it's like there's nothing there."

"It'll get better," she said. "I can help you."

"Yes, probably you can," he admitted. He thought about the storm she called in to stop the British fleet when they were caught in the battle at Brooklyn, or the furious wind that slammed the farmhouse when they needed to escape the German. "You've grown more powerful than I could ever imagine."

"Maybe," she said.

"There's no maybe in the recipe," he snorted. "You're powerful. No wonder the widow Nance wanted to recruit you for the Covenant."

"Don't say that," she said, suddenly angry again.

"It's true."

"I'm not a thing like her, like any of them. They're murderers. They killed my parents, and they tried to kill us."

"That's not what I was saying, and you're smart enough to know it. You're as powerful as she is—"

"No, I'm not!" She turned to Proctor and clutched his arm. "They are so powerful, and they're willing to do such horrible things. The German, he put a curse on thousands of soldiers, on the whole Continental army—you saw it yourself!"

"Yes," Proctor admitted.

"I can't even break the curse on one man, and I *tried*."

"If you'd had another chance, you would have found a way. You will find a way. We have to break that curse and stop the Covenant."

"We do. And I can't do it without you, Proctor. You have to keep trying to use your talent. If you stop trying to wrestle it into submission, and just relax and let it flow into you—"

"It's been pretty damned hard to relax," Proctor murmured.

"Halt," cried a voice ahead of them. Proctor saw two bayonet-wielding Continental soldiers step into the road to block their way.

Both men wore patched and weather-stained clothes. Neither appeared to have bathed in a long while, nor shaved recently. One was surly, looking for a fight, while the other was as twitchy as a cat watching birds from the wrong side of a window. But that was hardly the most remarkable thing.

Both men carried the curse.

Each man had a ghost chained to him.

An unnatural chill pricked over Proctor's skin. The surly soldier stepped forward, the bayonet on his musket aimed squarely at Proctor, who wasn't carrying any weapon at all. Proctor had to squint to see the ghosts at first, to make sure it was more than a trick of light and shadow.

But no, the ghost was there, a pale gray shade of an old man with his face slashed opened in several places—raw, open wounds that were all the more unsettling for being bloodless. The ghost's arm was draped over the soldier's right shoulder, and his body hung on the soldier's back, dragging its feet in the dirt behind him. The ghost's face was propped up on the soldier's left side, lolling over his other shoulder, licking its lips and leering at Proctor. It appeared to know that Proctor could see him.

The soldier almost seemed aware of the ghost's presence as well—twice, in the space of a few seconds, he reached up and adjusted the strap of his hunting bag where the ghost clung to him. And his head tilted slightly to the left, as if he were listening to the ghost.

"Who are you, friend or Tory?" he demanded.

"Friend," Proctor said, and Deborah answered, "Friends, in all meanings of the word, for we are of the Society of Friends."

The surly soldier sneered. "If you're that kind of Friend, you're no friend to us."

The second soldier—the thinner, twitchy one—laughed at that and then winced. It was harder to see the ghost that clung to him. It was a skinny lad, cowering behind the soldier as if it were afraid. When the soldier stepped closer to Proctor and Deborah, the ghost tried to pull away. It seemed that his hand was trapped in the soldier's chest—locked in the living man's heart, Proctor guessed. The cowering shade tried to pull away another time, and the soldier winced again.

"We're here to volunteer, to do what we can to help the army," Proctor said.

He had meant to discuss more specific plans with Deborah, but now that they were here, it seemed the only plan they could have. They needed to stay near the army long enough to find out how to break the curse.

"I don't know where you came from," the second soldier

said, his voice thin and reedy. "But you'd be better off turning your boots around and letting them take you straight back there."

"Thank you for the advice," Proctor said. "But we mean to help however we can."

"Don't talk them out of it," the surly soldier said. "We can always use extra hands to clean up after the horses and empty the jacks."

He kept an eye on Proctor as he spoke, as if he expected this to drive him away. But Proctor had lived his whole life on a farm, and he had seen the camps around Boston during the siege. It would take a lot more than that to drive him off. "If that's what we need to do. We all do whatever we need to do to help, right?"

Surly growled in disappointment. His twitchy partner laughed nervously and took a step away, looking up and down the road. His ghost was trying frantically to escape, tugging and pulling like a small dog on a leash. Pain flashed across the young soldier's face every few seconds.

Deborah glowed as she drew in power. The surly soldier's ghost stared at her, whispering something in his host's ear.

Proctor reached out a hand to Deborah, letting his fingertips brush her arm. He felt his skin tingle as it came close to her.

"Is now the right time?" he whispered.

"They're in so much pain," she said.

"What's that?" the surly soldier said, jabbing his bayonet at Proctor. "How do we know we can trust you?"

"Maybe you, we, maybe we should just take them to the officers and let them decide," the second soldier said.

"There's something wrong about them," the surly soldier said.

His companion laughed nervously again. "You say that about everybody and everything. Take them to the officers and let them decide."

The surly soldier grunted, thinking it over.

Twitchy put out his hand and gently pushed down the bayonet. "They're not even carrying weapons."

"What about watching the road?"

He lifted his head to the distance. As far as the eye could see, there was no one on the road behind Proctor and Deborah. "Who's coming? Besides, Zachary and Will are at the next post back. And we'll be back here shortly."

"If you just point the way, I'm sure we can find it ourselves," Proctor said.

The bayonet jerked in Surly's hand but didn't come up again. "No, we'll take you to headquarters and let them decide."

Proctor held out his hand for Deborah to go first. As she passed him, he saw that she still held on to the power—in fact, she held on to it almost all the time these days. He rarely saw her let it go. The two soldiers fell in behind them. After a few paces, the twitchy one said, "Go on ahead, if you don't mind."

"I do mind," barked Surly. "You talk us into this, and then—"

Twitchy put one hand over his stomach and grimaced. "It's that bad water I had when we were stationed down at the Battery. My stomach's still not right yet."

Surly frowned and reached up reflexively to cover his nose. "All right, then. But after the trots, you better gallop to catch up with us."

Twitchy laughed nervously again. "Sure, sure, I will, promise." He waited in the road a moment while they continued, then veered off into the cover of some bushes.

The widow Nance had put a sickness spell on the siege camp around Boston the year before. Everything had smelled of illness and fallen quickly into disrepair. Proctor had thought the effects of the curse on the Continentals' camp might be similar, but as they passed up the road and into the camp that wasn't what he noticed at all. There weren't thousands of ghosts as there had been at Brooklyn, not enough to chill the air and raise fog from the water. Yet something made his skin goose-pimple. Things felt wrong, even though they looked orderly and fine.

He had to relax and blur his eyes to see the ghosts clearly, but they were everywhere, hanging on to every soldier in the camp.

One clutched a man's ankles, dragging along behind him like a child in a tantrum; another had his hands tangled in the waistband of a soldier and would have tripped him had he been flesh—in the moments Proctor watched, the soldier seemed constantly off-balance; a third had his arms wrapped around his man in a bear hug. Many others were simply tied to their soldier: a rope running from one neck to the other neck, a sash of cloth binding one wrist to another. Some of the soldiers seemed unaware of the presence, or at least showed no outward sign. But in all, a pervasive sense of worry and gloom hung over everything.

Deborah swallowed air in little gasps, as if staggered by the extent of the sorcery. Proctor stumbled, suddenly weak, overwhelmed by the prospect of lifting the curse.

Surly led them to a farmhouse flying the Virginian regimental flag. Several horses were tied up out front. An officer ran out the door, carrying several orders. Proctor and Deborah stepped back as he untied his horse and mounted. His own ghost, badly wounded, arm limp and dragging a leg, floated out after him, grabbing the saddle just in time to be carried off. The horse kicked up dirt and was gone.

Surly stepped up to the door and knocked. Proctor moved into the doorway behind him. The room had been cleared except for tables and papers. One young officer lay on the floor against the wall, using his rolled coat for a pillow, snoring fitfully. His ghost squatted beside him, poking a finger in his head and stirring it around.

A solitary man in a neat uniform sat at the desk, writing with such painstaking care that he'd failed to hear them knock. His shoulders sagged in weariness or resignation, or both. Pain and hopelessness flashed in turn across his face.

No wonder, Proctor thought.

A dozen ghosts were latched to him, shackled ankle-to-ankle, like slaves in the market. They shuffled side-to-side, jostling for position, anxious, irritated, dead men full of restlessness and despair.

Surly knocked a second time. "General?" he said.

The man at the desk looked up, saw them in the door, and instantly composed himself. He lifted his head, squared his shoulders, and nodded recognition.

It was then, combined with the soldier's address, that Proctor recognized him. "General Washington."

"I'm sorry, have we met?"

Surly bumped Proctor out of the way, asserting himself as the center of attention. "We found them coming up the road, sir. They said they wanted to volunteer."

Washington stood and stepped around his desk. The ghosts shuffled out of his way and then pushed forward, crowding around him again. "We can always use volunteers."

"I think his name is Proctor Brown," said a black man over in the corner. It was Washington's slave, the excellent rider. Proctor hadn't noticed him because he'd grown attuned to looking first for the ghosts and this man had none, perhaps because he was a slave and not an enlisted soldier.

"Yes, that's it," Washington said. "Thank you, William Lee. Friend of Paul Revere."

"That's right," Proctor said.

"Did you find your aunt?" Washington asked.

Proctor's tongue knotted up in confusion for a moment before he recalled the story they'd told Washington when they'd met him. It took another moment to untie it, while he boggled at the man's memory, to recall a personal detail from a chance encounter during the middle of a complicated retreat.

Deborah spoke up to cover Proctor's confusion. "Yes, we did, and we saw her safely to the shelter of those who can watch out for her. Thank you kindly for remembering. Nor have we forgotten your kindness to us under the most horrible of circumstances when we sought to help her."

Proctor glanced at Deborah, once again amazed at her ability to turn on the fancy speech. He wondered if it was another aspect of her magic, but decided it was just a natural talent she had.

"After we took care of that, we decided to come back and volunteer," he said. "Help however we can."

"You don't happen to have about twenty brothers at home, do you?" Washington asked.

"It's no good, sir," Surly said. "They're Quakers."

"That doesn't keep a man from fighting. General Greene is a Quaker, and he's one of the best fighting men I have."

"If it's all right with you, I'd prefer to serve in some other way if I can."

Washington sighed, and for a split second the weight of the curse passed over his face like a shadow. But he smiled again as soon as he felt it, and all visible evidence of the weight he carried disappeared in the warmth of his smile.

"Of course. Corporal," he said, "perhaps you could take them to the captain for assignment."

"Not sure where he is, sir. Everyone's busy because of the fire."

"Ah," Washington said. "Well, then. Have you any skill with horses, young man?"

"Yes, si—" Proctor said, cutting off the *sir* in mid-syllable. It was hard to forget his militia training and remember to be a Quaker in Washington's presence.

His slip was covered by Deborah speaking over him anyway. "No," she said firmly.

Washington studied them carefully. The ghosts, some with ghastly wounds, surged forward at his shoulders. A chill wind ran over Proctor's skin.

"He likes to think he does," Deborah explained, dropping her gaze apologetically. "But he doesn't."

"What other skills do you have?" Washington asked.

Proctor sorted his brain for skills he could admit to that might be useful. He was glad for the excuse of being a Quaker—he didn't want to enlist to fight if it meant picking up the curse—but all the skills he had that might be of help came from his militia training. "I've got a strong back, and can build—"

"He's got good penmanship," Deborah interrupted, with her eyes still dropped to the floor.

"Is that so?" Washington said.

"No," Proctor said; he'd hated writing lessons with his mother. She'd spent every winter making him practice by copying Bible verses.

"He doesn't think so, but he does," Deborah said.

Washington leaned over his desk, sorting through sheaves of paper until he found one. He moved it aside from the others and tapped it with his finger. "Would you mind copying this letter for me?"

Proctor started to protest, but then Deborah glanced up at him with eyes so fierce and insistent he didn't feel up to dealing with the consequences of denying her. "Um, sure," he said. "What should I do?"

Washington pulled out the chair, reshuffling the crowd of ghosts every time he moved. "Copy this letter for me."

"Yes, s—" Proctor said, catching himself again.

He walked around the desk and sat down. The letter was a brief thank-you to a local patriot family that had hosted Washington and some of his officers for dinner the other night. Proctor picked up the goose quill, checked the tip, and found it blunter than he cared for. He almost used it as it was—if it was good enough for Washington, who was he to change it—but his mother's habits forced themselves on him, and he took out his pocketknife and trimmed it.

The ghosts crowded in around him while he worked, making a sound like whispers from a distant room.

Dipping the quill carefully in the ink, he copied the letter neatly and efficiently, making certain to get the lines straight—the draft slanted to the right—and not crowding it against the top of the page the way the draft was crowded. When he was finished, he sprinkled some sand on it and then shook it clean.

Only then did he glance up, hoping for Washington's approval. Washington picked up the sheet and studied it.

"It's slightly more legible than mine," he admitted finally, and Proctor felt a tightness he wasn't even aware of drain out of his neck and shoulders.

"Thank you," he said, choking once again on the *sir*.

"You'll do for now, as I can't afford to have any more officers exchange their swords for pens. As a civilian, I can only permit you to work on nonmilitary correspondence."

"I understand," Proctor said.

"Good," Washington said, seeming genuinely pleased. The ghosts shrank back for a moment, as far as the chain on their ankles would allow. "My compliments, miss," he said to Deborah. "I'm delighted that you seem to know your brother better than he knows himself. Mrs. Washington provides a similar service to me on occasion."

"Thank you," Deborah said.

"Do you know your own talents, or should I ask your brother?"

"I'm a fair nurse," Deborah said.

"Better than fair," Proctor said. "Her—*our* mother was a midwife and a country doctor. Deborah has helped her since she was, well, big enough to walk."

"Excellent," Washington said. "Most of our seriously injured are being dismissed to make their way home, but if you can get any who are staying in camp back into fighting condition, I'd be obliged to you."

"I'll do what I can," she said.

"Thank you for bringing these folks to me, Corporal," Washington said.

"Yes, sir."

"Take them to the quartermaster and have them put on the civilian rolls. He'll find you quarters and show you where to collect your daily rations."

"Thank you," Proctor said.

"We're glad to serve the cause," Deborah said.

Surly escorted them outside. His mood, which had lifted a bit while he faced Washington, soured again the moment they stepped through the door. He frowned, and his neck knotted up as he squinted at the sky. "You're too late for any rations today" was the first thing he said. "Not that they've been all too much to get excited over lately."

Another soldier stomped up the road from the way they'd just come, aiming right for Surly. He carried an extra musket and a Continental jacket.

"Where's Dewey?" snarled the newcomer. He had a smirking ghost on his shoulder, stroking a knife along his neck.

Surly snapped to attention. "Sir, he's right—"

He stopped in mid-sentence and stared with a mixture of hopelessness and fury back at the way they'd originally come.

"I'll tell you where he is—he's gone!" He flung the jacket to the ground at Surly's feet and shook the musket in his face. "We found these back where you were supposed to be guarding the road, and not a sight of him anywhere."

"Sir, he can't have gone far. It hasn't been more than a few minutes. He had the trots something awful—maybe he's just off somewhere private."

"You'd better hope he is—I put him with you so you could keep an eye on him. We can't afford any more deserters, by God. You bring him back and I won't whip you for it."

He tossed the musket to Surly, who snatched it out of the

air. The head of the ghost lolled on his shoulder; a horrific slash cut right across its dead mouth, but it lifted its eyes toward Proctor and grinned.

The other man stomped away. Surly shifted both guns to one hand and picked up the jacket, tossing it over his shoulder. Proctor half expected it to cover the ghost's face, but there was no such luck.

After taking a few quick steps back down the road, Surly remembered Proctor and Deborah. "The quartermaster is down thataway," he said. "You'll likely find him in the barn." With those simple directions, he was gone.

"Do you think desertions are a problem?" Deborah asked.

"I think that's what the curse is meant to do, to break men's spirits," Proctor answered. "When I was sitting in there, at the general's desk, it felt like a thousand ants crawling over my skin. I wanted to run away."

"They can't run away from it," Deborah said. "We saw what happened to that soldier in Gravesend—the fellow named Increase. The curse stayed with him after he went home."

"Yes, but they don't know that," Proctor said. He guided Deborah out of the road as two more officers rode up and dismounted, running into Washington's headquarters. Walking toward the quartermaster's barn, he said in a lowered voice, "No one but us even knows there's a curse."

"I don't know how to break it," Deborah said.

"We'll figure it out," Proctor assured her.

She nodded. "We'll have a better chance with you close to Washington. You'll be able to see the effects of the curse, learn more about who it affects, how many, and how."

"Ah," Proctor said, suddenly understanding why she'd made a fuss about his penmanship.

"And as a nurse, I'll have close access to men with the curse. I may learn something up close that will help me break it." She nodded again, sharply, to herself, as if having a plan was enough to keep her going.

Maybe having a plan was enough. "Once we get our bearings again, I want to find some way to rescue that orphan boy."

"And Lydia," Deborah insisted. "It's all part of the same curse. They're using power drawn from Lydia and the orphan for the magic that's sapping the army."

"Whatever we're going to do, we'd better do it soon then," Proctor said. "It won't be long till there's not any army left to save."

Chapter 16

Proctor thought he'd never worked harder than he did in Washington's headquarters, but he wasn't the hardest-working man there, not by a distance.

When Proctor woke up in the mornings, Washington was already awake and on the job. When he fell asleep at night, Washington was still going over his correspondence. Most of his work seemed to consist of talking to men and writing letters, not what Proctor would have imagined at all. But as commander in chief of the army, Washington had to manage not only his own officers but also the officers of the militia who coordinated with him. He wrote volumes of letters to the governors and legislators in the states, encouraging them to raise more troops and send more supplies, often with detailed lists. His communications with the Continental Congress included all that as well as their orders to him, which he frequently pressured them to change or adjust. And he never let his personal communication slide. Every gift was acknowledged, every visit remembered, every letter answered. Washington drafted most letters himself, but his handwriting suffered as a result, and so most letters were recopied before they were sent. Any changes between the original and the copy had to be marked on the original, which was then filed and saved for reference. The amount of paper alone was staggering to Proctor. It felt like they completed a book's worth every week. And all of it was done with this invisible curse hanging over them, this secondary army of ghosts intent on stopping their work and driving them away.

The headquarters had been nearly empty that first day as a result of Washington sending out everyone to gather information about the fire in New York. On most days, there were a dozen men inside at any one time, including many young officers who were Proctor's age. On the one hand, he felt a certain envy of them. He wanted to share their camaraderie and sense of purpose.

On the other, he didn't want to share the curse that hung over all of them. Though he tried to shut out the presence of the ghosts, he could not. They were spirits trapped in a world that should have released them: not all were soldiers, nor had all died violent deaths. Many men carried no more than an infant, tiny spirits dead in birth or cradle. Some of those were the worst, wailing in confusion, inconsolable. Some men carried mothers or grandmothers with them; Proctor often saw those spirits fail to intrude, as if this were just one more burden in a long life of burdens they needed to bear.

But in and around the headquarters, closest to Washington, the dead were all Continental soldiers, southern militia recognizable in their hunting shirts, hundreds of Marylanders killed at the old stone house covering the retreat from Brooklyn, and other faces that looked as familiar to Proctor as the faces around him. He felt a constant coolness in their presence that had little to do with the advancing autumn, and he often lifted his head to answer someone only to realize he'd heard the whispering of the ghosts passing through the room and nothing more.

Like the men he worked with, Proctor also had a mission: to break the curse so they could fight the war. Day to day, he felt like he was making as much progress against it as they were against the British.

He and Deborah usually tried to meet in the evenings, if only for a few minutes. Her experience was similar. After they'd been in camp a couple of weeks, he found her one night, sitting just outside the circle of a campfire's light, dabbing tears from her eyes.

He sat down next to her and said nothing for a while. Finally, she sighed, wiping both eyes with the back of her hand, and sat up straighter.

"How do you think they're doing on The Farm?" he asked.

"I hope that Magdalena is teaching them well," Deborah said. "I hope that Abigail can lift big stones, that Sukey has learned to keep her mouth closed, and Esther has learned to open hers. I hope that Ezra has finished the new rooms, and stays warm inside by the fire. I hope that Zoe is . . ." She started to choke up before she could get out the words. "I just hope she's still alive. I wish we had never made that rule about sending no letters."

Proctor nodded. "I wrote to Paul Revere, but he has been stationed in Maine and unable to check on them." He sighed. "This is the first year since I could walk that I haven't been in the fields at harvesttime."

"I hate this," Deborah said. "The world is too far out of order."

"You mean"—he looked around to make sure no one was too close, and then dropped his voice anyway—"the curse."

"Not just the curse, the cursed war. All wars are cursed." She covered her face with her hands again, holding them there for a second, then wiping the tears off her cheeks. "How is it going for you?"

Proctor started to tell her about his day, which included more time running menial errands than it did copying letters, and then stopped. "I haven't learned anything new in days."

Deborah nodded. "Only the soldiers are affected. Enlisted, militia—that doesn't matter. The curse doesn't lift once they leave. I've seen men who've gone away and come back—they all look haunted."

"Some don't have it so bad, but others—I don't know how they take it," Proctor said. "Washington especially. I can't tell how he thinks clearly with all those spirits leaning in at his shoulder and whispering to him. It's no wonder he doesn't sleep."

"I have noticed something."

"What?"

Deborah seemed to think about it for a moment. "Washington has one of his slaves with him, doesn't he?"

"William Lee—Lee was his hunting master in Virginia, I guess. He's a mad horseman, utterly fearless. Washington trusts him completely, more so than some of his officers."

Deborah nodded. "Some of the common soldiers have their wives with them, especially if they've been serving more than a few months."

"Some of the officers too," Proctor said.

"The men who have somebody unaffected by the curse seem to despair less and do better than those without, no matter what kind of ghost they carry."

Proctor shifted, scooting closer to the fire, holding out his hands to warm them. "How does that help us break the curse?"

"I don't know how to break the curse," Deborah said, her voice near to cracking. "I try. I spent all day today working on a man whose ghost was barely attached to him, a minister, I think, whose head was already lifted toward heaven."

"What happened?"

She held out her hands, as if she were trying to shape something between them, then let them fall back to her lap. "Nothing. All my efforts yielded me no more than frustration."

He rested his hand on her knee a moment in quiet sympathy. She took his fingers in her hand and stood.

"Come," she said. "I'll show you what I mean."

They rose and she led him to the tents. Most of the men were sick with camp fever or similar ills—he could hear one or two turning in their blankets; another suppressed his groans of discomfort. Proctor crossed his arms, resolving to touch nothing. One whiff of the sickly smell of their bowels and bedpans, and he tried not to breathe either. In the darkness, he could not see the ghosts, but he felt their presence as a chillness.

Deborah took a candle from a table at the entrance. She murmured "Let there be light," and fire leapt from her fingertip to the wick, setting it aflame. Proctor turned his head anxiously to either side at this casual display of witchcraft, worried that someone might have seen. But Deborah had shielded the candle with her body to prevent notice.

She looked up and saw the surprise in his eyes. "Sorry," she whispered. "I was in a hurry. Over here."

She took him to one cot apart from the others. As they passed the men, several faces turned hopefully toward her, and one or two smiled. She had a gentle nod, a touch on the leg or arm for each, and Proctor could sense the healing she did even in those brief seconds. He couldn't believe how strong she had become. It almost made him lightheaded.

At the same time, he could sense the ghosts surging at them from each man's spot. It was as if they grew stronger while the men grew sicker.

"Here is the one I was telling you about," she said, indicating a man asleep on a cot. There was a stool at the head of the bed. She gestured for Proctor to take a seat, then fetched herself a second stool and came to sit beside him.

"What ails him?" Proctor whispered.

"That's just it," she replied in similar tones. "Nothing as far as I can tell. Not beyond . . ."

Not beyond the curse.

She held the candle over the bed. In the flickering light, even with his best skill, it was hard for Proctor to see the ghost, in large part because the ghost didn't wish to be seen. It shifted as fast as the shadows, but from the glimpses Proctor saw it was indeed a minister in a black coat, with his arms folded like a corpse across his chest. His face was lifted toward heaven, and he strained upward as if he might reach it by sheer force of will.

"Watch this," Deborah whispered. She took a deep breath, closed her eyes, and *touched the ghost's ankle.* Saying a prayer, she gripped the ankle tight and tried to yank the ghost free of the patient. The ghost kicked and struggled to get loose.

The sick man moaned, drawing Proctor's eye just in time to see the man's image shift. It looked as if his spirit was attached to the ghost's. As the ghost tried to escape, it seemed to tug the man's spirit out of his body.

Deborah released the ghost's ankle. It relaxed at once, and the sick man stopped moaning. His spirit sank back into his body.

"Do you see how the two spirits are tangled together?" she whispered.

"How did you do that?" Proctor asked, still stunned.

She didn't hear his question, or chose not to answer it. "I think most of the spirits simply feel trapped or confused. They lash out, creating pain for the men. But this one has a certainty about it—he knows his destination and does not want to be deterred from reaching it. I think it's the only thing making this soldier sick."

The tent flap opened, and a pretty young woman in an apron entered. She went over to the side of another patient and encouraged him to drink. Proctor saw right away that the man had almost completely recovered despite the ghost attached to him.

"What do we do?" Proctor asked, with a nod at the patient on the cot between them.

"I was hoping you would have an idea," Deborah said.

"I'll think on it," he said, rising.

She tucked the covers up to the man's chin. "If we don't come up with something soon, I'm not sure we can save him."

Proctor thought all the following day, but he dwelled more on Deborah's power—she had touched a ghost as if it were flesh—than he did on thinking through solutions. How had she become so powerful, when he could scarcely do any magic at all? And why, strong as she was, did she think he had any answers?

When he met her at the tent the next evening, the sick man was awake. His eyes were white and healthy, even in the light of the candle, but his face was wasted and drawn, as if the life were being pulled right out of him. The ghost hovered over him, barely visible unless Proctor looked for it.

"Hello, Miss Walcott," the sick man said.

"Hello, friend Livingston," she answered softly. She sat on the edge of his cot and placed her hand on his. "I brought my brother Proctor to help me pray for you. Proctor, this is David Livingston, from Philadelphia."

"From Germantown," Livingston said weakly. "It's good to meet you, Mister Brown. I'd offer you my hand, but—"

Proctor sat on the opposite side of the cot and closed the man's hand in both of his. Livingston tried to give him a strong grip, but it was shaky at best, and his palm was clammy. "You're in the best possible care," Proctor said.

"Oh, I know that. Your sister is an angel."

"I thought adding another voice to our prayers couldn't hurt," Deborah said. "Can we all hold hands and bow our heads?"

She made eye contact with Proctor, and he understood

that she was going to show him what she had done to try to break the curse so far.

They took one another's hands, forming a small circle. They lowered their heads to pray silently, but while Livingston's lips moved in recitation of the Lord's prayer, Deborah went to work with spells. The cold energy that circled through Proctor from Livingston's hand now sparked and flowed the other way from Deborah.

She made eye contact with him, and he read her lips as she silently recited Mark, chapter 1, verse 25, where Jesus rebuked the spirit possessing a man, saying, *Hold thy peace and come out of him.*

She said it with force, with authority, and the ghost lurched upward, but as it did so it tugged Livingston's spirit with it. A spasm racked his body, and his hands jerked out of theirs as he folded his arms back in close to his body.

"I'm sorry," he said. "It's just too much of a strain."

"No, you're fine," Deborah said. "You should sleep. We'll sit here and pray over you for a while."

"You really don't need to go to all that trouble," he said. "I've seen enough men die now to know what's coming. I've made my peace with the Lord."

"And I've made my decision to change His mind if I can," she said, brushing the hair back off Livingston's forehead.

"See what she's like," he said to Proctor.

"Oh, I had a notion already," Proctor replied.

"Rest now," Deborah commanded, her hand on his forehead. The man's eyes blinked sleepily and he smiled, then his head sagged to one side and he fell instantly asleep.

"That was another—" Proctor left the word *spell* unsaid.

Deborah stared at him challengingly as she pulled up the man's covers and tucked in his arms. "It's easier for us to *pray* if he's resting."

Some of the other men looked their way. Deborah lifted a small blanket from the end of the bed and pulled it through the air as if drawing a curtain closed around them.

"They can't hear us now," she told Proctor.

It was hard to believe that was true—the other men weren't more than six feet away—but he saw how powerful she was becoming and accepted it. Nevertheless, when he spoke again, he still held his voice to a whisper.

"Is it safe, using so much . . . prayer?" he asked.

"I need to practice to grow stronger," she said. "So, yes, I practice every chance I have. Most of what I do makes these men better, helps them to heal faster, gets them back on their feet. Livingston here is the exception, because there is nothing wrong with him except the curse."

"What other . . . *prayers* have you tried over him?" Proctor asked.

"I've used every verse for casting out spirits that I can think of, but they all have a similar effect."

"Those are for evil spirits," Proctor said. "This may be an evil spell that ties these spirits to the soldiers, but this isn't an evil spirit in and of itself. It looks like a pious man."

Deborah looked at Livingston and his spirit thoughtfully. "Yes," she admitted. "He kind of reminds me of the Reverend Emerson."

Proctor smiled at the mention of the Concord minister who was responsible for the two of them meeting. That seemed like a lifetime ago, even though it had only been a year and a half. Not even that. He looked at the spirit and saw the resemblance. "He's a chaplain now, serving with the army at Fort Ticonderoga."

"I know," she said. "If he were closer, I would ask him for help with our prayers."

"Prayer-prayers or *prayers*?"

"Both."

"What other kinds of prayers could we try?"

Deborah folded her hands in her lap and bowed her head to think. "Are there verses for release or letting go?"

Proctor thought about it for a moment. "My God, my God, why hast thou forsaken me?"

"Very funny."

"Just choose a different focus." He pulled the little knife from his pocket and lay it surreptitiously on the edge of the blanket, next to Livingston. "Like that, for example."

"Cut the connection between the spirits?"

"It's worth a try."

Deborah nodded, placing one hand over the knife and another on Livingston. "Thine hand shall be lifted on thine adversaries, and all thine enemies cut off."

She was so powerful that Proctor felt the magic flowing through her, falling like the warmth of the sun on his skin. But nothing happened with Livingston, who slept, pale and frail, while the ghost twisted and turned above his bed.

"Let's try it again," Proctor said.

"No, that's not the right verse," Deborah whispered. "The ghost is not his enemy—whoever it is, he's just another casualty, trapped in the world when he should be freed from it. What's the verse, The Lord is righteous. He hath cut the something—"

"Psalm One Twenty-nine? The Lord is righteous. He hath cut asunder the cords of the wicked. Let them all be confounded and turned back who hate Zion."

"Yes, that's it. Neither Livingston nor"—she nodded toward the ghost—"is wicked, but the cords that bind them together are evil and filled with hate. Can you hold my hand and pray it for me?"

"Anything you need," Proctor said. He took her hand and bowed his head. When she whispered she was ready, he began reciting the verse. Hand in hand with her, he felt her power even more intensely than before. He called on his own talent, trying to add it to hers, hoping it was not too weak.

She placed Livingston's hand over the knife and held them both while Proctor recited the verse another time. He thought he saw something—the ghost stopped twisting, almost growing stiff or tensing. Livingston's spirit also rose in his body. The wind outside the tent picked up suddenly, snapping the fabric of the wall. Cold air flowed over Proctor's skin like water from a mountain spring.

Both spirits blinked out for a split second as he came to the end of another repetition of the verse. Livingston gasped at the exact same moment, but then his spirit and the ghost shimmered back into existence and he breathed more easily again.

"One more time," Deborah said. "We almost did something there."

Proctor nodded, although he was unsure what they had almost done, and began reciting the verse again. Deborah's eyes squeezed shut and her brows furrowed, and light seemed to flow into her like the flame lighting up a hurricane lamp. She was doing something with the knife as a focus; probably imagining a cutting of the tangle between the two spirits.

It was taking her a while to find her way to the proper spot. Her right hand squeezed Proctor fiercely as she lifted her left hand off the bed and mimed the kind of cutting gesture she might make with the cord of a newborn baby.

The spirit of the minister was agitated. He leaned toward Proctor, as if eagerly trying to speak, and then both spirits blinked away again. Livingston opened his mouth to take a breath and simply stopped breathing.

Proctor stopped in mid-verse and yanked his hand free of Deborah, who jerked back, startled.

"What? Why did you just do that? I was so close."

Coughing, hacking for air, Livingston swallowed air in deep gulps, half waking before he mumbled and rolled over. Deborah stared at him, eyes wide with a new uncertainty.

"I think that cutting the bond is too sudden," Proctor said. "I don't think it released the spirits so much as it destroyed them."

She leaned back, covering her face with her hand for a moment. "Dear Light," she murmured. "Thank you for stopping me, Proctor."

"It was working," he said. "Maybe the German has a trap built into the spell—"

"No," she said firmly, standing abruptly, turning once, then sitting down again. "It's like I was telling you. It's just impossible. There's no way to break it."

"We don't know that," Proctor said. "We only know that the ways we've tried don't work."

"What other ways are there? I've been trying for a fortnight and this is the closest I've come."

"Then we know we're on the right path," he said. He reached out and squeezed her hand again, but she let it lie limp in his fingers then tugged it free. "Look, there has to be a different way to do this."

"I'm not going to try again," she said. "Not if it means a spirit never gets where it's supposed to go, not if it means that a man might die."

"I'm thinking there's a gentler way," Proctor said.

Deborah raised her eyebrows.

"Releasing, casting out, cutting—they're all methods of power."

"It's a powerful spell—it will take power to break it."

"But there's power in slowness too. Have you ever made caramel toffee?"

"Huh?" She looked at him as if he'd lost his mind.

"I'm sorry. One of the officers, Tilghman, he carries some around in his pocket and never shares it, at least not with me, so it's been on my mind. But you know how to make toffee?"

"Sure . . . ," she said, clearly not knowing where he was going with the thought.

"You can't yank it apart suddenly. And it's hard to cut, and not only because your knife gets fouled. No, you have to pull it apart slowly. Slowly, but steadily, and the pieces come apart. Do you see what I'm saying?"

"If we could find a way to stretch the two spirits away from each other, they might naturally separate."

"Yes."

"But how do we know that the same thing won't happen, that just happened here?"

"It might. We'll watch and see, and if it's headed that direction, if there's any sign of that at all, we'll stop. But I'm thinking . . ." He trailed off, not sure if he could say what he had planned to say.

"Go on," she said.

He decided to just be honest. "The man who created this sp—*prayer* is powerful, very powerful. So he'll have defenses in place against powerful counterprayers. But if we think differently than he does, do it by our way instead of his, we might be able to break it."

"That's smart," Deborah said.

"Careful—my head may start to swell."

She rolled her eyes at him and smiled briefly, but only briefly. The deeply intense, focused expression returned. "We need a verse as a focus for our prayer, something about stretching things out. Something about the Exodus, you think?"

"Reaching the Holy Land after a long delay—it might work." Proctor reached for his pockets, feeling the frayed flaps under his fingertips, even though he already knew he'd left home without his Bible.

But Deborah understood his gesture. She lifted her head to one of the other patients. "Friend Hawkins," she said. "May we borrow your Bible, the one I see you reading each day?"

The young man with his leg bound up and his arm in a sling, in too much pain to sleep, was eager to help them.

His ghost was horribly mangled, like some of the men Proctor saw hit by cannon shot at Brooklyn. "I'm sorry," he said. "But all I have is this Bay Psalm Book. You're welcome to it, if it will help your prayers."

"It will indeed," Deborah said. She rose and went to his bed to take the book that he offered her. "Thank you muchly."

"David, is he going to make it?" Hawkins asked.

"That's in the hands of God, isn't it?"

"We have to have faith, don't we?" he said.

"Faith and prayer," she said with a smile, and placed a hand on him, whispering something that eased his pain.

She handed the well-thumbed Psalter to Proctor and waved the folded blanket through the air, reestablishing their spot of silence.

"There's nothing of the Exodus in here," Proctor said, tapping the closed book against his palm.

"We can use the Psalms," Deborah said wearily. "They do go on forever."

"There must be something." Proctor flipped through the pages. "They're all about protection and deliverance. Look, what about this one?"

"Psalm Thirteen?"

"Waiting a long time for God to deliver you from your enemies. It fits the bill."

"What do I do while we recite that prayer?"

Proctor looked at the body on the bed, and at the two spirits bound to each other. "You can touch them, right? So pull them apart like toffee."

She sighed and sat down. "All right then."

He placed the open Psalter on his lap and took her hand again. "O Jehovah, how long wilt Thou forget me aye? How long wilt Thou Thy countenance hide from me far away? How long shall I counsel, in my soul take, sorrow in my heart daily? O'er me set how long shall be my foe?"

Deborah inhaled, drawing in power with her breath, and

placed her folded hands over Livingston. To the others, it might look like she was praying, but Proctor could see that she was kneading the spirits where they connected, working them between her palms like dough.

". . . Illuminate mine eyes, lest I the sleep of death do take. Lest my foe say, 'I have prevailed 'gainst him.' And me those who do trouble, do rejoice . . ."

When he reached the end of the Psalm, he began again. He was on his third recitation before he could begin to see a difference due to Deborah's actions.

As the cord binding the spirits began to thin, the soul of the minister drifted away. Livingston, as far as Proctor could see, seemed to fall deeper and deeper into sleep.

Sweat beaded on Deborah's forehead, and her cheeks flushed red with effort. Proctor wanted to suggest that she take a break, but he was afraid to interrupt her.

He'd lost count of the number of times he'd recited the Psalm when the cord finally snapped. Deborah gasped and slouched forward, catching herself before she sprawled across the bed. The spirit of the minister hung in the air for a moment and then disappeared like smoke dispersed by wind with a sigh that Proctor thought audible to everyone in the tent. Livingston's body had gone completely still. Proctor could not see his spirit at all. He reached out his hand to assure Deborah that it was not her fault, that it was the work of the Covenant, their fault the man had died.

Livingston sighed again—the sound had come from him—and rolled over. His face was full of natural color again, and his cheeks no longer seemed so thin or sunken.

Joy sparked through Proctor. "You did it," he said.

"It was a lot harder than pulling toffee," she said. And then she looked at him and grinned. She was so beautiful when she smiled that way, and it was unique to her, something Emily could never match. "We did it! You figured it out for me."

She embraced him jubilantly and he hugged her back. Suddenly, he was very aware of the warmth of her body. She tilted her head up to say something to him, and he pressed his lips against hers. He kissed her hard, and she kissed him back hard, and for a second it was full of joy.

Then she seemed to realize what they were doing, and pulled away. They both glanced around nervously to be sure no one had seen them. Deborah touched her fingers to her lips and looked at her patient. "Do we have time to free every man in the army?" she whispered.

He shoved his hands into his pockets. "We'll do as much as we can. It will get easier. Most of the men have signed on until the end of the year. No matter how much they despair, I believe most will hold on until then."

"That's two and a half months. Maybe eighty days." Her face fell again, losing all the exuberance that had dressed the last few moments. "This was exhausting, Proctor. Even if it gets easier, I don't know that I can do it more than a few times a day."

"All we are asked to do is help those we can. The fact that we can't save everyone is no reason not to save anyone."

"Right," she said. She reached out and squeezed his hand again. "Thank you for reminding me of that. Thank you for everything."

"You were amazing," he said. "You *are* amazing."

It felt like everything was going to be all right between them again. If she would just lean forward and say that she loved him, if he could just find the words to reassure her that he felt that way toward her, it would all be all right. They looked into each other's eyes and stepped toward another embrace.

Voices sounded outside the tent, and Deborah pulled away instantly.

"Deborah?" he whispered, his arms still open.

"What will they think?" she whispered back.

The tent flap snapped open to reveal a sky lightening toward dawn and to let in the sound of a single bird singing. A man and woman in their mid-twenties stepped inside. The spirit attached to the man was a British soldier, clearly eager to escape.

"Thought we'd find you here," the woman said. She was the pretty young woman Proctor had seen the day before, and the man was the former patient.

Deborah rose to greet them. Proctor followed her, gently laying the Psalter on Hawkins's bed as he passed.

"Proctor, this is John and Margaret Corbin. John has been discharged. John, Margaret, this is my . . ." She hesitated a moment. "My brother, Proctor."

"Pleased to meet you," John said, vigorously shaking Proctor's hand.

"John had the camp fever," Margaret said. "I didn't think there was anything anyone could do for him better than myself, but your sister had him back on his feet in a day. It's like magic."

Deborah's smile froze on her face.

"It's nothing of the sort," Proctor said quickly. "Our mother was a healer, and her mother before her. There are things you learn, things that get passed down, that you hardly even notice or could explain."

"Well, she has a gift," Margaret said. "And she was a friend to me when I was a bit short with her too."

"It's nothing," Deborah said.

"It's something to us," John said. "That's why we came to say good-bye."

"Are you going?" Deborah asked.

"No, you are," Margaret said.

"The British are marching to attack," Corbin explained. "The orders were just issued. General Washington's going to take the main body of the army north to White Plains to meet them. I'm in artillery, so I'll stay here to defend the heights."

Margaret wrapped her arm through his and smiled at him. "And I'll be staying with him, in case they need an extra hand with the shells."

There was a moment of silence while this news sank in.

Proctor met Deborah's eyes and saw that she understood. "I work at headquarters," he said. "I've been here . . . praying all night. It's another hour till reveille, but I'd better report back."

"Of course," Deborah said.

"It was good to meet you," John called behind him.

Proctor didn't answer. Another battle with the Continental soldiers weighed down by the curse could end the war in favor of the British. He didn't mind the British winning as much as he feared the evil the Covenant might do if they achieved their goal. He sprinted all the way back to headquarters.

Chapter 17

The day was cold, gray, and blustery. Every boom of the cannons made Proctor lift his head to the skies to look for thunder, but it was only the British and American forces fighting for control of the big hill west of the little city of White Plains.

There was little for Proctor to do during battle, and there had been almost constant skirmishing for the ten days since their order to move. Part of him itched to be out there with a musket in hand, active in the fighting, but that would tie him down too far. Part of him wanted to flee the fighting and take up the search for the orphan boy and Lydia, still being held by the Covenant, though he knew he had no way to find or free them.

As a result, he never strayed far from Washington's headquarters, first at Jacob Purdy's little blockhouse and now on the hillside south of town that overlooked the British forces as they finally marched up the bucolic Bronx River valley below.

The main body of the Continental forces formed their lines behind a thick breastwork of cornstalks covered with earth. It was a strong position; which was why, Proctor supposed, early that morning after the first shots were fired, British General Howe had decided to flank them instead.

Since then the battle had raged all day on Chatterton's Hill, two hundred feet high, heavily wooded, and overlooking their defenses. Whoever controlled it controlled the battlefield. The leaves were brilliant hues of red and gold and orange, breathtaking and completely at odds with the bloody business taking place beneath them. Alexander Hamilton's artillery had formed a hasty battery in the trees and pounded the British soldiers and Hessian mercenaries as they attempted to make their way up the slope.

Hamilton was interesting—he was unaffected by the curse, but only because he already carried a ghost of his own from long before the war started. It had taken Proctor and Deborah some time to realize that, but once they did it explained much about his ability to stay strong and keep those around him motivated to fight.

Today it was dreadful fighting, like the kind Proctor had seen at Bunker Hill outside Boston, only with the British making a more cautious approach and better use of their field pieces.

As the wounded flowed back to the main camp, Proctor fought through the press of men to find Tench Tilghman, Washington's aide-de-camp. Even after all this time, Proctor found himself fighting not to address him as *sir*.

Tilghman, once he recognized Proctor standing at his side, seemed not to mind. "What is it, Brown?"

"My . . . sister is off nursing the wounded. If there's nothing I can do here, I'd like to go help her."

Tilghman nodded and waved his hand by way of permission, then turned to take a report from another aide. Proctor successfully fought the urge to salute, and he ran to the house where they were treating injured men. It overlooked the Bronx River and, across the river, Chatterton's Hill, so it provided a good view of the fighting. Many of the townspeople lined up nearby, watching the progress of the battle. Proctor paused beside them.

From this distance, half a mile away, it was all smoke and noise and brightly colored jackets moving slowly up the slopes or hiding in the trees. The British forces were taking terrible losses, but they continued their slow advance up the hill while their own cannons sent round after round over their heads into the Continental position in the woods. Each volley of the cannons, each hit by the cannonballs from the opposite side, shook the brightly colored leaves from the branches. They fell in a slow shower after each thundering boom.

"I can't watch," said a familiar voice beside him. "But I can't stop watching."

He turned instantly. Deborah. Exhaustion was reflected in every aspect of her appearance, from the dark circles under her eyes to the hollows in her cheeks to the weakened light of the magic she held in reserve, ready to use at any moment. "How are you?"

"I'm good," she said.

"I'm in awe of what you've done the past ten days," he said. "Over two hundred men cured."

"And hardly one of them over there, where the fighting is. If the British take the hill, it could all be lost."

"Don't worry, Hamilton will hold his men together." Every night for the past ten days, they'd worked together to break the curse. Luckily, few men were as difficult to free as Livingston had been. "Have you thought more about the way we might help more than one man at a time?"

"Yes, I think I've got it," she said. "Washington?"

They had talked about freeing Washington first, but Proctor couldn't figure out how it could be done without the general's cooperation. "There's no practical way to do it."

"It's all or no one then," Deborah said. "I'll need a day of sleep before we try. Or maybe a week. And I don't know if I'll get any sleep once the wounded start needing nursing."

"Why aren't you treating the wounded now?"

"Those well enough to make it back across the river to the camp are well enough to be treated by Doctor McKnight." McKnight was the army's surgeon. "But he's at North Castle, about eight miles away, so they send the wounded in that direction."

"Makes sense," Proctor said, only half attending, the rest of his attention consumed by the battle taking place across the river. "My God, look at Rall's jaegers!"

A collective gasp and similar exclamations came from others nearby.

The Hessian troops, in their green-and-red jackets, advanced up the hillside through the tall dry grasses. Sparks from the Hessians' muskets must have set the grass aflame, and a sheet of fire washed down the hillside. The American battery faltered for a moment at the sight of this imminent horror.

The Hessians stayed in formation and marched straight through the flames, covering ground quickly as they went.

"They'll burn alive," Deborah whispered. As they continued to march, she asked, "Are they protected by any—"

She left *spell* unsaid. Proctor answered, "No, no, I don't think so."

"Then how do they do it?"

"Discipline," Proctor said. "Discipline and courage."

All the things they'd been told about the cowardly Hessians were patently untrue. He didn't think the Continentals could have held together through that. Some of the men would end up horribly burned. All of them would take some hurt.

Deborah's fingers closed around his hand. He could feel her drawing on her talent again.

Cannons boomed, echoing across the sky for so long that Proctor finally realized it wasn't cannons but thunder. He looked up and the gray clouds overhead swelled and thickened, like a sponge filled with water.

"Deborah?" he said.

"Not . . . now . . ."

"No, you have to look—it's the German."

His free hand pointed across the river, to a spot behind

the British lines. A light flared there, supernatural and invisible to those without the talent to see it. But to Proctor it stood out as a beacon, shining like a lighthouse in the night off some rocky shore.

Deborah let go of him and stepped forward for a better view, as if six feet made a difference at this distance.

The air changed, and wind gusted up the valley, tearing the fire across the hillside and away from the Hessian soldiers. The Americans resumed their shooting, but the ground had already been won.

A few fat drops of rain splattered on Proctor's forehead, reminding him of the battle at Brooklyn when Deborah called in the storms. "Did you . . . ?"

She shook her head numbly. "I had nothing to do with that wind. How does he do it, Proctor? How does he hold so much power at once?"

"You saw the way Cecily—"

Deborah's head snapped around, glaring at him.

"—*that woman,*" he quickly corrected. "You saw the way that woman stole power from Lydia, making her a slave in two ways. You saw how they snatched up that little orphan boy because of his talent. The German holds so much power because it's not all his. Who knows how many people he is drawing on to do it, draining away their talent to augment his own?"

"How do we defeat that?"

"The same way we broke his curse on those men—by fighting his strength with cleverness. By outflanking him the way Howe's troops are trying to outflank us."

"In five days, it's the day of All Souls. That would be a very powerful day to attempt our"—she glanced at some of the townspeople nearby—"prayer."

"It's only three days to All Hallows' Eve," Proctor said, watching the Hessian troops advance another ten yards up the hillside. "That may be as long as we have to prepare."

Deborah's shoulders sagged, and her chin fell toward her

chest. "I'd better go rest now while I can," she said. She turned and left without any word of farewell

Proctor stood and watched the battle continue in the downpour, until the British and the Hessians drove the Americans from the hilltop.

By then the rain was too thick to see anything.

The rain fell for three days again, just as it had at the battle of Brooklyn. This was two months later in the season, and that much colder. Both armies bivouacked in the swampy conditions, too mired in the muck to continue the fight.

On Thursday, All Hallows' Eve, Proctor found Deborah in one of the nursing tents. It was empty, all the injured men evacuated north to the new camp. Even under cover of the tent, the ground was soaked, sloshing beneath Proctor's feet as he entered. Inside was empty, all the beds and tables removed, except for a couple of stools and a lantern.

"We'll have to do it tonight," he said. "With the British artillery on the high ground, there's no way we can hold our position here. The shelling will start as soon as the rain lets up, so Washington plans to withdraw tonight."

"I know," Deborah said. She sat on a stool in the driest corner, holding her hands up to the small flame of a lantern for warmth. "I've already been told to leave the tent. They'll be back to pack it up shortly."

"Are you ready?"

"Are you?"

"Yes." He had butterflies in his stomach as he said it. They had never attempted a spell this big before, or worked with forces this powerful. "I'll find a spot out in the woods just north of town where we can"—he checked over his shoulder out of habit—"pray together."

Deborah nodded. She still hadn't looked up or met his eye. He took it for deep concentration; it was obvious she had been thinking about the task ahead. In the silence, drops of rain pattered on the canvas of the tent, as if the sky were drumming its fingers.

"I've figured out why the Covenant wants to keep the British empire together," she said. "Something we spoke about the other day got me thinking."

That had been puzzling them for more than a year, ever since their encounter with the widow Nance. "What is it?"

"The German draws power from Lydia and the orphan, even though they're not willing, right?"

He shook the rainwater off his hat and held it. "I suppose so, yes."

"It's a focus," she said.

"I'm not following you."

"I knew we needed a big prayer tonight," she said. "So I was thinking about the biggest focus I could handle, and that had me thinking about the biggest focus that might be possible."

"The empire itself is a focus," Proctor said. It seemed too vast to be possible, but the moment he said it, he knew it was true.

"Imagine the power of people, millions of them, circling the whole globe, recognizing the same monarch," Deborah said. "On a day like Coronation Day, for example—"

"That was just last month, the twenty-second."

"Yes," she said. "With the Declaration of Independence just this past summer, this is the first year of my life we haven't celebrated the anniversary of King George's coronation."

"We didn't last year either, not after the rebellion started in Boston."

"We didn't, but we were still subjects of the king then and we should have. I felt guilty about not doing it," she said.

Proctor hadn't felt guilty at all, but he knew grown men, leaders in the rebellion, who'd had to hide their twitchiness. Some things became reflex over a lifetime.

"If you can get people around the whole globe acknowledging the same thing at roughly the same time, you can create a powerful focus for prayers."

It was her use of the word *prayers* that gave him a moment's doubt. "But if that's true, then you could use religion for the same thing. The Catholic Church covers the whole globe . . ."

She leaned forward eagerly in her seat, nodding. "Yes, *exactly*. You don't think the Papists use prayers the same way? Some of the most notorious wit—"

The word *witches* was interrupted by a slap on the side of the tent, and the flap yanked open. A head popped through the door, hat sagging with the wet and dripping rain. "Sorry, ma'am, we've got to take this down now and break camp."

He was one of the soldiers with the curse already broken. It startled Proctor to see a man with no spirit haunting him, but it also lifted his heart and reminded him of the importance of their work tonight.

"Thank you, Bryan," Deborah said, standing. "I understand."

She adjusted her bonnet, then pulled her shawl around her shoulders and over her head. She took the lantern while Proctor picked up the two stools, one in each hand, and exited the tent. He passed the furniture off to another of the soldiers, and then the two of them hurried over to the limited shelter of a nearby tree.

"But why do they need that big a focus?" Proctor asked.

"Do you need more explanation than simple greed? Think of the wealth they can amass. The widow Nance said they would make the whole world slaves. Why does any man have slaves, but to make himself rich at their expense?"

"So, just like Cecily drew on the power of Lydia for her magic," Proctor said. "Only magnified."

"I think that's exactly what she meant."

Proctor shook the water off his hat and put it back on his head. "There may be other reasons too," he said, now that he was running with the idea. "Think how the widow Nance was unnaturally young. Once her power was broken, her true age showed. A witch bound to the power of an empire might stay young for as long as that empire lasted, renewed with each new crowning of the king."

Deborah's face showed respect for this deduction, pleasing Proctor. He liked to keep a step ahead of her when he could, even if she didn't expect it.

"It's wrong, all of it," she said. "If this curse is any evidence of it, whatever they do with the power is wrong. We have to stop them."

"We'll take one step at a time," Proctor said. "We freed some of the men from the curse. Tonight we'll free them all. Then we'll find the German, and we'll free Lydia and that orphan boy—"

"Slow down," Deborah said. "I can't think more than one step ahead at a time right now, or it'll drown me."

"I'm sorry," Proctor said. "It's just that what they're doing to Lydia and that boy, taking their power against their will, leaving them weak, it just bothers me. We let Lydia down when we let Cecily escape with her. And nobody else cares about that boy or will protect him unless we do."

Deborah looked away to the distance. "One thing at a time," she said.

"I'll get our supplies and then we'll go out to the spot I found," he said.

She nodded, as distant from him again as when he'd first entered the tent. He saw her feet sinking in the mud as he left her there to run back to his own quarters one last time.

They joined the soldiers marching on the road out of town. The rain had finally stopped, but it was dark and cold, and the air felt saturated with wet. A gloom hung over the long train of men, but Proctor couldn't tell how much of it was another retreat and how much of it was due to the weight of the invisible burden most men carried.

Deborah carried a different burden, lost deep in concentration. Proctor tried to speak to her several times, but each time she ignored him.

There were many wives and other civilians, even some children, on the road, so Proctor and Deborah didn't stand out. Proctor couldn't tell the difference between them and some other young couples at first, but then as he watched more, he saw the couples hold hands, or exchange brief kisses of affection, and it bothered him that he and Deborah did none of that. He wanted to break the curse, return to The Farm, and continue a proper courtship with her, maybe take the next step, even if his mother didn't bless it.

The road was so churned that mud clung to their feet with each step. When they passed the copse of trees he planned to use, they left the road, stopping first to scrape their shoes clean on some fallen branches. Proctor held Deborah's elbow to help her climb over a stone fence and fallen logs. It was the only way he could touch her without causing suspicion.

"If we continue the fight, there's no reason for us to pretend to be brother and sister," he said as they made their way cautiously into the trees. The air around them smelled of the wet mold of leaves. "We could just tell people—"

"Now's not the time for this conversation," she said.

It wasn't. But there was never a right time for the conversation. "Are you sure the woods is the right place to do this? We could pick someplace more in the middle of the army."

"The army is so spread out right now, anyplace is the middle. But more importantly, what do you see around us?"

"Not very much in the dark."

"Crunch, crunch under your feet."

"It's more of a squish, squish—"

"Leaves," she said, impatiently. "Just as there's a time for leaves to fall from the trees, there's a time for these spirits to leave this world. This curse is unnatural. What we're doing is trying to set nature right again."

"Was that always part of your plan? Because . . ."

"No, I just thought of it now," she said with a shrug. "My original thought was that we just needed to be away from everyone. Where's our spot?"

"Over here, in this clearing."

He led her between the trees into a small clearing where the grass had been laid flat by the rain. From his bag, he took a handful of salt and began spreading a circle.

"Where did you get so much?" she asked.

"The commissary sent several complaints to headquarters but the thief was never found. Now please, let me concentrate while I do this."

Inside the circle, he made a star with lines of salt, both to mark the five points and as a symbol of the country. When that was done, he set his bag down and took out flint and steel, and a bit of dry tinder. He knelt next to the candle and struck a few sparks, but none caught.

"I'll do that," Deborah said.

Kneeling beside Proctor, she lit the candle the same way she'd lit the lantern in the tent: the flame leapt from her fingertip to the wick.

"What are you staring at?" she asked as she lit the second candle and moved around the circle to the third.

"The widow used magic like that—"

"I'm not her," Deborah snapped as she finished. "Hand me the other items."

He reached into the bag and passed her a heavy folded coat. "This is a Continental officer's jacket. Don't ask how I got it."

"I was more interested in how you didn't get caught."

"This is a blank letter of commission, the kind also used

for officers, and this is a muster sheet, also blank, but I thought they symbolized every officer and enlisted man serving. And this is a hat I got from a Pennsylvania militiaman. Here is a man's daily ration of food."

"What about weapons? No man is a soldier without his weapons."

Proctor wanted to disagree—he felt like he was still a soldier protecting their country even though he carried no weapons. "I'm supposed to be a Quaker. I couldn't just start bearing arms now, could I? Especially without enlisting."

She opened her mouth to argue, and then seemed to realize that they were both on edge because they were tense.

"Here," he said, reaching into his bag. "A powder horn and flints for a musket. Muskets are useless without powder and flint. I remembered the way the widow used lead balls for her prayers—her spells, I mean. She meant to spell all the lead shot that day, not just the pieces she touched. I thought we could do the same."

"That's good," Deborah said, arranging the items around the circle, inside the points of the star. She used the heavier items to pin down the papers. When she had placed everything the way she wanted it, Proctor handed her a folded blanket. She looked at him, puzzled. "Is this the common soldier's blanket?"

"No, that's for you. To sit on. To keep your dress dry."

"Oh! That was very thoughtful."

"You sound so surprised."

"I just hadn't given any thought to my dress." She stepped into the center of the circle, careful not to touch or break any of the lines. She placed the blanket on the ground and then sat on it, on her knees, as if in prayer. "You should go away now, Proctor."

He nearly laughed. "What?"

"If this goes wrong, if I draw all the spirits here and can't release them, they may attach to—or even attack—the nearest person."

"I won't let them harm you," he promised. Even though he didn't know how he'd keep that promise. His skin prickled at the thought of all those spirits chained to his own soul. He didn't know how Washington carried on.

"I was thinking more about harm to you," Deborah said softly. "If you go back to the army, keep moving north, when I'm done I'll catch up—"

"No."

"But I could—"

"No."

The candlelight flickered, throwing shadows across her face. Even more softly, she said, "Thank you. I do need you, more than you realize."

She actually said *thank you*. He let her words fill the air between them until they faded away. She drew a deep breath and then began to recite the verses from Ezekiel that they had agreed to use for the spell.

"Wherewith ye there hunt the souls to make them fly, and I will tear them from your arms, and will let the souls go, even the souls that ye hunt to make them fly. Because with lies ye have made the hearts of the righteous sad, whom I have not made sad; and have strengthened the hands of the wicked, that he should not return from his wicked way. Therefore ye shall see no more magic, for in the name of the Lord, I will deliver my people out of your hand."

Cut down a bit, and a word changed here and there, but it would do. Proctor lost track of time while Deborah recited it, though he checked on her several times and could see the power flowing through her. He did his part, standing guard to make sure they were unwatched and unapproached.

Which is why he noticed the lights flowing toward them,

twisting like eddies in turbulent water, carried downstream toward the rocks.

The cursed spirits were flowing to them. They came in a great semicircle, pulled like strands of toffee, from White Plains and the road and Fort Washington and places farther north. They came, like long snakes of light, writhing and squirming. Proctor quickly stepped around the clearing so that he didn't come between them and Deborah.

". . . no more magic. In the name of the Lord, I will deliver my people out of your hand."

She shone with power, like a hurricane lamp herself. Sweat and agony both poured over her face. The spirits were almost there, drawn so thin that surely they must break, just like the others.

But they were coming slowly. As she continued to recite the words of the spell, she began to pant for breath, straining to stay upright, and her words faltered.

". . . of the Lord . . . I will . . . deliver my people . . ."

The long, thin strands of light now turned into a mass of snapping, thrashing snakes, some lashing out as if they meant to bite, some pulling back toward the bodies they were unnaturally latched to.

". . . deliver my people, out of your hand," Proctor finished for her. She only needed a little bit more to start freeing the trapped souls. He reached inside to draw on his own magic and add it to hers.

And he found nothing. His magic was already drained.

Now that Deborah was weakened, now that he was looking for it, he saw his own talent flowing out of himself and into Deborah. She was draining him, the same way Cecily drained Lydia, the same way her master stole power from that little boy. And she was doing it without his permission, without even informing him.

In anger, he reached out to take it back.

Her head snapped up, eyes wide, afraid.

Before either could do anything else, a fierce wind

slammed into the woods, knocking the tops of the trees together and making them clatter like the rattle of spears. Then the wind rushed over the ground, turning over the leaves like a pack of dogs sniffing for prey.

With no magic, and no weapons to defend himself—to defend them—Proctor felt suddenly vulnerable and helpless.

The wind hit their circle, blowing out the first candle and knocking it over. Then it whirled around the circle, knocking the other candles over and scattering the salt. Around and around it spun, smashing all of it, tearing the papers away, tumbling the other items, spinning all of it and the leaves up in a whirlwind with Deborah at the center.

"He's found us!" she cried.

At the same instant the spirits stopped their twisting approach and snapped back to their scattered bodies. The air smelled like it did just before lightning struck, sharp and tainted. Through that smell, Proctor perceived another.

Cheap tobacco.

The whirlwind spun up and out through the trees and disappeared. Deborah sprawled on the ground, her cap torn from her head, hair tangled everywhere. He grabbed her under the arm and began pulling her to her feet. Her face turned toward him, dark hair spilling over her features. Her eyes were wide, panicked; her mouth hung dumbly open.

"Bootzamon," he said.

Her hands groped for her cap like a blind woman. He saw it nearby on the ground, and bent to snatch it up as he dragged her toward the road. She clutched it in her fist as they ran madly through the trees. She stumbled once, and fell, and he ran back to lift her up, and they ran again until they broke through the trees and came to the road.

With shaking hands, she tied her cap on her head as they climbed over the wall. Those nearest the road, especially the married couples, saw their mussed clothing and gave them knowing looks. Even though they were strangers, Proctor flushed with shame. Deborah was still too panicked to notice. They both kept checking over their shoulders as they plunged into the midst of a group of soldiers for protection.

"Miss Walcott," said a voice.

Proctor spun, his fist cocked to swing, but it was only the soldier who'd asked them to leave the tent. Bryan.

"Are you all right?" he asked. "You look like you've just seen a ghost."

They were staring at one. Bryan had been healed—Deborah had peeled his ghost off him and broken the curse. But now he was cursed again. A new spirit walked with him, propped up on Bryan's shoulder like a wounded comrade. The spirit had a horrible chest wound, a gaping hole where it looked like the body had been hit by grapeshot. It lifted its head, and a familiar face gazed back at them.

"Livingston," Deborah said.

"Yes, he was killed on the hill, fighting alongside Captain Hamilton," Bryan said. He got all choked up. "I didn't know him that well, but all of a sudden like, I can't stop thinking about him—how sick he was, and you prayed over him every day, and then he's dead, just like that, first day he goes back to the fighting."

Livingston's spirit tilted its head toward Deborah, in agony, pleading for release.

They were still walking, and Deborah turned her head away, to say something to Proctor, but then there were more spirits flowing past them, hundreds—as many as were killed in the battle. Just ahead of them, another spirit attached itself to someone else she had healed. They were seeking out those unaffected by the curse. Some spirits landed on officers who were already carrying another ghost.

Deborah began to cry. Proctor didn't respond, still too numb from his discovery that Deborah had been stealing his power from him. It explained so much: why every time he reached for his talent, it wasn't there. Bryan stepped up to put a hand on her shoulder and comfort her instead. But the presence of Livingston's spirit, pleading for help, only made her sob worse.

"We failed," Proctor mumbled.

He had never felt so sick, so hopeless, so betrayed. Deborah had used him like a slave. He had to check twice to be sure that one of the spirits had not become bound to him.

Just beyond the wall, a red glow caught his eye.

A pipe coal bobbed along the edge of the woods beside them, all the length of the road, until the woods finally ended. After that, hollow laughter followed them as they marched with the defeated army across the plains.

Chapter 18

They could see the jets of flame from the cannons first, and then seconds later the dull boom came across the broad waters of the Hudson and echoed off the cliffs below them.

The Hudson River was the route to the heart of the states, dividing New England from the colonies below. It was clear the British meant to sail upriver and do just that, so they could pick off the remnants of the Continental army bit by bit.

Washington's strategy had been to block the river passage by sinking hidden obstacles in all the channels—what the military men called a chevaux-de-frise. Two forts, one on the heights at the upper tip of Manhattan, and the other just across the river atop the steep cliffs of the New Jersey Palisades, protected the river and gave the Americans a place to fire on the British as they tried to navigate the sunken hazards. The fort on the New York side was named after Washington.

It had seemed like a sensible plan to Proctor, but the fort's adjutant commander had defected to the British just two days ago, giving them plans for safe passage through the maze of obstacles. Proctor suspected a compulsion spell—the German certainly was powerful enough—but he had no way to prove it.

Knowing the safe passages through the river would not have made a significant difference with the fort's cannons overlooking the ships. But the adjutant commander had also provided plans to the fort, and this morning the British forces, led by the Hessians, had begun their attack.

Again, cannons jetted flame in quick succession, and the dense smoke of musket and rifle fire rolled across the heavily wooded hills defending the main approach to the fort.

A rapid series of booms echoed off the cliff walls below.

Washington, who had been watching the progress of the battle through his telescope, lowered it from his face and knuckled something at the corner of his eye. Then he quickly lifted the spyglass and resumed watching the events.

Men stood back from him, but whether it was to grant him space out of respect, or because they felt the chill force of the spirits attached by the ghostly slave chain at his ankle, Proctor didn't know. The conversation had died as the day advanced. Colonel Magaw, the fort commander, had promised to hold it against all attack through the end of December. He would be lucky to hold it until the end of the day.

Meanwhile, watching was all they could do from this side of the river. Deborah might have been powerful enough to bring rain or storms, but ever since their failed attempt to break the curse she'd been distant, unwilling to do anything but quietly heal the physical wounds of soldiers.

"Damn it," muttered Tilghman. He stood next to Washington and watched through his own glass.

There was a chorus of demands for an explanation.

"They're striking the flag," Tilghman said. "The fort is lost."

Proctor strained to see. He could see the grand union flag of the Continental army in his head—thirteen red and white stripes, with the Union Jack of the British flag made small in the corner. It symbolized the thirteen states and their British roots.

The chorus of voices around Proctor insisted it didn't

matter; they could hold the river from their position at Fort Lee. It was only a matter of time until the British were driven back. Mere words. Proctor paid it no attention. He was focused instead on the next attack, which came rushing, invisible to all but him, across the river.

The spirits of the patriots killed defending Fort Washington sped across the water, some faster than cannon shot, as the flag made its slow descent. The spirits stormed up the Palisades and came over the ramparts like a strike force, hitting the soldiers at the exact moment the flag came completely down.

Every man up there but Proctor was already cursed. The spirits didn't shoot past them, but plunged through the men and joined with those already clinging to them.

One, showing horrible wounds, wrapped itself around Washington's neck as if it were trying to pull him over the wall and into the water.

His chin sagged forward to his chest.

He reached up and covered his eyes.

A gasp escaped his lips.

And then he sobbed. The general of the patriot army stood there, as the fort bearing his name fell bloodily into enemy hands while he was helpless to do anything about it, and he sobbed. Watching him, Proctor could have sworn he aged years in that moment. His brown hair seemed to thin and pale toward gray. Lines became etched on his face. His shoulders shook as he wept.

And the spirit yanked and tugged, holding frantically to Washington's neck. The other spirits chained to Washington's ankle pulled it slowly away, passing him back to the end of the mob and chaining it by the ankle to its spot in the line.

Washington's officers turned away from him, more out of respect than embarrassment. Or to cover their own senses of loss, despair, and fear. No man carried the weight that Washington did, but every one of them carried multiple spirits now.

Every one of them but Hamilton. The young artillery colonel from New York only had his own ghost, a guest from before the Revolution. It was settled so deep into him by something other than magic that Proctor could scarcely make it out as more than a vague haze.

Hamilton went and stood by Washington. Though much shorter than the general, he stood straight and tall. He stared unflinchingly at the fort across the river until Washington cried himself out and lifted his head again.

Much too formal to address the general without being spoken to first, Hamilton drew in a breath and turned his head away from Washington, as if he were planning to speak to someone beside him, though nobody stood there. "Well, that's done," he said. "We'd better go back to work."

Washington answered with a silent nod that Hamilton didn't even see. Hamilton took a few steps away, but Washington turned and wiped his cheeks clean with his fist. When the general spoke, his habitual voice of command sounded the same as it ever did. "Colonel, let us review the disposition of the artillery with an eye to discomfiting the British, shall we?"

"Yes, sir," replied Hamilton.

The two men walked toward the headquarters, followed by the rest of Washington's staff. Although Proctor was generally expected to keep himself available, he was not under the same rules of command as the soldiers, and he decided to go find Deborah instead.

He went to the tent he'd left her in earlier that morning, nursing the wounded. He opened the flap and peered inside. She was pacing, reciting something to herself, weaving air with her hands. The instant she noticed Proctor at the door, she rushed to the cot of a man and sat beside him, dabbing his head with a damp washcloth. He was the only patient in the tent—the other injured had been sent home to recuperate, left behind across the river, or returned to duty. The man was sleeping, but with a fever. His face was flushed and sweaty, and he tossed feebly in his bed. A sick stink filled the room like rotting flesh. The man's ghost was blurry, just a vague outline of a man, as if it had already half detached.

"Deborah?" Proctor said.

She didn't even look up to answer him. "I'm sorry, but I'm busy right now trying to save friend Donnelson. The surgeon sewed up his stomach wound and pronounced it healed but it's become infected. Maybe later."

"You've been saying *later* for days."

She wrung out the cloth in a bowl, dipped it in clean water, and wiped Donnelson's forehead again. "If you haven't noticed, there's a war occurring outside this tent. We've been on the move every single day."

"We need to discuss what happened on All Hallows' Eve."

"We will, just as soon as there's time."

"When will that be?"

She slapped the rag down on the little camp table by the bed and leaned forward, pressing her hand to her forehead. "I don't know—you're the one who can read the future, not me."

His hand knotted into a fist. It wasn't as if he hadn't tried to read the future, but if there was an egg anywhere near this army, somebody ate it before he could use it to scrye. At one time, he'd thought he didn't need any focus to read the future, but that had been pride; now he doubted his ability to do any spell.

He uncurled his fingers, flexing them. Then he stepped outside, flinging the tent flap shut behind him.

And stopped. Deborah had gotten exactly what she wanted again. She wanted to make him angry, so he'd walk away, and he'd let her do it.

He stomped back into the tent. "I can't believe you used me that way." His voice was choked, angry, but there, he'd said it; it was out.

"I told you I was very sorry." Her back was still turned to him. She held Donnelson's hand between hers.

"But you were doing the very thing we're fighting against, the use of others without their permission."

"Tell that to your precious General Washington who drags that slave Lee with him wherever he goes. Or to most of the officers in this army. They all own slaves."

His fist knotted up again. She was right—slavery was wrong, no matter who did it, but—"I'm trying to talk about us, about you and me."

"I'm sorry, Proctor. Do you want me to grovel for you? Do you want me to prostrate myself at your feet and beg forgiveness?"

"I don't want you to beg. I just . . . I feel betrayed." He unclenched his fist and held his open hand out to her. "I want to understand why you did it."

She rose so suddenly she knocked over the stool, spinning on him with her own hand raised in a fist. "What is there to understand? Nobody else at The Farm—not you, not Magdalena, nobody—is as powerful as me. And I'm not powerful enough!"

He took a step back and gestured for her to lower her voice.

Instead, she advanced on him. "You saw the widow— you've still got the scars on your arms from what she almost did. You saw what that southern woman did to those dead bodies. You've seen the monstrosities given life by the German." She pointed at the ghost hovering over the cot like a cloud of miasma. "You see that, right there, thousands of men cursed, all at once, as if it were child's play."

He glanced over his shoulder to make sure no one was coming through the door. If the word *witch* slipped from her mouth and someone overheard it, they could have even more enemies, and those among their friends. "Deborah—you don't want anyone to hear you. Quietly."

"You wanted to understand?" she shouted. "Well, now you understand—I'm afraid. I'm afraid of those people. They killed my mother and father for no reason at all. And they want to kill me too. And who's going to protect me?"

"I will."

Her eyes flashed like dark pieces of stone, her lips tightened, and she spun her finger once in the air. Instantly he felt bonds, as if thick cables were wrapped around and around him, pinning his arms to his sides.

"Protect me?" she said. "You can't even protect yourself. And they're more powerful than I am. You can't stop them if I can't stop them."

He thought he sensed a way to sever the bonds with a simple breaking spell, but he'd need to distract her to work it. "We've done all right," he said. "I've beaten Bootzamon twice."

"You got lucky."

"Together we found a way to free men from the curse—"

"Only so they could be killed or cursed again." Her face tensed in anger, and she whipped her hand in a circle, tightening the invisible bonds that held him until he could barely breathe.

"Is . . . everything . . . all . . . right . . . ?"

The voice came from the bed, where Donnelson sat propped up on one elbow. His ghost strained toward Proctor and Deborah, seeming to rub its hands with glee. Proctor wasn't sure what that meant—but if he didn't breathe soon, he'd pass out before he could find out.

"I . . . heard . . . shouting . . ."

Deborah dropped her hands to her waist, smoothing her dress over her hips. The bonds dropped from Proctor like severed ropes, and his knees almost buckled before he drew breath and righted himself.

"Everything is fine," Proctor said. "Just a small family disagreement."

"Can't you see you're disturbing a sick man?" Deborah said. "Leave now."

"They're still out there," Proctor said, softly enough that he hoped only she could hear him. "Bootzamon and the widow's ghost, Cecily, the German. They've got Lydia and that little boy. If we don't stand against them together, we'll surely fall to them alone."

Donnelson slumped back to the bed, gasping in pain. Deborah turned away from Proctor, uprighting her stool and sitting down again.

"I still may be able to help this man," she said, wiping his brow to cool him. "I know how to heal. I'll stick to what I know. You should do the same."

He walked over to the tent and held open the flap. "Funny," he said, pausing before he went out. "I thought I knew you."

He lingered a moment, hoping she would do something to change his mind, but she only sat there, back to him, pretending to take care of a man too far gone to help. He slapped the tent shut and stomped off. Let her be that way. If she wanted him to leave her alone, he would.

Nearby, a noncommissioned officer was instructing some of the men as they stored barrels of flour, all the army's provisions for the remaining winter. "Do you know where I can find General Washington's headquarters?" Proctor asked.

"At the river," the veteran said, jerking his thumb. His ghost echoed him, jerking its thumb the same direction. "Out by the Dutchman's gristmill."

"Thank you," Proctor said, tipping his hat. The other man looked at him oddly, and Proctor realized it was a wide-brimmed Quakerish hat. Quakers tipped their hats to no one. He walked away quickly without saying anything instead of trying to repair the fiction. As he followed the other man's directions, his head swirled with the thought that if he was done with Deborah, maybe he ought to be done pretending to be a Quaker too. But when he encountered others along the way, he was careful not to take off his hat for them.

He saw the gristmill from the road and then, as he came closer, spied the large, long gambrel-roofed house that flew the flag of the general's headquarters. He went in the open door and saw a small crowd surrounding a table covered with maps and papers. Colonel Henry Knox, who was taller than Washington and weighed three hundred pounds, filled the space of two men, bookishly holding a page up to his face to read it. Colonel Glover, the wiry-haired sailor from Marblehead, only half the size of Knox, stood on his toes trying to read along with the other man. Their ghosts jostled and fought with each other, though the two men restrained their own tempers to focus on their work. The room felt crowded by the restless spirits clinging to Washington and the other officers, all stirring as if the defeat of the army would mean their freedom.

The men all took their cue from Washington, who, somehow, ignored the great mob chained to him ankle-to-ankle like a line of slaves. Tilghman, bent over a table with the general, saw Proctor and greeted him with the slightest dip of his head before turning back to work.

A slightly built man with a cleft chin and calm, thoughtful eyes leaned against one wall, watching Washington and the others; he looked more like a schoolboy, intent on following a lesson, than an officer, but Proctor recognized him as a lieutenant from the Third Virginia. The ghost that clung to him was that of an old veteran, someone from the wars with the French and the Indians. The ghost also appeared calm and thoughtful, as if death were less of a burden than the one he'd carried during life.

Proctor struggled to recall the officer's name as he sidled up next to him. "James?"

The man's ghost thrust out a hand to shove him away. Proctor shivered as the spectral palm passed through him, just as the young man turned.

"Yes, Monroe, James Monroe," he said.

"Is there any place a fellow might catch a nap?"

"There's space in the rooms upstairs. But if you're cold, I'd grab a spot in the second parlor, nearer the fire. Bound to stay warmer there."

"Kindly appreciated," Proctor said, marveling how those Virginians always found the northern states so cold. Still, he agreed with Monroe: the fire sounded good. He was weary, and chilled beyond the air by the hovering presence of so many spirits.

He grabbed a quick bite of bread and a pint of watered rum from a sideboard set out to feed the flow of officers who filled the room, and made his way through the downstairs rooms looking for the other parlor. When he found it, there was only one thin officer there, the sharp angles of his knees and elbows hunched over a small folding camp table next to the fire. He was writing intently on a sheet of paper that hung over the edge of his table. Several other pages lay scattered at his feet.

"Do you mind if I come in?" Proctor asked.

The other man continued scratching words on the paper. Without looking up, he said, "Suit yourself. This is a country for free men."

"Thank you," Proctor said.

He had gone in and taken one of the other cane-bottomed chairs against the wall before he realized the other man had no apparent ghost. Somehow he had escaped the curse.

"Do you serve in the army?" Proctor asked.

The man finished what he was writing, held the sheet up to the fire to read it, then set it on the floor next to the others. "Aide-de-camp to General Greene," he said, taking another sheet of paper and sharpening his quill before continuing his composition.

Proctor didn't understand it. How did this one man escape the curse? He was studying the man and thinking about this when a new voice showed at the door.

"Mind if I join you gentlemen?"

James Monroe stood there, trailing his gaunt, angry spectral veteran from the French wars. Proctor had liked the warmth of the room, and he braced for a wave of cold as the cursed man entered. Also, Monroe's spirit was the most aggressive he'd seen, the first to try to actually attack him.

"Suit yourself," the writer answered, hunched over his table again. "This is a country for free men."

Monroe lifted his foot to step through the door.

And froze.

The moment he passed the barrier, a spirit rose up out of the writer's body, the shining figure of a woman, almost too bright to be seen. This was no thin, sexless angel: she was full-hipped, with rounded belly. Wings of pale fire, feathered with tiny dancing flames, unfolded from her back, and she snapped her hand toward the door as if swatting a fly.

Monroe's ghost recoiled as if the swat had hit him and had burned. Instantly it began tugging and pulling Monroe, trying to escape the room the way a whipped dog might flee its attacker.

Monroe cleared his throat. "No, I can see you are working. I'm sure it's important. I'll leave you to it."

The writer finished his sentence, dipped his pen in the ink, and paused a moment while a fat drop of liquid fell from the tip back into the bottle. "I'm very obliged to your kindness."

Monroe spun on his heel, leaving the doorway empty as he proceeded to another room. Proctor watched him go, tracing the vivid relief in the aspect of the ghost. When he turned back, the writer's spirit had disappeared. The man continued writing, as if oblivious to everything that had just transpired.

Well, they were all oblivious to what was transpiring. They felt the effects, but—unless they had the secret talent shared by Deborah and Proctor—couldn't see the cause.

Proctor put another log on the fire and stirred the coals. He was sick of this struggle, tired of the ghosts that haunted every step of the army. It was too much to face, too hopeless.

Yet here was a soldier, a commissioned officer and aide to General Greene, who was untouched. As far as Proctor could tell, the man had no natural gift, no direct control over magic, yet somehow he had a powerful protection against the curse. A powerful protector.

When the other man finished writing another sheet and set it aside, Proctor cleared his throat. "I believe we've met, but I can't recall your name."

The other man smiled, as if he had heard that before. "Tom Paine," he said.

"Pleased to meet you. My name's Proctor Brown."

Paine waited a moment. "Common sense."

Every time he used the false name, he was afraid someone would catch him, still, even after so many months. Licking his lips, he said, "I'm sorry, but that's my name. I'm not sure how it's common sense."

Paine tapped his chest. "No, I wrote *Common Sense*."

Proctor stared at him blankly.

"The pamphlet, arguing for American independence—"

Suddenly it clicked for Proctor. "Oh, you're Thomas Paine, the man who wrote *Common Sense*! Of course. Last year, before the Declaration of Independence. Now you're an aide to General Greene."

Paine stared at Proctor as if he were dim-witted. When he spoke again, it was slowly, with more emphasis on each word. "Yes, that's exactly as I told you. Now, if you don't mind, I should get back to writing."

He took a clean sheet of paper and smoothed it across the tiny desk. He dipped his quill and had it poised over the blank sheet.

"What're you writing?" Proctor asked.

A fat blob of black ink dripped onto the page. Paine grabbed a rag and was quick to blot it up. "I've been trying to write something new to inspire the soldiers and citizens of this great country to greater sacrifice in the hour of its need."

"How is it going?" Proctor asked

Paine held the blemished sheet up to the light and frowned. "Roughly. All inkspots and letters crossed out as soon as they're written. But that's the way of it. Sometimes the road to the right phrase leads through a thicket of wrong words."

"The way the path to peace and freedom leads through war and sacrifice."

"Well, yes," Paine said, now clearly annoyed with Proctor. "I'd best return to work. Don't let me disturb you any further."

While they talked, Proctor had been studying Paine closely for some clue to his protection, or protector, but he saw none. He only had the image, seared into his head, of the fiery-winged woman standing in the way of the cursed spirit. Paine began writing again. Proctor decided to approach the question directly. He waited until Paine held his pen above his ink, and then spoke.

"Do you believe in angels?"

Paine lifted his head, as if surprised to find Proctor still there. "I beg your pardon."

"Do you believe in angels?"

Paine sat up straight, squared his shoulders, and faced Proctor directly. "If this is about the passage I wrote in *Common Sense*, I stand by every word of what I said. Call me atheistic or vilify me by any name you choose, but I still contend that this country will never be strong so long as it gives primacy to any one religion over another. If we all held the same faith, there would be no opportunity for virtue in any of us."

"What?" asked Proctor.

"Huh," grunted Paine.

"So you're not—" Paine started at the same second Proctor said, "I wasn't—"

They both stopped.

"Angels," Proctor said. "I only wondered if you had ever experienced something you might describe as a divine presence."

Paine's mouth, creased in anger, softened at the corners, and then the ghost of a smile played across his lips. "Yes, I have known an angel."

Proctor shot forward in his seat. "Really?"

The other man laughed. "Mary, my wife. If there are such things as angels, then she was of their kind, bright and glorious, and left for a foundling with her dull parents."

Disappointment welled up in Proctor: Paine was speaking metaphorically when he spoke literally. The habit of empathy made him ask, "What happened to her?"

Pleasure disappeared from Paine's face. "She died giving birth to our first child."

The two men were silent for a moment. Paine leaned back in his chair and looked into the fire, rubbing his chin with his writing hand. Proctor awaited signs of the angel's return, wondering if naming her would call her, but nothing showed. He had the impression that she only acted when Paine was in danger, as when someone with the curse came too close. If it was his wife, she may have had the talent herself—many women who did had trouble conceiving, or passed away in childbirth. Deborah said that was the first thing that drew so many witches to midwifery. If she did have the talent, she might have attached herself to her husband on purpose, as a way of staying with him.

"She was a Quaker like you," Paine offered.

The voice startled Proctor out of his deep reverie, and then his reaction was amplified by his own uncertainty. Wasn't he pretending to be a Quaker anymore? Where did things stand with him and Deborah?

Paine saw his reaction. "It was not my intention to give offense. If I've misjudged you by your clothes . . ."

"No, you've not misjudged me, friend," Proctor said quickly. "You're a writer, are you not? You choose a cover for your book to reflect the interior, and good men do the same."

"Just remember, friend," Paine replied. "If God could clothe the world in myriad colors, as varied as all the flowers of the fields, as bright as the birds of the forest, then it can be no sin for you to wear something more cheerful than brown and black."

Proctor laughed aloud at that, and it was as if the act of laughing caused him to let down the dam of his defenses, so that the weariness he'd been feeling flooded over him again. He hid a yawn behind his hand. When it had passed, he lifted his head to Paine. "Will it bother you if I sleep on the floor for a while?"

"Not at all, it's a free country," Paine said, with considerably more warmth than he had used earler.

Proctor rose. "I'll go over there against the wall, out of your way."

"No, here by the fire, where it's warmest," Paine said, rising to gather his papers. "You'll sleep better, and I think I'm done for now."

There were a couple of threadbare blankets folded on another chair in the corner. Proctor took them to a spot on the floor near the fire, used one for a pillow, pulled the other to his chin. He shifted a few times, then lay there with his eyes closed but unable to fall asleep. He was think-

ing about Deborah, about his decision to stop their cha-
rade. All he had left to do was choose whether to stay with
the army awhile longer, or head back to The Farm to rejoin
the others.

Paine's pen scratched another sheet of paper or two, and
then the Scotsman rose and quietly stirred the coals, adding
a new log to the fire. In the renewed heat, with the sooth-
ing spit and crackle of the fire nearby, Proctor finally fell
asleep.

The room was cold and dim when he awoke abruptly. A
hand shook him roughly, and he was staring up into Tilghman's face. The officer's expression, usually calm and
thoughtful no matter the circumstances, was filled with
rage.

"Come on, Quaker boy," he said. "Howe's army is
across the river—it's another retreat."

"What?" Proctor said, grabbing his hat as he jumped up.
He was still drowsy, only partially grasping that the anger
was not directed against him. "How did they—?"

"No one knows," Tilghman said, gathering up the blankets and rolling them into a ball. "There are nothing but
our soldiers along the whole length of the Palisades. It's
like their progress was concealed by a fog, only there's no
fog. If some slave girl named Polly hadn't seen them first
and raised a warning, we'd still have been sleeping when
they fell on top of us." He grabbed Proctor by the shoulder
of his jacket and flung him toward the door. "Now go!"

"But my shoes," Proctor said, looking back to where
he'd kicked them off. He bent to put them on, and when he
looked up Tilghman was gone already.

Proctor hopped on one foot, buckling the shoe on the
other, and stopped, propped against the doorjamb. A cold
drizzle fell. "Of course," he murmured.

Rain blew in under the brim of Proctor's hat and ran
down his face. Outside, in the mud and the rain, discipline
collapsed like a straw house. Men ran, some shouting or-

ders, others curses; here and there solitary men stood still,
heads hung, dejected. Two couriers were shoving and
swinging at each other over who would take the last sad-
dled horse.

Then the men blurred to Proctor's vision, and for a second all their ghosts emerged in sharp relief. They all were
agitated, attacking their unwilling and unwitting hosts,
dragging them one way or another, twisting their heads to
see every slight, tripping them so they fell in the way of
every random strike or blow.

Proctor wiped the rain out of his eyes, but he could still
see the ghosts. Whether a puppet master somewhere, his
hand inside their spectral forms, stirred them to violence,
or whether they savaged on their own initiative, spurred on
by the prospect of release at the American army's ruin,
Proctor couldn't guess. Nor did he think it mattered. Even
though he was not cursed like the soldiers, he felt cold fear
rushing through him just from being so near it. He was
close to the bridge—if he crossed it, he could escape the
British forces and eventually make his way back home
again.

Of course that would mean abandoning Deborah at the
fort.

The two men were still fighting each other over the
horse. Proctor grabbed the reins from their hands and
knocked them both sprawling into the half-frozen mud.

The horse was equally eager to escape. As Proctor swung
into the saddle, it bolted from the camp. He turned it
toward Fort Lee, bent to its neck, and let it gallop.

Chapter 19

The first refugees Proctor passed coming out of Fort Lee restored his hope. Several hundred men marched in orderly file, making good time toward Washington's headquarters and the nearby bridge. Proctor reined in his horse, easing over to the verge of the road to let the men pass. Several called out the news to him, urging him to turn around. Only when they came close to him could he see that they carried very little more than the clothes they wore and personal weapons—all their gear, the tents, the stores, the winter supplies, must have been left behind.

He ignored them the same way they ignored the frantic and ineffective struggles of their own cursed companions. When the end of the line passed him, he kicked the horse on again, throwing up clods of mud as they rushed on. Within half a mile, he had to rein in a second time. Stragglers filled the road in all manner of dress and organization. Some ran away in their bare feet and underclothes, as if British bayonets were nicking their heels and elbows.

No, not British bayonets, but cursed spirits. The dead souls trapped with the men stabbed numinous daggers into their tender spots and tore futilely at the mortal flesh with translucent, bony fingers. The men, unaware of the ghosts that Proctor saw so clearly, were driven to panic and lost all sense of purpose. Trunks lay abandoned in the road, along with scattered clothes, military supplies, and even weapons. Someone in a panic was trying to unhitch a team of horses from its carriage in order to escape more quickly.

The crowd fighting over the wide-eyed, stamping animal saw Proctor and surged toward him.

Though no horseman, he closed his eyes and ran the horse straight at the low wall bordering the road. He took a breath in relief as it leapt over the barricade. Now free of the mob, Proctor took off across the fields toward the fort. It sat in the distance, a low, brown wall flattened by the hard iron of the sky. Like a dropped wallet at the side of the road, waiting to be picked up.

The gates stood wide open. Proctor walked the horse inside. Under one porch roof, protected from the drizzle, a solitary officer sat eating breakfast off a table covered with a linen cloth; his slave, in better clothes than those worn by many of the ordinary soldiers, cleared the dirty plates away while his master carefully wiped the corners of his mouth with his handkerchief. Not twenty feet away, a mob had broken into the rum stores and were already drunk. With their arms around one another, they swayed back and forth, singing "Yankee Doodle."

The ghosts swirled around, weaving in and out of the mist. It gave Proctor a headache just to watch them. One man they grabbed by the ear, whispering things only he might hear. Another man they led by the nose toward some plate of bacon abandoned in the rush to escape. The next one they dragged by the collar, flinging him against a man who immediately spun around with his fists.

It was as though they gained strength from the nearness of the necromancer who ruled them. Or perhaps, knowing that their last hours on earth were numbered by the impending defeat of the American forces, the cursed spirits wanted to experience life one last time, and so they seized it by proxy, dragging their cursed hosts any direction they could. The more intense the experience, the better.

Proctor used the horse to push his way through the looters, drunks, and lost souls. The last were men standing vacant-eyed, the cursed spirit overlapping their own souls so far they no longer knew who or where they were. He came to the tent where Deborah had been treating the sick, and he dismounted.

On his way in, Proctor ran into another man staggering to the entrance on his way out. The man was barefoot, wearing only trousers held up by suspenders and a shirt with more holes in it than fabric. His chin rested on his chest. For a second Proctor took him for a lost soul; the spirit shackled to him had merged so far into his body, it was hard to see. Then Proctor caught the stink of rum, so strong it made his stomach turn.

"The woman here, the nurse," he said, unable to squeeze past the man. "Have you seen her?"

The man lifted his head.

He was not a lost soul, but a soul possessed. The spectral eyes behind his eyes burned like white-hot flames; the grin behind his own mouth twisted into a leer.

"Get in line," the man said, his words sounding like a voice layered upon another voice. "A fine peach like that, I intend to finish pitting it myself before it's wasted on a British prick."

Proctor swung his fist at the man's face, as a reflex. Despite the stink of rum, the man laughed, easily dodging the blow. Proctor pulled back his fist to punch again, but stopped when the man lifted his hand to show the fascine knife he held there. The wicked curve on one end matched the uneven smirk on the drunk's doubled face. A stain on the sharp edge might have been blood.

"Oh, lookee, the Quaker's angry," the man taunted in the same echoey voice. "I'm shaking in my boots." He looked down. "Oh, wait, I'm not wearing any boots."

While the man admired his own rough humor, Proctor drew on his talent, swallowing the power like a man about to drown.

"He only is my rock, and my salvation," he quoted from the Psalms. "He is my defense."

The drunk sneered, laughing at Proctor. "What good do you think a Bible verse can do you?"

The last syllable was not even out of his mouth when a fist-sized rock that Proctor had summoned from a pile across the yard slammed into the side of the man's head.

The ghost must've felt it coming, turning the man's head at the very last second, because the rock only glanced off his cheek instead of laying him flat. It threw him off-balance, though. Proctor hurled his body into the man, knocking him to the ground, where he gripped his wrist and slammed it down until the knife came loose. He jammed his knee into the drunk's gut and pinned his throat to the ground, squeezing as hard as he could while he lifted his head and scanned the tent.

"Deborah?" he called out. "Deborah!"

Something like icicles pierced his arm, and he gasped. The man, too drunk and stunned to resist hard, did little to free himself, but the cursed spirit possessing him thrashed like a cat in a sack. Its arms flailed, struggling to get a grip on Proctor, stabbing chills through him every time it grabbed at him.

The spirit's bright eyes flared brighter, and the sneering grin on its face twisted into laughter of triumph. Proctor's right arm, pinning the man's neck, went tingly and numb. All the air rushed out of his lungs.

The dead soul had grabbed hold of his own living spirit and was tearing it out of the flesh of his arm. The numbness shot up his arm and through his shoulder, almost touching his heart.

With a choked cry of fear, Proctor rolled off the possessed man and away from him, tearing his soul free from the spectral grasp. Blood thundered back through his arm, followed by burning pain.

The other man rolled over to his knees, holding his throat, gasping for breath. The spirit trapped in his body corkscrewed around, trying to drag him back into the attack on Proctor.

When he and Deborah had first seen the curse, and tried to cure the volunteer in Gravesend, they had stopped short because they feared destroying the man's own soul.

Proctor didn't stop to worry about this man's original soul. The original spell, which Deborah had taken from the gospels, came back to his tongue.

"By the finger of God, I cast out devils!"

He felt the power flow through him, filling his numb arm with life, and he pointed it at the man on the ground. He saw the spirit start to rise out of the body, and his joy rose with it.

But it was not to be so easy. In the same instant, the man stirred, and Proctor hesitated, afraid for his soul. The spirit snapped back into the body of the drunk, who lurched to his feet. The spirit trapped inside him gave him an oddly doubled image, as if Proctor's eyes were crossed. The outer body was sluggish and heavy-limbed, but the inner body twitched like flame, white-hot and quick with rage. When he spoke, the doubled voice became one, echoing from far away, as if through the canyon of the man's throat.

"What do I care for your Bible verses when I am trapped in this hell?" it growled

He lunged at Proctor, raising his fist.

"By the finger of God, I cast out devils!" Proctor cried again. The spirit was willful, but the flesh was weak, and Proctor stepped inside the drunk's slow lurch to punch him in the jaw.

The man flew backward, falling over a cot and breaking its leg, to lie motionless on the ground. There was a burst of dust, or maybe a flash of pale light, and then nothing.

Proctor shook his hand, which hurt knuckles-to-wrist. "All right, so that was more my fist than my finger."

He stepped cautiously over the body. After a second he poked it with his toe, ready to leap back. But nothing happened. The cursed spirit was gone, and Proctor did not think it had gone to a better place.

"God forgive my soul," he whispered. Now that the fear had left him, the possible evilness of his act appalled him. He knelt quickly beside the body, checking for a pulse, for a breath, and found none. The shock of breaking the curse might have killed the man as well as casting out the other soul. Both were victims of the German necromancer who had placed the curse on them.

The sound of gunshots outside snapped him to attention. "Deborah!" he cried, spinning around, checking every corner of the tent, under the scattered piles of blankets. He was both relieved and alarmed when he didn't find her.

He ran out the entrance and saw the officer who had been eating breakfast calmly riding out the gate on Proctor's horse. He sprinted after him for a few steps then stopped when he realized how futile it was.

During his fight, the rest of the fort had emptied, even of the drunks, who staggered, arms linked, out of sight, down the road, or ran singly, like thieves caught in the act, across the sodden fields and away.

"Excuse me, sir, but are you a Friend?"

Proctor turned at the voice; it was the officer's slave, who had been left behind. Proctor considered answering that he was no Quaker, but thought better of it.

"Yes, I am a friend," he said.

"Am I wrong to assume you are looking for Miss Deborah, the Quaker nurse?"

Proctor's heart leapt up. "Yes! Have you seen her?"

"Yes, sir," the slave said, calmly removing his white gloves and folding them into his pocket. "She left shortly before you arrived, helping one of the sick men along to the bridge."

"Thank you kindly," Proctor said. "If I find her, may I tell her who I am to thank for the news?"

"Caesar, sir," the slave said. By mutual unspoken consent, he and Proctor hurried to the gate. As they went, Caesar stooped to pick up a musket that had been dropped. "Tell her not to worry 'bout me none," he said. "Tell her I gone over to the British side to be a free man."

He spied a powder horn and flints among the scattered items, stopping to retrieve those too.

Proctor opened his mouth to argue, then shut it again. "I'll tell her that, Caesar," he said finally. "But if you stay with the American side, you'll have your freedom too."

Caesar looked away and laughed. "Someday, maybe. But why wait for freedom someday when I can have my freedom today? That's what Howe promises." He turned his face back to Proctor. "You give my best to Miss Deborah now. She's a true friend to slaves, but no friend to slavery."

"Did she tell you that?"

"She spoke a word or two. Said I could trust you, if you came this way."

Proctor stopped and shook his head. He was never going to understand Deborah. She'd been drawing on his talent, making his power a slave to hers, for months, but now she was against slavery. Proctor thrust out his hand. After hesitating a moment, Caesar took it and they gave each other one solid shake.

"Good luck to you then," Proctor said.

"Next time you see me coming, keep your head down, sir," Caesar said.

"I'll do that, friend."

They went separate directions. Caesar turned toward the advancing British lines, walking with his head held high and an eagerness to his step. Proctor watched him go for a second, then checked the sky. Somewhere behind the heavy blanket of clouds, the sun had passed noon. There would be an early nightfall today. He set a quick pace the way he had just come, back toward the Hackensack River and their last bridge to freedom. Inwardly, he swore at himself for wasting time. He must have just missed Deborah originally, when he cut over the fields and away from the road. Now while he ran through debris abandoned by the army as it fled, he didn't know where he'd find her again. She could have been forced to leave the road for the same reasons he had, and there would be no signposts to point her way.

He had almost caught up with the drunken stragglers when he heard a loud huzzah and the rattle of drums behind him. It brought back the rush and fear he had experienced at Lexington, during the battle that started the Revolution. Only this time, instead of British Redcoats, German jaegers, mercenaries, their green jackets brilliant against the brown-and-gray landscape, crested the road behind them. It would be nothing for them to overtake the last remnants of the Continental army and defeat it. The Americans had already done half their work for them, leaving a trail of plunder like bread crumbs along the road.

The non-uniformed rabble ahead of Proctor broke in a panic, shouting, shoving men aside and trampling one another in their mad rush to escape. The cursed spirits shackled to their flesh displayed everything from despair to glee. He hurried after them, taking frequent glances over his shoulder. He watched the enemy soldiers enter Fort Lee.

The fort on Brooklyn Heights, White Plains, Fort Washington, and now Fort Lee: one after another, every American stronghold had fallen. With every fall, there were fewer men left to fight.

He looked ahead, at the men fleeing across the wet winter landscape in bare feet and shirtsleeves. It scarcely seemed to matter if the Hessian mercenaries overtook them—they were already defeated. No wonder so many of the spirits were gleeful; Proctor bet that the condition of their curse was nearly fulfilled. When the American army was no more, they would be free to go on to heaven or hell, each as his due.

As the mob cleared, Proctor spied two figures struggling arm in arm along the edge of the road, resuming their journey now that the panicked soldiers had passed. He came closer, confirming his first impression. It was Deborah, acting as a human crutch for a soldier. The soldier limped along, his ghost driving a spectral bayonet into his leg with each game step, drawing a grimace and beads of sweat along his forehead.

Deborah, slight compared with the soldier she supported, poured her magic into him, trying to heal him a little bit with each breath. But it was a fight between her and the spirit, and the spirit was slowly winning. If the soldier fell down, and the advancing jaegers bayoneted him when they passed, as they had so many other wounded, the spirit would be freed.

"Here, let me help," Proctor said, coming up beside them.

"Proctor?" Deborah flinched at the sight of him. Her voice was strained from the physical effort she expended, and from the magical effort she drew on as well. He stepped in to take her place, but she turned her shoulder to block him. "I wouldn't want to steal anything from you again, not even your labor."

"That's the point. You can't steal it if it's freely given." He reached out again. "Here, I want to help."

"Why must you always be so obstinate?" she murmured.

"Why do you always resort to flattery?"

She scowled at him but moved aside, permitting him to take her place.

With Proctor's support, the wounded soldier didn't have to put any weight on his bad leg and they began to make swifter progress. The hairs on the back of Proctor's neck prickled as the soldier's spirit tried to shove him away. It wasn't as powerful as the one in the tent that had tried to yank out his own soul; in fact, he noticed little more than a chill against his skin. But the cursed souls had clearly grown more aggressive. For months, they had been content to torment their hosts. Now Proctor felt himself regularly assaulted by them. They could sense that the end was near, and grew stronger and bolder as they drove their hosts out of the conflict.

The three of them—Deborah, Proctor, and the soldier—continued down the road more easily, if not more swiftly. Deborah continued to try to heal the man, touching his arm as if to steady him, but really to murmur prayers to keep his spirit from causing greater pain. All three continued to look behind them. Though part of the enemy forces had broken off to take the fort, others continued after them.

The soldier stopped walking and shoved Proctor away. He leaned against a fencepost, his face red and lined with pain. Tears rolled down his cheeks, though he had not uttered a word of complaint.

"You two go on without me," he said. "You know what they'll do when they catch up to us."

"We wouldn't dream of abandoning you," Deborah said. But she glanced over her shoulder as she said it. The rumors were that the Hessians killed stragglers when they found them, and the British soldiers did worse to the women they captured.

"You must abandon me, Miss Walcott, for your own sake. You done a good job nursing me, and if I was to keep the leg, it'd be because of your care. But there's no more to done for it now, and you must go. It's every man and woman for hisself."

Proctor wrapped his arm around the man and practically lifted him off his feet. "We're no nation if we act that way," he said. "We'll escape together or not at all."

"It might be not at all," the soldier said, his voice strained.

"Not if I have any say in it," Proctor said, setting a quick pace down the road again.

Deborah's eyes met his, and he saw the gratitude in them.

"Thank you," she said.

"Let us talk less," he replied. "And walk more."

They hobbled along as the enemy forces advanced steadily behind them without gaining. Bearing the weight of the wounded soldier on his shoulder, feeling the man's heavy breathing in his ear, and smelling his sickly sweat, the distance seemed to pass beneath Proctor's feet like water moving through a mill wheel, constant motion without any progress.

But that was merely an illusion. Soon the thin gray curtains of drizzle parted, and the long low house of Washington's headquarters emerged into view.

"Come on, we're almost there," Proctor said.

"Almost where?" Deborah asked.

"The bridge and the ferry are just ahead up here. Once we cross the river—"

"Once we cross the river," interrupted the wounded soldier, "we still got nowhere to go."

The cursed spirit hung arms over his shoulders. It tilted his face up to Proctor and cackled silently.

Chapter 20

Proctor felt a light pressure on his arm and jumped, but it was only Deborah. Whether she was trying to reassure him or herself, he couldn't say. Then he followed the line of her gaze and realized they were both past reassuring.

Hundreds of men were lined up, waiting their turn to cross the Hackensack River. With the cursed spirits attacking them in a frenzy, they would surely have broken and run if not for the calm example of General Washington watching over them.

Washington's calm demeanor was the mystery.

Thirteen cursed spirits were shackled to him now. They attacked him like an angry mob eager for a lynching. They swarmed around the neck and flanks of his horse, leaping, tearing, and pulling at him. As hand after invisible hand sank into his living flesh, he must have been pierced by a thousand painful icicles. And then there was the mounting sense of fear and panic that came with the spirits attacking you. Even one of them drove Proctor mad. He could not imagine a dozen more.

Washington's horse felt their presence too, shifting nervously from foot to foot, tossing her head, her skin twitching. Breath frosted from her nostrils each time she snorted, not because the temperature was dropping so fast, though it was dropping, but because the presence of so many spirits chilled the air that much.

Despite all this, Washington sat straight in the saddle. He looked irritated at the horse, frustrated with the retreat, and angry to be surprised again by the British. But somehow, through force of will, he mastered his feelings as he organized another orderly retreat. The men around him, seeing his example, tried to do the same as they waited their turn to cross.

William Lee, Washington's stocky, round-faced slave, galloped up on his mount, hooves tossing mud as he pounded past the ranks of men. He leaned his red-turbaned head in close to Washington to report, and Washington's gaze turned back down the road toward Fort Lee.

"They've stopped marching," the wounded soldier said.

They had! A few green coats of Hessian scouts were visible in the distance, but the main body had stopped advancing. It made no sense to Proctor—they could overrun the Americans and destroy their forces in a short battle. The Americans were unprepared physically or spiritually for a protracted fight.

Maybe that was the point. Why fight when the Americans were already beaten?

"Maybe they've stopped, but we haven't," Proctor said. He heaved the wounded soldier over to the line waiting to cross the small bridge.

Deborah followed after, but her face was pale and her step uncertain.

"What's wrong?" Proctor asked.

"It's too much," she whispered, casting glances at the men around them. She didn't mention the curse, but she didn't need to. It was visible in the men, even to those who were blind to the powers of magic. Their faces were drawn, their eyes full of fear. Every third man looked ready to bolt.

Proctor knew exactly how she felt. He'd felt the same way, hopeless and helpless, and he had seen someone who changed his mind. "There's an officer in Greene's command who's protected."

"One man . . . ," Deborah said.

"If we understand his secret, we'll have the solution."

Then they were pressed into the mob of soldiers crossing the bridge, pulled along with them to resist being crushed in their wake. The water churned beneath the bridge, sending up eddies of cold air, though that was not what made Deborah and Proctor shiver. The shivers came from the dozens of invisible hands that pinched, prodded, gripped, and groped them.

On the far shore, they would have broken free of the other soldiers and set their own pace, but it was easier to be pulled along by the current, pieces of flotsam in the river of refugees. Washington was one of the last to cross, just as he had been at Brooklyn. The sound of hoofbeats in the mud prompted Proctor to move to the side of the road in time to see Washington and his officers hurry past them to the head of the column.

With the thick clouds overhead and the lateness of the year, night fell early while they were still on the road. Proctor was practically carrying the wounded soldier along; the man's leg wound had started seeping blood again. Deborah's constant attempts to pour strength into the man's spirit were having a diminishing effect. The cursed spirit draped across his shoulders whispered in his ear at all her efforts, draining his will as fast as she could lend to it.

"How much farther must we go on?" Deborah asked.

"Until we reach someplace safe where the army can resupply and regroup," Proctor said.

The wounded soldier groaned and held his arm across his belly. "I can't wait that much longer. Do you two mind waiting here for me while I do my business?"

Deborah turned her head away. "Of course we will."

"Do you need help?" Proctor asked.

The soldier shook his head, grimacing. "There are still some things a man has to do himself."

"Well, sure," Proctor admitted.

Deborah grabbed a fallen branch from the side of the road for the soldier to use as a crutch. He accepted it with a thank-you and hobbled off behind a thick mound of brush and trees. The darkness was so thick they couldn't see him.

Proctor shifted his head to speak to Deborah and she turned her body away, not so far as to be rude, but enough to prevent him from speaking. He could get so angry at her for the way she made the simplest things difficult for him. But she had her arms wrapped tight to her chest, shivering, and looked so cold and comfortless that all he wanted to do was reach out to help her.

They stood there in awkward silence, watching the line of soldiers pass. It stretched out like an earthworm, growing thinner the longer it became. As the men marched—no, Proctor realized, he couldn't call it marching. They plodded on. The mud clumped heavy on their shoes, those who had them, for some were barefoot. He imagined that they felt much as he did. The wet air seeped through all their clothes, and the natural cold settled into their skin like ice forming on a lake. Their bellies were empty, and though damp was everywhere, their throats were dry.

On top of that, every one of them carried a dark and unwilling passenger, a spirit meant to do nothing more than drive a wedge between them and the cause of independence. As the stragglers passed them, the spirits showed more energy than the men.

"How do they keep going?" Proctor asked.

Deborah shook her head. "I don't know." The catch in her voice as she spoke made him think that she might have been referring to herself.

He wanted to tell her that he could forgive her for turning him into a witch-slave, that all he wanted was to hear the apology from her directly. But it was hard to find the words. "Deborah—"

"Don't." Her voice sounded on the verge of a sob. "Just don't. Proctor, I—"

Whatever she was going to say was drowned out by the

approach of a horse. Proctor stepped in front of her and pulled her back to the side of the road. William Lee, Washington's slave, rode past them and down the road just out of sight, then turned and came back, reining in his horse as he approached them.

"You're end of the line," he said, giving Proctor a nod of recognition. "We're camping for the night in the village of Hackensack, about a mile ahead."

"That's it?" Proctor asked, looking back down the road. "But there were so many more."

"I figure about one in three thinks they can do better on their own if they go home," Lee said. "If that's your plan, this'd be the time to go."

Proctor had been thinking about just that. Neither he nor Deborah had enlisted. They could leave, use their connections along the Quaker Highway, making their way back to Salem and to The Farm. He wondered how Magdalena was doing with all the other witches, how their training was coming. With everything he and Deborah had learned, they might be able to work with them to find a way to break the curse.

Lee's horse was restless. He circled it, pointing the way they had just come. "Back that way half a mile is a turnoff that will take you north back toward New England."

"No, friend," Deborah said. "We'll join you at the camp."

"The fight's not over yet, is it?" Proctor asked.

Lee shrugged, as if maybe it was. "See you in camp then." He spurred his horse, bending low over its neck as it leapt down the road.

"Why do you want to stay?" Proctor asked Deborah.

"If I can't defeat the Covenant by myself, I can at least help those who are fighting against it. If all I can do is save one life, or help one man heal to fight again, that's what I'll do."

"We can do more than that," Proctor said. "You see how

General Washington carries on, despite the burden he carries. You see the strength that some men have to keep fighting despite the curse. As long as a few men remain free, we've not lost completely."

Deborah shook her head as if she disagreed, as if she'd already accepted defeat, but she said, "We'll do what we can to give strength to those who still wish to carry on the fight." She called out the wounded soldier's name, leaving the road to follow him into the brush. "They've set up camp ahead," she explained. "There will be fires for warmth, and maybe something to eat."

Proctor eased around her and pushed farther off the road, calling the man's name, but the dark returned no answer. He searched for a body, thinking the man might have passed out or fallen sick. But when he bent close to the ground, his fingertips found footprints in the mud leading away from the road. "I think he's deserted."

"But how?" Deborah asked. "He could barely stand, much less walk."

"When he's marching with the army, the curse holds him back and weakens him. The moment he decides to run, it gives him strength and purpose."

"But escape doesn't break the curse. We know that from the farmhand at Gravesend."

"It's meant to break the will of the Americans to fight, not just now, but forever."

"We have to find a way to lift it."

"I know." They had climbed back onto the road and were hurrying toward the camp. He thought about the man he'd found at Fort Lee, and the strength of the spirit that had almost torn his soul from him. He had freed the man from the curse, but he was sure it had killed him.

When they entered the camp, Deborah was ready to stop at the first fire where she saw some of the other women, but Proctor told her no. "We have to find the man I was telling you about."

They weaved through the campfires scattered around the village, with Proctor searching men's faces. Everywhere he saw signs of despair, mixed with a sort of grim determination to fight on anyway. That was a rare trait, but not so rare among frontier farmers who planted their fields again every year despite the storms, frosts, and pests that attacked the previous year's crop. The sounds were quiet for a camp this large: just the crackle of the fires, the occasional clink of metal on metal. There was no laughter, and only whispered conversations. This was the whole army, what was left of it, and it was smaller than the garrison at Fort Washington had been.

"Is that him over there?" Deborah asked.

She pointed toward a fire where men in full uniform gathered around artillery they had carried with them on retreat when other men dropped their muskets. A slight young man, head cocked to one side, stood beside a cannon, caressing it the way a man might stroke the neck of a favorite horse. He carried no cursed ghost, but a dark shadow flowed around him, independent of the firelight.

"No, that's Captain Hamilton," Proctor said. "The one who already carries a ghost. Whatever that is attached to him, it gives him strength, and lends courage to those around him. But it makes me uneasy."

Deborah unconsciously and wearily slipped her hand around Proctor's arm. He was afraid to say anything or draw her attention to it, but for a moment he felt closer to her. They walked through the camp, circling Hamilton. "It is not a good spirit. But he does not seem to be a bad man."

"It's your Quaker ways," Proctor said. "You think no one is, at heart, a bad man. It's so opposite of what I was brought up to believe, that we are all sinners."

"We are all broken," she said. "But that is something different. Even a broken lamp can still hold oil to give light."

"Or spill it everywhere, setting the house ablaze and burning it to the ground."

He covered her hand with his, and she pulled away startled, crossing her arms. He was confused, unsure whether she reacted to his gesture or his words, and angry—even Emily, when they had their differences, didn't withdraw from him so completely. But when he opened his mouth to confront Deborah, she whispered.

"Oh, my."

She was staring at a man who sat alone at a small fire. A group of three soldiers had approached him, and instantly an angel appeared as a numinous light in the dark, driving back their cursed spirits. The men fled.

"That's him," Proctor said, called away from his own dark thoughts and back to their greater task. "Let me introduce you."

The fire had been built in the shelter of an old corncrib that offered some slight protection from the wind. Thomas Paine sat beside it on a log, with a drum for a writing table propped between his knees. He was wadding up the pages of his manuscript and tossing them into the fire, one by one.

"Hello, friend," Proctor said.

Paine looked up, startled to be spoken to. Despite his guardian, he appeared to be as worn as the other men, if only by the force of seeing his hopes crushed. "You're the young man from headquarters, just last night. Proctor, right?"

"Yes. This is my friend Deborah Walcott."

"Tom Paine. I'm pleased to meet you." He belatedly shifted his work aside and started to rise.

"Please don't bother yourself on my account," she said, sitting down instantly across from him. "Are you the author who wrote *Common Sense*?"

"That would be me," he said. He wadded up another

page of writing and flung it into the fire, where it crackled and curled as it was consumed.

"You wrote that 'The cause of America is in a great measure the cause of all mankind,' " Deborah said. Her eyes glittered with thought, and Proctor could see that she was thinking of the Covenant. The words were even truer than Paine realized. "Your words inspired the whole country."

Paine offered her a weak smile. "I have been fortunate to have your whole country to inspire me."

"What are you doing now?" Proctor asked him, gesturing to the manuscript.

Paine crumpled another sheet. "I've been working on a new pamphlet, but everything I've written so far is inadequate to the crisis we now face. I need to throw it all away and start over again. Everyone has been thoughtful about interruptions, leaving me in solitude to write, but I don't even know where to begin."

They were all so beaten down that no one knew where to begin. Paine grabbed the rest of the sheaf of papers and spilled them all into the flames at once. The sheets writhed like tortured souls, disappearing in a fountain of ash and sparks.

Deborah tilted her head toward the rest of the camp, where cursed spirits hovered over the dark humps of the exhausted men. "*Crisis* is the only word for it," she said. "Those poor souls."

Paine followed her gaze and nodded thoughtfully. "These are times that try men's souls."

The fire crackled, filling the silence left in the absence of words.

A second later Paine grabbed a half-burned sheet of paper from the edge of the fire and hurriedly put out the smoldering flame. He took out his pen and ink, setting them on the drumhead between his legs. Smoothing out the sheet of paper, he began to write.

Proctor looked at Deborah, expecting to exchange a

glance of wonder. Instead he saw her pouring her strength and power into him, the way she'd poured it into the soldier before. She was drained, exhausted, but somehow she had discovered extra reserves and was giving them away.

Paine lifted his head, his eyes alight. "I'll need more paper."

It took Proctor a second to realize he was being asked to help. "I'll go get some from Washington's secretary."

"Thank you," Paine said, bending back over his work.

Deborah could not break her focus long enough to say a word to him. The angel that protected Paine shone in him as a light, leaning over him and placing its hand upon his shoulder as he wrote. Deborah took a deep breath and closed her eyes.

Something wet landed on Proctor's cheek. Snow flurries swirled through the air.

He walked off into the camp alone.

Chapter 21

Washington had set up his headquarters in an open-sided tent. If the rest of the army was exhausted and defeated, the men around Washington were busy enough for all of them. A row of makeshift tables had been erected, and men sat at all of them, inscribing letters that Washington dictated rapidly one after another. Couriers stood at the ready, cleaning their horses and readying them for departure.

Under the tent canopy, Washington was surrounded by his "family," the men he trusted most. Colonel Robert Harrison, the well-born Marylander, and Colonels Meade and Webb had maps spread across one end of a table. They argued about the army's next location with Washington even as he was sending out letters to all the states calling for volunteers and supplies. Proctor recognized the three men by their voices: Harrison's southern enunciation, Meade's deep bass, and Webb's blunt language. It was hard for him to make out individual men in the tent. He saw the cursed spirits crowded everywhere, making the whole of it a confused and jangled mob of double images. He finally glimpsed a pair of white silk stockings—spattered with mud—among the legs of the other men. Pushing through the crowd, he found the man he sought seated at a table, sealing a letter. The man handed the sealed letter to a courier; the lantern light caught his full cheeks and high, thoughtful forehead.

"Colonel Tilghman," Proctor said.

Tilghman seemed startled to see him. "You've followed

us on this folly, have you?" His smile was genuine, but his face strained.

"Is there anything I can do to help?" Proctor asked.

"We're near done with letters—"

"Tench!" It was Washington's voice, cutting through the jumble of words like a saber. The general turned from his letters, holding up his hand to silence Harrison and the others.

"Sir!" Tilghman replied, jumping to his feet.

"While I'm thinking of it, who was that young New Yorker, looks like a schoolboy, who brought the cannons with him?"

"Captain Alexander Hamilton, sir."

"Hamilton? He held the hill for us at White Plains when the Germans marched through that awful fire."

"Yes, sir. He held his men together and brought off all their supplies."

"Keep him close," Washington said. "And see if you can't find more like him." With that he turned right back to Harrison, Meade, and Webb, shooting down their next suggestion for a camp because it was too easy to cut off.

Tilghman chuckled, and his ghost, as if offended by this slightest sign of merriment, reached down into his chest and twisted its fist. Tilghman's chuckle turned into a hard, thick cough. He covered his mouth, leaning his head away from Proctor. When the coughing subsided, he wiped his mouth on the back of his hand.

"Excuse me," he said. "It's this pernicious damp."

"I just arrived in camp. I'm sorry I wasn't able to help earlier." He and Deborah were trying to find a way to defeat the Covenant, but the men here were also trying to win the war. Every time he reported to Tilghman, Proctor felt like he should be doing more to help them too.

"Not at all," Tilghman said, clapping his clean hand on Proctor's shoulder. "We're nearly done with the despatches. Most of the men have terms of service ending before the new year. If the states don't send us new drafts of men, it'll make the army we have tonight look large by comparison."

"Is that what all these letters are?" Proctor asked.

"Those are mostly written," Tilghman said. "But it's no secret to say that the mood here is darker than the night around us. So some of the officers are taking this chance to revise their wills, and some are writing letters absolving their relations of any treason. A few are sending notes to their families, informing them of their safe escape, but that's only a few. If you need to send a letter to someone, we can include it with the couriers when they go."

Proctor looked at the dwindling supply of paper and thought about who he might write a letter to. He wondered if his mother would even read a letter from him. Was he as dead to her as she pretended? Probably so. If he had any family at all now, it was the family of witches who had gathered in Salem, and he couldn't send them any letters—with The Farm hidden, there was no way to deliver them.

"Actually," Proctor said. "I wonder if I might take some sheets for Mister Thomas Paine."

"Paine? Is he here?"

"He is," Proctor said. "He's sought solitude away from the rest of the men so that he might work on a new pamphlet, and he asked me to bring as much paper as I might find. I know supplies are limited—"

Tilghman grabbed a stack of blank pages from the table, yanking one from beneath the pen of a young officer just beginning to write. "We'll have more paper sent up from Morristown or Newark. Take all of this and come back if he needs more."

"Thank you," Proctor said.

Tilghman started to speak, but the spirit riding him shook his fist around in his chest again, and the words disappeared in a spasm of coughing.

Proctor drew power into himself and thought of a spell

he might use to sever the cursed spirit from Tilghman. Then he thought of the dead man back in the tent at Fort Lee and opened his fist, letting the power flow out of him again.

If they didn't find enough power to break the curse soon, he doubted the army would survive until the end of the year. And if the army didn't survive, he doubted the witches in Salem would have any chance at all. The Covenant would send Bootzamon and their other assassins to pick them off one by one. He had to pour out his worries to someone—

He turned back to Tilghman. "I would like to write a letter to a friend," he said. "Captain Revere, of Boston. Although he may be a colonel by now."

Tilghman cleared a space for him at the table. "Use whatever you need. We'll send it out with the next post rider."

Proctor breathed a sigh of relief and sat down to jot a quick letter saying that he and Deborah had been struggling in the service of the war, and the situation looked bleak unless they found help somewhere before the end of the year. He thanked Paul for his friendship and wished him well.

Innocent enough, if anyone else read it, and all true. But he trusted Revere to do the right thing with that knowledge if he could.

When he returned to the campfire, Paine was scribbling intently in the margins of salvaged sheets. He looked up at Proctor with a mixture of impatience and anger, taking the offered paper without a word of thanks, going to work instantly on a clean sheet. The drumhead vibrated with each tap of his pen to the page.

Despite Paine's gruffness, the presence of his guardian had an instant and amazing effect on Proctor. He hadn't realized how much being surrounded by the cursed spirits had a suffocating and corrosive impact on him. But he felt his tension ease and his anxiety fade the moment he stepped into Paine's presence. The angel was no longer visible to him the same way, but he could sense her there, imbuing Paine's work.

He opened his mouth to say something, but Deborah put her finger to her lips and rose, leading him a few steps aside.

"That presence is amazing," she whispered. "What is it?"

"I believe it's the spirit of his wife," Proctor said. "She died giving birth to their first child."

"And stayed with him of her own accord, tied to the man and not the place?" She watched Paine with new regard. "Amazing," she repeated. "I think if he were at the gallows tree, she'd find a way to save him."

The comparison only made Proctor think of that hapless soldier pretending to be a Quaker in New York, the one they'd seen hung outside the mansion the day after the fire. He did not want to share a similar fate. "What did you do, right before I left?"

"The same thing I had been doing with the wounded soldier earlier," she said, hiding her mouth with her hand, though Paine seemed too preoccupied to notice anything they said. "I poured my hope and strength into him. 'But I will hope continually, and praise Thee more and more. I will go in the strength of the Lord God.'"

He recognized her spell as a quote from the Psalms, but he couldn't say which one. "I'm surprised you have any left."

"That's the remarkable thing," she said. "I had so little left to draw on, but everything I poured into him came back to me increased."

"How?"

"Through her power. I've been thinking . . ."

That hardly counted as news—when did she ever stop thinking? "Yes?"

"The Covenant wants to keep the British empire together as a focus, a way of channeling magic through the symbol of the king to achieve the power they crave."

"Right."

"What focus do we—as Americans—have? We all belong to our separate states, follow our separate churches and faiths, identify with our separate regions."

"We have the Declaration of Independence," Proctor said, remembering the way it had been published in every newspaper and read in every church, at least in Massachusetts.

"And we have *Common Sense*."

"Paine's pamphlet."

"Yes," she said. "That was read by people in every state. Without it, would we have had the Declaration?"

"I see what you're saying. His new pamphlet could be a focus, allowing us to pour magic into the soldiers to break the curse."

"I don't know that we could break it," she said, shaking her head. "I don't know that you and I together could channel that much power."

"But we could strengthen the army against the effects of the curse."

"And buy us time to find a solution." She looked at him with eager, intense eyes—a way she had not looked at him in months. "We have to find other ways to focus the good that is here and fight this evil power."

"Why—" He bit off the question in his mouth, afraid to say too much.

"Why? I think that is self-evident. These are the people who murdered my parents, who murdered the Walker family, who would have killed you. They mean to—"

"That's not what I was going to ask." He took a step back, angry at himself.

"What is it? Spit it out."

He spun on her. "Why have you been so distant from me? Why have you been holding back?"

Her own face grew dark with anger. "I know why you hid your visit to Emily Rucke from me in New York. You still have feelings for her. You like her fine clothes and scented perfumes and delicate manners. You—"

"You don't know what you're talking about."

"Oh, don't I? You should have seen the puppy-dog look on your face when you stared at her. I can't be like her, Proctor. I will never be a fine lady or own those fancy clothes. And I'll never own slaves to tend my hair—"

"You're a fine one to talk about slaves. You never asked my opinion, never asked my permission. You just used me like a slave."

He regretted the words as soon as they left his mouth, and he wished he knew a spell to call them back. But her accusations about Emily hurt. Maybe because they were a little too close to the truth. He couldn't say that he hadn't thought of her at all, especially when Deborah kept him at arm's length and made him feel so alone.

"I am sorry I did that to you," she said tersely. "I was afraid, afraid I would have to stand against the Covenant alone, and I knew I was not strong enough. That doesn't make the way you look at Emily Rucke a lie."

She wiped her eye quickly, then seemed ashamed that she had done so. She turned her back to Proctor.

"Deborah—it's not like that."

"Save your words," she said. "I don't need them."

As she walked off toward one of the fires where some of the other women gathered, Paine looked up from his work. "A very agreeable young woman," he said. Then he picked up another sheet and bent back over the drum to continue writing.

Proctor just stared at him

He'd had thoughts of Emily, but they were idle thoughts, for a world that might have been, not for the world he lived in. Emily could run an estate and keep order among the servants, but he couldn't imagine her marching miles in the dark, giving all her strength to others to keep them going. She had the courage to face down cheating shopkeepers, but he couldn't imagine her fighting for her life against a scarecrow animated by the soul of a dead witch.

Paine looked up from his work again. "You're welcome to sleep next to the fire again, if you like. It was no trouble last night."

Deborah had already disappeared among the campfires and shadows; Proctor could no longer make out which of the figures moving in the distance was hers. What would he say to her if he caught up with her right now? Best to give her peace tonight and try to talk to her again tomorrow.

He sat across from Paine and held his head in his hands. "Thank you," he said.

Proctor woke late the next morning to the sound of distant gunfire. His neck was stiff and his back sore from sleeping curled up against the corncrib. He had mud plastered to his cheek, stubble rough on his fingers as he tried to brush it away. The fire was long cold, not even coals among the ashes, and Paine and his drum were both gone.

As Proctor sat up and rubbed the sleep from his eyes, he saw that the camp had already woken. Far from the others, the fire dead, and Paine too distracted by his writing to remember him to anyone, it must have been easy to overlook Proctor. He entered the tiny village, hearing the distant boom of guns again.

"What's that?" he said to one of the Maryland companies as he passed them.

"Cornwallis is attacking our rear guard at New-bridge," answered one of them.

"Aren't we going to provide support?" Proctor asked.

"And put the whole army at risk? Not a chance."

"Are we going to retreat then?"

The Marylander shrugged. "Not yet. I suspect it will come to that."

Proctor wandered through the village, which seemed startled to discover an army in its midst. Children in winter coats stood at the gates of their yards, worried looks on their faces as they watched the soldiers in their summer uniforms stand shivering in the streets. Outside barns and storefronts, local farmers argued with quartermasters over the matter of supplies.

"If we feed the army, we'll go hungry," one of them complained as Proctor passed.

"We're already hungry," the officer argued back. "You should do your patriotic duty and sell us whatever you can spare."

"What do you have to buy it with?" the farmer said. "Patriotism? That won't feed my children—"

Proctor continued past them, turning his head anytime he saw a woman in case it might be Deborah. Likely enough, she'd been invited into someone's home. The women, at least, might expect to be fed and given warm blankets.

"Excuse me," he said to a group of three soldiers when he came to the spot where he'd last seen her the night before. "There was a woman here last night, in plain clothes, she'd been nursing the wounded. Have you seen her?"

"Oh, we sent the women off first thing this morning to Morristown," one said, wearing his ghost draped around him like a winter coat.

"Philadelphia," mumbled a second man.

"Some went to Newark too," said a third, chewing a plug of tobacco just like the ghost that haunted him. "Though anyplace is better than here. This is no place for women, not with the Hessians at our heels, and the Redcoats coming on theirs." He looked north, toward the sound of the guns.

"Sweet on one of them, were you?" asked the first man.

"No," Proctor said. "No, she was . . . my sister. That's all. I want to be sure she's safe."

"She's safer in Newark than she is here, that's for certain," the tobacco chewer said. He turned his head and spat.

"Bet she's in Morristown," insisted the first. "Safer, warmer, *and* better fed."

Proctor marched with them across New Jersey. Everyone was tense, with Cornwallis nipping at their rear guard like a dog at the seat of their pants.

Proctor stumbled to the head of the line, thinking to pursue Deborah, but Tilghman saw him and called him over. "Good to see you, Brown. We sent a lot of men off last night as couriers. Would you mind lending a hand until we get a few back?"

"I'll be glad to," Proctor said.

Deborah was safer away from the army, but he needed to stay here until he found a way to beat the curse. He thought he'd do it with Deborah's help, but if she was gone for a while, he'd carry on by himself.

It was easy enough to fall into the new routine of the camp. Every day they moved locations again, sending out scouts to find the position of Howe's troops. Proctor was busy copying letters and delivering messages.

He looked up from his desk to rub his hands together and blow on them for warmth. Through the frosted window, he saw another group of new arrivals, riflemen from Virginia's western valleys.

All of Washington's desperate letters for aid were beginning to have some effect. The militias had risen in both northern and southern Jersey, ambushing the Redcoats and Hessians the way the militia had beaten them at Lexington and Concord. In the main body of the army, what was left of it, soldiers were still deserting, but they were thin, hungry, and dressed in summer clothes. The new arrivals coming in were cut from tougher leather. The bunch outside were riflemen—tall, broad-shouldered, auburn-haired, in heavy coats with heavy beards. All but one of them. He was still a boy, too small for his clothes, outsized by his own rifle. Proctor would bet that under all that dirt, his face was as smooth as a girl's. Proctor smiled. The newcomer reminded him of Arthur Simes back home, who could have passed for twelve, tagging along with the militia to Lexington Green.

The smile faded from Proctor's face.

Out at the edge of their camp beyond their quarters, a swirling wind kicked up veils of snow. To any other eye, that's all it was, a mere caprice of winter.

But Proctor was in tune with the curse placed on the Americans, and he could see the truth of it: the ghosts of dead men, trapped in the mortal world, had been cursed to follow the army until they found a mortal soul, cursed to haunt that mortal until the war ended.

The newcomers were signing papers of service, reporting to duty. And the ghosts were drawn to them like crows to a carcass. Pale troops came racing over the fields, kicking up swirls of snow, eager to be the first to reach fresh souls to haunt.

It was one thing for a youngster, someone Arthur's age, to volunteer to fight. The world was already a hard place, with injury or disease ready to strike a man down at any time. If a boy wanted to go off to war and face that, he might be no worse off than he was at home. But Proctor couldn't let someone that young take on a cursed spirit.

Proctor bolted out the door. He heard voices in the howling wind as he walked toward the Virginians. "I beg your pardon," he said, rounding the group of men to reach the boy hiding in the back.

A ghost shot past him, raking fingers like claws of ice along his back. He shivered and one of the Virginians laughed at him, asking, "Need a warmer coat?"

The first ghost attached itself to the leader of the group, grabbing hold of his rifle barrel like a drowning man trying to pull himself to shore. The Virginian registered the change only in his bright blue eyes, which were suddenly wary, shifting from side to side as if he'd felt someone brush against him and stick a hand into his pocket.

A second ghost stepped inside another man, who grunted as if he'd been hit. The men around chuckled at the unexplained noise, and he frowned back at them.

Proctor put his hand on the shoulder of the boy, who had watched what just happened. "I beg your pardon, friend."

The boy spun around and his bright eyes popped wide open. "Proctor?"

Proctor's jaw dropped. "I—"

He knew the face, the girlish curve of the jaw, the auburn curls of the hair even cut short, the bright green eyes. A mixture of surprise, shock, and relief washed over him. He had traveled so far to find her, had given up when he found her parents murdered, and now here she stood in front of him. Alexandra Walker.

"Hi, Alex—" He couldn't say *Alexandra*, not if she had disguised herself as a man. He stumbled over his words. "Alex Walker . . . right?"

Anger and fear flashed across her face. She punched him in the chest, knocking him back, then turned and ran away.

Proctor started after her, but the group of men blocked his way. He tried to push through, but the biggest grabbed Proctor by the arm and tossed him back on his heels.

"What do you want with my brother Alex?" the leader said. His ghost still held on tight to the rifle, as if eager to lift it and use it.

Proctor tried to look past them. "That's not your brother—"

His words were cut short by a bright burst of light and the taste of blood in his mouth, and he found himself on the ground. The Virginian who'd punched him towered over him, daring him to stand up and say anything again. But the leader—Alex's brother—knelt down beside Proctor.

"Now what were you saying about my brother?"

Proctor pushed himself up to his knees, remembering too late how Alexandra had often spoken of her overprotective brothers. He wiped the blood from his mouth and flung it onto the dirty snow that littered the ground. "Redeem their souls from deceit and violence, and let their blood be precious in your sight."

The Virginian's brows drew down in puzzlement.

Proctor's mouth was still bleeding, so he swiped the blood onto his fingertips and flung it again, this time making sure to get it across Alexandra's brother's boots as he repeated the protective spell.

The elder Walker stood up and took a step back, and the men around him—Alex's brothers and cousins and others from their part of the Shenandoah Valley, Proctor guessed—laughed uncertainly. They were all cursed now, every one of them carrying a spectral rider. His protective spell wouldn't work on them all or last forever; except for the brother with blood on his boots, it would start to fade in power as soon as they walked away from this spot. But it was all he could do.

"What's going on here?" blustered an officer's voice.

"Nothing, friend," Proctor said, rising up to his feet. "I misspoke, and my friend here corrected me."

The officer looked at Proctor with a mixture of pity and disgust before he turned on the Virginian volunteers. "What's wrong with the lot of you? Beating up on a Quaker who won't even defend himself or name his attacker. Save it for the Redcoats."

"Yes, sir," Alexandra's brother said, managing a look of genuine chagrin.

The officer looked over the group and counted them

again. "Are we one short? I thought there was one more of you."

"No, sir, this is all of us."

"All right then." The officer told them where to report and yelled at them to get moving. Before they followed his orders, the oldest brother turned back to Proctor. The rest of the group formed a wedge behind him, their numbers doubled by the presence of the cursed spirits that only Proctor and other witches could see.

"I'm sorry about the misunderstanding," Walker said.

"It's no worry of mine," Proctor said, running a tongue over his swollen lip and spitting the last of the blood from his mouth. "But when you see your brother Alex again, you tell him that he has a friend in headquarters who would like to see him."

Chapter 22

He left before the Walkers could waste any more of his time with argument or denial. Alex knew he was here. If she decided to run away, there was no way he would find her again. But surely she would come to him. Maybe the two of them could break the curse, even without Deborah's help.

Soldiers turned their heads at the sight of his face as he walked back into headquarters and took his place at the desk where he had been copying letters. He blew on his hands to warm them once more, then picked up his pen, cleaned the tip, and resumed copying the letter where he'd left off. Men around him fell silent, which suited Proctor fine. He was deep in thought, dividing his attention between the letter and ways to break the curse, when Tilghman came over to the table and leaned close to his ear.

"If you go pack snow on that, it won't swell as much," he said so softly no one else could hear it.

Proctor started, pulled out of his thoughts. "Pack snow on what?" he said, for a second genuinely puzzled.

By the time he realized it was his swollen lip, Tilghman straightened up, laughed, and clapped Proctor on the back. The other men grinned and resumed their conversations in normal tones. A moment later, one of the side doors opened and Washington emerged with General Greene. His head doubled back at the sight of Proctor, and he said, "By God, if I can get just a few more Quakers to fight, we'll win this thing yet."

Greene, who was one of the "fighting Quakers" who'd joined the army at the beginning, laughed at Washington's quip as they went outside to continue discussing their plans.

Proctor watched them trail the chain of ghosts behind them. It would take a lot more than fighting men to turn the tide of the war.

He looked at the window and hoped Alex Walker came to find him sooner rather than later.

In the first good sign he'd had in a while, she didn't disappoint him. She showed up several mornings later, tapping at the door when everyone else had gone out to mess.

"Sorry," she said without any preface of greeting as she slipped inside. "I was just surprised to see you is all."

"There's more to it than that," he said.

She dipped her head and kept her eyes hidden by the brow of her hat. "I know you fought with the militia at Lexington and Concord, and I should've expected you'd volunteer after we abandoned The Farm. I'm glad to see you fighting for the cause of liberty too. My brothers want a free country, and I mean to help them. So I came by, 'cause . . . well, I hope you won't say nothing to none of the officers here, is all."

She finished, and when he didn't say anything right away, she peeked out from under the brim of her hat to check his response. She'd grown a couple of inches taller in the last year and a half, and her face had lost all its baby fat. It was longer, her cheekbones more pronounced. Still, he wondered how anyone could see her and take her for a boy.

"I won't say anything," he promised. "I'm glad to see you safe."

She shrugged. "We haven't been in any danger. A few skirmishes against backcountry Tories, but nothing of consequence."

"I meant what happened to your parents."

She tilted her head forward, so the brim of her hat hid her face again. "Did James say something to you about the Indians?"

It was Proctor's turn to be surprised. Remembering the tomahawk dangling in Bootzamon's hand, he said, "It wasn't Indians."

She tensed up, as if she couldn't decide whether to fight or run. He felt sorry for her, but he thought she needed to hear the truth, just to know the evil they were up against.

"They weren't Indians, no more than it was Indians who attacked us on The Farm summer before last." The assassins who came to kill Deborah's parents had been dressed as Indians, a poor disguise seen up close, but there were meant to be no survivors, only witnesses from a distance.

"I knew it," she said after a pause. "I tried to tell my brothers, but they wouldn't listen."

Proctor nodded. "I'm sorry."

Her head came up, her eyes narrowed, fierce and angry. She thumped the butt of her rifle hard on the floor "I knew it. There was a hiding spell on the house. We came home from a muster upvalley, and we couldn't find our own house until I found and broke the spell. It was primitive, something you or Deborah could have taken apart in minutes, but—"

"I was the one who made that spell."

The anger in her face widened into mistrust, and she took another step away from him. "Why were you there?"

"I was looking for you. You hadn't responded to any of our letters—"

"What letters?"

"Deborah had been writing you for months, asking you to return to The Farm. We needed—*we need*—your help."

Alex waved her hand in the air and Proctor froze, thinking it was part of some spell, but it was no more than a throwaway gesture. "My mother probably burned them. I told her I was done with the talent, done with Deborah and her kind. I want no more part of that world ever again."

"You can't just bury your talent," Proctor said.

"Can't I? It's a poison. It gets your family killed. Look what happened to Deborah. Look what they did to Magdalena." She looked at him suspiciously, taking a step toward him and raising her gun as if she meant to use it. "Did you bring the killers with you? Are my parents dead because of you?"

"No, they were dead when I arrived, looking for you." He quickly revised his idea of how much to tell her. Did he dare describe Bootzamon? "The assassin was waiting for you. He's from the Covenant. They're trying to kill everyone with the talent."

"All the more reason never to use it again," she said. Some of the anger drained out of her. "What happened?"

"He tried to kill me too, but I was able to . . ." He paused, choosing his words carefully. ". . . drive him away. Then I hid the house. I knew you could find it if you came back, but he couldn't. Alex, you can't mean what you said, about never using the talent again."

"I haven't used it since the fall before last except to break the spell that hid our house."

"But that's not natural." He thought about Abby, the young witch back at The Farm. "Doesn't the talent spill out at night? Don't you find yourself waking up, floating above your bed?"

"Sleepwalking is all it is," Alex answered. "And the night fear. Easy enough to understand after some of the cruelty and bloodshed I've been witness to."

"That explanation may answer to some, but I know you aren't fooled by it. The talent is rooted in our very blood, it's part of us. To deny your talent is to deny yourself."

"Sin is part of who we are, but we are taught to deny that."

"It's not the same," Proctor said.

"It's exactly the same. Suffer not a witch to live—it's right there in the holy book. God gives us the talent, but it's only a test. It's wrong to use it, and God punishes us when we do, killing our families, making us feel hunted. Don't you think all these men coming after witches are doing holy work?"

"Some of them are witches too," Proctor said. "They're doing it because they mean to kill or make slaves of us all, just like the Redcoats. We need your help to stop them."

She lifted her gun. "I can load and shoot this rifle as fast as any over-mountain man, and I can hit a target as small as a rabbit at three hundred yards better than two of my brothers. I'm doing my part for the war."

"That's not the kind of help we need. We have to break the curse. Unless we do, the American army is finished, and the cause of freedom is lost."

The wind kicked up outside, blowing through the cracks around the doors and windows. Proctor's skin goose-pimpled.

Alex walked over to the table and chair. She propped her rifle against the wall and sat down, burying her face in her hands. "The curse—are those the spirits I see around my brothers?"

Proctor scraped a chair across the floor, spun it around, and sat down across from her. "Yes."

"I guess that's why I came to see you." She looked up, her eyes full of tears. She took off her hat and pulled at a fistful of her short-cropped hair. "I've lost a lot of the sight by not using my talent. But I thought I could see . . . I don't know. Around my brothers. All the time."

"They're dead men, mostly dead soldiers. Their souls are shackled to every man who enlists in the army. They fill them with fear and drive them to desertion."

"My brothers are afraid of nothing and would never desert the cause once they decide to fight for it."

"Then they'll fit in with General Washington and the

men who've stayed with him. And the curse, unable to break their wills, will seek ways to find them dead. I'm sorry."

"Is this because of Deborah and her mother too?" Her words choked in her throat.

Proctor shook his head softly, and spoke softer still. "No, we're nothing to the Covenant. They would be doing this regardless. They want to keep the empire alive as a focus, allowing them to draw on the power of men around the globe, in order to cast their spells. They're killing anyone who might stand in their way. Any witch who doesn't join them is against them."

"Miss Cecily joined them," she said.

Proctor nodded.

"And Lydia too."

"No, not Lydia. She was Miss Cecily's slave in more ways than one, body and soul. She's forced to serve Miss Cecily in spirit, but Cecily also draws on Lydia's power, adding it to her own. That's the kind of thing the Covenant does, and it's wrong." It's what Deborah had done too. Had he forgiven her for that yet? Had she forgiven herself?

"Is that why you fight them?" Alex asked.

"As long as there's breath in my body," he said. "For that, and for what they did to Deborah's parents and yours. But everyone who serves them is slave to another. Cecily is bound to a German necromancer, the same way that Lydia is bound to her, and all her power flows into him. I am certain he's the one who set the curse."

"Can't we kill him and break it?"

Proctor thought about the time they'd faced him at Gravesend. He didn't think he was ready to face the German again, not yet. And there was another problem. "A curse outlives the witch who cast it. As long as its focus remains—a house or a family—the curse continues. From everything Deborah and I could tell, this curse was placed on the Continental army, and it will last until the army is gone. Or until we find a way to break it."

Alex seemed to shrink as they spoke. She looked like a young girl again, not even twenty, one who'd lost her parents and seen too many other people die violently and now faced the loss of even her brothers, the last friends and protectors she had in the world.

"I need your help to break the curse," Proctor said.

She shook her head. "I can't help you."

"We'll need a circle, as big as we can make it, to draw enough power to break this necromancer's power."

"And who do you have for this circle? You and me?"

"We'll go get Deborah." As he said it, he knew it was true. Alex had lost all confidence in her talent, and didn't want to use it. But with the three of them—with Deborah, frankly, since she was the most powerful of them—they might be able to draw enough talent to break the curse.

"You, me, and Deborah?" Alex said, with a snort of miserable laughter. "The three of us?"

Proctor leaned forward. The three of them might be able to do it. "Yes."

"That's no circle, it's a triangle. If this German necromancer has Cecily and Lydia and whoever else he has enslaved—I'm right in assuming he has other witches to draw on?"

"Yes," Proctor admitted weakly.

"Then the three of us can't draw enough power to break that. Cecily alone nearly killed us all."

"Alex, please—"

"No! It's foolish and plain wrong. I'm sorry I was ever drawn into this. I'm sorry for what happened to Deborah. But I won't use my talent again, not ever."

"Then there's nothing anyone can do to help your brothers," Proctor said.

Her eyes flashed anger at him. She opened her mouth to speak, but before she could say anything the door flew open. Alex instantly grabbed her hat and pulled it down over her head, hiding her face. She stood up and slammed her chair against the wall, grabbing her rifle.

The figure coming through the door scarcely seemed to notice. His long, intelligent face was worried, distracted. It was Tom Paine. "There you are."

Proctor stood, ending up beside Alex, who couldn't rush out the door until the other man moved. "It's good to see you again, friend. What can I do for you?"

"You've already done it," Paine said, approaching Proctor. Alex started to leave, but Proctor grabbed her arm and held her. "You found me the paper I needed to write my latest pamphlet. I've just come from Philadelphia, where, after more struggle than I expected, it's been typeset for printing. I could never have finished it if I hadn't written so much that first night. I felt a great spirit guiding my hand."

"I'm glad to have helped," Proctor said, holding on tight as Alex tried to pull her arm free without making a scene. "But you've already thanked me for that. You didn't need to come find me again."

Paine snapped his fingers as if trying to recall something. "It was your friend," he said. "That very pleasant young woman."

Proctor dropped Alex's arm and grabbed Paine's hand. "Deborah?"

"Yes, that's her name," he said. "I saw her in Philadelphia, in an upholstery shop of all places."

Deborah was still alive. Thank God. "Is she well?"

"She is, and she asked about you, or I would never have recognized her."

"Where is she?"

"John Ross's shop, on Mulberry Street, between Second and Third, close to the waterfront. His wife Betsy is a Friend, but also a friend to liberty, like you." Paine turned toward the door. "I have to go report to General Greene. Philadelphia is ready to quit the fight, if we don't do something to change their hearts at once. But I wanted to find you and let you know Deborah was well and asking after you."

"You've done me a greater favor than you know," Proctor said.

"As you did for me," Paine replied. He dashed out the door as fast as he'd entered it, forgetting to close it as he left.

Alex stood there rubbing her arm. "You didn't have to hold me so tight," she said.

"I'm sorry," he said. It felt like the only thing he had said to her since she arrived.

"You were very worried about Deborah," Alex said. "You didn't even know where she was."

"No, I didn't," he admitted.

"Do you think she can break the curse on my brothers? I don't want to see them hurt by this. They're all the family I have left."

"If anyone can help them, it's Deborah."

"She'll have to do it without me," Alex said. "I'll go with you to find her, but I won't touch the talent again, not for anything."

"Not even if it touches you?"

She didn't answer that.

Proctor looked out the window at the sky. They could travel for a couple of hours yet tonight, be halfway there by morning. He grabbed his bag from under the table and slung it over his shoulder. "Do you need to tell your brothers that you're going?"

"If I do, they won't let me go," she said. "Not without explaining, and I don't think I want to explain the curse to them. So the sooner we leave, the better."

He nodded. "If you meet me at the edge of camp, just past the smithy, in half an hour's time, I'll have supplies and a horse. Can you ride double?"

"If you've got a horse that will carry us," she said. "If

you don't, I've walked a few hundred miles already. I can walk a few more."

"It might come to that," he admitted. Two horses would be impossible, and even one might be difficult. It made him wish for Singer, who'd been so indefatigable on the trip to Virginia and whom he'd left behind in Massachusetts.

Looking either direction to make sure she wasn't seen, Alex stepped out the door and dodged behind the next house. Proctor watched to make sure she was headed in the right direction before he followed her.

The air was cold and dry on his lungs as he stepped outside, and he squinted against the bite of the wind and the brightness of the sun on the snow. He stopped by stores and talked the quartermaster's aide into giving him a few extra measures of biscuit and salted meat. "We're short of couriers, so we're taking important letters to Philadelphia."

"What about the regular couriers?" the quartermaster asked. "They just left this morning."

"It's a critical letter, and can't wait until tomorrow," Proctor said. He was thinking about a spell he might use to persuade the quartermaster's aide, but the man recognized his face from Washington's headquarters and served out the supplies.

He stopped at the stable, hoping for similar results. "I've got letters to—"

"That's the mount over there," the stable boy said as he shoveled the stall. "Don't push it too hard and it'll be fine."

The horse was clearly intended for someone else, but Proctor didn't stop to explain. Instead he moved quickly, before the other rider showed or the stable boy realized he wasn't the right courier. It didn't matter what the other man's message was: Proctor's mission was more vital to the success of the army, even if no one knew it.

Leading the horse out of the stable, he swung into the saddle and directed it around to one of the back streets. A new group of carriages and wagons waited on the main road, visible between the houses. One of the horses was a sturdy bay, reminding him again of Singer. Even the way the horse tossed her head and looked smartly around was similar. But it was only a trick of desire, seeing what he wanted to see.

He leaned forward and patted the heavy gelding on its neck. This was the horse he had, and it was big enough and strong enough to carry two of them to Philadelphia, which was all they needed. Although he hoped to reach Alex unseen, luck brought Colonel Tilghman hurrying down the street just as Proctor passed. Tilghman, recognizing Proctor, waved him to stop.

Proctor briefly flirted with the notion of riding past Tilghman as if he didn't see him, but the officer stepped into the road to block his progress.

"Yes?" Proctor said.

"You're lucky I caught you," Tilghman said, tilting his head up and shielding his face from the wind with a gloved hand. "Some fellow just stopped by headquarters looking for you. I told him you were around. I didn't realize you were leaving."

He must've meant Paine, although Proctor was sure Tilghman should recognize Paine. "He already found me," Proctor said.

Tilghman looked puzzled, as if this wasn't possible. He checked over his shoulder at headquarters, expecting to see Paine there perhaps, and then let it go. "Ah, good," he said. "Where are you headed?"

No reason to lie. He'd be back soon enough, if it all worked out. "To Philadelphia. Someone saw my sister there, and I mean to go see how she's doing."

"Of course," Tilghman said. Even the officers and enlisted men took leave to see their families. "We'll see you soon."

"As fast as I can return," he promised.

Alex waited for him behind the smithy, just as they had planned. She had her arms wrapped tight around herself, looking small and cold. "What took you so long?" she asked.

"Someone was looking for me," Proctor said. He pulled her up in front of him. They set out on the hard mud of the frozen road at a pace the horse could keep for hours.

Chapter 23

After a short night's camp, they continued their ride across the snowy landscape. Alex sat in front of Proctor, with her rifle resting across her legs. She'd held herself rigid, not daring to lean too much into him, despite the bitter cold. Proctor passed the miles by thinking about Deborah and how it would be good to see her for Christmas.

He and Alex approached Philadelphia from the north, passing through rich farmland until at last they saw chimneys rise like row on row of cornstalks, from rooftops spread out like a furrowed field alongside the broad, deep waters of the Delaware River. Proctor thought Boston and New York were big cities, but Philadelphia looked twice as big as either.

"They say forty thousand people live there," Proctor said.

"It's wrong," Alex answered.

"They've got to live somewhere, I suppose."

"No, not the number," she said. "See how few of the chimneys are in use."

She was right. Though thousands of chimneys rose into the sky, smoke rose from fewer than half. It was late December, with snow on the ground, and the air below freezing for days. What house would not keep a fire going?

As they passed through the outskirts and into the city, the answer became obvious. Empty houses did not require fires. Up and down the streets they roamed, with every other house boarded up. Whole streets appeared to be abandoned. In the houses that were occupied, faces peered out and, seeing Alex's rifle, disappeared again. A few men moved here and there through the streets, but when Proctor called out to them, they hurried away.

"What do they fear?" Alex asked.

"You'd think the British army was one street over," Proctor said. "Not a state away."

They made their way into the center of the city. Proctor finally spied the offices of a printer. A man stood out front, smoking his pipe and watching the street.

"Can I buy a paper?" Proctor called.

"None for sale," the man said. "No one wants to be held to account when Cornwallis comes marching down the street tomorrow or the day after."

"The British army will never reach these streets," Proctor said.

The man blew out a ring of smoke, then stepped inside his door and locked it.

"Where's Mulberry Street?" Proctor yelled. The man pulled his curtains shut.

Eventually, they identified Second and Third Streets, and made their way inward from the docks until they came to Mulberry. There was one upholstery shop on the street, advertised only by the wares in the window. It was a bandbox house, one in a row of similar buildings, two windows wide and winding upward several narrow stories. The windows weren't boarded up, which was promising. The store was in the front of the first floor: whoever worked here lived in the back half of the house and on the upper floors. He hoped they could lead him to Deborah, tell him where she had gone.

They dismounted, and Proctor tied the horse up out front. The bell hanging above the door rang as they entered.

"Hello," Proctor called. He heard voices in the back.

The showroom was crowded with goods. In the window

and on the shelves near the front were stacked items no one could afford to purchase during wartime—curtains, umbrellas, Venetian blinds. On the worktable at the back of the room were spread a variety of more practical items: folded tents, blankets, and cartridges, all for the army. Strips of leftover cloth had been rolled for bandages. A pair of shears used for the work lay nearby.

A door opened into the private quarters at the back of the building. The voices of two women came through the doorway, but only one woman entered the showroom as the other stopped short.

The second woman withdrew into the shadows of the back room, but Proctor recognized her at once. His skin tingled all over as he felt her draw power to defend herself. It rolled through the room like heat lightning across a stormy sky, and then went still again, shut off.

"Deborah?"

She didn't answer, but the shopkeeper, a pleasant young woman with dark hair and a quick smile, turned and looked back. If she wanted direction, she must have received it.

"You must be mistaken," the shopkeeper said. "There's no one named Deborah here."

"Deborah Walcott," Proctor said. "She's a friend, and more than a friend."

The shopkeeper hesitated, then put on a false smile. "If anyone comes by with that name, whom shall I say came calling?"

"Proctor Brown," Proctor said. Paine had told him that Deborah was asking after him, so why was she hiding? "But she saw me, and knows me by sight."

Alex took off her hat and shook the snow out of her auburn hair. "Tell her that Alexandra Walker was here also."

Deborah appeared in the doorway at the sound of Alex's voice, and then rushed forward, wrapping her arms around the younger woman. She kissed her cheeks, saying, "Alex, praise the Light. I feared you were dead."

So that's how it was, then, Proctor thought. He was as good as dead to Deborah. She would rush out to embrace Alex, but she would hide from him. Her eyes met his, and she looked away at the floor.

"So these are friends of yours?" the shopkeeper said.

"They are," Deborah said. She took a ribbon from her pocket and circled Proctor and Alex, whirling it around them, saying, "The God of my rock, in Him will we trust. He is our shield, and the horn of our salvation, our high tower, and our refuge, our savior, who savest us from violence."

Proctor could not say which of his senses had been touched, but he felt a numbness, like the kind that happened to a foot that had fallen asleep. Alex felt it too. "What did you just do?" she asked.

"Agents of the Covenant are here in Philadelphia, searching for women with the talent. I just created a shield that will keep them from sensing your presence, the way I sensed it when you walked through the door."

"I feel like there's a layer of oilcloth between my body and the world," Proctor said. "It's . . . odd."

"I don't like it," Alex grumbled.

"The sensation will fade," Deborah promised. "And it keeps us hidden, and protects our hostess from unjust retribution for coming to our aid. Proctor, Alex, may I introduce you to my dear friend Betsy. She and her husband, John Ross, own this shop."

Betsy's head swiveled from Proctor to Deborah and back again. "*This* is the young man you were just telling me about?" she asked.

Deborah blushed, confusing Proctor.

Before he could sort that out, Alex asked another of the questions that was on his mind. "Why were you hiding from us?"

Deborah reached out and squeezed Alex's hand. "I'm sorry. It was because I thought you were a soldier, yet you did not carry the curse, and yet you had the talent—"

Proctor cleared his throat.

"No, it's all right," Deborah said. "Betsy's family have long been guides on the Quaker Highway. She knows everything."

"Samuel and Becky Griscom, my parents," Betsy said. "There were seventeen children. With so many people in the house, no one noticed when an extra person or two stayed with us a day or two passing through."

"She knows Magdalena," Deborah said.

Betsy nodded. "She stayed with us for a night over a year ago, on her way from Lancaster to Salem. I hope she's well."

"I haven't heard from her lately," Proctor said. "The last we saw her, she was teaching the students that Deborah left behind."

The mention of her students touched a raw nerve for Deborah, who seemed eager to change the subject. "When I saw you with a witch disguised as a soldier, I thought it was someone from the Covenant, come to find me at last."

"What did you think, that they'd made a slave of me, without me knowing?"

She flinched. The accusation cut deeper than he intended, hitting another, rawer nerve. "They've been spreading panic among the leaders of the rebellion," she said.

"Another curse?" Proctor asked.

"There are not enough tormented souls to spare," she said, still refusing to meet his eyes. "But the effect is very similar. Someone has been moving through the city, casting seeds of fear among the leading men. From there it spreads like a fever, leaping house-to-house upon each street, even though we are yet far from the front lines of the war."

"I am lucky that Deborah came to us when she did," Betsy said. "She was able to protect our shop."

"You must say nothing to her husband, John, when he returns," Deborah said. "He knows nothing of the talent."

"Is he not a Friend?" Proctor asked.

"He is not," Betsy said. "He was raised in the Church of England. We were apprenticed together, in Webster's upholstery shop. We fell in love and married against the wishes of our families."

Proctor's respect for Betsy increased. Few people were that brave, and fewer still prospered after, with the judgment of the community against them. "Do you ever regret your decision?" he asked.

"Not once, not even for a second," she said. "We've been happy together, and have done good work. He is serving with the militia now, readying the city against a possible attack. He only knows that Deborah is an old friend of my family."

"I was lucky that Betsy recalled the code of the highway," Deborah said.

Shadows paused outside the shop's display window, a group of three or four—a man and wife, perhaps a servant and child. Proctor, seeing them, said, "Maybe we should continue this conversation in back, in case someone enters."

"Business has been slow," Betsy admitted. "I'd be grateful for any sale."

"We'll stay out of your way," Proctor said.

Deborah chivvied Proctor and Alex into the back room while Betsy went to answer the bell at the door. Muted voices came from the front room. Another table, also covered with work, crowded the back room, along with a pair of chairs. The tight space forced Proctor and Deborah to stand near each other. He hadn't been this close to her in weeks. For the moment, it was as though they stood alone.

"I'm sorry," Deborah said softly. She blinked back tears. "What I did was wrong. No circumstance excuses it."

He found his breath taken from him. "You don't have to ask for my forgiveness."

"No, but I do need to earn it. I have to find a way to make things right."

Make things right? She'd been gone for weeks, without sending any word to him. "You can't make things right by running away."

"I'm not running away." She turned to the table and picked up a piece of fabric. "I've been looking for other ways to defeat the Covenant."

"You plan to distract them with brightly colored bits of cloth while the rest of us sneak up and bang them on the head?"

She scowled at him. "No, I was thinking about the things we'd talked about, how the Covenant wants to use the empire, King George himself, as a focus for their magic. In America, we have no such focus for the common power. We all identify each with our separate states. Every state has a different leader, a different capital, a different flag."

"We have the grand union flag," he said.

"Yes, and it includes the Union Jack. As if we've never let go of Britain. Think about it, Proctor. Even with the Continental Congress, we all look to our local representative, not the body as a whole. Our national focus is divided, and that makes us more vulnerable to the curse."

Deborah could be so smart. "There's the Declaration of Independence," Proctor offered. "We all shared in that."

"We did," Deborah said. "And we shared in Tom Paine's *Common Sense*. Those words united us as a people. But it's not enough; those two things have passed."

"There's Paine's new pamphlet," Proctor said.

Deborah nodded eagerly, as if he understood now. "I opened the floodgates and let the full measure of my power flow into Paine as he wrote that first page. I couldn't help myself, not with his . . . guardian angel lending her hand. Only later did I consider the possible benefits of it. But I doubt that any soldiers will stop to read his words during the smoke and slash of battle, and that's when their course is most easily changed by the spectral riders at their reins."

He saw the point she was driving toward. "There needs to be a simple focus, a symbol that all men share."

"Yes," Deborah answered, holding up a piece of cloth with red and white stripes, and stars on a field of blue. "Then I met Betsy and she was working on a banner for the Pennsylvania navy—"

"Uh," Alex said, conveying a world of panic with that single syllable. She stood in the doorway, peering into the front room. A muffled squeal of fear came from Betsy as Alex turned to run, her eyes as big as silver dollars.

Proctor and Deborah leapt forward together, pinning Alex between them and carrying her into the doorway, where they all froze.

In the front room, Betsy was bound by strips of cloth, hands tied to her sides, ankles wound together, mouth gagged.

That would have been remarkable by itself, but she also floated a full foot above the floor, the toes of her shoes dangling, stretching for something to touch.

Yet what made her squeal through the gag were the shears. The pointed ends floated in midair an inch from her eyes, scissoring open and shut.

Across from Betsy stood a petite blond woman, wearing a silk dress worth more than a farm. The glee written on her face at Betsy's fear and discomfort chilled Proctor like the coldest wind. Cecily Sumpter Pinckney. Behind her stood Jolly, Lydia, and the orphan boy.

"You," growled Deborah.

Cecily stepped back, startled. Her expression flashed from glee to fury, as though there was little difference between the two. Betsy collapsed against the floor. Cecily flicked her fingertips, and the shears flew at Deborah's face.

Proctor snatched them out of the air, clicking them shut in his fist. There was no magic involved, just his reflexes.

Deborah drew on her talent, flinging items at Cecily the way she'd flung stones at the barn. Folded curtains flew across the room, rolls of cloth unfurled in the air, and a set of Venetian blinds clattered as they came at Cecily from every direction.

Cecily passed her arm across her body, and the items all flew back at the doorway where Deborah and Proctor stood, the heavy fabric pelting them. The blinds smacked Proctor across the face, and when he shook off the stars and saw clearly again, yards of cloth were swirling around Deborah, binding her tightly.

He lunged forward with the point of the shears, slashing down through the fabric. Long curtains lifted off the floor, winding around her, pinning her arms to her sides, and covering her mouth. He desperately tried to pull them off, just enough for Deborah to speak, to cast a spell, but his hand had no more than touched the fabric when knuckles crashed into his jaw, knocking him to the floor.

"Sometimes the older ways work best," said Jolly's rough voice.

Proctor rolled over, dazed. Jolly's huge fist lashed out at him again. Proctor rolled to the side to dodge it, and the blow glanced off his ear. Then he felt fingers in his hair, and knuckles crashed into his temple several times until everything went black.

Proctor woke up choking, a huge knot of cloth shoved in his mouth and tied so tightly his jaws ached. He tried to reach up to pull it out and found his hands tied to his waist. He attempted to stand before he realized his ankles were bound. Spots swam before his eyes, and he crashed back against the wall, panting through his nose.

A body pressed against him. Deborah. He glimpsed Betsy just beyond her. The three of them were propped against the wall in the front room of the shop like so much merchandise.

As his vision cleared, he noticed the other four people in the room. Cecily sat primly on a chair in front of them, her lace gloves folded on her lap. Her face wore the façade they had grown to accept as fact when she'd been part of their group at The Farm, a particular closemouthed smile that Proctor now realized signaled neither happiness nor agreement, nor necessarily anything pleasant at all.

Behind Cecily stood Lydia, the lean, weathered slave who had served her for so many years. She wore a checked dress meant more for summer than winter, with no more than a thin shawl on top of it to keep her warm. A forlorn boy of nine or ten, his face as sad as an empty bowl, leaned against Lydia's hip. He rubbed a thumb across his lower lip like a much younger child. The orphan Revere had sent them to find on Long Island, William Reed. Lydia rested a hand on his untidy hair.

Lydia had helped Proctor on The Farm, introducing him to magic that no one else would teach him. She'd even tried to warn him about Cecily.

But Cecily had grown in power during the past year. Lydia and the orphan stood passively at her side, their faces emptied of passion and volition. Behind the dead surface of Lydia's eyes, Proctor thought he glimpsed something furtive, like the flight of birds in a cage.

Over at the door, peering out the window, was the man who'd punched Proctor: Jolly. He'd come dressed as an Indian to The Farm to assassinate them; on Long Island, he had dressed in the colors of the Loyalist rangers who served King George; now he wore a buff coat with gold trim like a gentleman.

Cecily stared at Proctor. "I confess I find myself surprised," she said in her slow southern accent, "that someone of your unusual and remarkable talents would not even attempt to use them to preserve yourself, much less protect your especial lady friend."

Proctor lurched forward, meaning to lash out, but the bonds immobilized him even without the benefit of magic. He strained until sweat formed on his brow, then fell back against the wall.

Cecily laughed, a high tinkling sound, genuine as her smile, as though he'd made a hilarious jest. Tilting her head over her shoulder, addressing Lydia without actually looking at her, she said, "Doesn't that just go to show? You can take the boy off the farm, but you can't scrape the farm off the boy."

He didn't care if Cecily was a lady, he'd scrape her off his boots given a chance. He just doubted he'd get one.

Cecily inclined her head toward Deborah with similar condescension. "And you—if you had only drawn on him, the two of you might have been as powerful as me," she said, opening her palm toward Lydia and the orphan boy. Lydia's eyes revealed a present will, but it moved within tight constraints. The boy had a dreamy look about him, a ship unmoored from the world.

Jolly stepped away from the door. "Let's just kill them and get it over with. I don't like it here."

"Don't be in such a careless hurry, my dear man," Cecily said. "You wouldn't butcher a cow just because you were tired of milking it. I believe these two can be useful to me, in the same way that I am useful to our master."

There was an edge to her voice at the end of her sentence. Though she enslaved others, she didn't want to be treated like a slave by anyone. She was much like some of the southern officers in the Continental army in that respect, Proctor thought. Not that those thoughts helped him.

He shook his head. How muzzy were his thoughts? Cecily had said *these two*—did that mean Alex had escaped in the confusion? Should he expect help or just be glad of her escape? The latter, he decided at once. There was nothing Alex could do alone against this witch and her assassin.

"Let's just kill her then," Jolly said, jerking his head toward Betsy.

"Is killing your answer to everything?" Cecily asked. "We'll have a hard time making it look like the work of Indians here in Philadelphia."

He grunted in complaint but not in contradiction.

"A simple spell of forgetting will render her harmless to our purposes," Cecily said, rising. "But these others may yet serve me, willingly or not. Fetch the carriage around to the front."

"Yes, ma'am," he said, relieved to finally take some action. He opened the door to the shop.

A rifle cracked outside, and Jolly was thrown back against the wall, bleeding from his chest.

That stupid Alex, Proctor thought. She hadn't run.

Cecily shrieked, a sound of fear mixed with fury. She grabbed Lydia and the orphan by the shoulders and moved them in front of her, blocking the door.

Jolly pressed his fist into the bloody hole in his chest, kicking his way back from the door, leaving a smear of blood across the floorboards. "God damn it," he said between clenched teeth and short, sharp breaths. "God damn it."

Deborah had rolled over onto her knees and crawled toward the back room. Proctor reached out with bound hands and grabbed Betsy by the shoulder, tugging her toward the door. She'd been paralyzed with fear, like a climber stuck at some precarious height, but the moment Proctor started her in motion, she understood his intent and moved as fast as she could.

It wasn't fast enough, not for any of them.

A charge shot through Proctor's skin, like someone pulling on all his hairs at once and locking him in place. A muffled gasp from Deborah meant she'd felt the same thing. Only Betsy continued to crawl.

Cecily chanted in some foreign language Proctor didn't recognize. It was not French or German or Dutch or any of the other tongues he'd heard in Boston among the docks, but he didn't care for the sound of it. To judge by the way Lydia went rigid and clutched the boy in front of her, neither did she. Cecily's voice rose, until it sounded like a chorus of voices.

Golden light filled the room, not the gold of jewelry but a polluted radiant yellow streaked with brown. Proctor's head spun dizzily, and his vision blurred. He thought he saw the light swirling through the air, flowing like sewer streams across a muddy street. Lines poured out of Lydia, the boy, Deborah, and himself, and flowed into Cecily.

Whatever she was doing, Proctor had no desire to help her, willingly or not. He lifted his bound hands through the light flowing from him, trying to wrap it like a loose rope around his wrists and wind it back to himself.

Cecily shrieked and slapped her hand in his direction. The invisible blow hit him, throwing him back against the wall, and the flow of power from him increased.

"Attack me!" she screamed at the door. "I defy you to show your face and challenge me!"

Shapes moved outside the window, a body of people, close together, crossing the street. Maybe it hadn't been Alex at all. Maybe it had been the local militia—Betsy's husband, on his way home, had seen what happened and called for aid. Jolly saw them through the open doorway and rolled over in a last effort to escape. As he turned, he gasped in agony, and blood poured out of his mouth and his chest. He collapsed on the floor and lay, eyes open, perfectly still.

Cecily took no notice of him. She coiled power into her like a whip, ready to lash out.

The faces moved up the steps, and into the doorway.

Feet scuffed over the stone steps, and a shadow passed in front of the door. Proctor gritted his teeth, ready to try to attack Cecily again the moment she lashed out at her attackers.

The foremost shadow entered the room and immediately shrank in size. It was a small old woman in a gray dress and a white cap. She walked with a cane.

"Magdalena?" Cecily said, surprised.

Chapter 24

The other witches from The Farm filed into the room behind Magdalena. The old sailor Ezra and the hardy farm girl Abby stood on one side. The two cousins, storklike Sukey and short, doughy Esther, stood on the other. The five were linked together, forming an open circle. Their faces revealed a mixture of terror and determination.

Alex trailed in behind them. Her rifle was aimed over their shoulders, at Cecily's head. Cecily flinched from the rifle, backing away as she gathered words for a spell.

Magdalena, however, began speaking the moment she came through the door. "Oh, Lord, fight against them that fight against me. Take hold of shield and buckler, and stand up for mine help."

Proctor felt the surge of power through their circle, more powerful than anything they had ever done before. The walls of the building shook as in a high wind, and Proctor's ears popped. He longed to add his own talent to theirs. For a second he thought he might wrest it free from Cecily, but then he felt her yank it back to herself. With a sweep of her arm, she flung every item in the room—curtains, blinds, chairs, shears.

At the very least he expected it to break their focus, to see one or more of them fall, perhaps stricken by the chair. But they stood their ground and everything bounced off them as harmlessly as rain off a roof.

"You have no power over us," Magdalena said. She leaned on her cane for support, looking frail and old. Ezra stood at her side and supported the arm that held the cane. Advancing like martyrs into flames, they held hands and surrounded Cecily. Esther trembled and averted her eyes as she stepped over Jolly's corpse.

Cecily grabbed Lydia and the orphan boy by the shoulders, using them as a shield.

"You're being foolish," Cecily said. "You have no idea of my master's power."

"I doubt sincerely that it is greater than the power of the Lord God," Magdalena said. "There is still time for you to repent the evil that you've done. Let the two of them go and surrender, and I promise that no harm will come to you."

Cecily laughed, a mad sound.

"We can protect you if you repent of your deeds," Magdalena said.

"Don't let her," Alex said, stepping forward. She pulled back the hammer on her rifle.

Anger flashed over Magdalena's face, and she reached up to push Alex's rifle aside. The effort threw her off-balance, but it would not have been enough to tip her over if Cecily had not chosen that moment to act.

Cecily made a grabbing motion in the air, and Jolly's body slid across the floor. The deadweight of his boots hit Magdalena's legs, knocking her over. Ezra and Abby collided as they tried to catch her, and all three fell down. Alex's gun went off into the ceiling, knocking loose a spray of plaster.

With her hand on Lydia's collar, Cecily leapt for the rear door. Proctor, still unable to touch his talent, thrust out his long legs into the mass of Cecily's thick skirts.

She tripped and fell.

Deborah threw her body across Cecily, trying to pin her to the floor. Ezra was still tangled up with Magdalena. Abby leaned over them, trying to haul them up by their collars. Sukey and Esther held hands, chanting a shield spell that protected them from Cecily's magic. Sukey spoke it loud and clear, and Esther echoed her timidly, half a word behind.

Proctor wiggled across the floor to help Deborah pin Cecily. But before he could reach them, Cecily shoved Deborah aside and retreated to the corner of the room.

"Lydia, William," Cecily shrieked. "Come to me now!"

Lydia defied her. Although it was only four or five steps, her powerful legs struggled like someone making way against a headwind. When she reached the shelter of the cousins' spell, she collapsed to the floor, gasping in relief.

But the orphan boy, in a dream world all this time, seemed panicked. He ran to the only person he knew, to the woman who called for him, to Cecily.

She removed a knife from her dress and held it at his throat. The tip of the blade cut his skin, but he didn't seem to notice. Cecily petted his hair, and he rubbed his thumb against his lips, staring at the others in fright. The pins and needles scattered on the floor around his feet trembled and rose into the air.

"Don't you dare hurt that boy," Lydia cried. She lunged forward with her arms outstretched. One step past the cousins, she left the protection of their spell. Cecily flung her against the wall, where she lay moaning, cradling an arm bent at an odd angle.

"You won't hurt that child," Magdalena said softly. She stood with her oak-knob cane held before her. Ezra and Abby stood tight at her back. Alex hid behind them.

"Will I not?" Cecily said with a smile, a forced smile, as false as all her others. She kept a shield in front of her: her magic could not touch the others, but theirs could not touch her either. "Do you even know what power the blood of an innocent holds in leash? I think all of you will clear a path to the door for me or I will spill his blood and we shall all see for ourselves."

Magdalena's mouth set, hard as mortar, in the old brick of her face.

Abby, who had many brothers and sisters, said, "You can't let her do that."

"Hush, child," Magdalena said. "It is bad enough that we had aught to do with the killing of her soldier. But a man who lives by the gun can fairly expect to die by one. We'll have naught to do with the death of an innocent child. Everyone clear the door for her."

They all stepped back, except for Abby. Magdalena rapped her on the ankle with her cane, and she stepped back too.

"See, we've cleared your way," Magdalena told Cecily. "But I think you will discover, once you're through the door, that there is no place for you to escape. So why don't you put down your knife?"

Cecily had thought through the same options. Without her driver, with only one witch-slave to draw power from, and surrounded by eight other witches, she had no real chance of escape. "You do not know my master. If I surrender, he shall see that harm comes to me as harvest comes to those who sow."

"Let us protect you," Magdalena said firmly.

Cecily had another option—an innocent's blood to spill. She murmured a spell under her breath. Her knuckles were white on the handle of the knife. When she reached the end of the spell, Proctor knew she meant to slit the boy's throat and use his power to slice through their shield like a cannonball shot through wooden ramparts, killing as many people in the room as she could.

Proctor struggled against his bonds, rising to his knees. He could ram her, roll into her, do something to distract her.

Only it was too late. Her lips stopped moving. Her eyes narrowed. She drew the knife back an inch to rip open the boy's throat.

The knife turned red hot in her hand.

She screamed and flung the knife away, but the lace cuff of her sleeve had caught fire. She clawed at it, trying to tear it off or beat out the flames.

Zoe—little Zoe, Captain Mak's daughter—rushed in from the back room. The orphan boy was the same size, the same age as she was. She wrapped her arms around him and dragged him back through the doorway. Betsy Ross, untied and on her feet, covered both of them protectively and hurried them out of harm's way.

Proctor didn't think he would lecture Zoe for using her fire talent in the house, not this time.

However, they were not safe yet. The smell of burned fabric and scorched flesh filled the room along with Cecily's shrieks. She flailed her arm around, in danger of setting the curtains or the walls aflame.

Ezra grabbed her by the waist and slapped at the fire. "A pitcher, get a pitcher, or a bucket!"

Proctor and Deborah struggled against their bonds, unable to help. Sukey and Esther were doing a dance of panic, trying to hide behind each other. Alex helped Magdalena to the doorway, hoping to force the old woman to escape.

But Abby, like any girl who'd grown up on a farm and seen the damage done by fire, knew the danger. She bolted up the steps, looking for the bath pitcher. She returned seconds later with a pot and poured it on Cecily's arm. It doused the flames enough for Ezra to throw Cecily to the ground and beat them out.

"My God, girl, the stink," he said.

Abby set the chamber pot on the floor. "It was all I could find."

"Bind her mouth at once," Magdalena ordered.

"She's hurt bad," Ezra said, trying to hold Cecily, who rolled around on the floor, weeping. "She needs care."

"We'll set to healing her as soon as we're certain she can't hurt us," Magdalena said.

Abby handed Ezra strips of cloth, the leftover bandages that had been scattered on the floor. He gagged her mouth and then started tearing off her burned sleeve.

Alex came over to Proctor. She pulled out a hunting knife with a blade as big as her forearm and sawed through his bonds. "C'mon," she said. "The easy part's done. Now we have to break the curse and save Washington's army."

He pulled the gag off his mouth. "Is that all?"

An hour later, as darkness fell, the shop looked, except for its occupants, as though nothing unusual had happened.

The cousins took on the task of cleaning up, putting back every item that wasn't broken, torn, or ruined. Abby scrubbed the floor clean of any sign of bloodshed and burning.

Ezra had rolled Jolly's body up in yards of canvas and was sewing the canvas shut. "I don't have any cannonballs to put in the sack," he said. "But these bricks from out back ought to do the job just as well, sink him straight down to the bottom of the river."

Magdalena saw to the healing. She set Lydia's broken collarbone and applied salves to Cecily's burned arm. Cecily sat, gagged and tied to a chair, in the corner of the room. Alex hid Cecily's carriage in the alley behind the shop, and then stood sentry at the front window in case anyone came out of the deserted city to investigate.

Betsy served hot coffee and cold food to everyone, while Zoe tried to play with William, the orphan boy, who was back in his dream world again. That left Proctor and Deborah with little to do. They sat next to each other, rubbing circulation back into their limbs.

"I owe you an apology," Deborah said to Magdalena. The others continued to work as though they'd heard nothing, including the old Dutch woman. "Truly, Magdalena, I must beg your forgiveness."

"You must do nothing of the sort," Magdalena said brusquely. The situation clearly embarrassed her.

"No, I must," Deborah insisted. "I thought myself more fit to teach our students than you were. But in a year of instruction, I was never able to get us to work together as well or powerfully as you did just now."

Magdalena wrapped a poultice around Cecily's burned arm, ignoring the woman's whimpers. She stopped just long enough to wave a finger at Deborah. "You must instruct each woman to do her best, not to do *your* best. You cannot develop *their* talents if you want them all to have *your* talents."

She slapped the next wet bandage on Cecily's arm, drawing a yelp of pain behind the gag. Everyone else in the room, including Proctor, held their breath, waiting for Deborah to snap. But Deborah only bowed her head and accepted the rebuke. When Proctor finally breathed in again, he felt that all the other witches had done the same.

"What I don't understand is how you knew to come here," Deborah asked Magdalena after the silence.

"He's the one you ought to ask," the old woman replied, indicating Proctor.

"You?" Deborah said, turning toward him.

"After the fall of Fort Lee, I knew we needed help," Proctor said. "So I wrote a letter to Paul Revere. I'm glad he was able to deliver the message. I wasn't sure it would make it."

Magdalena tied off a bandage around Cecily's burned hand. "I could not let these evil Hexen hurt any more people."

Sukey looked down her long, narrow nose at Proctor. "When Magdalena asked Ezra to accompany her, Esther and I decided that we were not about to be left behind. Were we, dear?"

"Oh, no, we weren't," said Esther, her jowls shaking in

affirmation. She indicated Abby and Zoe with a wave of her chubby hand. "We *all* came."

Proctor sipped the scalding-hot coffee. "That's why we started the school, isn't it? So we would have good witches trained to defeat the sorcery of the Covenant."

"Yes, but . . . ," Deborah said, although she seemed unsure how she intended to finish.

"We arrived in your camp the same day you left for Philadelphia," Ezra said to Proctor. "Must have just missed you. Your officer, Tilghman I think, he told us where you were going, and we followed you here."

The other conversations, the other work, had stopped. Zoe's voice broke the silence, coming through the doorway to the back room.

"Ip dip dip, my fast ship, sailing on the water, like a cup and saucer."

There was a hard *thump* as she bounced a small ball on the floor and then a boy's laughter as he tried to snatch up stone jacks.

Proctor could see Deborah digest all of this. "So you've seen the curse?" Deborah asked Magdalena.

The old woman nodded grimly. "It is a worse necromancy than the one that woman attempted on us. I have never seen the kind. It is an abomination."

"Do you know a way to break the curse without bringing harm to the men who carry the weight of it?" Deborah asked.

Before the old woman could answer, Proctor said, "Should we have this conversation where Cecily can hear it?"

"She's not going anywhere she can betray us, lad," Ezra said. "Nor do I care to be carting her around the house like a bale of silk."

Cecily struggled against her gag, trying desperately to speak. Magdalena studied her thoughtfully, then indicated that she should be allowed to speak. Ezra reached down and pulled the knot in her mouth aside.

"Allow me to listen," Cecily said, panting, spitting out words between winces of pain. "Please—I can help you if I know what you plan to do."

Magdalena turned her head toward Deborah as the two, together, appeared to consider this offer of aid. But Proctor looked to Lydia, who was stiff and stony-faced. She would never speak up, but her reaction was unmistakable.

"No word comes out of that woman's mouth that isn't a lie," he said. "We don't dare trust her, even if she has no way to speak to her master."

He took Cecily's chair in his hands and spun it around to face the wall. "Please," Cecily begged. "I know I can help you. Just give me a chance to prove myself."

She continued to beg as he picked up a bandage and tore it in half, wadding up two small strips to plug her ears. As he reached down to stuff the first ear, he saw more clearly the jewels that dangled from her lobes. What he had taken for pearls were tiny heads carved of marble or maybe alabaster. They reminded him of the skulls fashioned from lead balls he had used in the battle of Bunker Hill. Reaching out on impulse, he took an earring in his hand to remove it before plugging her ear.

"Please," she begged. "You must trust me—No!"

As soon as he touched the earring, she twisted her head around to bite him. She fastened on to the soft skin between thumb and forefinger, thrashing her head back and forth and drawing blood.

"What—?" Ezra said, hesitating, then grabbing her head.

Proctor shoved his free hand in the corner of her mouth, prying her jaws open. He jerked his hand free, squeezing one of the bandages over it to stop the bleeding. Ezra shoved the gag back into Cecily's mouth, knotting it tighter. She thrashed back and forth, trying to kick away from the wall. When Proctor reached for the earrings again, she thrashed until Ezra held her still. Proctor removed the earrings and Cecily sobbed, even more than she had at her burns.

The earrings were warm in Proctor's hands, holding light inside their translucent forms. Now that he examined them closely, he could see the heads were one each, a man and woman, both with their hair pulled back. The ears were etched grotesquely large. As the gems sat in his palm, the light inside them faded. They turned from pearlescent white to a cold, dull gray.

"What are they?" Deborah asked.

Proctor poured them into her cupped hand. "That's for you to discover. Some sorcery of her master's. Whatever they are, or were, I care not for them."

He stuffed cloth strips into Cecily's ears. Her chin fell onto her chest, and she sobbed through her gag.

"There's a pantry in the kitchen," Betsy said. "Perhaps we could shut her inside it."

Proctor was relieved at the suggestion. He expected someone to protest, but no one did, so he quickly asked Ezra to help lift her chair. They carried her sobbing into the kitchen. The cupboards were already bare. Her chair fit neatly inside, and the shut door muffled her cries.

"The streets are empty outside," Alex said at the window.

"Perhaps I should be giving the soldier a proper burial then," Ezra said, pointing to the shrouded body on the floor. "We're but a couple of blocks from the docks, and it'd be best to do it soon. With this cold in the air, the river could freeze over solid."

"Give me a moment and I'll help you," Proctor said.

"I'll help him," Alex said. "You can stay here."

"Are you sure?"

"I'll lend an extra hand," Abby offered. "Won't be the first burying I've helped with, and I'd just as soon have

Mister Jolly's body out of here." The look she exchanged with Alex indicated that the latter had told her what had happened to the bodies of Jolly's fellow assassins when Cecily's necromancy raised them from the burial plot on The Farm to kill Deborah's mother.

"Let me run and fetch her carriage," Alex said.

She ran out the door. Ezra and Abby picked up either end of the shroud and dragged it to the entrance. The girl might have been the stronger of the two.

"We'll go upstairs," Sukey said, covering a yawn. Together she and Esther supported Lydia up the narrow stairs. That left Zoe and the little boy by the fire nibbling at honeyed bread. Betsy went to the children and said, "Come with me. We'll find a warm room for you to sleep in tonight."

"C'mon," Zoe said to the boy. She made eye contact with Proctor as they stood. He gave her a slight nod. They had saved him, just as they'd promised. Zoe winked back as she put her arm around the boy's shoulders and led him after Betsy.

"A remarkable girl," Proctor said.

"Hrm," Magdalena responded. Proctor suspected that she'd been frustrated beyond endurance by Captain Mak's independent daughter. It gave him his first smile, however small, since Cecily's appearance.

"You have a plan?" Deborah asked the two of them, lowering her voice to a whisper.

"Not a plan, but a thought," Magdalena said. "It's the opposite of a baby at childbirth. That soul is trying to enter this world so it can enter the body, and sometimes a gate has to be opened to coax that soul inside. But these spirits, with the soldiers, they're trapped in this world against their own nature. If we open up a gate for them, they'll be able to continue on their way."

"It would take all of us in a circle to open that wide a gate," Deborah said.

"Then it's good that all of us are here, yah?" Magdalena replied.

For the first time in almost two months, since their attempt on All Hallows' Eve, Proctor felt truly hopeful. They might really be able to break the curse. "Can we do it tonight?" he asked. "The sooner it's done, the better."

Magdalena shook her head. "No, we will have to be much closer to the spirits. Not to all of them, but to most."

"So we'll return to the army's camp on the Delaware River," Deborah said.

"Yes," Proctor said, feeling a little of the hope drain out of him. "But that doesn't give us much time. Tomorrow is Christmas. It may be the last time all the men are gathered together. Their enlistments are up in another week and most of them are likely to resign, especially with the weight of the curse on them. It'll take us all day to ride back to the camp."

"We can't travel on Christmas Day," Sukey protested, holding a thin hand over her shocked and incredulous heart. "It's disrespectful to our Lord. One more day of waiting won't make a difference. We simply can't—no, we won't—travel on a holy day, will we, Esther dear?"

Esther opened her trembling mouth to agree, just as she always did, and then her chin stopped trembling and her face took on a serious expression Proctor had never seen before.

"Yes, we will," she said.

"See!" Sukey crowed triumphantly. "It's just like I . . . *What?*"

"If a lamb falls into a pit on the Sabbath, you pull it out," Esther said. "Our good Lord said that it is lawful to do good on the Sabbath, and if our army needs saving on Christmas Day, then we must save them."

"Well, I never," Sukey snapped.

"Perhaps it's time you should," Esther said. "If the army

will be gathered tomorrow for Christmas, then we should go to them tomorrow."

"If we leave before dawn," Proctor said, "then we should reach them just after nightfall. It could be our last chance. On the day after Christmas, I think many of them will consider their enlistments up and depart." They were going to do it—they had rescued Lydia and the boy, and they were going to break the curse. "Let us all get what rest we can tonight."

Deborah frowned anxiously. "Should we wait?"

"We all need the rest," Proctor said.

"But if *that woman* is in the city," she answered, indicating the pantry where they had locked up Cecily, "can Bootzamon or the widow Nance be far behind? How can we be sure they won't attack us here tonight? Especially once their master realizes we broke the spell of her earrings."

"Ezra and I will sleep downstairs and guard the doors," Proctor said. "It's the best we can do."

Ezra nodded confirmation. "I'll sleep by the pantry and make sure there's no mischief from that one." He put a hand on the knife in his belt. "I won't hesitate to take care of her if there is."

"We'll be more prepared tomorrow if we all rest well tonight," Proctor said.

Deborah glanced at him and replied with a small nod. Then she looked away, reaching up to make sure her hair was tucked in.

He didn't know how to read her expression. He couldn't tell whether things were better between them, or damaged irreparably.

"We should all go to bed now then," Magdalena said.

Ezra slept in the back room, and Proctor took the front. Hardly ideal sleeping conditions, but he'd faced worse.

He propped himself up against the front door with bolsters and rolls of cloth. Though he closed his eyes, he didn't expect to get much sleep. The air out of doors was bitter cold, and the wind prowled around the house like a fox outside a chicken coop, looking for a way inside. Before long the fire died, as if it too wished to settle under its blanket of coals and go to sleep. Proctor's breath frosted, and little claws of icy air scratched at him through the narrow cracks in the door. Ezra's rumbly snore echoed from the other room, which only made Proctor want to be alert enough for them both.

He wrapped his coat and blanket more tightly around himself and settled in for a long, discomfited night. His head was spinning too much for sleep anyway.

The Covenant's plan was to have a victory by the new year, when all the army's enlistments were up and the men went home. If the army was broken then, its spirit would be broken for good. That gave them mere days, barely a week, to undo the curse. If their first attempt wasn't successful, they wouldn't have much time to try again.

Every noise outside, every trick of the wind, made him jump. He knelt at the window, looking for shadows in the street, when he heard footsteps in the house.

Bootzamon could easily leap to the top floor and make his way inside through a window or a chimney or a vent in the attic. Proctor tightened his hand on his knife.

And then nothing. He had settled back against the door, cursing his too-active imagination, when he heard the footsteps again. Stocking feet padded gently and slowly down the stairs.

He rose to a crouch, ready to strike. Then Deborah peered around the corner, wrapped in a heavy blanket.

"I couldn't sleep," she said so quietly that not even Ezra could hear her, not over his own snoring.

"Neither can I," Proctor said. He settled down again, back against the door, sliding the knife under a blanket so she wouldn't be alarmed.

"It's going to be a cold night," she said.

"It is December," he replied, a bit inanely, but he couldn't think of anything else to say. She had a sleeping cap on, tied loosely, with her hair tumbling down from the back. She stood at the bottom of the stairs, framed by the doorway.

"Well, I just wanted to check, to be sure you were all right," she said. "I'd better go back upstairs and try to sleep."

She turned to go, but as she did, he held out his hand, saying, "Come here, Deborah. Please."

She dropped her eyes to the floor, avoiding his gaze, but turned and came at once. He held his blanket open, and she settled on the floor beside him. A quiet sigh racked her body, and then she leaned in close and rested her head on his shoulder. He settled his face on her head, smelling her hair. He folded his arm around her and pulled her close. She laid her hand on his chest.

"See, that's warmer," he said.

"I've missed you so much," she said. The words were spoken over his, her mouth pressed against his body. He felt them as much as he heard them, like a deep ache that had been growing for a long time, finally pushing to the surface.

"I've been right here, the whole time," he said.

"That's not what I mean."

"What do you mean?"

She lifted her head, eyes closed, lips parted, and kissed him, wrapping her arms around his neck to pull him close. It was long and deep and satisfying, like nothing he'd ever done before. When they stopped to take a breath, they were both panting. They swallowed one gulp of air apiece, then kissed again. He didn't want it to ever stop.

Her fingers crawled across his chest, deftly unbuttoning his shirt. She slipped her hand inside, sliding it over his bare skin.

He reached out and moved the bolsters, placing them behind her, and began to undo the stays of her nightshirt. He was eager to go forward, but too aware of the irrevocable change it would mean. His hand faltered.

"What will Magdalena think?" he whispered. "Or the others?"

She pushed his shirt half off and leaned up to kiss the scar across his neck, where the musket ball might have killed him. Her mouth traced it hungrily, hot against his skin. Then she rolled up his sleeves and, taking his arm in her hand, kissed the scars on his forearms, where the widow had tried to use him as a sacrifice for her spell.

"I've been a fool to care," she said, pressing his scarred arm to her cheek. "I don't believe they could think any less of me than they already do."

"You're still a fool," he said. But he nudged her nightdress off her shoulder and kissed his way across her collarbone to her throat.

Her fingers combed through his hair, grabbed hold, pulled him tighter and lower.

He pushed her gently back onto the pillows and, for a little while, forgot that there was anyone or anything in the world but the two of them.

They woke, curled on the floor, Deborah inside Proctor's arms. It was still dark outside.

A cough sounded. Proctor, groggy, realized it was the second cough: the first one had woken them both. He lifted his head. Magdalena stood at the bottom of the stairs, just at the corner, without entering the room.

"We need to leave soon," she said, her voice cast low. Deborah tensed at the sound, pulling the blankets over her head.

"Yes, ma'am," Proctor answered. He braced himself for her righteous anger, but a second later, without saying another word, she turned and slowly climbed the stairs.

Her footsteps had scarcely reached the top landing when Deborah threw off the blanket and frantically began to dress. Proctor watched her, a dumb grin on his face—he could tell by the way his cheeks hurt from it—and worry in his heart.

"Deborah, we have to—" He stopped, unsure what they had to do. What church would marry them? Who would stand in for their families to approve?

"Don't just sit there." She glared at him, the same old, familiar Deborah, and he grinned again.

The cold began to settle on him, though, so he pulled on his own layers of clothes, never taking his eyes off her. In the back room, Ezra's snoring had stopped. There was a bump as he rolled over. Deborah tossed the blankets in a panic.

"What do you need?" Proctor said as he buttoned his shirt.

"My cap," she said.

He found it tucked inside one of his pant legs and tossed it to her.

"Everything all right out there?" Ezra said, thumping to his feet.

"All's well," Proctor answered as Deborah slipped her cap on and turned to go up the stairs. He snatched at the hem of her skirt, and she turned back, the habitual short temper on her face melting when she saw him. She bent to give him another quick kiss, then darted up the steps.

Ezra stomped over to the doorway and saw the mess of blankets and pillows scattered about as Proctor pulled on his shoes.

"Christ, lad, you look like you tossed all night," the old sailor said. "You must be exhausted."

"On the contrary," Proctor said. "I don't think I've ever slept better."

Chapter 25

Betsy was up to see them off before dawn. "Are you sure you have to travel today?" she said. "Never mind that it's Christmas Day—the wind outside makes it fit for neither man nor beast."

"We must break this curse as soon as possible," Deborah said. "It's the only thing that matters now if we mean to defeat the Covenant and preserve our independence."

When she saw that they could not be dissuaded, Betsy embraced her. "Thank you for your help in my shop."

"Thank you for your advice," Deborah said. "You were right. About a lot of things."

"I'm so happy to hear that," Betsy said, grinning. She handed a rolled bundle of striped fabric to Deborah. "Here is the flag we were working on. Will you deliver it to General Washington?"

"I will see that it's delivered," she promised. She turned and handed it to Proctor.

"The flag," he asked.

"No Union Jack in this one," she said. "Thirteen stripes for the thirteen states, just like before. But Betsy added stars on a field of blue. In a circle."

Proctor's thoughts went to a witch's circle. But Betsy, who was eavesdropping, said, "A circle, because a circle is unbroken."

Proctor smiled and tied the rolled bundle to his horse.

They made an odd parade on a bitter Christmas morning. Cecily's carriage was a calash, pulled by one horse. It had four seats covered by a folding fabric roof. It would be the only cover any of them had in the cold, so Magdalena, Sukey, and Esther claimed three of the seats. Zoe and William were to squeeze between their legs on the floor. Ezra would take the driver's bench.

The farm wagon, pulled by Singer, was open with only a driver's seat. Proctor was happy to see the horse again. She immediately nuzzled his hand for treats.

Abby and Alex agreed to drive the wagon. They had discovered that, growing up on farms with several brothers, they had many stories to trade. Cecily was bound and wrapped in blankets in the back of the wagon.

"It's better than she deserves," Alex said. "And we can keep an eye on her there."

Deborah approached Cecily. "It will look odd for such a fine lady to be seen in the back of a wagon," she said. She wrapped a ragged scarf around Cecily's head, and touched her finger at the corner of her eye to make it droop. She said a spell and created the illusion of an old hag. "But no one will look twice at a vagrant given a ride on Christmas Day."

Cecily's eyes burned with hate. Proctor thought they completed the bitter-old-hag illusion perfectly.

Deborah waved a ribbon around Cecily and repeated the verse about God as their shield. "And if your master does send anyone for you, that will keep them from seeing your spark."

The hate in Cecily's eyes turned to despair.

"You must take the fourth seat in the carriage," Deborah told Lydia. "Given your injury, it will be best for you."

"This is nothing," Lydia said. "Not after the way you and Miss Magdalena did your medicine on me. But I'm not letting Cecily out of my sight. That woman is plain evil. She's done evil to me, and done evil to those children, and I plan to keep an eye on her until she can't do nobody no harm no more."

So it was settled. Deborah took the last seat in the calash and Lydia sat in the front of the wagon, across from Cecily, just like a guard on a prisoner. Proctor rode the horse that he had borrowed from the army, and they all set out through the deserted streets of Philadelphia in the hour before dawn. They left the city and took the country road north for the long, tedious ride through the bitter, lip-cracking, finger-numbing cold.

By midday the children were bored and restless, and Magdalena chased them out of the carriage. At first they rode on the bench with Ezra, then they ran up and rode on the bench with Abby and Alex. And then Zoe insisted that Proctor let them take turns riding on the horse with him.

It was late in the day, and they were passing through woods. The trees shielded them from the wind, but the parade moved slowly. Cecily's horse and Proctor's mount were both played out. Cecily's horse was worse, and the carriage had fallen a way behind. Only Singer had any bounce left in her step.

Zoe sat in front of Proctor, with his coat wrapped around her. "This has been about the best Christmas ever," she said wistfully.

Proctor laughed, though the cold made his lips split to do it. "How can you say that?"

"Usually it's a bunch of us sitting around, listening to boring sermons and singing boring songs." She grinned. "This has been interesting."

He grinned back at her.

William sat on the wagon, squeezed between Alex and Abigail. "Zoe, I'm freezing," he said. His teeth were chattering.

"Here, I'll take you both back to the carriage," Proctor said, leading his horse over to the wagon. Cecily glared at him, but her disguise as an old hag made her almost pitiful. Proctor stretched out his arm and William clung to it, clambering onto the horse, which staggered under the extra weight, near spent. Singer tossed her head, showing off that she could pull all night.

Proctor walked the horse back to the calash. Inside, the women huddled in blankets, Sukey and Esther sitting opposite Magdalena and Deborah. They scooted aside to let the children squeeze in between their legs. Esther reached down to rub their shoulders.

Deborah unwrapped the scarf from her face. "How much farther is it?" she asked.

Proctor pointed to smoke rising, black just beyond the trees. "Over there, I'd say. Less than a mile. Do we have a plan?"

"We have a spell," Deborah said.

"If we can hold enough power, it should work," Sukey said. The tip of her long nose was turning blue from the cold, but she seemed too excited to notice. "We can hold that much power, don't you think, Esther dear?"

"We can do it," Esther said firmly.

Magdalena nodded in approval. "Deborah has formed a good spell. She learned much during these past few months."

"Proctor always had good suggestions," Deborah said. He felt a bit of pride that she would praise his talent. He'd had some good ideas when they were trying to break the curse.

Magdalena patted Deborah's knee with a gnarled, liver-spotted hand. "Not in magic," she said. "You have always had a gift for that. What you've learned these past few months is humility, how to trust the wisdom of others."

Proctor held his breath, expecting Deborah to explode the way she would have six months before. Instead, she lowered her eyes and murmured, "I think that's what I said."

Magdalena snorted, either in disbelief or laughter. Proctor turned his horse away before anything else could be said—compliments from Deborah would never come much better than that, and he wanted to enjoy it for a moment.

"Hey," Ezra said. He sat steady on the seat of the calash as it bounced over the frozen roads. "If we're so close to the army's camp, why aren't we raising any sails on the horizon?"

"Because there's no ocean and no ships?" He was still feeling light-headedly hopeful.

Ezra frowned in reply. "You know what I mean. There are no soldiers on the roads, no wagons, no horses."

The old sailor had a point, but Proctor wasn't convinced. "Maybe it's because it's Christmas?"

"Maybe it's because their Christmas present was, they all went home? What if there's no more army to save?" He licked his lips nervously and rubbed his chin. "Whatever it is, something don't feel watertight to me."

Proctor looked ahead at the smoke. There were maybe one or two fires going, but not a camp of two thousand men. Noticing that worried him too.

"Pick up the speed," he said, kicking his horse to the lead.

Singer lurched forward, yanking the wagon along, and the calash rattled after. They covered the last mile in the darkness, finding nothing they expected—no sentries, no songs, nothing.

They entered the camp only to find it empty. The tent flaps hung open, the horses were gone, even the equipment and artillery were missing. The fires had burned down to coals.

"You're too late," crowed a harsh voice.

Proctor wheeled his horse. A veteran in a worn uniform sat in the doorway of a tent with a whiskey jug at his side, a pamphlet in his hand, and the bloody-bandaged stump of an amputated leg propped up on a stool. His face twitched at invisible twinges of pain—invisible unless you could see the sadistic ghost of a backcountry Loyalist, dead from some wasting disease, as he danced around the soldier and stabbed him repeatedly with his hunting knife. Every time the spirit blade pierced a joint or muscle, the ghost cackled in delight.

The sight was extraordinarily unsettling, but not as much as the empty camp. If the army had been dispersed, it would be impossible to break the curse on all of them. "Have they been sent home?" Proctor asked, dismounting from his horse.

"Home?" The man laughed, his unshaven face broken by another wince. "No, son—they've gone to take back Trenton from the Hessians."

Trenton? So Washington was crossing the Delaware . . .

"Where is everyone?" Deborah asked, hopping from the calash before it came to a complete stop. Behind her, the children's eyes were wide as they stared at the veteran and his ghost. William started to say something—it was possible he hadn't been around cursed American soldiers until now—but Esther shushed him and held the children back with her big arms.

"The army is making a surprise attack on the Hessians in Trenton," Proctor explained. His head was spinning. Washington must know that if he didn't do anything, the remaining bulk of his army would disperse in the next few days as their enlistments ended, and then the war would be lost. If he attacked Trenton, and they were beaten, the war would probably still be lost, so they'd be no worse off. But if they attacked Trenton and won . . .

Men would be inspired. Most would reenlist. The Revolution would still have a chance. Proctor took Deborah aside. "We have to break this curse *right now*," he said. "To give the army an even chance in the attack."

Deborah nodded. "Where can we set up?"

Proctor turned back to the wounded soldier. "We've been riding all day in the cold. Where can we stretch our legs and warm up?"

"Take your pick of the fires," he said. "We ain't got no particular use for them tonight."

"We'll use that fire over there," Deborah said, pointing to a muddy spot trampled out of the snow in the middle of the camp. She turned to the wagon. "We won't find a better focus than the camp where they've been living. Magdalena, will you set up our circle around that fire?"

The old woman nodded and climbed stiffly out of the carriage. "Sukey, you'll help me," she said.

"Ezra," Deborah said. "Gather wood and build up the flame."

"There's a pile over thataway," the old soldier suggested, pointing the way between some tents.

"Abby, can you lend a hand?" Ezra asked.

"Of course," she said, and Alex added, "I'll come too," and the three of them took off. Lydia climbed out of the farm cart, and stood guard over Cecily.

"You—" the soldier said to Proctor, pointing to the retreating form of Alex, "and that other young fellow might still catch up with the troops if you hurry. They've just gone a few miles upriver to the ferry."

Proctor nodded absently. "Maybe after we get the women settled and, um, say our Christmas prayers."

"Isn't it a bit late for that?" the soldier said, twitching as the ghost stabbed his amputated leg another time.

"Not yet, but it will be if we don't hurry quick," Proctor said.

Magdalena, hobbling along on her cane, directed Sukey as she poured out a circle of salt around the fire. Inside the circle, she built a star, with the fire at its center. The wood gatherers returned and, stepping carefully over the lines, built up the flame in the center. Then, at Magdalena's direction, they built smaller fires, in the place of candles, at each point of the star. Deborah walked around the circle and lit them from her fingertips.

"Hey," the soldier said to Proctor. "How'd she strike that fire so fast?"

"She keeps her tinder dry," Proctor said. "Can I help you inside—?"

But the soldier grabbed a nearby crutch and pushed himself up off his stool for a better look, spilling his pamphlet onto the ground. Proctor picked it up, intending to hand it back to the soldier, but as the soldier hopped toward the fire, Proctor shoved the folded pamphlet into his back pocket and moved to stop the other man.

"You don't need that many fires," the soldier said, nervously, angrily. He looked worried about the flames spreading to the camp. "One will keep you just as warm."

His ghost, aware that the witches could see him, inflicted cruel wounds against the other man's spirit. Deborah had looked up at him in annoyance, but, seeing the ghost twist its knife into the man's shoulder and elbow, her expression changed to one of compassion.

Reaching out her hand, she grabbed the ghost by the wrist—its eyes went wide—and held its blade short. You could see the soldier's face relax as pain he expected to come, didn't. The ghost tried to pull away in fear of her.

"I am a healer," Deborah said quietly. "If you let me see to my sisters, and friends, that we may warm ourselves, and say a prayer for the army on this Christmas night, I will come to you afterward and see if I can ease your pain."

The soldier nodded numbly and, with a shiver, turned back to his tent.

Deborah held on to the ghost. It struggled to get away from her, to return to the soldier it was bound to, but she held tightly to its wrist. With her other hand, she took hold of the spectral knife; pulling slowly, like toffee, she separated the spirit blade from the spirit. She held it for a second, and then it faded away like mist in the sun.

She released the ghost, but now it was the one who trem-

bled and twitched. It held up its hands to placate her, retreating at once to the side of the soldier.

"How did you—?" Proctor started to ask.

"Come, we'd best hurry," she said.

All the little fires were burning now. She placed Magdalena at one point of the star, then Sukey, Esther, Abby,
and Ezra at the others.

"Where do you want me?" Proctor asked.

"At my side," Deborah said. "I expect some of the spirits, freed from their hosts, may try to attack us. As we complete the circle, I want you to stay at my right hand as my
shield."

"And do what if they come?" he asked.

"Whatever you must do to gain me time to finish," she
said.

Proctor nodded and quickly scanned the camp. The two
children stood with Lydia, over by the cart. Alex stood
with them, her rifle over her shoulder. The soldier sat in his
tent nearby. They would have to help him remember things
differently once they were done.

"We're going to do a very similar prayer to the one that
Proctor and I tried on All Hallows' Eve," Deborah said.
"But this time, as I chant each line of the prayer, I want all
of you to recite the phrase from Exodus, *Let my people go*.
Are we ready?"

"I'm no Moses, ma'am, meaning no offense," Ezra said.
"Are you sure that's the chorus we ought to be reciting?"

"Are you an American, Ezra?" Deborah asked.

"Rhode Islander by birth," he said.

"This war—not only our war for independence, but the
war the Covenant makes on us to prevent it—means we are
all one people now. Americans are your people. We—not
me, not our group here, but all of us, Americans—we need
you to recite that chorus and mean it. Can you do that?"

Proctor didn't expect the old sailor to agree so easily, but
her tone brought out in him the ship-born habit of obedi-

ence. He ducked his head and touched his brow, saying, "Yes, ma'am, when you put it that way, my duty couldn't be clearer. Let my people go, just like in Exodus."

"Good," Deborah said. "Then we're ready."

Or as ready as they were likely to be. Proctor checked over his shoulder to see if the ghosts were already attacking him.

Deborah began to pace counterclockwise around the circle.

"Wherewith ye there hunt the souls to make them fly, and I will tear them from your arms, and will let the souls go, even the souls that ye hunt to make them fly," she said.

"Let my people go," came the response.

"Because with lies ye have made the hearts of the righteous sad, whom I have not made sad; and have strengthened the hands of the wicked, that he should not return from his wicked way."

"Let my people go."

Something was happening. Proctor could feel the invisible flow of power as Deborah paced around the circle, connecting all the witches together.

"Therefore ye shall see no more suffering, for in the name of the Lord, I will deliver my people out of your hand."

"Let my people go."

The fires crackled, flames leaping up, and spit out showers of sparks. A hole, but a hole made of light instead of darkness, formed in the air above the circle. The soldier's ghost clung to him now, desperate and afraid. But as Deborah began reciting the spell again, it stretched out, drawn toward the light. The more that it was drawn, the more furiously it fought to stay behind.

"Let my people go."

Sweat formed on Deborah's brow as she concentrated, focusing all the power of the witches in the circle through her. Other spirits were drawn to the light now, lines as thin as shooting stars across the sky, pulled from miles away.

"I need more power," Deborah whispered to Proctor between repetitions of the verse.

Proctor looked around frantically. He waved Alex over. "We need you in the circle," he said. "We need your power."

She shook her head, afraid, watching the flow of spirits, stretched out like snakes, toward the hole in the sky. "I can't . . . I won't . . ."

"I will," Lydia said. Her arm was in a sling, and a threadbare blanket was all that covered a thin dress made for southern climes. Her breath frosted the air as she spoke.

"Follow me," Deborah said, and she continued the circle, chanting the next verse again.

Proctor felt the power flow through him, into Deborah. More and more ghosts appeared above them, stretched thin across the sky, but still tethered to the living soldiers miles away. The ghost with them in the camp thrashed and flailed like a child throwing a tantrum, clinging desperately to the soldier with the amputated leg. The soldier stood up with his crutch and moved away from the fires, back toward the wagons.

The spell was working. A power resisted them—the German himself perhaps, as if he was nearby, just across the river. But Proctor knew they could break through it with a final push. "Alex, please?" he begged.

She took a step away, afraid, and shook her head.

Remembering the way the widow Nance had drawn on Deborah, he realized they had an untapped source of talent. "We can draw on Cecily," he whispered.

Deborah missed a step. ". . . will let the souls go, even the souls that ye hunt . . ."

Lydia firmly said, "No."

And the power faltered. The ghosts pulled back, held by

the power of the German's magic to this world until the curse was fulfilled.

"Let my people . . . ," said the chorus of voices, but there was doubt in their words, and the unity fell apart before they completed the verse.

"That woman made a slave of me," Lydia said, "but that does not give us any right to make a slave of her in turn, and I will not be part of that."

Deborah nodded at once. There was justice in Lydia's argument. They would not win against evil if they were unjust.

"One more time," Proctor said. "We can do it."

He'd been holding back, afraid to let go with Deborah because of what she'd done to him before, but this time he opened the floodgates and poured everything he had into her. She started the circle again, trailed by Proctor and Lydia; she started the spell, and this time when the chorus came back, it came with power, and everyone pushed their talent through her.

The ghosts all surged toward the light again. Proctor pushed harder. Deborah, instead of trying to hold his power and control it, let go, opening up so that it flowed straight through her.

". . . go!"

The ghost in the camp peeled loose from the soldier and flowed into the light like water spiraling down a drain. A keening cry built to a crescendo and then he was gone. The fires in the circle flared and sparked.

A grin splashed across Proctor's face, and all the witches cheered. At that instant, their focus broke, the hole blinked out of existence, and all the other ghosts stretching toward it snapped back to their living hosts miles away.

Deborah turned around and threw herself into Proctor's arms. He hugged her back, reveling in the smell and feel of her body against his, amazed at her power and talent. Now, even more than their night together at Betsy Ross's house, he knew that things were finally right between them, the way they were meant to be.

"We must finish this now," Magdalena said, pounding her cane in the ground. "One is not enough when there are thousands."

Deborah stepped away from Proctor and nodded. "We're very close. I just need one more element to my focus—what's this?"

She grabbed the pamphlet from Proctor's back pocket. As she held it open, he saw the title that Deborah had noticed. It was Paine's new essay, *The American Crisis*. She read the first line. "*These are the times that try men's souls* . . . He has no idea how true that is."

"I bet Washington had all the men read this before they marched tonight," Proctor said. "That's why he ordered up copies from Philadelphia."

"A focus of our own, against the Covenant."

"Now," Magdalena said. She had directed Ezra to feed wood to the fires, to keep them going strong.

Deborah held up the pamphlet. "I think I have what we need right here—"

A child's scream interrupted them.

The soldier lay sprawled on the ground at the back of the cart. It was empty, and Cecily was gone. William and Zoe knelt beside him.

But that was not the vise that squeezed Proctor's heart.

Bootzamon stood at the edge of the camp. He had watched the end of the curse-breaking, the release of the trapped soul. The scream and the sight of everyone turning toward him seemed to snap him to his senses. As Proctor watched in horror, the scarecrow covered the distance to the children in a single leap. He scooped them up, one under each arm. "I've got the young ones," he cried. "Find the master's pretty."

His sentence was addressed to the widow Nance, who

emerged from one tent and entered another. "She's already gone."

A rifle cracked.

Alex stood with her gun at her shoulder, smoke trailing from the barrel. The ball smashed through Nance, doing no more harm than a piece of hail in a bag of straw.

Nance turned on Alex, but before she could call up the first flame, Deborah attacked. As she ran toward the widow, her hands plucked at the air, unmaking the widow where she stood. Straw stuffing flew out of a pucker in Nance's dress and scattered every direction, while invisible hands tugged off her gloves and pulled the wooden bones out of her sleeves. The widow screeched, but her empty sleeves flapped loose when she tried a counterconjure.

"There're too many of them," Bootzamon said. The children under his arm screamed and struggled.

"Proctor!" Zoe yelled.

Proctor was already running toward them, but the scarecrow-man turned and jumped twenty feet at a step. At the edge of the camp, Bootzamon turned and yelled at Nance, "We have what we came for—run!"

Nance slithered from side to side in a desperate attempt to dodge Deborah's magic. She was a near-empty bag of clothes with a feedsack skull, shrunken and brown, more snake-like than anything. With a shrill scream of fury, she turned and fled after Bootzamon.

Proctor untethered his horse and mounted. The other witches ran toward him. Ezra lurched from one direction to another, dazed. "It happened so fast," he said. "God almighty, what am I going to tell Captain Mak?"

"You'll tell him how we rescued his daughter," Proctor said. "Deborah?"

Her fists were clenched. "I'll take them both apart. I'll take them both apart piece by piece."

"Leave that to me," he said. "You need to break the curse."

She hesitated. "What? We can't do it without your talent."

"You have to," he said. "If I have to face the German, I'll need him to be distracted. It's the only thing that will give me a chance."

He didn't say *a chance to live,* but he and Deborah were looking directly at each other, and she saw the meaning of his words.

"Go," she said. She held her hand to her heart, as if to keep it from splitting. "We'll break the curse, I promise."

Chapter 26

Proctor kicked the horse hard and took off after Bootzamon and Nance. They followed a trail through the forest,
and he chased them recklessly. The moon was full, the skies
clear, but the trees blocked the light, turning everything
into a webwork of gray. He leaned close to the animal's
neck, his hand resting on the pulse in its throat. He willed
it the courage to make blind leaps and drove it to keep running until froth flecked its mouth and its energy flagged.
Two dark figures dashed through the trees ahead of him.

"More," Proctor whispered to the horse. "Give me a little more." The horse bent its head and struggled, spit flying
from its mouth as it strained. Branches tore against Proctor's face and legs, and he prayed. The figures appeared
again, much closer.

And then they plunged out of the trees into an open field.
The horse stumbled and fell, giving Proctor just enough
time to leap free. He rolled over the frozen furrows and
came to his feet bruised and stunned. Bootzamon and
Nance had crossed the field to the river's edge. Moonlight
reflected off the snow, giving details an eerie blue clarity.
The lights of Trenton burned faintly on the far shore. The
falls of the Delaware, an eight-foot drop over gray boul-
ders, rumbled in the night.

"Proctor!" Zoe screamed. Immediately she started beating the scarecrow's arms, trying to tear him apart with her
hands.

Bootzamon turned back and stared at Proctor. Proctor

saw through the illusion to the gourd face, which was incapable of showing emotion. And yet this one seemed to register surprise.

"Mein Gott, I have never seen such a relentless mortal."

"You forget our master," the widow Nance said. She danced in her near-empty clothes like a snake about to strike. With a hiss, she turned and slid onto the river. Near the falls, the water was choked with chunks of thin ice lodged among the rocks.

"Too true," Bootzamon said. The little boy hung limply, his thumb rubbing his lip, too afraid to respond. But Zoe redoubled her fury, trying to set the scarecrow on fire. He tightened his grip on her, saying something in another language. She grimaced in pain and her flames sputtered out.

Proctor stumbled across the field toward them. "Drop her now."

"You're welcome to follow us if you wish," Bootzamon said. The cockfeather on his hat bobbed as he bowed his head. As Proctor lunged for him, he turned and jumped out onto the ice, leaping from block to floe, rock to rock, crossing to the other side. Proctor stepped on the edge and broke through. Frozen water sloshed up to his ankles. There was no way he could follow.

But there was a ferry a few miles upriver. Where the army was crossing. He turned and ran back to the horse. It lifted its head at his approach, but its chest was still heaving as it tried to catch its breath.

Proctor laid a hand on the neck and, after a moment, it started to breathe easier. But there was no way it would rise or run again tonight. He would have to walk.

"There you are, thank God."

He looked up at the voice. It was Alex, riding bareback on Singer, her rifle across her legs.

"I followed as fast as I could," she said. "Where are they?"

He pointed to the distant lights of Trenton. "Across the river. I couldn't stop them."

"Then we have to follow," she said. Singer stamped and circled, ready to go. Proctor began untying a roll of cloth from the other horse's back. "What's that?"

"Betsy's flag," he said, rising with the bundle in his arm. "If the army is crossing, they've got the ferries and every boat on this part of the river. We'll need something to get to Washington so we can talk our way across. This is it."

Alex offered him a hand, and he climbed onto Singer. The horse braced herself against the extra weight, but she was sturdy and could carry them both a short way. Her hooves kicked up snow behind her as she headed north along the river.

A few dark miles later, they found the army. A sentry stopped them, but Proctor said, "Message for General Washington," and they were waved on through.

It was eerily quiet despite the chaos. Horses and artillery had been loaded onto a ferryboat, which struggled, almost capsizing, as it moved away from shore. The current slung the boat downriver and banged chunks of ice at its sides until the guide ropes snapped taut. Without a word, crews on the distant shore began to slowly pull it across.

Proctor and Alex rode past the ferry landing. Along the riverbank shadowy lines of men waited to crowd into several Durham boats, heavy craft meant for shipping ironwork up and down the river. Farther on, they saw other boats, some larger, some smaller. The scene reminded Proctor of the armada that evacuated the army from Brooklyn only a few months before. The mood on the shore tonight was no less desperate. That there were only a tenth as many men in the army now, and that they were going toward battle rather than away, amplified rather than diminished the feeling.

The ghosts they carried had much to do with that. As Proctor and Alex rode along the bank, faces glanced at them then turned grimly back to the task of crossing. Not so the ghosts—they were agitated, some of them angry, cruelly stabbing, punching, or choking their hosts. These spectral faces, the same color as the moonlight, turned toward Proctor and Alex, showing glee in their torments.

"Do you see my brothers?" Alex asked.

"No, I don't," Proctor said. "Maybe they've already crossed the river."

"This is horrible," she whispered. "What can we do?"

"We have to trust Deborah," Proctor said. "She'll find a way to break the curse. But we have to cross and stop the German before he uses the children to do something worse." He shifted uncomfortably. "We need to find Washington, and fast." Raising his voice, he shouted, "Message for General Washington."

"Quiet," snapped one of the officers as he chivvied men into his boat. He was one of Smallwood's men, from Maryland. Proctor couldn't recall his name, but he recognized the one-eyed ghost that followed him around like a child hiding behind a tree. "The order's for silence."

Proctor dropped his voice. "We're looking for—"

"I heard," the man said, scowling. He waved his hand upriver and went back to work, packing men into the boat. Many of them still wore their summer jackets, which was all they had. A few had wrapped their feet in rags because they lacked shoes.

The little ghost stood behind the officer, following Proctor and Alex with his one good eye until they were out of sight.

Neither Zoe nor the boy William would end up like that, Proctor promised himself.

Another boat splashed into the water as Proctor and Alex rode past. The passage of so many ghosts across the river was starting to raise a fog, as it had at Brooklyn. A small crowd of men stood just ahead—Washington, surrounded by his young officers. They in turn were ringed by a crowd of ghosts.

The men, following Washington's lead, were outwardly stoic and calm, but the ghosts were frantic. They hurled themselves at their hosts, clawing at them with cold, spectral hands. The men were so numb with the frigid air, or so determined to see this through, that they didn't flinch.

Alex shuddered and averted her eyes. "Why isn't Deborah's prayer working?"

Proctor shook his head. Surely they had enough power to do the spell, even without him. Enough power to have some effect. But the only effect he saw was the wrath of the ghosts from the previous attempt.

Washington remained calmest among the men, at the center of the worst fury. The thirteen ghosts shackled to him tore at him, tearing at his clothes like a fierce wind. Washington ignored the distraction. He stood with his hands folded behind his back, watching the boats disappear into darkness and fog.

"Message for General Washington," Proctor said.

"It's our prodigal Quaker," Washington replied, looking up. "Tench asked if we had seen you."

Proctor dismounted with the rolled bundle. "A flag for you, sir, sent by Miss Betsy Ross of Philadelphia."

"Blankets would do the men better," Washington said.

"A blanket can warm one man, but the right flag can warm the hearts of the entire army." Proctor knew it sounded like enthusiasm, but he also knew it to be true. He unfolded the corner. "It's a new design, with thirteen stripes and thirteen stars on a field of blue, for the thirteen states."

After a pause, Washington nodded. A young officer— James Monroe, another Virginian—stepped forward and took the rolled banner from Proctor's hands.

"Make a note to convey our thanks to Missus Ross if the outcome tonight shows favor on those thirteen states,"

Washington told Monroe. Then to Proctor, "It ought to be no secret to you that we mean to fight tonight. If that offends your conscience, now is the moment you should turn back."

He had to get across the river if he had any hope at all of finding Zoe and William before the German necromancer performed some abomination with them. The memory of that little boy in Boston, the one murdered by the widow Nance for her spell, was strong in his mind. "I'll go along and do what I can, if you don't mind," Proctor said, glancing at Alex. "We both will. Just tell us who to report to, and what boat to take."

Before Washington could answer, a man ran up from the shore. "Excellency, sir," he said. "Most of the men have departed now. We'll need you on the other side."

Washington nodded, then he looked to Proctor and said, "Climb aboard then, if you're coming."

Proctor touched Alex's arm and said, "This is our chance."

Alex had dismounted from Singer, but she couldn't move away from her side. "I . . . I can't."

The ghosts. She'd seen the ghosts, and knew of the curse, but it was a different thing completely to be in the middle of thousands of specters, to see them whipped into frenzy, desperate to scare their hosts away. Anyone would run, which was why ninety percent of the army was gone.

The sailors were waving them aboard. It was a small boat, light enough to move quickly, but made to carry no more than a dozen men. Washington wouldn't wait while Proctor tried to persuade Alex to join them.

"I understand," he said. "Go back to the others, help them any way you can."

He clapped her on the shoulder and hurried to board the boat before Washington changed his mind. There was no way under heaven that he was leaving those children in the hands of Bootzamon and his necromancer master.

"So you're still around, are you?" said the man holding the boat steady on the shore. He was a black man with a round, intelligent face, wearing a tarpaulin seaman's jacket, and he spoke with a familiar Massachusetts accent—a sailor from Glover's Marblehead regiment. But Proctor couldn't place him. Seeing the puzzled look on Proctor's face, he said, "The passage from Salem port to Gravesend."

"That's it," Proctor said. "Only we stopped short of Gravesend and you rowed us ashore. Cuff, isn't it? From the *Bluejack*."

"That's right."

"It's good to see you again."

"You too. Grab an oar and pull, if you don't mind. These southern boys don't know how to handle themselves in the icy water."

"Glad to," Proctor said, and put his hands on the gunwales to climb into the boat.

The icy water was not just in the river. The boat was ankle-deep in it, and the air was cold enough to freeze. Proctor shivered as the water shot up his ankles and flowed down into his shoes. The other men in the boat crouched low and stomped, not just to break the ice, but to keep their sodden feet warm.

Proctor picked up an oar and braced the end against the shore, ready to push off. Cuff leaned against the boat and it lurched forward, throwing everyone in it off-balance. He shoved again and it slid over the icy mud of the bank toward the water. Before he could jump in, Alexandra ran down from the shore and splashed through the water. Surprised, Proctor reached out a hand to pull her aboard.

"Deborah would kill me if I let you out of my sight," she said before he could ask. The other men shifted aside to make room.

Proctor reached out and pulled in Cuff, who was now soaked to his thighs in the icy river water, but he didn't say a word of complaint. He bent low, rocking the boat from side to side as he made his way between the other crouching bodies to the front to help pole their way across.

Proctor glanced at the boat. Most of the men were attached to Washington's headquarters staff, but they represented a mix of the whole army. Captain Blackler and another private from the same Marblehead regiment as Cuff worked the oars. Lieutenant Monroe, from the Virginia regiment, carried the flag. Two other lieutenants, from Haslett's Delaware and Smallwood's Maryland regiments, were there, ready to convey Washington's orders to their commanders as soon as they landed: Washington relied on his Chesapeake troops to take the brunt of any fighting, and he liked to keep their junior officers close to hand. Backwoods Pennsylvania riflemen, like Alex's brothers, in hunting shirts and fur caps, sat at either end of the boat, pushing off ice and paddling. All of them carried ghosts with them, so many that they blurred together into a mist.

A pair of Jersey farmers, armed with shotguns, huddled under blanket coats, filling the last two spots in the boat. Proctor guessed that they were locals, men Washington had recruited to be his guides once they reached the far shore. One had his head bandaged, probably a knock to the skull in some recent skirmish with the Hessians. He was sick the instant the boat started to rock, leaning over the side to empty his stomach.

No, the farmer wasn't sick from the rocking of the boat—he felt the presence of the ghosts. The confines of the boat held more ghosts than men, and the fear they created was enough to set Proctor's teeth on edge. They were too mixed together to stay distinct, but when they brushed up against him, like a cat on the stairs in the dark, it made him feel that he was ready to tumble and break his neck, a feeling that washed through him every few seconds. At least he could see and recognize the cause. These other men could only sense it and blame their own cowardice. He glanced back at shore. Why hadn't Deborah and the others broken the spell yet? What was taking them so long?

Beside him, Alexandra's teeth chattered, and not just from the cold water. She felt it too, and felt it worse because she hadn't had months to grow accustomed to it.

"Give me your oar," she said. "I need something to do."

He handed it to her and turned to crouch behind Washington and Monroe, who hunkered low against the wind in the center of the boat. Proctor looked out across the water. The rising fog obscured the moonlight, and the black water absorbed the rest, so that they were surrounded by darkness. A steady wind, bitter and frosty, pushed them backward.

Alex grunted, pulling on the oar against the current and the wind. They were slowly moving across the river.

Suddenly the wind turned into a storm. Sheets of sleet hurtled out of the sky into their faces. The gale kicked up waves on the river, slamming chunks of ice against their sides hard enough to rock the boat. The storm raged as if to capsize and drown the entire army in one fell swoop.

Perhaps it was meant to do that. Proctor had seen the kind of weather Deborah summoned, and the German was more powerful than her. During the battle at White Plains, he had summoned rain to douse the grass fires as his Hessians marched up the hillside against Hamilton's cannons.

He had to assume that Bootzamon and the widow Nance had returned to their master and warned him of the attack. He had to assume their master was intent on stopping it.

Proctor felt the cold of the ghosts pass through him again. He looked up in sick worry. The curse still held. Had Deborah failed? Worse, had Cecily returned, or Bootzamon and Nance been sent back to stop them? Proctor felt trapped, unable to reach the children, unable to go back to Deborah's aid.

"Victory or death," Washington said. He was kneeling

in the boat ahead of Proctor. It took Proctor a moment to realize that the general had addressed him.

"I beg your pardon," he said.

"Victory or death," Washington repeated. "That's the password tonight, if I need you to run messages to Tench for me."

"Yes, sir," Proctor said, forgetting his Quaker guise. Or rather, dropping it. He would be no pacifist tonight, not when those he loved were in danger.

Washington caught the *sir*. He glanced back at Proctor with a very small smile.

Victory or death. With the curse on them, and enlistments about to end, it was more than a password. Icy water sloshed about their feet, freezing as they stood in it. Sleet and wind clawed at their faces. Cursed spirits fought to hold them back, and a well-trained enemy waited ahead. It was hard to believe in the possibility of victory.

Where was Deborah? What was she doing?

Proctor lowered his head against the bitter wind. The men—and woman—at the oars tugged onward. The men with poles pushed off ice and steadied the balance of the boat. Proctor guessed they had reached the halfway point in the river, but they could see nothing. One shore was blank behind them, and the other hidden by the fog and the weather ahead.

Monroe, crouching next to Proctor, suppressed a gasp as if at some unexpected hurt.

Proctor looked up. His ghost grappled with him as something tried to pull it away.

Deborah! Their spell was working.

Monroe's ghost clung desperately to the living soul, but it was not enough. It was stretched thin, and then whipped away. In quick succession, three more ghosts went flying, from the Marblehead private, the Marylander, and the rifleman at the rear of the boat, like ships' pennants torn from their stays in a gale.

Proctor snapped his head around. He thought he saw a brightness above the far shore. They had done it! They had completed the spell and opened the gates to the afterlife.

But the ghosts did not go gently into that good light. They hung on to tethers of spirit torn from their hosts, fighting like salmon at the end of a fishing line. The Marblehead captain lost his ghost, which ripped at his soul the same way. He hesitated in mid-stroke. With three men frozen at the oars, the boat's forward progress stopped and the current turned the prow of the boat to carry them downriver.

"Row on," Washington ordered. Obeying the sound of his voice, the men dug in mechanically and the boat surged forward again.

One by one, the other ghosts were torn away but not torn free. Long lines of spirit snaked away from their bodies, like yarn being spun into thread. The strain on the men showed in their faces—it was a physical pain, an agony of doubt in the heart, and every man believed he suffered it alone in shame.

Only Washington's ghosts held on tightly.

Washington's ghosts were shackled to him. Deborah's spell pulled them backward, like a line of buoys dropped from a ship in a fast wind, but they refused to let go. The first ghost in the line buried his hands in Washington's shoulder blades like some demon ripping out an angel's wings. Each ghost behind that one reached out and clawed its way back to Washington.

If Washington's ghosts held on, Proctor was certain they all would. He had a sick fear in his stomach about the children, but he feared that he made a mistake. If Deborah's spell failed because he should have stayed behind and added his power to the others, he would never forgive himself.

The pull of the ghosts was so strong that they slowly dragged Washington physically backward, as if they meant to tug him overboard and drown him before they would be cut loose.

Washington's head came up into the wind. He squared his shoulders, found his balance, and rose to his feet, bracing one leg in front of him. But the ghosts could pull him no farther.

The wind shrieked and howled. The air spit water and ice like a fountain of misery. The other men's ghosts began to climb their way back along the tethers to their human hosts.

Young Lieutenant Monroe, embracing the flag in his shaking arms, rose to stand beside Washington. The flag began to unfurl, its striped corners snapping in the wind. Proctor scooted forward, behind the two men, ready to catch them if the ghosts should try to drag them down. Deborah's spell wasn't strong enough. It wasn't strong enough because she wasn't in the middle of the army.

Fog closed in around them. Neither shore was visible, and the other boats disappeared into shadows as gray as the fog. The ghosts pulled themselves back together into a cluster behind Washington. The other men's ghosts came out of the dark toward the boat, like fish swimming upstream against diminishing rapids. Proctor knew he had to help Deborah break the curse, but he had no idea how to do it.

"Put your backs into it now, my good fellows," Washington said. He removed his telescope from his pocket, though he didn't bring it to his eye. "I can see the far shore."

Alexandra nearly wept as she rowed. The private at the front of the boat cried openly as he pulled on his oar.

The loose flag whipped against Proctor's face, and he shoved it angrily aside. He had to do something to help Deborah's spell. He needed a focus—

He needed the flag. Deborah had poured magic into it while Betsy sewed, creating a focus to sustain men's spirits.

Thirteen stripes and thirteen stars, meant to represent all the states. Just as the men and woman in the boat came from every part of the country.

The flag snapped against his face again. This time, Proctor grabbed a fistful of the fabric and jammed it down into the spot where the spectral shackles wrapped around Washington's ankles.

"Let my people go."

He felt power surge through him as he had never felt before, as if he were drawing not just on his own source but also, through the flag, on Deborah and Magdalena and all the other witches of the circle. It ran through him like fire set to a trail of oil leading to a gunpowder keg, and it hit the shackle and the shackle shattered.

The first ghost turned and looked at Proctor, the eyes in his ruined face a mixture of relief and dismay. Still he held on to Washington's shoulders, and the ghosts behind clung to him. They would not go so easily.

The wind swirled like mad, spinning the loosely rolled flag out of ice-numbed Monroe's hands. It whipped out of the young lieutenant's grasp, snapping between the ghosts and Washington. Only Proctor still held on, one end knotted in his fist.

He raised his fist to the face of Washington's first ghost, the Virginia gentleman with his jaw shot away. He looked at the bully blacksmith's ghost looming over his shoulder, at the Connecticut minuteman still trying to stuff his organs back into his torso. The flag whipped in the wind, beating against all of them. Proctor stared down the long line of ghosts and thought about the friends he'd lost in the war, the men he'd seen die, Amos Lathrop and Joseph Warren and David Livingston. He thought of all the men still fighting—from men like Cuff and Alex's brothers to officers like Tench Tilghman and Paul Revere.

"Take my talent," Alex whispered, in tears. "Do it."

The flag threatened to rip out of his hand. This was his

only chance. He opened himself to Alex's talent and let her power flow through him. But it wasn't only her power. He was connected to Deborah and Magdalena, Esther and Sukey, Abby and Lydia and all their power. He was connected, through the flag, to Betsy Ross and every other man and woman who still believed in the cause of liberty. He was connected, by their presence, to the men in the boat, and to General Washington. And through Washington, he was connected to every man still in the Continental army, every man who kept the faith and kept on fighting despite the defeats, the deprivations, the terrible odds.

All that power flowed into Proctor Brown and through him. He held his fist up to the ghost at Washington's back, the speechless Virginian mutilated by the war.

And he said, *"Let my people go."*

His words were snatched away by the howl of the wind, but it was a howl of despair. All around them, ghosts thrashed in the fog, ripped from their human hosts. Their screeches filled the night. But Washington's ghosts still hung on. The flag flapped one way, then the other in Proctor's fist, wrapping around the ghosts. Washington turned his head as if he felt something. The voiceless Virginian with the ruined face, pale as the moonlight, brittle as ice, stared down at Proctor as though he wanted to speak. Proctor clutched the flag with both hands, gritting his teeth as he struggled to hold tight.

The wind gusted, tearing the banner out of his fists. He grabbed for it and missed.

The flag flew away into the dark. But it had twisted around Washington's ghosts and carried them away. The Virginian's spirit reached out to Proctor with an open hand before he disappeared. The other ghosts in the boat let go and flew up into the icy fog, and then all the spirits abandoned the fog at once and followed Washington's ghosts toward a bright light that hung like a haze-covered moon above the western shore.

Proctor caught his breath.

The Jersey farmer with the bandages lifted his head. He felt the difference instantly. Alex stared at Proctor, her eyes dry and full of wonder.

The wind swirled again but this time it lifted the fog, revealing the other boats. Men all across the river saw Washington standing, and they shouted and pointed at him. Henry Knox's great voice boomed out instructions across the water, indistinct like the roll of thunder. Up and down the river, men bent to their oars with new vigor. The makeshift armada, frozen in place on the icy river, surged forward as one toward the far shore.

Proctor fell back to his seat, his hands in the ice water. He didn't notice the cold. His heart was pounding, and he felt light-headed and exhausted and full of joy. He'd done it. With Deborah and the other witches and Alex, he'd broken the curse.

Victory or death. They might have a chance at the former after all.

"Sir," Monroe said apologetically to Washington, gazing toward the lost flag. "I—"

"Never you mind, Lieutenant," Washington said. "We'll requisition another from Missus Ross as soon as we have the opportunity. There's our shore."

Alex laughed aloud in relief. The Marblehead captain at the helm began calling out the stroke, and the rowers bent into their oars, shoving ice aside each time they pulled. The dark line resolved into a bank, where the men who had already landed had fires waiting.

"You did it," Alex whispered to Proctor. "I saw you, you did it."

"We did it," Proctor said. It was all of them—Deborah, Magdalena, the others. It was Betsy Ross and Thomas Paine. It was all the men in the boat, all the men in all the boats who defied the despair of the curse and kept on fighting. It was Washington at their head. "We all did it."

The boat landed and they disembarked. He and Alex ran up the shore to the nearest fire, which was fed with wood stolen from the fences that lined the roads in this part of the country instead of stone. The air was so bitter that the side facing the fire would get warm while the other side froze. Men turned around and around, like meat on a spit, trying to dry their wet clothes and keep from freezing. Proctor copied their motion.

The rest of the horses and artillery still had to be brought over before they could march. But despite the cold and the delays, Proctor felt a sense of joy for the men around them. It was as if the entire army had set down a heavy burden. Men were laughing while they stomped their soaked feet to stave off frostbite. Even if they didn't understand why, they could feel that the curse had lifted.

"So we've won, right?" Alex said. "We broke the curse."

"We broke the curse," Proctor said, glancing around to make sure no one had overheard her. "But we haven't won."

"Deborah is fine," Alex said. "We broke the curse."

Proctor hoped Deborah was fine. He wanted to believe that she and the others were fine. But he was thinking about Zoe and the boy, William.

"Bootzamon and Nance are still out there somewhere," he said. "Cecily escaped and who knows where she is. The German is in Trenton, surrounded by Hessians. If we don't defeat them—if we don't defeat *him*—he'll just do it all over again."

And he'd use the blood of the children to do it.

The wind picked up, raging like a drunk. It spit needles of ice at them. Alex's teeth chattered. She turned to the fire and rubbed her hands together while Proctor stared into the dark toward Trenton, miles away.

Chapter 27

Proctor and Alex and the other wet-footed soldiers fresh off the boats tried to warm themselves, while all around them the army moved with purpose. Adam Stephen's Virginia brigade fanned out into the woods, setting up sentry points around the landing. Other units formed a line of march. The artillery was landed and moved into positions where it could be used to provide support to the infantry. It was hours past midnight already, but men moved with energy and purpose they had not shown in months.

Through the dark and the swirling snow, Proctor recognized the familiar silhouette of Washington's slave, William Lee, as he led horses to the general. He recognized one of the horses as well.

"Excuse me," he said to Alex. "I'll be right back."

"I'm coming with you," she said, picking up her rifle and falling in behind. He was in no mood to argue. He pulled his hat down over his face and folded his arms tight to his chest against the cold.

"—they never left my sight," Lee told Washington as Proctor approached. Lieutenant Monroe and the other junior officers from the boat still surrounded Washington. "I liked the look of this one and brought it along," Lee added.

"A bit small, but I like the cut of him," Washington said. More than any other man, he'd carried the burden of the curse without revealing it. Proctor could see the difference in him now, a difference that he suspected had as much to do with seizing the initiative of battle as it did with letting go of the chain he'd carried. There was delight in Washington's eyes as he considered the horse. "If he had another hand or two, I'd want to try him myself."

"This one, I wager she'd carry you fine," Lee said.

"That's my horse," Proctor interrupted as he pushed his way between the horses. He rubbed Singer on the withers and checked his gear. Singer snorted, blowing a cloud of frosted air out her nose, and shook the sleet off her back. "I didn't realize she was going to be brought over."

"I wasn't leaving this fine an animal on the far shore," Lee said. "Not with what's at stake tonight."

"Where'd you get her?" Washington asked Brown before anyone questioned Lee's forwardness.

"From a music teacher in Massachusetts, name of Morgan," Proctor said. "He's got a wild-air dam that breeds well, and is trying different stallions with her. This one's not quite the horse he's looking for yet, but she does fine for me."

"He's got a better eye for horses than any music teacher I've known," Washington said, meeting Proctor eye-to-eye. "We can find a use for this pony tonight."

Proctor knew that Washington was asking to use the animal, and that most men in the army wouldn't refuse their general. But he needed to reach the German, ahead of the fighting if he could, to rescue Zoe and the orphan and put a stop to the Covenant's plan. And the fact was, the army still respected a man's individual will and his individual rights. "I'm not willing to give her up."

The junior officers behind Washington bristled. But the general adapted instantly, as he had a way of doing.

"Then we can find a use for you."

"Anything you need of me, I'm willing to do," Proctor said. *The closer to the front, the better,* he might have added, but he didn't want to seem too pushy.

"You're from the North, and I daresay you've seen a

blizzard or two before. Can you handle yourself in the snow and ice, and ride quickly if you need to?"

"I have, and I can, and she can too."

Washington nodded toward the young Monroe for a moment. "I'm sending the Third Virginia out as scouts. Go with the lieutenant here. If you encounter the enemy, or any surprises at all not of our making, you carry the news back as fast as that pony can carry you."

"Yes, sir," Proctor said. Washington had given him a direct order, and he responded out of reflex, forgetting his Quaker guise.

Washington laughed. "You see," he said. "We'll get a musket in your hands before you know it."

The junior officers laughed then too. They all felt the relief of the curse lifted off them. Proctor hoped it didn't make them too foolhardy or blind to danger.

Lee handed him Singer's bridle, giving the animal one last pat of appreciation, then turned his attention to preparing Washington's horse, the large sorrel he liked to ride when he expected there to be shooting. Proctor led the horse away, following Monroe, who glanced once, twice, at Alex without saying a word. It was clear that Monroe didn't think he needed Proctor assigned to their company, and that he was even more skeptical of the tagalong who appeared younger than himself.

"He's with me," Proctor said. He might ruin his own counterfeit as a Quaker, but he wouldn't wreck Alex's disguise. "I promised his brothers I'd look after him."

"I'm the one with the gun," Alex said. "We'll see who looks after who."

Monroe let the matter go. "We'll be in Captain Washington's company."

"William Washington?" asked Proctor. The general's cousin had been wounded during the battle at Harlem Heights. "Has he returned to duty?"

"You couldn't keep him out of this fight," Monroe said.

"We'll have about forty men, and we're to move ahead of the main company, securing the road and making sure no travelers go into or out of Trenton." He glanced at Proctor and Alex one more time. "If anything goes wrong and the Hessians discover us, we'll be on the sharp edge."

Alex shielded her face against the raging wind. "It's hard to imagine anyone leaving their quarters in weather like this."

"Hopefully, the Hessians are thinking the same thing," Proctor said.

At that point, Monroe seemed to accept that he could not discourage them. "Let's go report."

William Washington was a large man, though not so tall as his cousin, and inclined to fat despite the hardship of the campaign and the scarcity of supplies. He had a round face, and the cold make his cheeks more red than the last time Proctor had seen him. Monroe gave him General Washington's orders. Captain Washington accepted Proctor and Alex as two more volunteers, much like the Jersey farmers who were going to lead the way across miles of frozen country.

They were the first group to set out. Proctor's intention to ride Singer quickly faded. The weather, bad enough for the crossing, intensified as though a malevolent will drove it like a pack of dogs against them. They marched uphill into a fierce gale, which hounded them through the bare trunks of the thick woods. Noticing Alex sheltering behind Singer as they walked, Proctor dismounted and used the horse as a moving windbreak.

It proved a wise decision. The trail was steep, and the path icy and uneven, so that they slipped despite going slowly. The storm came at them over the heights like a barrage from battlements, intended to drive back an enemy's attack. The snow, which had been falling steadily, turning to stinging sleet again and then, for a few agonizing minutes when they had no place to shelter, into hail that hit them like icy rounds of buckshot.

But the storm could not sustain that fury. Once they crested the hill and turned south, the ice and hail abated. It started to snow again, big, wet flakes like scrapings off a block of ice. In a short while those flakes turned into fat drops. Rain fell, as cold as ice, turning the road to a morass of mud so that they had to make their way single file along the edges. A second group of forty men, many of them local militia, followed behind and found the going no easier.

They came to a crossroads at a little hamlet, where Captain Washington met briefly with the commander of the second group. The other unit took the lower road, toward the river, while Washington led their group eastward. "It's up to us to cut off the road to Princeton before they send for or receive reinforcements," Monroe explained.

The British had a large garrison at Princeton. If they came down at the right moment, the Americans would be crushed between the pincers. "Are forty men enough to do that?" Proctor asked.

"They'll have to be," he said.

As they continued the march, Alex approached Proctor, lifting her musket just enough to draw his eye. "It's too wet to fire," she said under her breath.

Proctor looked around. The other men's weapons could not be in better condition.

Even if the army failed in its attack on the Hessian units, he dare not fail in his own, private mission. But he would have to get closer to the city before he tried to get inside.

Despite the weather, the roads were busy. The first man they caught was a farm boy about Proctor's age, sneaking home shamefully after falling asleep at the home of some girl he was courting. The second was a woodcutter old enough to be the first one's grandfather; he said he was out trying to pick up the windblown branches before some other fellow got them. The third was a haggard old woman in clothes little better than rags. She said she was a midwife, going to attend a birth, but she stank of witchcraft to Proctor. When she was taken prisoner with the others and forced to join their party, she grew belligerent, hurling epithets and threats of doom at the soldiers, reminding Proctor of Cecily or the widow Nance.

Proctor reached for the knife he carried under his jacket. Alex's hand, cold even through her gloves, fell on his.

"Careful," she said. "Sometimes a crone is just a crone."

It was his fear for Deborah taking hold. He had no idea where she was or what she was doing, whether she was safe or not. "The German is going to attack us again, I can feel it," he said.

"But she's not," Alex said.

After a moment's pause, he withdrew his hand and thrust it into his pocket again for warmth. As they continued walking, he looked east. Dawn was starting to show on the horizon, like a redheaded child rising from the dark blankets of his bed. Any minute could bring an alarm.

Ahead of them, dogs started barking angrily. Dogs had barked at them from a distance all night, but it had been one or two, and their voices curious. This sounded like a hunter's kennel loosed on a fox. A large house sat beside the road just ahead of them. A lantern lit the window, and a door banged open.

"For God's sake," yelled the man. "Stay off the road, damn you! If you won't go back to Hesse, at least go back to Trenton and give me a single night's decent sleep."

Through these and other words, it became clear that the man thought they were either a British or Hessian force, both of which had frequently been on patrol of late. This was the crossroads they'd been aiming for, the road connecting Trenton to Princeton. When Washington finally conveyed their true nature to him, the man immediately ran to silence his dogs. He grabbed a coat before he rejoined them, maybe taking it for granted they would hold him prisoner.

"The name's John Riker," he said. "Doctor John Riker. I'll come along, if you allow. Maybe I can help some poor fellow."

"You could help a poor fellow now with a bite of warm food," Monroe said.

Riker nodded and went inside to order his servant to prepare something. Outside, Washington ordered the men to set up barricades across the roads. While the men went to work in the tapering rain, dragging fallen trees and borrowed wagons into place to block passage, Proctor took Alex and drifted away from the others. If he was going to sneak into town, he'd have to do it soon before it got too light or the shooting started.

"If anyone asks," he told Alex. "I rode back to Washington to report."

"You can't just leave me here!"

"I have to," he said. "If we both go, it'd be too suspicious. Once you enter the town, come find me."

"How will I find you?"

He didn't have time to fashion a finding charm, and he wasn't sure she would use magic in any case, despite what she'd allowed him to do in the boat at the crossing. "Look for the loudest commotion," he told her.

He took Singer aside, into the trees, and mounted her back. The horse seemed to welcome either the warmth or presence of a rider again. With Proctor bent low to her neck, she took off through the woods, finding a trail easily with sure steps.

The smell of cheap tobacco braced him for an attack.

"You are indeed persistent, aren't you?" said the hollow, oddly accented voice from the trees behind him.

Proctor twisted in the saddle, bringing Singer around. The red coal appeared first, bright as a small sun against the dark background of the woods. The figure of the scarecrow Bootzamon stepped out of the woods. In the dawn light, Proctor could see that the raggedy clothes were different than in Virginia or New York, less elegant and more decayed perhaps, but once again he had a cockfeather in his cap.

"I assumed you've raised the alarm among the Hessians," Proctor said. Could he escape Bootzamon and get back to the advance party to warn them? Would General Washington change his plan now even if the Hessians had been warned?

Bootzamon did a jaunty side-step to flank Proctor. "Why would you assume I've raised any kind of alarm for anyone?" He plucked at his sodden waistcoat with a gloved hand. Damp straw spilled from his jacket cuff. "You'll find it hard to set anything on fire tonight."

"When did I ever set anything on fire—?" Proctor asked.

From the corner of his eye, he spied a ball of flame missile toward him. He tumbled off Singer to dodge it, got tangled in the reins, and was dragged through the snow. Another missile burst in front of the horse, showering her face with sparks. Proctor untangled himself and rolled free as Singer reared, whinnying in terror. The scarecrow form of the widow Nance jumped out of the trees in front of the horse. As Proctor staggered to his feet, Singer dashed off into the woods in fear.

"I wasn't actually speaking to you," Bootzamon said.

"I should have killed you the first time I saw you," Nance sneered at Proctor, words pouring like maggots out of her feedsack mouth. The pipe stuck in her inhuman face, shifting from side to side. "I should have slit your throat in Boston and bled you instead of that little blond boy."

She summoned pinecones to her hand from the forest floor and flung them at him, one after another. Each one sparked in the air and then drowned in wet smoke before it reached Proctor. He batted them aside, until Nance stopped where she stood and screamed, a disembodied sound like the wind between rocks.

"I could make some snowballs for you to throw, if you think they'd work better," Proctor said. He stepped sideways to prevent Bootzamon from sneaking up behind him.

Nance reacted with rage and flung herself at Proctor. Her scarecrow body slammed into him like a wet straw mattress, smelling of dust and mold and smoke. Her soft fists battered at him, while the ends of his hairs began to sizzle and curl with heat. She was trying to set him on fire!

He grabbed one of her arms and spun in a circle, tossing her at a tree. She slammed into the trunk and crumpled to the ground. Snow fell off the branches and covered her. Her head popped up out of the snow, pipe clamped in her teeth, and shook it off.

"Why aren't you attacking him?" she yelled at Bootzamon.

"But you're doing so well," he said.

Proctor had two choices: he could either run or attack. If he ran, they would be behind him, and they could chase faster and kill quicker than he wanted to think about. So when Nance spoke to Bootzamon, he charged her. He slipped as he ran over the snowy ground, but he stretched out his arm as he fell and snatched the pipe from her mouth.

"Damn you," she cried. She stretched out her hand, like a falconer calling to her bird.

The pipe tried to leap from Proctor's grasp but he squeezed his fist around it and ran away from her. The pipe yanked at his arm, like a big dog trying to break its leash, but he held on tight.

"Give that to me," she demanded, rising from the snow like an angel of wrath.

"Give it to you or what, you'll threaten to kill me? You've already played that card." He circled as he spoke, keeping both Nance and Bootzamon in his sight. He tried to break the pipe in his hand, but it was unnaturally strong, bound together perhaps by the same magic that animated Nance's scarecrow form.

"Give it to me or I'll strip the skin from your meat a few inches at a time, you stupid boy."

She advanced on him, but she was wary of coming within his grasp now, so she spoke words in a language he couldn't understand, summoning the pipe back to her. It leapt about as if alive, twisting and yanking his hand to escape. He closed both hands about it to hold it tighter, one fist around the bowl and one around the stem, but still it pulled his arms straight out in front of him in its desire to return to her. Unable to take another step back, he dug in his heels and held on to it like a man trying to control a wild horse.

"I'll take that now," she said, snapping her hand in the air as if yanking it from his grasp.

Proctor gritted his teeth, refusing to let go, even if it yanked his arms out of joint. He felt a great pull and then a tiny snap as the force of her own magic broke the bowl and stem in two.

"That's not good," Nance said, and then she collapsed in a pile of rags and cast-offs.

Proctor fell back, sprawling in the snow. He dropped the broken pipe and scrambled to his feet at once, braced for the attack from Bootzamon.

"She's not dead, you realize," Bootzamon said, walking toward Proctor. His feet left no mark in the snow. "Her soul is still shackled to our master. He'll make another body, sacrifice another foal, breathe her into life again."

"I've noticed how hard you are to get rid of," Proctor said.

"Rotenhahn," Bootzamon said.

The word meant nothing to Proctor. He looked about for a weapon, anything to strike Bootzamon with. He might not be able to kill him, but he could slow him down again.

Bootzamon lunged at Proctor, laughed when he jumped, and stopped short, stalking him slowly, keeping pace step by step with Proctor as he tried to get away.

"Rotenhahn was my name," Bootzamon said. "I've been so long outside my own flesh that I had stopped using it."

"It's a good name," Proctor said uncertainly. He spied Singer in the woods and wondered if he could trick Bootzamon to within kicking distance of her again.

"I was a canon at the cathedral in Bonn," Bootzamon said. "I was a witch, but only because the talent came upon me, breaking in on my will like a thief entering a house at night. I didn't know what was happening to me, didn't know how to control it. The good people of the city, my own friends, even my family, beheaded me and burned my body."

"You need better friends," Proctor said. He had a large branch in his hand now.

"But my master, the prince-bishop, was there, and trapped my soul. I discovered later that he had arranged for the witch hunt so that he might trap many of our souls to do his bidding. He was new at necromancy then, and it took him numerous attempts to master the skill. It turned out that he had to visit me in jail beforehand and mark me as his own in order to harvest me. Put down that cudgel."

"I don't think so," Proctor said, lifting it to strike.

Bootzamon gave one flick of his finger, and the staff flew out of Proctor's hand and into the scarecrow's glove. He patted it on the palm of his open hand.

"You freed the souls, the cursed souls shackled to the soldiers in your army," Bootzamon said. He had stopped advancing. He blew out a cloud of smoke, and the coal in his pipe flared bright.

"A group of us did that, but yes," Proctor said.

Bootzamon took the pipe from his mouth and tossed it to Proctor. "Free me."

The pipe scorched his hand, twice as hot as the widow's had been. "What?"

"I thought it only natural to serve; that was our lot in death as well as life. But this strange country of yours is full of men who would rather be dead than serve another. I have no pleasure in anything I do, owning only others' pain, collected in debt to my master. I would rather be dead than serve him or anyone else again."

Proctor was waiting for the trick, for the subterfuge. "I can't guarantee where you'll go, to heaven or to hell."

"You think this is not hell enough? I serve a devil and depend on the demon Dickon to stoke a flame that keeps my soul on constant fire."

"It's not the same kind of curse."

"I have faith in you, boy. You've bested me twice, and I have no one else to have faith in. You'll find my master in town, in the small house on King Street across from Colonel Rall's headquarters. The children may still be alive."

"How do I defeat him?"

"You can't. You can only escape him." He flung the stick aside, and his voice took on an edge of anger. "Now be quick about it, before he realizes what I am about and summons me back to his bottle collection."

Proctor snapped the pipe in half, breaking the focus of the spell. "Let my people go."

Nothing happened.

Bootzamon stared at him. "*Let my people go? Dimitte populum meum,* that's your spell?"

"It worked the first time," Proctor said.

"But you're not any kind of Moses," Bootzamon said.

"I don't want to reach the land you're promised," Proctor answered. Bootzamon's anger was making him tense.

"Try this verse instead," Bootzamon said. He fell to his

knees and lowered his head. "*Quoniam peccavi super numerum harenae maris, multiplicatae sunt iniquitates meae, Domine, multiplicatae sunt iniquitates meae.* My transgressions, O Lord, are multiplied. My transgressions are multiplied, and I am not worthy to behold and see the height of heaven for the multitude of mine iniquities. I am bowed down with many iron bands, that I cannot lift up mine head, neither can I have any release. For I have provoked Thy wrath, and done evil before Thee. I did not do Thy will, neither kept I Thy commandments. I have performed abominations, and have multiplied offenses. Now therefore I bow the knee of mine heart, beseeching Thee of grace. *Et nunc flecto genua cordis mei, precans ad te bonitatem Domine.*"

"What is that?" Proctor asked.

"Don't they make you learn the Prayer of Manasseh anymore?" Bootzamon said.

"I don't know it."

Bootzamon shook his head in disappointment and sighed. "I'll say it, and you can repeat it after me."

"All right." Proctor clutched the broken ends of the still-warm pipe in his fists and stumbled badly through the prayer in Bootzamon's wake. "My transgressions, O Lord, are multiplied . . ."

They finished and sat there silently as the icy rain continued to fall.

After a moment, the scarecrow's shoulders sagged, his head drooped forward, and water poured off the brim of his hat. Then he stood and dusted the snow off his knees. "Oh, well," he said. "It was worth the attempt. I'll have to kill you now, but I promise I'll make it quick."

He took two steps toward Proctor with his tomahawk raised.

But Proctor finally realized the verse he needed to use. He opened his palm and saw that the pipe bowl still glowed faintly. He dropped to his knees and bowed his neck. Plunging the pipe bowl into the snow, he said, "Father, into Thy hands I commend this spirit."

There was a sound in the air, like glass breaking. Bootzamon stopped, startled, and stared at the sky where a light appeared in the clouds. The tomahawk tumbled out of his gloved hand and landed upside down in the snow.

Behind the illusion of Bootzamon's human face, always faint to Proctor's eyes, behind the pumpkin head and stickbones of the scarecrow, a spirit appeared. It was long-chinned and gaunt, with hollows for his watery eyes and a mouth opened in shock.

"You can feel hell," Bootzamon whispered. "It scorches the bottoms of your feet like hot coals. *Domine, remitte mihi, remitte mihi.*"

His spectral head toppled off his body, and the whole form of his spirit rose out of the scarecrow like a blue flame, fading in the air like steam from a cup. The light in the sky faded away.

When it was dark again, the gourd rolled off the scarecrow's shoulders. A second later, the body collapsed into pieces, a pile of harmless rags at Proctor's feet.

Chapter 28

Proctor was shaking, not shivering, but shaking. Sweat poured from his forehead, and his hands were wet and clammy.

He staggered over to a tree and propped himself up, trying to catch his breath. There was no time to spare. The German might not know he was coming yet. What was it that Bootzamon had called him?

No, not Bootzamon. Rotenhahn. He had earned back his own name.

Rotenhahn had called him the prince-bishop. He was in Trenton, in the small house on King Street across from Colonel Rall's headquarters. Proctor might still surprise him if he moved quickly enough. He might still be able to rescue both the children.

He called for Singer, but she was long gone, spooked by Nance and Bootzamon. Did he waste valuable time searching for her or simply make his way into town? It was best to go straight for the goal. He stuck a sprig of evergreen in his hat and spoke a spell of concealment, meant to turn away any eyes who chanced upon him. Not a perfect spell, but snow flurries filled the air again, and in this weather it would have to do.

He staggered out of the woods and found the road. A cooper's shop sat at the edge of town, with the shadows of the other rooftops spread behind it. He was headed the right direction.

Proctor had almost passed the shop when the door

opened and a Hessian in his tall, stiff cap popped out. Proctor froze—the concealment spell was more effective when he didn't move. The Hessian stared through him, then dropped his gaze to the snow. Proctor had left a trail of footprints behind him, leading right to where he stood.

The Hessian started forward with his gun raised. At the same moment, the wind intensified, sweeping snow before it and wiping clean Proctor's footprints like waves over sand. The Hessian shielded his face against the blast, and looked again, but the prints were gone. He peered through Proctor as he scanned the roads one more time, then turned and went inside.

As soon as the door slammed shut, Proctor hurried into town, hunched over against the wind. He followed the sign to his right down King Street. Here and there, he saw early smoke rising from chimneys, but on the day after Christmas, in the cold with the storm holding back the dawn, the residents were late to stir.

In the middle of town, he saw a large mansion that filled half a block. The Hessian commander Rall's regimental colors snapped in the wind outside. Directly across the street, lights burned in the lower windows of a small house.

Proctor climbed over the little picket fence around the yard and went to the back. He checked his supplies—some salt, some sand, a knife. He couldn't do anything with a direct attack. His plan, if you could dignify it by calling it such, was to sneak in, grab Zoe and the orphan boy, then escape through the American lines before the shooting started.

He eased the door open silently and stepped into the kitchen.

A voice from the front parlor chilled Proctor to the bone.

"You've been a thorn in my side, boy. You've deprived me of a servant who's been my obedient dog for almost two hundred years. For that, I think you owe me."

Proctor still had his hand on the latch. He pushed

against it, intending to leave, but the door slammed shut. The latch turned under his fingers and against his will, sealing it as tight as a cork in a bottle.

"You won't be leaving that way," the voice said. "Come out here."

Maybe it was time for a new plan. He fumbled in his pocket as he walked slowly to the doorway. He stopped there, leaning against the jamb.

The parlor had been turned into a stage mockery of a palace. A thick, imported rug woven with elaborate vines covered the simple wooden floor from wall to wall. Two tapestries of archers on horseback hung from hooks in the ceiling, one against each wall; because the walls were too short for their length, fabric bunched up on the floor. Two ornately carved tables set with gleaming candelabra sat on either side of the doorway. The glow from the candles was almost as bright as the flame from the fire in the hearth, and the greasy smell of them filled the air. Next to the hearth sat a cumbersome upholstered chair, and in that chair sat the large, heavy figure of the German. The prince-bishop.

A simple box sat against the wall behind the chair. Black silk was draped over it, and half a dozen glass bottles were arranged across the top. The bottles were filled with a liquid, and in the liquid floated bits like locks of hair and fingers. One of the bottles lay shattered, broken glass spilled across the floor.

Zoe and the orphan boy sat on the floor at the German's feet. Silver chains about their throats connected to leashes that draped loose over one of the prince-bishop's meaty hands. His other hand drummed restlessly on the arm of the chair. Proctor tried hard not to look at the children directly.

"It's humble," Proctor said. "Not too ostentatious."

"You make joke," the prince-bishop said, spitting out the words. "But I despise this rude country of hovels and barns. Even the best men here—if such a phrase has any meaning at all—live like animals, sleeping with their hounds in wooden shacks and wearing a perfume made of piss and *Scheiße*."

"You don't have to stay," Proctor said. He pulled a fistful of sand from the bag in his pocket and cast it into the room in the shape of an inverted V. "Let your house be built on foundations of sand."

He hoped to weaken or deflect any spell that the prince-bishop cast at him. And maybe purchase enough time to come up with another plan.

The prince-bishop chuckled, his big chest shaking as he sat in his chair. "If that's all the skill you have to offer, I have to wonder how you ever caused me so much trouble."

"Run," Zoe whispered. Her eyes were large and dark and wet. The prince-bishop gave almost a disinterested tug on her chain and her tongue clove to her mouth. The boy, his hair a wild mess and his eyes desperate, strained against invisible fetters to touch his hand to hers.

Proctor wondered if the prince-bishop, like all men seduced by power, relied too much on his servants. Jolly was dead, Cecily was trapped, Rotenhahn was released, and Nance was made useless for a time. Maybe he could just grab the children and run. "Give them to me," Proctor said.

"Come and get them," the prince-bishop said indifferently.

Proctor stepped across the threshold into the room.

As he passed the boundary, the archers in the tapestries came to life. Their tiny bows twanged and miniature darts flew at him from both sides. Proctor flinched, but when the arrows reached his lines of sand they dropped to the floor.

The prince-bishop's amused chuckle stopped and the smile at the corners of his mouth folded downward. His fat fingers stopped drumming on the arm of his chair. Before he could lift his hand, Proctor stretched out his arms.

"Bring to light the hidden things of darkness," he said.

The candlesticks flew to his hands, one to each. There was no reason for them to be lit, not with the fire burning, so Proctor reasoned that they formed part of the German's protective spells. As soon as the heavy gold slammed into each palm, he blew out the flame, wrinkling his nose at the fatty stench of the wax.

He dropped the snuffed candlesticks. When they hit the floor, the tapestries crashed with them. Tiny arms and the legs of horses protruded from the folds of cloth. The arrows were only the first wave of their attack, but now nothing moved.

The prince-bishop frowned. His hand turned into a fist.

"The only good thing about this country," he said, "is that so many young talents may be plucked from it, like an orchard full of low-hanging fruit. When your little rebellion is over, I shall go about the country gathering baskets of them. In five years, I'll have more power than I had before. If only you were a few years younger, I might try to break your will too. I could teach you the sort of power over other men that you only dream of." He stroked Zoe's head, like a hungry man polishing an apple. She cringed but was helpless to move.

Proctor took a step forward, his toe touching the line of sand. "I don't dream of power over other men."

"How sad," the German said. His fist thumped on the arm of his chair, and the carpet sprang instantly to life. Vines swirled up from the floor, twining around Proctor's ankles, lashing at his hands and face.

Panicked, Proctor jumped back toward the door. A vine snapped at him, snaking around his leg and dragging him down to a knee. Proctor pulled his knife and slashed at the vines, but more of them wrapped around his arm, holding it in the air while a dozen viny fingers tried to pry it from his hand. He jammed the other hand in his pocket for the salt, ransacking his memory for a verse about salting the land.

Hope leapt to his throat ahead of the words—the first vines that came at his second hand shied from the salt as it spilled from his fist. Then one shifted direction, winding around his head like a gag, covering his mouth so he couldn't speak. The vines dragged him down, both knees on the floor like a penitent, one arm staked out wide, his head pulled back. With the last effort of his free hand, he flung the salt across the room at the prince-bishop's face.

The children ducked and the prince-bishop turned his head aside. The salt scattered harmlessly. Then vines shot up Proctor's free arm. He was pinned to his knees, his arms staked out to either side, his head pulled back, and his mouth gagged by the vines.

He could see the light glisten on the tears welling in Zoe's eyes.

"You're somewhat resourceful," the prince-bishop murmured. He rose slowly, moving his great bulk with care and deliberation. When he stood, he looped the silver leashes around a nail in the wall and then calmly walked over to Proctor. He paused on the way to scatter the sand with the toe of his polished leather boot. He did nothing in a hurry, as if living centuries had taught him there was no need to rush. He was studying Proctor when a cannon boomed outside.

The prince-bishop turned his head.

Cannons roared again, one volley and then a second in quick succession, from the lower end of town. From the other direction came the shouts of the army and the crack of musket fire. The army was coming.

Proctor hoped they came quickly enough.

The Prince-Bishop's face registered disbelief. He walked over to the window and pulled the curtain aside. Close at hand, the Hessian kettledrums beat out the warning. There were shouts in German as the soldiers poured into the streets.

Still in no hurry, the prince-bishop watched events unfold for a few moments. Proctor finally dared eye contact with Zoe and the boy. Zoe sat very still, her shoulders folded forward, but the boy struggled, jerking his hands from side to side to loosen the invisible bonds that held him. No words passed between the children and Proctor, but he understood that they were begging for his help. And that he, by coming there, had made a promise that he would rescue them.

The prince-bishop turned away from the window and, without warning, slammed his fist into Proctor's head, knocking him dizzy. "Damn you and damn your countrymen."

Proctor shook it off. The blow had loosened the vines gagging his mouth. "You already tried that, and it failed," he said back, spitting out bits of leaves.

But the prince-bishop was done with him. He went to his box, carefully sweeping the broken glass aside and removing the bottles. Lifting the lid, he set them inside. The last one was black glass, a New York globe bottle. A figure seemed to swirl in the liquid inside.

Proctor struggled against the vines as the sounds of battle intensified. Cannons fired in the street just outside their door. Men shouted in several languages. A musket ball shattered the window and thumped into the plaster just above Proctor's head.

Through it all, the prince-bishop moved with calm deliberation. He was ready to seal the box when he glanced at Proctor with a gleam in his eye. With a small, empty bottle in one hand, he approached. He stooped to pick up Proctor's knife on the way. Taking Proctor's right hand in his fist, he jammed the tip of the blade into the second joint of Proctor's pinkie. Proctor was too stunned to scream, but he turned his head away, gritting his teeth until his jaw ached.

"Ordinarily, I prefer the forefinger," the prince-bishop said. "But your hands are rather large and I have only this small bottle left."

Then he sawed through the joint with a practiced motion. Proctor's finger popped off and fell to the floor, rolling among the unnatural vines. The prince-bishop dropped the knife and bent to retrieve the finger. He squeezed it through the tight neck of the little bottle. Then he placed the bottle in his box, closed the box, and tucked it under one massive arm.

"After I step out the door a musket ball or cannon shot will come through the wall and strike you," the prince-bishop said to Proctor. "But if it doesn't happen today, it will happen someday. You may expect to see me again."

His smile returned, and with it his disturbing chuckle. He shifted the box of bottles under his arm for balance, then took the silver leashes from the nail in the wall and jerked the children to their feet. He led them toward the rear door, away from the fighting.

"Don't go with him, Zoe," Proctor said through the pain. "You have to fight him—you have to get away."

Zoe dug in her heels, refusing to go. "Fight him, William," she said. "We have to fight him."

"Enough of this foolishness," the prince-bishop said. "It is time for us to leave."

He tugged on the chains, and they were pulled off their feet. But the boy raged, screaming until his face was red, one loud, continuous, inchoate No.

Objects rose from the floor. First one candlestick flew at the prince-bishop, followed instantly by the other. He brushed them out of the air with a toss of his head, and yanked the chains impatiently. Which is how he came to miss the knife. It lodged in his leg with a meaty *whack*.

The boy yelled in triumph.

The pain broke the prince-bishop's focus. The vines retreated, melting back into the rug like ordinary images.

Proctor shoved his bleeding hand into his shirt, squeezing it tight against his chest. The prince-bishop reached for the knife protruding from his leg, and Zoe yanked the chains out of his hand. Both children scrambled across the floor toward Proctor.

The prince-bishop yanked the knife out of his leg. "I'll take what's mine now."

He held out his hand, covered with blood that might have been either Proctor's or his own. The children were drawn across the floor toward him like iron filings toward a magnet.

Proctor grabbed them, one in each hand. Zoe held on to his left hand, and William the right. Whether it was slick with blood or weak from the loss of his finger, the boy slipped out of his grip. His little hands reached out to Proctor for a second chance.

Zoe was being torn from his other hand.

Proctor hesitated.

He could grab for the boy and lose them both . . .

He wrapped both arms tight around Zoe and rolled to the floor, pinning her there.

"Zoe!" the boy screamed. He was dragged across the floor and into the prince-bishop's hand.

A cannonball smashed through the wall, flying through the spot Proctor had just been. The prince-bishop had Proctor's finger and William with him. Proctor started to rise to chase after him, but another ball smashed through the house.

Suddenly all the prince-bishop's possessions—the tapestries, the rug, the chair, and the tables—began to writhe and crackle, like parchment fed to the flames. Zoe screamed, and maybe Proctor screamed too. He covered her protectively, dragging her through the doorway.

When they looked back, the room had been reduced to bare floors, plaster dust, and broken glass. The prince-bishop and the boy were gone.

"We have to save William," Zoe said.

Proctor's teeth were clenched in pain, too much pain to answer. But he staggered to his feet, hand jammed under his arm to stop the bleeding. He and Zoe ran outside. And then, with their feet slipping out from under them, they skidded to a stop.

Hessian corpses littered the ground. The rain had frozen on top of the snow: blood flowed over its glassy surface, forming a thin, translucent film of red that covered the streets and yards. Lieutenant Monroe lay on the ground by the Hessian cannons, blood-soaked at throat and chest. Doctor Riker straddled him, with clamps shoved into Monroe's slashed neck. Gunfire still sounded off to the east. General Washington rode through on his horse, yelling for the men to follow him. Men who'd been awake all night, who'd crossed a river choked with ice, who'd marched through miles of sleet and snow, ran breakneck after Washington and toward the light of a new dawn.

But there was no sign of the prince-bishop or William anywhere. They had disappeared.

"Come on," Zoe said, tugging at his sleeve. Tears welled in her eyes. But she made no effort to move. Even she could see there was no way to follow the missing pair.

"Proctor!"

He turned at his name and saw Alex on the back of Singer. She rode up to them and reined in the horse.

"When she came back alone, I feared the worst," she said, jumping off the horse. "You're injured."

"I'll be fine," he said. He spoke the words through a grimace and collapsed to his knees. "The German escaped."

Alex tore a strip of cloth from her red shirt, pinioned his arm, and started binding his bleeding hand. Zoe dodged behind Alex and watched with wide eyes. New pain spiked all the way to Proctor's shoulder, but all he could think about was whether or not he was doomed to become a slave to the will of the prince-bishop just as Rotenhahn had been.

Musket fire rattled the air east of town, and officers called to men to continue the fight. As Alex tied off the bandage, a group of American soldiers surged past, following Washington as he pursued the retreating Hessians. A voice sounded from the crowd. "Alex!"

Her brothers—free of the curse and free from harm— emerged from the group.

"Thank God you're safe," she said, throwing herself at them.

Seeing that she was covered with blood, they spun her around, looking for the injury. "No, I'm fine," she said, pointing to Proctor. "It's his blood."

The biggest brother, the one who'd punched Proctor, said, "Don't you know there are places to cut him that'll make him bleed a lot more."

She started to explain, but another soldier ran into the street and cheered. "We've won," he shouted. "The Hessians are routed. We've won!"

Elation spread like the early sunlight spilling over the rooftops. Even Proctor, who struggled to rise to his feet, felt joy rising in him. This was better than the curse being lifted, the sense of a burden set aside: this was a feeling of triumph, of overcoming some impossible obstacle.

"We've won!" Alex cried, shaking Proctor by the arm. Alex and her brothers, the soldiers in the street with their wounded comrades, a company running toward the fighting—they all raised their fists at the news and cheered. When they cheered again, Proctor let the feeling sink in. The curse was broken and the army had its first victory in months, just days before enlistments were up. Now men would be willing to sign on for another year and keep fighting the British. More important, the Covenant had been stopped and the prince-bishop had lost Bootzamon's services forever.

The soldiers cheered a third time, and Proctor added his raw voice to their jubilant chorus.

A small voice sounded at Proctor's side. "We've won?" Zoe asked. Her face was a wreck of worry and tears. She kept glancing back to the house as if she expected to see William emerge at any moment.

Proctor turned toward the river, toward Deborah and the others, and prayed quickly that they were safe. He rested his good hand on Zoe's shoulder and cradled the other against his chest.

"We aren't done yet," he told her, suddenly sobered. "But yes, we've won. For now."

Chapter 29

May 1777

Proctor sat in the main room of the new addition to The Farm in his new suit of clothes. A fire burned in the hearth, although the wall wasn't completely plastered. Proctor leaned forward in his chair and stirred the coals with an iron.

He looked up when Deborah entered. She was beautiful, wearing a white dress that set off the flowers that she had woven into her hair.

"Let me see it," she said.

He held out his injured hand for her to examine. She cupped it in her own smooth, small palms, turning it over, running her fingertips over the scar of his missing finger. The joint hadn't become infected, and had healed better than he expected.

"How's the strength?" she asked.

He pulled his hand back and shifted the iron to it. He bounced it a few times, showing the power of his grip.

"It looks better," she said.

"It is." He propped the iron up in its place by the hearth. "Still no word on the prince-bishop or the boy?"

A rider had come in that morning. Proctor heard the warning chimes, but didn't go to answer them. He assumed there was a message.

"General Washington has his spies searching for them," Deborah said. "But he sends word that they haven't been seen. We still have no idea of where he's from, or what he's the prince-bishop of."

"Did Washington say anything about Cecily?"

Deborah frowned, an expression he didn't want to see on her face today, and he immediately regretted the question. He could tell from Deborah's expression that there was no news about her either.

"There was no reply from your mother," Deborah said, changing the subject.

"I am dead to her," Proctor said. She would never forgive him for pursuing his talent. But that was all right. "I accept that's how it is."

"Are you sure you want to do this?" she asked.

He saw the worn-out pair of shoes where she had set them. He reached down and picked up his own old pair, sitting by the chair. The heels were cracked and the soles were peeling off. The leather had been rubbed through in places.

"Entirely certain," he said, making his voice as cheerful as it could be. "These carried me all the way to Alex's farm and back, and then from here to Gravesend and back again."

"Then why are we waiting?" she said.

Together they lifted their shoes up to a hole in the plaster and dropped them into the wall. Bowing their heads, they each said a silent prayer in the Quaker fashion. Proctor held an image in his head, of anyone coming to do Deborah harm being kicked away by shoes. In truth, they had already done all their other preparations and had just been waiting for today to finish the spell.

After a moment's silence, Proctor said, "Once we patch that up, The Farm should have stronger protections than ever."

"Only as long as we live here to protect it," Deborah said. She swallowed hard and looked away. "When I asked if you were sure you wanted to do this, I didn't mean the spell."

"I know," he said. "And when I said I was certain, I didn't mean the spell either."

Abby poked her head in the door. "Deborah—there you are! Don't you know it's bad luck to see the groom before your wedding?"

"Not for Quakers," Deborah said.

Abby rolled her eyes at Proctor, as if to say, *See what you're in for.* He laughed.

They walked outside together, hands carefully at their sides. A bower had been built beside the orchard, where the apple trees were covered with blossoms. A long table had been set up between the trees. It was covered with almost equal amounts of flowers and food. Abby ran to join Alex, who stood with Sukey and Esther. Magdalena waited next to the bower along with Ezra, as stand-ins for Deborah's parents. Zoe held a big bouquet in her hand. She started bouncing up and down when she saw Deborah.

Deborah turned and wrapped her arms around Proctor, taking him by surprise.

"Aren't you worried what people will think?" he said.

"Not anymore. Not ever again."

Acknowledgments

It's not necessary for a writer to invent new details to make the struggles of 1776 seem more heroic, even when it is a lot of fun. For those interested in historical sources, I depended on David Hackett Fischer's *Washington's Crossing*. *Washington's Spies: The Story of America's First Spy Ring*, by Alexander Rose, also provided essential background, as did *Patriot Battles: How the War of Independence Was Fought*, by Michael Stephenson. In the early stages of planning this book, I had a wide-ranging conversation with historian Mark V. Kwasny, author of *Washington's Partisan War, 1775–1783*. Mark, I know the New Jersey militia deserve more than two men in a boat, but I swear that's all there was room for.

Dr. Thom and Deborah Mak won the right to name a character in this novel at a charity auction for St. Joseph Montessori School. I want to thank them for their generous contribution to SJMS and for giving me Zoe, who, in turn, contributed more than I originally expected.

The American Revolution was born, in part, in the coffee shops of Boston; in turn, much of this book emerged at my local coffee shop. Thanks to everyone at Luck Bros this past year, especially Justina, Mary, Chester, Sarah, Tim, Tony, and the Allisons, meek and tall. Good luck in the Peace Corps, Allison.

I could not have finished this book without the help of the 2008 Blue Heaven writers, especially Daryl Gregory and Paul Melko, who struggled through a draft as rushed and rough as the retreat from Fort Lee, helping me regroup it into a more coherent and polished story. Chris Schluep once again made great suggestions. Thanks to my sons, Coleman and Finlay, for keeping their sense of humor and adjusting to my long hours. The no-pun zone is for you. Rae Carson Finlay reads every word of every draft I throw at her, always holding me to a higher standard and insisting that I write better, for which I am deeply grateful.

Read on for an excerpt from

TRAITOR TO THE CROWN

THE
DEMON
REDCOAT

by

C. C. FINLAY

Published by Del Rey Books

All the furniture had been pushed to the edges of the room and neatly stacked out of the way. Deborah walked—no, waddled—around the open space, with Abigail supporting her on one side and Magdalena on the other. Magdalena, small and frail, supported herself with her cane, and looked as if she might topple under the weight. Proctor went to take her place, but Lydia put down the blanket and basket and got there first.

"Oh, you don't need to do that—" Deborah protested, but the last word was interrupted by a wince as she felt another contraction.

"Just keep breathing through it," Abigail said.

Deborah nodded and continued her small circuit of the room. Magdalena shuffled over to a chair and collapsed into it.

"What can I do to help?" Proctor asked.

All four women looked at him as if he had just asked them how to fly. "Maybe you could go check outside," Magdalena said.

"Check for what?" he asked. "We've set spells protecting our borders against any physical intruders, man or animal, living or dead, accidental or intentional." They'd learned their lesson after Bootzamon's probing of their hideaway some years before. "It's been over a year since we heard or saw any indication of the Covenant."

Magdalena raised the knob end of her cane at him.

He threw up his hands in surrender. "I'll go check the borders," he said.

"Thank you," Deborah said. She paused and smiled at him, but the effect was weakened by the sweat beading on her forehead.

Proctor grabbed a bucket and climbed the hill to the orchard to gather the fallen apples. Clouds rolled in, deepening the gloam before he'd gathered them all, and the wind whipped through the branches, threatening to break more limbs. He plucked a ripe apple and tucked it in his pocket for Singer, their mare, then took the rest and dumped them into the pig trough with their other kitchen scraps. Inside the barn, he rubbed Singer's nose while she ate out of his hand and then checked the cows in their stalls. When he was done, he took a lantern from the wall and went outside.

He meant to light it with magic. He had almost mastered the talent, but he wasn't going to make the attempt in the barn with all the straw around. Shielding the lantern with his body, he tried the spell that Deborah had taught him.

A prickling unease shivered through his skin the moment he spoke.

Before he could stop the spell, flame exploded from his hand, a ball of fire that hung suspended in the air. Wind swirled, drawing straw and grass up in a spiral to feed the flame. The new-fed fire, leashed to the ground, wavered toward the barn, then veered abruptly at the house.

Coming to his senses, Proctor kicked and stamped, scattering the dried grasses. Deprived of fuel, the flames quickly sputtered and died.

Hair prickled on the back of his neck, but he told himself he was imagining things. Worries about Deborah had him on edge. Still, he decided that he knew the land well enough to walk it in the dark. He put the lantern down and set out to check the fences.

The Farm was hidden by an illusion that blurred its presence to passing eyes. To anyone on the other side of the fence, Proctor would seem no more than a stray shadow or a bobbing will-o'-the-wisp. There were also physical barriers, thorny hedges just beyond the fence. Spells had also been set to discourage visitors from going any farther. If someone did press through the thorns and spells, their presence would set off warning bells. A variety of other protections would delay or trap them while the witches in the house responded to the warning.

In short, no man or creature not explicitly blessed or excepted by Deborah could approach them unawares. No wonder the Covenant had given up.

He finished his inspection at the gate, the weakest spot in their defenses, but he saw and sensed nothing unusual there, either. Satisfied, he passed through the gardens and returned to the house in the dark. The wind was as fitful as his mood, gusting and twisting along the ground in his wake.

Proctor entered the new wing so he wouldn't disturb the women. He couldn't wait until Deborah made up her mind to move into this part of the house. The main room was dominated by a huge fireplace built out of fieldstone and protected by an ancient spell that he and Deborah had performed on the day of their wedding.

He put logs on the grate and started a fire—using flint and steel this time. Wind whistled across the chimney top, but the shaft did not seem to be drawing smoke very well. He let the sparks burn down instead of feeding them.

He went through the back door into the old house. He saw Deborah in the bedroom, or at least he saw her knees poking up in the air. Abigail sat on the bed beside her, holding her hand.

Magdalena stepped in front of him to block the view. "Done already?"

"I checked all our boundaries. We're shut up tight for the night."

"Then go make sure we have fresh water, and kindling for the fire."

"But—" He looked at the pitchers of water already full and ready, and the stack of firewood by the hearth, and then he realized it was just more make-work to keep him out of their way. He decided not to be irritated by it. "How's Deborah?"

"She's fine," Magdalena said. "Why do you think she's not fine?"

"I didn't think she wasn't fine."

Deborah's voice came from the other room, high-pitched, breathless, and short. "I'm fine."

"Is she supposed to sound like that?" he asked Magdalena.

"Sound like what?" the old Dutch woman snapped angrily.

"I'll go get water and firewood," Proctor said.

"That would help a great deal, yes."

The pitchers were all full, so he carried the kettle outside and filled that at the well. Then, since there was plenty of firewood inside already, he started moving one of the piles over to the porch where they could get at it easier.

He'd seen plenty of births—his mother had a sure hand with the lambs and calves, especially during difficult deliveries. But as an only child, he had never attended a baby's birth before. Deborah's pregnancy had been hard enough, but this—the hours of pain, sweat, and blood, the uncertain outcome . . .

Actually, it reminded him a lot of being in battle.

Best not to mention that.

He tossed the split logs onto the new pile and went back for two more. All that mattered was keeping Deborah safe, keeping their baby safe. He wondered if they were going to have a boy or a girl. If it was a boy, he wanted to name him after his father. Lemuel. Now, that was a good strong name. Lemuel Brown.

Lydia stepped outside. "She's asking for you."

He dropped the wood. It clattered on the ground, banging off his shins, but he hardly noticed because his heart was pounding so hard. "Is everything—"

"Everything's fine," she said.

Proctor ran inside and stopped at the door to Deborah's bedroom. Magdalena sat between Deborah's feet, and Abigail frowned at him, rising immediately to block his view. "Deborah?" he said.

"Proctor, is that you?" she answered, panting between words.

"Yes, Lydia said you wanted me."

"Yes, I did," she said, gritting her teeth through a painful contraction. "Now go away."

Abigail reached out and squeezed his arm, not as a gesture of reassurance, but as a means of turning him around and pushing him out the doorway and across the room. "She just wanted to know where you were. Now she knows. Don't you have water to fetch or wood to split?"

The hearth had burned down to coals. "I could tend the fire," he suggested. It would keep him near Deborah, and no one could argue that he wasn't doing something.

"Good," Abigail said, and she shoved him out of the way.

He moved a chair over in front of the hearth and added a log from the basket. He prodded it into flame, then added more logs on top. This chimney was drawing just fine.

Lydia pulled up another chair beside him and took out her knitting. "It's not that cold outside," she said.

"It felt chilly enough when I tried to see how my wife was doing," he muttered.

The wind rattled the shutters, which banged against the

house like someone knocking to come in. The wood in the fire crackled and split, shooting sparks out into the room. The draft from the chimney drew the flames into wild and unusual shapes. Proctor stared at them, the way he might stare into someone's face, while Deborah shouted and panted her way through ever more frequent contractions.

Abigail popped her head out of the bedroom door. "I think it's time," she said eagerly.

Proctor jumped out of his seat.

"Not you," she said. "Lydia—she'll want to see the baby being born."

Lydia sighed, then put her work aside and joined the women. With all of them crowded into the tiny room, they couldn't close the door.

Deborah cried out.

Proctor plopped down in his chair and stabbed the iron into the fire. He flipped over a log, sending up a spray of sparks.

"This time, you push," Magdalena said. "Just like you're doing your business."

Deborah cried out again.

Proctor stirred the coals. Sparks shot up again, but this time a ball of fire rose with the sparks. It was just like the strange flame that had formed when he tried to light the lantern. In a split second air spiraled around it, drawing fire from the logs, making the flame larger and stronger.

And more man-like.

The flame had limbs and a head. Proctor watched, frozen, as fiery fingers formed at the ends of its arms. Eyes as black as charcoal popped open in its head. The arms and legs, rooted in the burning logs, stretched and pulled like a creature escaping a trap.

It reminded him of the imp Dickon that had kept the evil Bootzamon's pipe lit.

Only it was the size of a man, and it was crawling out of a hearth that had once been used as a black altar.

Proctor's tongue came unfrozen. "Demon!"

Deborah cried out in reply from the other room.

He tipped over the kettle on the fire. Steam rolled out of the hearth, but the demon twisted and dodged, avoiding most of the water. It was a creature of spirit—it needed the flames to manifest. If Proctor drowned the fire, he could kill it.

Proctor grabbed the nearest pitcher and doused the flames again. The creature roared and spit, but it yanked one leg free of the burning logs. If it escaped and became a free creature of fire—

"Demon—we're under attack from a demon," Proctor yelled.

He looked for more water, wishing that he'd brought in more water—why hadn't he brought in more water? He ran for the washbowl, but it was empty. He grabbed the half-empty pitcher from the stand and turned back to the fire. The demon was almost free.

"There, you're almost there, one more push," Magdalena said.

Proctor flung the pitcher. The ceramic shattered into a thousand shards, and the water washed over the rest of the logs.

Which set free the demon's other leg.

Deborah cried out, louder than before.

The demon floated above the hearth, staring at Proctor eye-to-eye. Horns rose from its head and its mouth gaped in a snarl of white flame and orange tongue. Red fire rippled from its shoulder to its waist like a coat, and it moved on legs of smoke. It glanced away from Proctor, at the bedroom, and licked its lips.

Proctor drew all the power into himself that he could summon. Sweat poured from his body. He would smother the demon with every stone in the house. He would call rain out of the sky. The demon took a step toward the bedroom and Proctor blocked its way.

"No. You will not have my wife or my child."

The demon hesitated and fell back.

Abigail's voice sound behind him. "Proctor, it's wonderful, come see your baby—"

Her sentence ended with a scream.

The baby—his baby—cried out in the other room, its first sound, so small and vulnerable. Proctor's heart jumped, and he turned his head. Magdalena had emerged from the room, smiling, oblivious. She held a knife out handle-first for Proctor, inviting him to cut the baby's cord.

The demon lunged past him.

Proctor clutched for it, his right hand sliding down the flames until they closed on the creature's ankle. Heat knifed up his arm, and the scar of his missing finger felt like a hot coal had been hammered into it. The demon twisted and lashed at him like a frightened snake. Proctor tried to drag it toward the front door, but the pain was blinding. His knees buckled beneath him and his vision blackened like the night. Everything in the room went dark except for the flames.

Abigail screamed and screamed. Deborah shouted his name. His baby cried out, tiny and helpless.

The demon's ankle slipped through Proctor's hand. He was holding on to no more than a heel. He tried to grab at it with his other hand, but he needed it to hold on to the floor lest he spin away into the dark and the shadow. The demon twisted around and slashed at his face with red talons. Proctor rolled away from the blow, but he couldn't hold on much longer.

A cool white light, smooth and round as a pearl, emerged from the darkness.

The light came from the knob of Magdalena's cane. She blocked the way to the child. She spoke out in German, words Proctor couldn't understand, though the tone was clear enough: *Clear out.*

The demon shrank back and roared, a sound like the wind building up to a tempest. The demon pulled free of Proctor's hand, and Proctor collapsed to the ground.

Magdalena threatened the creature with her cane. The light brightened, a full moon, filling the room. The demon bounced from corner to corner, like an anxious cat, desperate to escape and equally ready to strike.

"Grab it," Magdalena shouted, and Proctor realized she was shouting at him. "I told you to grab it und hold it!"

He lunged for it, and the demon dodged away. The baby hiccuped in the other room, and the demon seemed to cry in anguish, a whistling sound like the wind scraped over a roof's edge. Proctor grabbed at it again with his left hand but it was hot to the touch and he flinched. It slipped through his fingers.

The demon, swollen with flame, charged at Magdalena. Proctor yelled out "No!"

"You will not have this child!" she cried.

The demon tried to bull past her, but she stepped into its way and slammed the knob end of her cane into its face. The white light hit the shadowy fire of the creature like water hitting hot oil. The sizzling crackle was followed by a burst of power that knocked everyone to the floor.

When Proctor pushed himself upright again, the baby was wailing, the demon was gone . . . and Magdalena lay broken at odd angles on the floor, surrounded by the shattered pieces of her cane. Lydia knelt over her a moment, then shook her head.

Magdalena was dead.

"God, dear God in heaven, what was that?" whispered Abigail. She sat in the corner, knees pulled up to her chin.

The baby squalled.

Deborah! Proctor lurched up and lunged to the doorway.

He flung it open. Deborah sat there in a pile of wet and blood-tinged sheets, holding the baby to her breast with the uncut cord snaked across the bed. Tears wet her cheeks.

"I wanted this to be a happy day," she said. "I wanted this to be our happiest day."

Her voice wasn't sad or scared. It was angry.